Sign of Seven Trilogy
Blood Brothers • *The Hollow* • *The Pagan Stone*

Bride Quartet
Vision in White • *Bed of Roses* • *Savor the Moment* • *Happy
Ever After*

The Inn Boonsboro Trilogy
The Next Always • *The Last Boyfriend* • *The Perfect Hope*

The Cousins O'Dwyer Trilogy
Dark Witch • *Shadow Spell* • *Blood Magick*

The Guardians Trilogy
Stars of Fortune • *Bay of Sighs* • *Island of Glass*

Chronicles of The One
Year One • *Of Blood and Bone* • *The Rise of Magicks*

The Dragon Heart Legacy
The Awakening • *The Becoming*

EBOOKS BY NORA ROBERTS

Cordina's Royal Family
Affaire Royale • *Command Performance* • *The Playboy
Prince* • *Cordina's Crown Jewel*

The Donovan Legacy
Captivated • *Entranced* • *Charmed* • *Enchanted*

The O'Hurleys
The Last Honest Woman • *Dance to the Piper* •
Skin Deep • *Without a Trace*

Night Tales
Night Shift • *Night Shadow* • *Nightshade* • *Night Smoke* •
Night Shield

The MacGregors

The Winning Hand • The Perfect Neighbor • All the Possibilities • One Man's Art • Tempting Fate • Playing the Odds • The MacGregor Brides • The MacGregor Grooms • Rebellion/In from the Cold • For Now, Forever

The Calhouns

Suzanna's Surrender • Megan's Mate • Courting Catherine • A Man for Amanda • For the Love of Lilah

Irish Legacy

Irish Rose • Irish Rebel • Irish Thoroughbred

Jack's Stories

Best Laid Plans • Loving Jack • Lawless

Summer Love • Boundary Lines • Dual Image • First Impressions • The Law Is a Lady • Local Hero • This Magic Moment • The Name of the Game • Partners • Temptation • The Welcoming • Opposites Attract • Time Was • Times Change • Gabriel's Angel • Holiday Wishes • The Heart's Victory • The Right Path • Rules of the Game • Search for Love • Blithe Images • From This Day • Song of the West • Island of Flowers • Her Mother's Keeper • Untamed • Sullivan's Woman • Less of a Stranger • Reflections • Dance of Dreams • Storm Warning • Once More with Feeling • Endings and Beginnings • A Matter of Choice • Summer Desserts • Lessons Learned • One Summer • The Art of Deception • Second Nature • Treasures Lost, Treasures Found

Nora Roberts & J. D. Robb

Remember When

J. D. Robb

Naked in Death • Glory in Death • Immortal in Death • Rapture in Death • Ceremony in Death • Vengeance in Death • Holiday in Death • Conspiracy in Death • Loyalty in Death

• *Witness in Death* • *Judgment in Death* • *Betrayal in Death*
• *Seduction in Death* • *Reunion in Death* • *Purity in Death*
• *Portrait in Death* • *Imitation in Death* • *Divided in Death*
• *Visions in Death* • *Survivor in Death* • *Origin in Death*
• *Memory in Death* • *Born in Death* • *Innocent in Death* •
Creation in Death • *Strangers in Death* • *Salvation in Death*
• *Promises in Death* • *Kindred in Death* • *Fantasy in Death* •
Indulgence in Death • *Treachery in Death* • *New York to Dallas*
• *Celebrity in Death* • *Delusion in Death* • *Calculated in Death*
• *Thankless in Death* • *Concealed in Death* • *Festive in Death* •
Obsession in Death • *Devoted in Death* • *Brotherhood in Death*
• *Apprentice in Death* • *Echoes in Death* • *Secrets in Death* •
Dark in Death • *Leverage in Death* • *Connections in Death* •
Vendetta in Death • *Golden in Death* • *Shadows in Death* •
Faithless in Death • *Forgotten in Death* •
Abandoned in Death

ANTHOLOGIES

From the Heart • *A Little Magic* • *A Little Fate*

Moon Shadows
(with Jill Gregory, Ruth Ryan Langan, and Marianne Willman)

The Once Upon Series
(with Jill Gregory, Ruth Ryan Langan, and Marianne Willman)
Once Upon a Castle • *Once Upon a Star* • *Once Upon a
Dream* • *Once Upon a Rose* • *Once Upon a Kiss* • *Once Upon
a Midnight*

Silent Night
(with Susan Plunkett, Dee Holmes, and Claire Cross)

Out of This World
(with Laurell K. Hamilton, Susan Krinard, and Maggie Shayne)

Bump in the Night
(with Mary Blayney, Ruth Ryan Langan, and Mary Kay McComas)

Dead of Night
(with Mary Blayney, Ruth Ryan Langan, and Mary Kay McComas)

Three in Death

Suite 606
(with Mary Blayney, Ruth Ryan Langan, and Mary Kay McComas)

In Death

The Lost
(with Patricia Gaffney, Ruth Ryan Langan, and Mary Blayney)

The Other Side
(with Mary Blayney, Patricia Gaffney, Ruth Ryan Langan,
and Mary Kay McComas)

Time of Death

The Unquiet
(with Mary Blayney, Patricia Gaffney, Ruth Ryan Langan,
and Mary Kay McComas)

Mirror, Mirror
(with Mary Blayney, Elaine Fox, Mary Kay McComas, and
R. C. Ryan)

Down the Rabbit Hole
(with Mary Blayney, Elaine Fox, Mary Kay McComas, and
R. C. Ryan)

ALSO AVAILABLE . . .

The Official Nora Roberts Companion
(edited by Denise Little and Laura Hayden)

THE RISE OF MAGICKS

NORA ROBERTS

St. Martin's Paperbacks

This is a work of fiction. All of the characters, organizations, and events portrayed in this novel are either products of the author's imagination or are used fictitiously.

Published in the United States by St. Martin's Paperbacks, an imprint of St. Martin's Publishing Group

THE RISE OF MAGICKS

Copyright © 2019 by Nora Roberts.

All rights reserved.

For information, address St. Martin's Publishing Group, 120 Broadway, New York, NY 10271.

www.stmartins.com

Library of Congress Catalog Card Number: 2019024266

ISBN: 978-1-250-12305-3

Our books may be purchased in bulk for promotional, educational, or business use. Please contact your local bookseller or the Macmillan Corporate and Premium Sales Department at 1-800-221-7945, ext. 5442, or by email at MacmillanSpecialMarkets@macmillan.com.

Printed in the United States of America

St. Martin's Press hardcover edition / November 2019
St. Martin's Griffin edition 2020
St. Martin's Paperbacks / December 2021

10 9 8 7 6 5 4 3 2 1

For Bruce, and the home, the family we built together

Our books may be purchased in bulk for promotional, educational, or business use. Please contact your local bookseller or the Macmillan Corporate and Premium Sales Department at 1-800-221-7945, ext. 5442, or by email at MacmillanSpecialMarkets@macmillan.com.

Printed in the United States of America

FREEDOM

Of old sat Freedom on the heights,
The thunders breaking at her feet:
Above her shook the starry lights:
She heard the torrents meet.

—Alfred, Lord Tennyson

PROLOGUE

On the shield, one of seven forged in the timeless past to hold back the dark, fell a single drop of blood.

So the shield weakened, and the dark, spider-patient, waited as the decades passed, and the wound spread under the grass and ground.

And on the last day of what had been, a good man, in all innocence, broke the shield open. The dark rewarded him with deadly infection, one that would pass from man to wife, from parent to child, from stranger to stranger.

While the dying world reeled, its framework—governments, technology, laws, transportation, communication—crumbled like bricks of dust.

The world ended with bangs and whimpers, with blood and pain, with fear and dread. A cashier handing change to a customer, a mother nursing her child, businessmen gripping hands over a deal—these and so many simple contacts spread death like a poisoned cloud over the world.

And billions fell.

They called it the Doom—for so it was—a murderously speedy sickness with no cure that killed villains and innocents, statesmen and anarchists, the privileged and the penniless with equal glee.

While billions died, those who survived—the immune—struggled to live one more day, to find food, to protect whatever shelter they might have, to escape and evade the unchecked violence unleashed. For some, even in their most dire hour, would burn, pillage, rape, kill for the sheer pleasure of it.

Through the poisonous cloud that enveloped the world, light sparked. Darkness pulsed. Powers, long dormant, awakened. Some bloomed bright, others black through choices made. But they bloomed.

Magicks began to hum.

Some embraced the wonders while some feared them. And some hated.

The other, the not-like-me, would always spark hate in some hearts. What came to be known as the Uncanny faced the fear and hate of those who hunted them. Governments, desperate to hold their own power, sought to sweep them up, imprison them, experiment on them.

Magickals hid from or fought against those who called on a fierce and bitter god to torture and destroy, from those mated to their own bigotry like a lover.

And from and against those who bloomed dark.

On a storm-lashed night, a child whose light sparked at the moment of a good man's death drew her first breath. She came from love and sacrifice, from hope and struggle, from strength and grief.

With that loosed cry of life, a mother's tears, the strong hands of the man who held her, the warrior, the leader, The One took her first step toward destiny.

Magicks began to beat.

In the years that followed, wars raged between men, between dark and light, between those who fought to survive and build and those who sought to destroy and rule the rubble.

The child grew, as did her powers. With her training, her mistakes, her triumphs, she took the next steps. So a young girl full of faith and wonder reached into the fire and took up the sword and the shield. And became The One.

Magicks began to rise.

CHAPTER ONE

A storm raged. It crashed around her with wild, wind-whipped rain, sizzling strikes of lightning, bellowing booms of thunder. It whirled inside her, a torrent of anger she knew must be suppressed.

She would bring death tonight, by her sword, by her power, by her orders. Every drop of blood shed would be on her hands—that was the weight of command, and accepted.

She was not yet twenty.

Fallon Swift touched her fingers to the cuff she wore on her wrist, one she'd conjured from a tree she'd destroyed out of temper, and carved to remember never to destroy out of anger.

It said: *Solas don Saol.*

Light for Life.

She would bring death tonight, she thought again, but she would help others live.

Through the storm she studied the compound. Mallick, her teacher, had taken her to one similar enough on her fourteenth birthday. But while that one had been deserted, with only the stink of black magicks, the charred remains of the dead, the dying cries of the tortured left, this one held more than six hundred—two hundred and eighty personnel, and three hundred and thirty-two prisoners.

Forty-seven of those prisoners were, according to their intel, under the age of twelve.

She had every inch of the compound—the containment center—every room, every hallway, camera, alarm, in her head. She'd made detailed maps, had spent months planning this rescue.

It would be, in the three years since she'd begun to raise her army, since she and her family had left their home for New Hope, the biggest rescue attempt by her resistance forces.

If she failed . . .

A hand gripped her shoulder, steadied her as it always had. She turned her head, looked at her father.

"We've got this," Simon told her.

She let out a breath. "Bespelling the surveillance cameras," she murmured, and relayed that to the elves mind to mind so they'd pass the word.

Now those at security monitors would see only the trees, the rain, the swampy ground.

"Take down the alarms."

She and other witches worked the spell, painstakingly, while the storm blew.

When the all clear ran through the ranks, she ignored the pang, gave the order. "Archers, go."

The guard towers had to be taken out, swift and silent. She felt Tonia, lead archer, friend, blood of her blood, nock an arrow, release.

With eyes gray and focused, she watched arrows strike, men fall, in the towers on the four corners of the prison walls.

Moving in, she took the electronic gates, using power

to disarm. At her signals, troops flowed through the opening, elves scaled the walls and fences, shifters leaped, tooth and claw, faeries glided with a whisper of wings.

Timing, she thought as she spoke to the elf commander Flynn, to Tonia in her mind. They would breach the three doors simultaneously, and each team leader would focus their troops on priorities. Destroy communications, eliminate security, take the armory, secure the lab. Above all, shield all prisoners.

After one last glance at her father, seeing the courage and determination in the face she trusted completely, she gave the order.

Drawing her sword, she blew the locks on the main doors, charged in, blew the secondary doors open.

Part of her mind overlaid the now with the prison on Hatteras, the visions she'd stirred there at fourteen. So much the same.

But here, soldiers lived, reached for weapons. Even as gunfire rang out, she struck, enflaming sidearms that left hands blistered and men screaming with pain. She struck out with sword, swung out with shield to cut through the enemy.

Fighting through, she heard the shouts, moans, pleading from behind the steel doors, and felt the fear, the terrible hope, the pain and confusion of those locked in.

Drenched in it, she cut down a soldier as he rushed to his comm, sliced her sword across the radio, sent a bolt of shock through the entire system.

Sparks showered, monitors blanked to black.

Boots clanged on metal stairs, and death, more death, met them as arrows sliced through the air. Fallon took a bullet on her shield, sent it flying back and into the shooter as she pivoted to the iron door someone inside the prison had managed to secure.

She blasted it open, taking out two on the other side and, leaping over the smoking twists of metal, cleaved her sword through a third before she rushed toward the stairs leading down.

War cries followed her. Her troops would spread out, swarm through—barracks, offices, mess hall, galley, infirmary.

But she and those with her surged toward the lab and its chamber of horrors. There, another iron door. She started to punch her power through, stopped a breath away from the blast as she sensed something more, something dark.

Magicks, black and deadly.

She held up a hand to halt her team. Forcing patience, she searched, tall in elf-made boots and leather vest, black hair short, eyes blurred with power.

"Stand back," she ordered, and shouldered her shield, sheathed her sword to hold her hands to the door, the locks, the deep frame, the thick metal.

"Booby-trapped," she murmured. "We push in, it blows out. Stand clear."

"Fallon."

"Stand clear," she told her father. "I could unwind it, but that would take too long." She swung her shield up again, and her sword. "In three, two—"

She shoved her power, light against dark.

The doors erupted, spewing fire, raining out jagged, flaming metals. Shrapnel thudded on her shield, whizzed by to impale the wall behind her. Into the torrent she leaped.

She saw the man, naked, eyes glazed, face blank, shackled to an exam table. Another in a lab coat flung himself back, sprang on his hands, then scaled the back wall in a blur of speed.

She flung power at the ceiling, brought the one in the

lab coat down in a heap as Simon dodged the scalpel swipe by a third before taking him out with a short-armed jab.

"Search for others," Fallon ordered. "Confiscate all records. Two to secure this section, and the rest move out, clear the rest of the level."

She approached the man on the table. "Can you speak?"

She heard his mind, the struggle to form words.

They tortured me. I can't move. Help me. Will you help me?

"We're here to help." She watched his face as she sheathed her sword. Blocked out the chaos of fighting from above while she kept her mind linked to his.

"Got a woman over here," Simon called out. "Drugged, cut up, but she's breathing."

They hurt us, hurt us. Help us.

"Yes." Fallon laid a hand on one of the shackles so it fell open. "How long have you been here?"

I don't know. I don't know. Please. Please.

She circled the table to release the shackle on his other wrist. "Did you choose the dark before or after you came here?" she wondered.

He reared up, glee on his face as he struck out at her with a bolt of lightning. She simply swatted it back with her shield, impaling him with his own evil.

"I guess we'll never know," she mumbled.

"Jesus Christ, Fallon." Simon stood, the woman limp over his shoulder, his gun drawn.

"I had to be sure. Can you get her to a medic?"

"Yeah."

"We'll clear the rest."

When they had, the count was forty-three enemy prisoners to transport. The rest they'd bury. Medics moved in to treat wounded from both sides while Fallon began the laborious process of vetting those held in cells.

Some, she knew, might be like the ones in the lab. Others might have had their minds broken, and a broken mind could bring danger to the rest.

"Take a break," Simon told her, and shoved coffee into her hand.

"There are some shaky ones." She gulped down coffee as she studied her father's face. He'd mopped off the blood, and his hazel eyes held clear. He'd been a soldier long ago, in the other time. He was a soldier again in this one.

"They'll need to move into one of the treatment centers before they're clear to go. Why does that always feel as if we're keeping them prisoners?"

"It shouldn't, because it's not. Some are never going to be right again, Fallon, and still we'll let them go unless they pose a real danger. Now tell me how you knew that bastard on the table down in the lab was a bad guy."

"First, he wasn't as powerful as he thought, and it leaked through. But logically, the spell on the door, witchcraft. The other magickal in the lab was an elf. Bad elf," she said with half a smile. "Elves are good at getting through locks, but they can't bespell them. I felt his pulse when I released the first shackle, and it was hammering. It wouldn't have been if he'd been under a paralytic."

"But you released the second one."

"He could've done that for himself." She shrugged. "I'd hoped to question him, but . . . well." She downed the rest of the coffee, and blessed her mother and the other witches who'd created Tropics to grow the beans. "Do you have the status of the woman they'd dumped off the table?"

"Faerie. She'll never fly again—they excised most of her left wing—but she's alive. Your mom's got her at mobile medical."

"Good. The faerie's lucky they didn't just kill her instead of tossing her off. Once our injured prisoners are cleared, I need you to debrief. I know it's hard for you," she added. "They're soldiers, and most of them are just following orders."

"They're soldiers," he agreed, "who stood by or even abetted while their prisoners were tortured, while children were kept in cells. No, baby, it's not hard for me."

"I could do this without you because I have to do it, but I don't know how."

He pressed a kiss to her forehead. "You'll never have to figure it out."

She spoke to magickal children who'd been ripped away from non-magickal parents, reunited two whose parent—by blood or choice—had been locked in another cell.

She spoke to those who'd been locked in for years, others who had been swept up only days before.

She checked each one off the very precise records kept by the—now deceased—prison commander, reviewed the horrific records of experiments done in the lab.

Both Dark Uncanny—the witch, the elf—who'd worked there had hidden their natures, so her intel hadn't shown any magickals on staff.

Intel only went so far, she thought as she marked the witch as deceased, the elf as a prisoner of war.

The storm passed and dawn broke when she did a last pass through the building. Cleaning crews already worked to scrub away the blood staining the concrete floors, the walls, the stairs. The supply team had gathered everything worth taking—the rations, the equipment, the vehicles, the weapons, clothing, shoes, boots, medical supplies. All would be logged, then dispensed where most needed or held in storage until it was.

The burial unit dug graves. Too many graves, Fallon

thought as she walked outside, across the muddy ground. But today they dug none for their own, and that made it a good day.

Flynn slid out of the woods, his wolf Lupa by his side.

"Seven of the prisoners need more treatment," he said. "Your mom's helping with their transport to Cedarsville. It's the closest clinic that can handle their injuries. The rest are on their way to the detention center on Hatteras."

"Good."

Flynn, she thought, fast—an elf, after all—efficient, and solid as the rock he could blend into, had met her mother and birth father when he'd been a teenager.

Now a man, he stood as one of her commanders.

"We'll need a rotating security detail here," she continued. "Hatteras is close to capacity, so we'll need this facility. And they may come and check when they can't get through, or just bring in another load of prisoners."

She rattled off several names for the detail, including her brother Colin.

"I'll set it up," Flynn said. "But Colin took a hit in the op, so—"

"What?" She whirled around to Flynn, grabbed his arm in a vise grip. "I'm just hearing this?"

"You're The One, but the mother of The One is downright scary, so when she says keep it to myself, I keep it to myself. He's good," Flynn added quickly. "Took a bullet in the right shoulder, but it's out, and he's healing. Do you think your mom would go with enemy wounded if her son wasn't okay?"

"No, but—"

"She didn't want you distracted, and neither did your brother, who's more pissed off than hurt. Your dad already shoved him in the mobile heading back to New Hope."

"Okay, all right." But she pushed her hands through her short crop of hair in frustration. "Damn it."

"We freed three hundred and thirty-two, and didn't lose anyone." Tall and lean, eyes of sharp green, Flynn looked back toward the building. "No one will be tortured in that hellhole again. Take your victory, Fallon, and go home. We're secure here."

She nodded, and walked into the woods, breathed in the smell of damp earth, dripping leaves. In this swampy area of what had been Virginia, near the Carolina border, insects hummed and buzzed, and what she knew to be sumac grew thick as walls.

She moved through until she stood within the circle of the shimmering morning sun to call Laoch.

He glided down to land, huge and white, silver wings spread, silver horn gleaming.

For a moment, because despite victory she was bone weary, she pressed her face to his strong throat. For that moment she was just a girl, with bruises aching, with eyes of smoke gray closed, with the blood of the slain on her shirt, her pants, her boots.

Then she mounted, sat tall in the saddle of golden leather. She used no reins or bit on the alicorn.

"*Baile*," she murmured to him. Home.

And he rose up in the blue sky of morning to take her.

When she arrived at the big house between the New Hope barracks and the farm where Eddie and Fred raised their kids, their crops, she found her father waiting on the porch, his boots up on the rail, a mug of coffee in his hand.

He'd had a shower, she noted, as his mop of dense brown hair still showed damp. He rose, walked down to her, laid a hand on Laoch's neck.

"Go on in and check on him. He's sleeping, but you'll

feel better for it. I'll see to Laoch, then there's breakfast for both of us keeping warm in the oven."

"You knew he'd been hurt."

"I knew he'd been hurt and I knew he was okay." Simon paused when she dropped down. "Your mom said not to tell you until you'd finished. She said that's that, and when your mom says that's that—"

"That's that. I'm going to see for myself, grab a shower. I could use that breakfast after. Travis and Ethan?"

"Travis is at the barracks working with some new recruits. Ethan's over at Eddie's and Fred's helping with livestock."

"Okay then."

And now that she knew where her other brothers were, she went in to check on Colin.

She went inside, turned for the stairs in the house that served as home, but one she doubted would ever really be one. The farm where she'd been born, had been raised would forever be home. But this place, like the cottage in the woods where she'd been trained by Mallick, served a purpose.

She walked to Colin's room, where he sprawled over his bed wearing an old, fairly disreputable pair of boxers. He snored heroically.

She moved to him, laid her hand lightly—very lightly—over his right shoulder. Stiff, achy, she noted, but a clean wound already well healed.

Her mother had serious skills, Fallon reminded herself. Still she took another minute, touched his hair—a darker blond than their mother's and worn these days in what he thought of as a warrior's braid: short and fat.

He had a warrior's body—muscular and tough—with a tattoo of a coiled snake on his left shoulder blade. (Done at sixteen without parental permission.)

She stayed a moment in the chaos of his room—he

still collected whatever small treasure appealed to him. Odd coins, stones, pieces of glass, wires, old bottles. And had never learned, apparently, to hang, fold, or put away a single article of clothing.

Of her three brothers he was the only one without magicks. And of the three, the one who seemed born to be a soldier.

So she left him sleeping, walked downstairs, down again to her rooms on the lower level.

Unlike Colin's, her room was scrupulously neat. On the walls she'd pinned maps—hand drawn or printed, old and new. In the chest at the foot of the bed she kept books, novels, biographies, histories, books on science, on magicks. On her desk she kept files on troops, civilians, training, bases, prisons, food supplies, medical supplies, maneuvers, spells, duty schedules, and rotations.

On the stand by her bed sat a white candle and a ball of crystal—gifts from the man who'd trained her.

She shed her clothes, dumped them in the basket for later laundering. And with a heartfelt sigh, stepped in the shower to wash away the blood, the sweat, the grime and stench of battle.

She dressed in jeans, worn at the knees and barely hitting the ankles of long legs, a T-shirt that bagged a bit over her slim frame. She pulled on her second pair of boots until she could clean the ones she'd worn to battle.

She strapped on her sword, then went upstairs to have breakfast with her father.

"Your mom's back," he told her as he moved to the oven to pull out plates. "At the clinic, but back."

"I'm heading over there after breakfast." She chose juice, as she wanted something cool.

"You need sleep, baby. You've been up over twenty-four."

Eggs, scrambled, bacon, crisp. She dug in like the starving. "You, too," she pointed out.

"I caught some sleep on the way back—and had a nice porch doze, as my dad used to call it, before you got here."

She shoveled in more eggs. "I don't have a scratch on me. Not a single scratch. Soldiers I led bled. Colin bled. I don't have a scratch."

"You've bled before." He laid a hand over hers. "You will again."

"I have to see the wounded, and they should see me. And the rescues. Then I'll sleep."

"I'll go with you."

She glanced at the ceiling, thought of the soldier who slept. "You should stay with Colin."

"I'll pull Ethan back to sit with him. Your mom said he'd likely sleep until afternoon."

"Okay. Give me a sense of the prisoners," she said, and he sighed.

"A mix. Some hard-asses with a lot of hate and fear of magickals. They skew older, and it's not likely we'll have much luck turning them around. But we may be able to educate a few of the younger ones."

"They need to see the lab recordings. They need to see people being drugged, strapped down, tortured, experimented on just because they're different."

Though what she'd reviewed at the prison turned her stomach, she continued to eat. She needed fuel to function.

"Let that educate them."

He couldn't miss the bitterness in her voice, rubbed her hand again. "I agree. It should wait a few days. A lot of them expect torture and execution from us. We show them we treat our prisoners humanely, decently."

"Then show them proof of the contrast," she finished.

"All right. But some won't ever change, will they?"

"No."

She rose, took his plate and hers to the sink to wash. "There's no point asking why, but I keep circling back to it. Twenty years ago the world you knew, Mom knew, ended. Billions died terrible deaths from the Doom. We're what's left, Dad, and we're killing each other."

She turned to look at him, this good man who'd helped bring her into the world, who'd loved her, fought with her. A soldier who'd become a farmer, now a farmer who lived a soldier's life again.

He had no magicks, she thought, and yet he was all the light stood for.

"You didn't hate or fear," she said. "You opened your home, then your life, to a stranger, a witch, and one who was being hunted. You could have turned her away, and me inside her, but you didn't. Why?"

So many answers, Simon thought. He settled on one. "She was a miracle, and so were you, inside her. The world needed miracles."

She smiled at him. "It's going to get them, ready or not."

She rode into town with him, taking Grace to give her mare some attention and exercise. The hills rolled around them, green with summer and surging wildflowers. She smelled earth, freshly turned and planted, heard the shouts, the clang of metal from the barracks where recruits trained.

A small herd of deer slipped out of the trees to crop their way along a steep ridge heavy with trees. Above, the sky held soft and hopeful blue after the night's storm.

The road, cleared of abandoned cars and trucks—all laboriously towed to an outlying garage for repair or dismantling, wound toward New Hope.

Houses, she thought, most in good repair now, and most occupied. Those that couldn't be salvaged had been—like the vehicles—scavenged for parts. Wood, pipes, tiles, wiring, anything that could be used. On the reclaimed land, beef cattle, milk cows, goats, sheep, a few llamas, more horses grazed behind carefully tended fences.

At a bend in the road, the pulse of magick thrummed from the Tropics her mother had helped create. There grew groves of citrus trees, olive trees, palm, coffee beans, pepper, and other herbs and spices. Workers on harvesting detail paused to wave.

"Miracles," Simon said simply.

After passing the security checkpoint, they rode into New Hope, once, at the height of the Doom, occupied only by death and ghosts. Now it thrived with more than two thousand people, and a memorial tree honored the dead. The community gardens and greenhouses, a site of two vicious attacks, continued to bloom and grow. The community kitchen her mother had established before Fallon had been born served meals daily.

The Max Fallon Magick Academy, named for her sire, the New Hope schools, the town hall, the shops open for bartering, the homes lining Main Street, the clinic, the library, the life reclaimed through sweat, determination, sacrifice.

Wasn't all this, she wondered, another kind of miracle?

"You miss the farm," she said as they guided the horses to the hitching posts and troughs.

"I'll get back to it."

"You miss the farm," she repeated. "You left it for me, so every time I come into New Hope, I'm glad you left it for a good place with good people."

She dismounted, gave Grace a stroke before looping the reins around the rail.

She walked with him to what had once been the elementary school and now housed the New Hope Clinic.

They'd made changes over the years—Fallon had gone back through the crystal to see how it had all begun. The entrance hall held chairs for those waiting for an exam or checkup. A section held toys and books collected from abandoned houses.

A couple of toddlers played with blocks—one had wings fluttering in delight. A pregnant woman sat plying knitting needles and yarn over the mound of her belly. A teenager sprawled in another chair, looking bored. An old man sat hunched, his breathing a rattling wheeze.

As they turned toward the offices, Hannah Parsoni—the mayor's daughter, Duncan and Tonia's sister—hurried down the right corridor, a clipboard in one hand, a stethoscope around her neck.

She had her luxurious mane of dark blond hair pulled back in a long tail. Her eyes, already a warm brown, deepened with pleasure at the sight of them. "I was hoping to see you both. We're swamped," she added, "so I've only got a minute. Rachel has me working with the scheduled patients and walk-ins, but I helped with the first triage on the wounded. We haven't lost anyone. Some of the people you freed . . ."

Compassion rolled off her, so deep Fallon felt the waves on her skin.

"Some of them are going to need extended treatment, and counseling, but none of them are critical now. Lana—she's amazing. How's Colin?"

"Sleeping," Simon told her.

"No fever, no infection," Fallon added.

"Make sure to let your mom know. She does know, but it would help her to hear it."

In the way she had of offering care, Hannah reached out to touch them both. "You look so tired, both of you."

"Maybe I should do a—"

As Fallon lifted a hand to her face, Hannah took it. "A glamour? I wish you wouldn't. They should see the effort. They should know what it costs, what freedom costs. That you pay the price for it, too."

She gave Fallon's hand a squeeze, then moved on. "Hey, Mr. Barker, let's go back, have a look at you."

He rattled, wheezed. "I can wait for the doctor."

"Why don't we go back to an exam room, just have a look? I can get you started for Rachel."

Soothing, cajoling instead of insulted, Fallon thought. That was Hannah—Hannah who'd been studying, training to be a doctor, essentially since her childhood, and who'd served as a field medic on rescues for years.

Patience, Fallon realized, was just one form of Hannah's magick.

She saw the girl in the office, working briskly on a computer—a skill she herself had yet to fully master. April, she remembered. Faerie, about her age. Wounded in the attack in the gardens two years before.

An attack instigated by Fallon's own blood, her cousin, the daughter of her sire's brother and his woman. Dark Uncannys who wanted her death above all.

The girl looked up, beamed a smile. "Hey, hi. Are you looking for Lana?"

"I wanted to see the wounded—any who are up for it."

"We have the freed prisoners who were treated and cleared holding at the school auditorium, and the troops treated and cleared sent home or to the barracks. The rest are in the ward. Jonah and Carol are doing rounds, and Ray's monitoring the ones we released medically. It's been kind of an all-hands-on-deck morning. And right now?" She smiled her bright, faerie smile. "Rachel and Lana are delivering a baby."

"A baby?"

"One of the prisoners—"

"Lissandra Ye, wolf shifter," Fallon finished—she'd read every report. "She's not due for nearly eight weeks."

"She went into labor in the mobile heading here. They weren't able to stop it." As some worry leaked through, April pressed her lips together. "They've got a kind of NICU set up for it, as best they can. But I could tell Rachel was worried even though Jonah said he didn't see death.

"He'd see it, right?" April reached out for reassurance. "Jonah would know."

Fallon nodded, stepped out.

"Death's not the only consequence." She spoke softly to Simon. "Lissandra Ye was in that prison for fourteen months. She was raped inside there, and they kept right up with experiments on her after she got pregnant."

"You need to trust your mother and Rachel."

"I do."

She walked down another corridor. Classrooms converted to exam rooms, treatment rooms, surgeries, storage for supplies, another for medications and drugs.

Labor and delivery. She laid a hand on the door, felt the power simmering. Her mother's power. Heard Rachel's calm voice reassuring, and the moans of the woman in labor.

"I do," she repeated, and because that fate was in their hands, continued to the sprawling cafeteria set up as a ward for patients who needed continued treatment or observation.

Curtains—scavenged or fabricated—separated the beds and made an oddly festive show of color and patterns. The monitors beeped. Not enough, not nearly enough for so many patients. They would rotate them as needed, she knew.

She saw Jonah looking as weary as she felt, hanging a fresh IV bag.

"Start on Jonah's side," Simon suggested. "I'll start on Carol's."

So she walked to Jonah, and to the stranger with her eyes closed in the hospital bed. Under her eyes circles spread dark and deep. Her skin had a gray cast, and her hair—deep, deep black—had been shorn brutally short, like a skullcap.

"How is she?" she asked Jonah.

He rubbed tired eyes. "Dehydrated, malnourished— that's common throughout. Burn scars—old and fresh— over about thirty percent of her body. She's had her fingers broken and left to set on their own. Your mother worked on that, and we think she'll get the use of her hands back. Her records show she was in there for over seven years, one of the longest in the facility."

Fallon glanced at the chart. Naomi Rodriguez, age forty-three. Witch.

"The records listed an elf she'd taken into her care."

"Dimitri," Jonah told her. "He doesn't know his last name, or remember it. He's twelve. He's okay, if any of them are. He finally agreed to go with a couple of the women we were able to release."

"Okay. I want to—"

She broke off when the woman opened her eyes, stared at her. Eyes nearly as dark as the shadows dogging them.

"You're The One."

"Fallon Swift."

When the woman groped for her hand, Fallon took it.

Not physical pain, she realized—the medicals had taken care of that. But they couldn't touch the mental anguish.

"My boy."

"Dimitri. He's all right. I'm going to go see him soon."

"We'll bring him to see you," Jonah added. "As soon as we can. He's safe now, and so are you."

"They held a gun to his head, so I had to go with them. They said they'd let him go if I did, but they lied. Full of lies. They drugged me, and my boy. He was just a boy. They wouldn't let me see him, but I could feel him, hear him. They kept us drugged so we couldn't find our power. Sometimes they kept us gagged and blindfolded and shackled for hours, maybe days. They'd take us to that jackal and his devils to torture us. Some looked ashamed, but they took us to him. And they knew what he did to us."

She closed her eyes again. Tears leaked out, trailed down her cheeks. "I lost faith."

"There's no shame in it."

"I wanted to kill, at first I lived by imagining killing them all. Then I only wanted to die, just end it."

"No shame," Fallon repeated, and those anguished eyes opened again.

"But you came, even though I had no faith."

Fallon leaned in. "Do you see me? Do you see the light in me?"

"It's like the sun."

"I see you, Naomi. I see the light in you." When Naomi shook her head, Fallon laid her free hand on the woman's cheek, let some of that light flow in. "They dimmed it, but I see your light. I see the light that shined, that took in a frightened boy, a small, confused, grieving boy, and gave him a home. I see the light that was willing to sacrifice herself for the boy. I see you, Naomi."

Fallon straightened. "Now rest and heal. We'll bring Dimitri to you."

"I'll fight with you."

"When you're well," Fallon told her, and moved to the next bed.

It took nearly two hours. She joked with a soldier who claimed being shot, then kicked and stomped on was just a day in the life. She comforted the distraught, reassured the confused.

Before she left she saw the boy, the bone-thin boy with dark skin, sitting on the side of Naomi's bed. Haltingly, he read to her in a voice rusty with disuse from one of the children's books in the waiting area.

She slipped outside for some air, saw her father had done the same and was currently kissing her mother.

"You know, you guys don't need to get a room. You've got a whole house."

Lana turned bluebell eyes on Fallon, and smiled. "There's my girl." She moved quickly, gathered Fallon up tight. "You're so tired."

"I'm not alone."

"No, you're not." She drew back. "We didn't lose anyone. Thank the goddess."

"Including the premature baby?"

"Including. It was rough, but I finally got the baby to turn. Rachel wanted to avoid a C-section unless he stayed breech."

"He."

"Brennan. Four pounds, three ounces, sixteen inches. Rachel's still monitoring, but she's pleased with him, and his mother. She's one tough lady."

"So are you. Now go home, check on Colin, then get some sleep."

"I'm going to. We're about to rotate here. Let's all go home."

"I need to talk to the people in the auditorium, then I'll be home."

With a nod, Lana ran her fingers through Fallon's hair. "You're going to find some of them need more time to acclimate. Katie's working on housing—there are so many, and many of those shouldn't be left on their own yet."

"We've got volunteers who'll take some in," Simon pointed out. "Those who seem steadier can take some of the housing we prepped before the rescue. But some may just want to go."

"They shouldn't, not yet, but—"

"I'll talk to them," Fallon assured her, and guided her mother to the horses. "Wanna flash?"

"Actually, a ride would be good." Lana waited until Simon mounted, held up a hand and swung up behind him, as if she—once an urbanite, a New York native—had been riding all of her life. "Come home soon," she said, and nuzzled into Simon's back, wrapped her arms around him.

Love, Fallon thought as they rode off. Maybe that was the biggest miracle. Feeling it, giving it, knowing it.

She swung onto Grace and rode toward the school, hoping to convince the tortured, the exhausted, the sick at heart to believe.

CHAPTER TWO

When Fallon arrived home, she spotted Ethan coming out of the stables, the dogs Scout and Jem trotting at his heels, as usual. His recent growth spurt still gave her a little jolt. She remembered, clearly, the day he'd been born, at home, in the same big bed where she, Colin, and Travis had come into the world.

He'd let out a cry that had sounded to her ears like a laugh. When she'd been allowed to hold him the first time, he'd looked at her with those deep, deep newborn eyes, and she swore—still swore—he'd grinned at her.

As the baby of the family, his sunny nature revealed itself in that first laughing cry and every day since. But he was, Fallon admitted with some reluctance, no longer a baby.

Though he remained slight of build, he'd put on some muscle. He had their mother's butterscotch hair and lovely blue eyes, but it looked as if he'd inherited their father's height, as he'd sprung up inches in what seemed to be five minutes.

She smelled the stables on him—he'd been mucking them out, no doubt—as she dismounted.

"How's Colin?"

"Mom says good. He slept the whole time she and Dad were gone. Probably still asleep." As he eyed her, Ethan took Grace's reins while the dogs leaped, leaned, and looked for attention. "You should sleep, too."

"I will. Travis?"

"He came home for a few minutes, just to check in. He's taking Colin's schedule with the recruits, so he had to get back."

Her middle brother may not have lost his penchant for a good prank, but he stood up. Travis always stood up.

"Grace is happy you took her for a ride," Ethan said as he managed to nuzzle the dogs and the horse at the same time. When it came to animals, Ethan understood their thoughts, feelings, needs. That was his gift. "Now she's hoping for a carrot."

"Is that so?"

Fallon imagined the garden, the rows of carrots, the orange spears in the ground, the springy green tops. Choosing one, she let the words form in her head, flicked out a hand.

And held a carrot, fresh from the ground. Beside her, Ethan laughed.

"That's a good one."

"I've been working on it." Fallon swiped the dirt off the carrot on the thigh of her jeans, fed it to her sweet, loyal mare.

"I'll cool her down, get her settled," Ethan said. "Go get some sleep. Mom said to tell you there's leftover pasta if you're hungry. They're conked, too."

"Okay. Thanks, Ethan."

He started to lead Grace away, paused. "When Eddie got back—when I was over helping Fred with the farm, and he got back—he said what they did to the people you rescued was an abomination. That's his word for it."

"It was. It's exactly the right word for it."

"He said there were little kids locked up there."

"There were. Now they're safe, and they're free, and nobody will hurt them."

Those lovely blue eyes, so like their mother's, clouded. "It never makes any sense, you know? Being mean never makes any sense."

For Ethan, she thought as she walked to the house, the first choice and the last would always be kindness. She hated knowing he trained every day for war.

She considered the pasta, decided she was more tired than hungry, so went straight downstairs.

And found Colin waiting for her in the family room. Obviously he'd woken with an appetite, as an empty bowl, plate, glass stood on the table.

A good sign, she thought, as was his color, the clear look to his hazel eyes.

"How's the shoulder?"

He shrugged with the good one, lifted the other arm in its sling. "It's fine. Mom says I have to wear this dumb-ass thing for the rest of the day, maybe tomorrow, so I don't jerk it and screw things up. Pain in the ass."

"She'd give you a bigger ass pain if you screwed things up."

"Yeah." He might be a fearless soldier, but he wasn't stupid enough to take on their mother. "Hell of a fight, huh?"

She let him talk it out. He'd need to, she knew, as most of the men and women she'd visited in the clinic had needed to.

"We were basically on cleanup, you know? Man, we had them on their heels, Fal, on their fricking heels. This is when you were down in the torture chamber, right? Eddie said you were down there."

He paced as he spoke—a nervous habit she understood, as she often did the same.

"So, a couple of the faeries are working on the locks
on the cells because we've got it under control, right?
You could hear some of them who were drugged to shit
and back calling for help. And kids crying. Jesus."

He paused at that. "Jesus, kids. You just never get over
that part. Anyway, this guy drops down, put his hands up.
I'm not going to neutralize some dude who's surrendering,
so I move in to take his weapons—he laid them down, for
Christ's sake. And, Jesus, Fallon, one of his own shoots
him, and wings me before I could take him out."

A soldier to the bone, one who'd formed a strong band
of brothers—and sisters—in arms, Colin's disgust came
with a lacing of fury.

"He shot his own man. His own, unarmed, man. Who
the fucking fuck does that?"

"True believers," she said simply. "Don't underesti-
mate the true believer."

"Well, whatever the son of a bitch believed, I believe
he's burning in hell now. He shot his own man, a man
with his hands up. No threat. Anyway." He gave her that
one-shoulder shrug again. "We got them out. Did you
talk to Clarence?"

"Yes. He's doing fine."

"Good. Good. I saw him go down, but I couldn't get
to him."

"Most of our wounded have been treated and released. The others need a little more time in the clinic,
but they're going to be fine."

"Yeah, Mom said. I think I'll go into town, see how
everybody's doing anyway."

"Tell Ethan so he can tell Mom and Dad if I'm still
sleeping."

"Sure." With his free hand, he stacked the plate, bowl, glass, balanced them. Then his eyes met hers, warrior to warrior.

"It was a good mission. Three hundred and thirty-two prisoners freed."

"Three hundred and thirty-three. One of them just had a baby."

"No shit?" He grinned. "Good deal. See you later."

She walked back to her room as he started upstairs. He'd been raised a farmer, she thought, one who loved basketball and bragging and finding little treasures. Once he'd claimed he'd be president. He wouldn't, Fallon thought as she stripped to the skin. He was, and always would be, a soldier. And a damn good one.

She dragged on an oversize T-shirt she'd scavenged years before and used for sleep with a pair of boys' boxers. After countless washings the image of the man and his guitar on the shirt had faded like a ghost. Her dad called him The Boss, said he'd been—or was, who knew?—a kind of rocking troubadour.

She didn't have any musical talent, but she knew what it meant to be the boss.

So she slid into bed thanking the gods no one she loved or commanded had died. And as the voices, the stories, the nightmares of those she'd helped save rang in her head along with their fears, their gratitude, their tears, she ordered herself to shut them out.

And sleep.

She woke in moonlight with the chill of fall in the air. Fog grazed along the ground, thin smoke that wound through the stone circle. Frost, sharp as diamonds, sparkled on the high grass of the field.

The woods beyond rattled and moaned with the wind.

"Well." Beside her, Duncan scanned the field, the woods, then turned to study her with dark green eyes. "This is unexpected. Did you pull me in?"

"I don't know."

She hadn't seen him in nearly two years and then only briefly when he'd flashed back to New Hope to report. She knew he'd come back at Christmas to see his family because Tonia mentioned it.

He'd left New Hope two years ago come October, after the battle in the gardens when he'd lost a friend who'd been a brother to him. When she'd struck down her father's brother, his murderer—and Simon Swift had finished him.

He'd gone to help train troops, to work with Mallick, her own teacher, at a base far enough away to give them both time and space.

"Well," he said again. "Since we're here." He kept his hand on the hilt of his sword as he spoke, as he went back to scanning the woods, the shadows, the night. "I heard the rescue mission hit the marks. Big one," he added, glancing at her again. "We could have helped."

"There were enough of us to handle it. More are coming. You . . ."

He wore his hair longer than he had, she noted, or just hadn't bothered with a trim. It curled over the collar of his jacket. He hadn't bothered to shave, either, so his face—all the strong angles of it—carried a scruff.

She wished it didn't suit him. She wished she didn't feel this . . . want for him.

"Me?" he prompted.

"I'm disoriented. I don't like it." She heard the angry edge in her voice, didn't care. "Maybe you pulled me in."

"Can't tell you. Wasn't intentional either way. For me

it was summer, evening. I was in my quarters thinking about capping off a long day with a beer. We've got a nice little brewery going on base. You?"

Ordering herself to calm, she answered in kind. "Summer, the day after the rescue. I'd just gotten home. I was sleeping. It could be evening by now."

"Okay then, we're likely on the same time both ways. It's not summer here. MacLeod land, my mother's blood's land. The first shield, the one my grandfather broke."

"The dark broke the shield. The boy and the man he became was a tool, innocent. He was innocent."

Her voice changed, deepened, when a vision came on her. She changed, all but glowed. He'd seen it before. "Here she goes," he murmured.

"You are of him, Duncan of the MacLeods. I am of him, for we are of the Tuatha de Danann. As our blood and the taint of the blood of what waits opened the shield to magicks, bright and dark, so will blood close it again."

"Whose?"

"Ours."

"Let's get to it then." He drew his knife from its sheath on his belt, prepared to score his palm.

"Not yet!" She gripped his arm, and he felt the power in her, through him, pumping. "You risk opening all, risk the end of all. Famine and flood, scorched earth and the ash of the world. There's so much more to come. Magicks rising, light and dark, dark and light. The storm whirling, swords slashing."

Now she laid her hand on his heart, and he felt too much. Every muscle in his body quivered when her eyes, dark with visions, met his. "I am with you, in battle, in bed, in life, in death. But not this night.

"Do you hear the crows?"

He looked up, watched them circling. "Yeah. I hear them."

"They wait, it waits, we wait. But the time is coming."

"Can't come soon enough," he muttered.

She smiled at him, and something in the look was sly and seductive and full of power.

"You think of me."

"I think of a lot of things." God, she made his mouth water. "Maybe you should snap out of it."

"You think of me," she repeated, and slid her hands up his chest until her arms circled his neck. "And this."

Her body molded to his; her mouth brushed his once, twice. Teasing, alluring. A damn laugh in her throat. He ached everywhere, all at once, and wanted, needed more than he could bear.

"The hell with it. All of it."

Now a sound like triumph in her throat as he took those offered lips.

She tasted of the wild, and made him crave it. The savage and the free, the unknown, the always known. Desperate, his hands ran up her body, over it—at last—while he changed the angle of the kiss, deepened it.

Crows circling overhead, the stones swimming through the fog, the wind like mad music over field and wood.

Hard against her, his heart beating like thunderclaps, he would have dragged her to that frost-coated ground, taken her at the entrance of doom.

But she knocked him back, and nearly off his feet with a sudden jolt of outraged power.

Breath heaving, he stared at her, saw the visions had drained. What stared back at him was a very pissed-off female.

"What the hell is wrong with you?" she demanded.

"Do you think we came here so you could move on me and—"

"I don't know why the hell we're here, but you're not going to put that on me. You started it, sister. You moved on me."

"I . . ."

He watched the temper change to confusion, then— some satisfaction, at least—some shock and shame.

"I wasn't myself."

"Bullshit. You're always yourself, visions or not." And he remained so hard, so damn needy he had to fight not to tremble with it. "The vision card doesn't play for me."

"I'm sorry." She said it stiffly, but she said it. "I don't know why . . ."

"More bullshit. We both know why. Sooner or later we'll finish this and see if that takes care of it, or not. Meanwhile . . ."

"I'm not a diddler."

"A what?"

So much heat still inside her, she realized. From lust—she wasn't so stubborn she wouldn't acknowledge it—and from embarrassment. "It's what Colin calls girls who come on to guys, then flick them off because they can. I'm not like that."

"No, you're not like that." Calmer, he looked at her again. "We feel what we feel, you and me. One of the reasons I left is because I'm not ready to feel it. I figure it's the same for you."

"It'd be easier if you stayed mad."

"It'd be easier if you let me have you. Too bad for both of us." He tipped his head back, studied the circling crows. "We've been here before, you and me."

"Yes. We'll be here again. What we do then, what we do between now and then, and after? It all matters so much. I can't think about . . . sex."

"Everybody thinks about sex," he said absently. "I told you I'd come back to New Hope, and I will. I told you I'd come for you, and I will."

He drew his sword, enflamed it, shot fire at the crows. He turned to her again as they erupted and fell. "You think of me, too."

She woke in her bed with the evening light of summer slipping soft through her windows. She sighed, rolled out of bed to dress and find her family.

Duncan popped back to his quarters with the same rude jolt he'd popped out of them.

"Son of a *bitch*!"

He dropped down on the side of his bunk to get his breath back. Not like flashing, he thought. That brought a little zip to the blood, but this had been—coming and going—like being shot out of a cannon.

He damn well didn't appreciate it.

He needed a beer, maybe a good, long walk. He needed his hands on Fallon again. No, no, wanted his hands on her, and that was a lot different than need.

He'd kept them off her for damn near two years, he reminded himself, and got up to pace around the bedroom of the house he shared with Mallick. He'd have kept them off her longer if she hadn't moved on him.

Not her fault—not altogether anyway. He wasn't stupid enough to think otherwise. They'd gotten caught up in something—best to just leave it there.

How many times had he been to that place in dreams, in visions? The stone dance, the fields, the woods. He'd never been inside the farmhouse where the MacLeods had lived for generations before the Doom, but he knew it.

Tonia knew it—because she'd told him.

Did Fallon?

He should've asked. If he found himself in that field again, he'd go to the house, look for his ghosts. Look for the family who'd worked the land, lived and died there for generations.

He knew their names because his mother had told him. Their names, their stories. But it wasn't the same.

He strapped on his sword. Strange, he'd worn it at the stones, but he'd taken it off to shower after the long training day. He'd worn his prized leather jacket—one he'd scavenged when he and some troops had flashed to Kentucky on a scouting mission.

Dressed for weather and defense, he considered. Fallon, too, he recalled. Brown leather vest over a sweater, wool pants. She sure as hell hadn't been sleeping in cool-weather clothes.

So that was interesting. Magicks were, for him, endlessly interesting. A science, an art, a wonder all wrapped up with power.

He glanced at the pile of books—most loaned to him by Mallick. Study, the man said, constantly. Read and learn, look and see, train and do.

His own personal Yoda.

Man, he missed DVD nights back at home.

He wandered the room, looking at the sketches he'd pinned on his walls. His mom, his sisters, friends, one of Bill Anderson outside Bygones. One of the memorial tree. It held his father's name, and the name of the man who'd stood as his father for a brief time.

The man his mother had loved, for that brief time. And Austin had given him an art set—even more prized than the leather jacket. He'd long since worn the colored pencils, the charcoals, pastels to nothing. But he'd scavenged more.

Mallick had surprised him, as he'd expected a man who was that hard a taskmaster to scoff at sketches, and to complain about the waste of paper and supplies.

Instead, Mallick found an alchemist who could create more.

Art, he'd said, was a gift.

Of course, it didn't hurt that Duncan drew maps as well—minutely detailed. Or could re-create an enemy base on paper to help plan a mission.

Still, Duncan hadn't shown him the sketches of Fallon. Not even the one he'd done of her drawing the sword and shield from the fire in the Well of Light.

He nearly opened the drawer where he kept sketches of her, then drew back. Just asking for trouble, he decided. So he dragged his fingers through his disorderly mop of black hair, considered it groomed, and walked out to the living room where Mallick sat by the fire.

He knew Mallick had chosen what was basically a vacation cabin for the fireplace, the trees, a plot of land he used for a garden, for beekeeping. And it had a loft for his workshop.

Duncan, who'd considered himself pretty well versed in magicks—hell, he'd taught the younger magickals back in New Hope—had learned a hell of a lot in that loft.

The place wasn't much—they had to bespell it in the winter to keep from freezing half to death—but they did well enough. Maybe neither of them could cook worth a damn, but they didn't starve.

"I'm going out for a beer."

"Have wine instead," Mallick said, "and tell me about Fallon."

Duncan stopped in his tracks. "You sent us there? Goddamn it."

"No, but I saw you, both of you, in the fire."

"You didn't send us?"

"No." Leaning forward, Mallick poured the second

glass of wine—a nice, tart apple wine he'd helped make the previous fall.

Duncan dropped down on the other end of the battered sofa. He'd rather a beer, but the wine was okay in a pinch.

He took a swallow, sized up Mallick.

The man didn't lie, so there was that. Now he sat, patient—he often displayed the patience of a damn cat at a mouse hole. Gray threaded through his dark hair, worn longer even than Duncan's. The white streak in his beard added a strange sort of . . . pizzazz, Duncan mused. He kept his body soldier fit.

Duncan supposed he looked pretty good for a guy with a few centuries under his belt.

"I was thinking about the beer, and *pop*. There we were. She said she'd been catching some rack time. She'd have earned it, from what Tonia told us."

"Yes."

"While we were there she had a vision."

Mallick nodded. "Tell me. I could see, but I couldn't hear."

Instead of the beer and the walk, Duncan drank wine by the fire and spoke of visions.

"Her blood, mine, Tonia's probably because of the twin deal. No surprise there. How and when," Duncan mused, "that's the mystery. Visions are a bitch more than half the time. More questions than answers with the cryptic bullshit."

"The answers are there," Mallick corrected. "You are of the Tuatha de Danann, as is Fallon. As was your grandfather. His blood, innocent blood, played a part in opening the shield. Yours, and the blood of The One, will close it."

Duncan tossed back more wine. "How and when?" he repeated.

"Courage, faith. These are the what that lead to the how. When you have them, when all that must be done has been done, leads to the when."

More cryptic bullshit, Duncan thought. "I put my life on the line, and will again. So does she. So do the people of New Hope, the people here, at every base we've established. So do the people who're fighting who we haven't been able to reach."

"The gods are greedy, boy," Mallick said mildly.

"Tell me about it. I don't ask why—what's the point— some people kill, torture, enslave other people. They just do."

"Fear, ignorance, a thirst for power."

"Just words." Duncan dismissed them as he might a thin layer of dust. "It's nature, for some it's just how they're wired. I've read the histories. People did the same as far back as those histories go. Before magicks faded and after. Maybe especially after. The world goes to hell, and they still do it."

"Life is long."

Duncan smirked. "Yours anyway."

Amused, Mallick shook his head. "The life of all, of worlds, of gods and magicks and men. But since mine has been long, I can tell you there have been times of harmony and balance, and always the potential for it. Faith and courage build that potential."

"Faith in gods and their cryptic bullshit?"

"In the light, boy. It's what it holds and offers. You would fight and die for your beliefs, your ideals, to defend the innocent and oppressed. But after the battle, the blood, the wars, will you live for them? Light for life."

"*Solas don Saol*." Duncan thought of the words engraved on the wooden cuff Fallon wore.

"The One came to understand the fight won't be enough." Leaning forward, Mallick poured himself more wine. "You've failed to report the rest of your time with her tonight."

"Not relevant." Annoyed, Duncan decided he could use a little more wine himself. "Besides, you saw for yourself."

Mallick said nothing, just sipped his wine. Damn cat-and-mouse patience.

"She moved on me. I kept my hands off her until she made the move. And I took them off her when she said no. Except she didn't say no. She never says no, exactly. And I'm not getting into that with you. It's weird."

"You're young and healthy, as is she. This alone creates attraction. But there's more between you than a desire for physical release, and you both know it."

"Physical release." Duncan rubbed his hands over his face, left them there. "Jesus."

"Do you think because I haven't indulged in the pleasures of the flesh I don't understand desire?"

"I don't want to—" Dropping his hands, Duncan stared, those green eyes both fascinated and appalled. "Ever? No sex, as in seriously ever? No, no, don't tell me. Talk about weird."

"Body," Mallick continued easily, "mind, spirit. There are some who find a mate in all three."

"I'm not looking for a mate."

Mallick nodded, sipped more wine. "When you don't look, you don't see."

Enough, Duncan thought as he pushed to his feet. Just enough. "I'm going for a walk."

Mallick sat where he was as Duncan strode out. The boy would brood, he thought. He'd also check the sentries, the security levels, do a spot check on the newer recruits.

The boy was a born soldier, a born leader, though he still had much to learn.

He would walk off his frustration and his brood, just as he would, eventually, meld his considerable courage with a faith he didn't yet trust. He'd make his way to where he needed to be.

The world depended on it.

CHAPTER THREE

Fallon spent time with her maps, studied images in her crystal—and slipped into it to gather more intel. Out of habit, she trained before her family rose, in the dark before dawn, conjuring ghosts to battle.

She helped mix balms, potions, tonics because they were needed, and the skill in creating them needed regular honing, like a good tool. She went on hunting parties, scouting parties, scavenged, as those skills required practice as well.

She'd learned from her parents that she couldn't lead a community without being part of it. From Mallick she'd learned that training, studying, looking could never cease.

As she walked to the barracks, the air sang with the ring of steel against steel, the *thump, thump* of the dummy bullets (real ammo remained too precious for training), the whiz of arrows in flight.

She watched soldiers and potential soldiers fight their mock battles, with Colin shouting orders and insults with equal fervor.

"Fuck it, Riaz, you're dead. Get the damn rocks out

of your boots and move your feet! Get off your ass, Petrie. Catch your breath?" She heard him layer in so much incredulity, she snickered as he grabbed Petrie's sword and used the enchanted blade to mock-slit Petrie's throat. "Try breathing without a windpipe. Now give me fifty."

Petrie, easily twice her brother's age, rolled over. He may have snarled—silently—but he started counting off the push-ups.

The brand on Petrie's wrist gleamed with sweat. He'd train, she thought, and would take orders from a teenager because he knew what it was to be a slave of the Purity Warriors.

The cult formed by the fanatical Jeremiah White branded magickals on the forehead with a pentagram. Then tortured and executed them. People like Petrie, the non-magickals, they marked as slaves, used as they chose—in the name of their merciless god.

So Petrie would train, he'd do the fifty, pick up his training sword, and fight back.

Some wouldn't. Some freed from slavery or oncoming death wouldn't pick up a sword or bow. That, she thought, was their choice. There were other ways to fight back. Planting, building, tending stock, teaching, sewing, weaving, cooking, treating the sick or injured, tending to children.

Many ways to fight.

Petrie had chosen the sword, and as he sweated out those fifty—arms quivering on the last five—she saw the potential soldier.

He'd train, she thought again, then she glanced over at the shouts.

Travis whipped another squad out of the woods, across the field, and through the last, brutal section of the obstacle course. A girl held the lead—maybe sixteen, Fallon judged, pale, pale white skin flushed now with effort. Delicate features, and a fierce determination in exotic eyes as she high-stepped through the old tires. She had a red streak—like a slash of defiance—in her hair while the long black tail of it bounced as she leaped onto the rope wall.

Climbed it like a lizard up a rock, Fallon noted with approval. Sweat soaked her shirt, ran down her face, but she swung over the ropes, charged up a narrow ramp to vault onto the next wall. She found her handholds, flipped over and down, then bolted over the finish.

A spotter called out her time. Twenty-three minutes, forty-one seconds.

Impressed, Fallon walked over, offered a canteen as a couple others hit the final wall.

"Thanks."

"Marichu, right?"

"Yes."

"That's a damn good time."

Marichu swiped away sweat. "You still hold the record at twenty-one twelve. I'll beat it."

"You think?"

"I'll beat it." She handed back the canteen. "I want to go on the next mission."

"How long have you been here? About three weeks?"

"Five. I'm ready."

"That's up to your instructors, and you have three more weeks to meet the minimal eight."

"I'm ready," Marichu repeated and walked away to stretch.

Fallon waited for Travis, waited until he'd seen the last man over the course, ordered his squad to hit the showers before the next round—tactics, the classroom session their father taught today.

"Marichu," she said.

Travis nodded, guzzled water. Lanky, his hair sun-streaked, and lately sporting a trio of thin braids on the left side, he glanced toward Marichu as she headed for the barracks with the others.

"Strong, smart, and freaking fast. Damn near elf fast. Well, a slow elf."

"But she's not an elf, right? Faerie."

"Yeah. She's the one who escaped the PWs before they got her to one of their compounds—but not before they'd raped her, knocked her around, and busted one of her wings beyond repair."

"Yes, I remember."

"She was in pretty bad shape when we stumbled on her—heading here, she said. That was me, Flynn, Eddie, and Starr. Fever from infection, half-starved, still hurting bad. Still, she had a stick she'd sharpened like a spear, and would've jabbed the shit out of us if she could before we convinced her we were the good guys."

"I wasn't here when you brought her in. The healers tried to fix her wing. Mom tried."

"Couldn't. Too much damage, too much time between the break and when we got her back. Rough for her, but I gotta say, she's compensated. She's good with the bow—not great, but she could be. Sloppy with a sword yet, but . . . She's got speed, endurance, agility—nobody in her group comes close."

"Thoughts, feelings?"

He blew out a breath. He'd been raised not to poke into people's private thoughts—not that he hadn't done so now and then. Now, since Petra had infiltrated and attacked, it was part of his job.

"She's good at blocking out the poke, I gotta say. But I get she's pissed, more determined, but pissed, too. She wants to fight. She likes learning to ride, wants to learn to drive. It's normal stuff, Fallon. No underbelly there, I can feel. Oh, and she's figured out Colin's got a thing for her."

"What?"

"He keeps it to himself, because she's kind of young, and a recruit. But he's got a little thing there. I didn't poke in—I could see it. Anyway."

"Anyway," she echoed for lack of anything else. "How many are ready for a mission?"

"You should ask Dad."

"I will. And Poe and Tonia and Colin and all of the instructors. Now I'm asking you."

He hooked his thumbs in his front pockets as he chewed it over, bite by bite. The fact he'd think carefully was the very reason she'd asked him first.

"Four, maybe five. Anson, Jingle, Quint, Lorimar—and maybe Yip. NM"—non-magickal—"elf, witch, NM, and shifter. In that order."

"Okay, thanks. See you later."

She moved over to where Tonia's archery group rotated out.

Duncan's twin—and it was impossible to look at her and not see him even though Tonia's features were more delicate, her eyes a summer blue instead of a forest green. The humidity had her hair curling wildly as if it fought to free itself from the restricting band.

She nocked an arrow, let it fly. And hit the straw-man target heart center.

"How's it going?"

Tonia nocked another arrow. "Not too bad. I've got one or two in the batch I just finished with who probably won't shoot an arrow or bolt into their own foot."

"Do you work with Marichu?"

"Sure. She's got potential, and I'm thinking of switching her to a crossbow. She's got the strength, and I think she'd work better with a crossbow than a compound. She tends to drop her left shoulder—and that's probably from the damaged left wing. We're working on it."

She shot a third arrow. The second had pierced the straw head between the eyes. The third went straight through the groin.

"No straw babies for you," Tonia said, and smiled. "Music in the gardens tonight. How about we hang?" Before Fallon could answer, Tonia laid a hand on her arm. "We reclaimed it, Fallon. We won't let Petra or her bitch of a mother take it from us. You said it yourself."

"Yeah, I did."

Petra, she thought, her cousin, daughter of her birth father's brother—and murderer. Blood of her blood.

She pushed it back. "I did," she repeated. "We won't."

"But you hardly ever come. Plus, there's a guy I'm looking over. You could give me your take."

Fallon envied how naturally, easily Tonia could "look over" a guy. And if the looking over part hit the mark, move to the next step.

"What guy?"

"Anson, recruit, worked his way up here from Tennessee. Totally cute accent, killer abs, and so far not an asshole."

"Travis said he was about combat ready."

"I'd agree there. So come check him out tonight. Come hang with me and Hannah."

"Next time," she said and meant it. "I can't tonight."

"You've got something else cooking?"

"Yeah. I'm still working out the details, and I need to talk to my dad, to Will, to some of the others—including you. To start, how many do you think are ready for a mission?"

"Of the boots? A lot of greenies, still." Tonia signaled so Fallon walked with her to retrieve the arrows. "I'd say

Anson with the studly abs. He's got nearly two months of training—an NM, fearless but not stupid. There's Quint, who came in about the same time. Witch, damn good swordsman. He's still learning to harness his magicks, but he keeps it wrapped well."

"Just the two?"

"Thinking," Tonia replied, and swiped at sweat on her forehead. "There's Sylvia—no," she said with a shake of her head. "Not yet there. Shit, Hanson Lorimar. He's a show-off, and irritates the crap out of me, but he's solid. NM," she added. "There's Jingle—very fast elf. She's a little goofy, but she gets down to it when it matters."

"What about Yip?"

"Shifter. Possible. What's the mission?"

Fallon started to evade. But this was Tonia. "PW enclave, Arlington."

Tonia's eyes widened. "Arlington? It's huge, and it's cozied right up with D.C."

"That's right."

"Word is they've formed alliances with Dark Uncanny and Raiders, fortified the shit out of the place."

"That's right, too."

Like Travis, Tonia took time to think. A fat jay winged by to perch on the straw man she'd killed, peck at it.

"Fallon, I'm with you, but we just don't have enough to take it."

"I'm working on that. Keep it quiet, okay, until I talk to my dad, Will, a few others."

"No problem. If we could take Arlington . . ."

"It would be a major kick in their ass," Fallon finished. "That's the idea."

With her father, Colin, Poe all doing instructor duty, she walked back home.

To her profound surprise, she found her mother, Fred, Arlys, and Katie swimming in the backyard pool.

"Caught us," Lana said with a laugh. "So join us."

"What's going on?"

"Committee meeting." Katie, town mayor and one of its founders, who'd given her dark curly hair to Tonia and her green eyes to Duncan, dunked her head back and giggled.

"Somebody's been into the wine," Fallon concluded.

"Oh, yes we have!" Fred, naked, flowed out her wings, fluttered up, shaking her curly red mop, then dived back in.

"Come on, baby, give yourself a break, too. Fred's youngest two are napping." Lana gestured to where Eddie and Fred's youngest slept on a blanket in the shade. "The rest of the kids are doing what kids do on a hot summer day."

"And we're having a little private party," Arlys finished. New Hope's chronicler, workhorse, founder wasn't naked. She wore a tank top and underpants as she floated blissfully on her back.

"I can't think of the last time I swam in a pool just because," she added.

It occurred to Fallon she'd never seen the four of them this relaxed—and she wondered if, now and again, they had their little private parties when she wasn't around.

God knows they'd earned them.

"Come on in!" Fred waved her hands, added little fountains to the water. "We're talking about men. And sex. I really like sex. Makes me all sparkly."

"I haven't had sex in . . . Who knows?" Katie finished. "The men I have sex with end up dead." She slapped a hand over her mouth as a laugh erupted, as Fred slid over to wrap an arm around her. "Oh, it's not funny. It's just true. I'm not sad," she assured Fred. "I loved them both. You know how that is, Lana."

"I do."

"I was thinking about having sex with Jeff Barlow."

Arlys sank, came up spitting out water. "Jeff Barlow!"

"Considering it. But, Jesus, I don't want to kill him." Katie laughed again, pushed back her wet ropes of hair. "But since it's a little lust and not love, maybe."

"He's a good soldier," Fallon said, she hoped helpfully.

Katie shot back an indulgent wink. "I was thinking more he has a nice ass, honey."

"Oh. Well." She could feel her mother's amusement as Lana treaded water and smiled. "I'd say Mark McKinnon has a better one, and he doesn't have a wife or woman, either."

Arlys let out a wild roll of laughter as Katie shook her head. "He does have a better ass," Katie considered, "but he's at least ten years younger than me."

"What difference does that make?"

"That's my girl. Mark McKinnon." Lana pointed at Katie. "Go for it."

"I couldn't . . . maybe."

"Try not to kill him," Fallon added, and after a shocked beat, all four women roared with laughter.

"You're now, officially, a member of our private party." Arlys sent a splash of water in Fallon's direction. "Into the pool, girlfriend."

She needed to get into town, needed to talk to Will, check on the rescues. She needed to— What the hell.

She unstrapped her sword, pulled off her boots. After a moment's consideration, she stripped down to the skin like her mother and Fred. And for the fun of it, leaped, rolled twice in the air, and dived in.

Later, when she rode into town, Fallon thought how much she'd enjoyed that half hour of silliness with a group of women. Her mother's circle—minus Rachel, who hadn't been able to get away from the clinic, and Kim, who had an herbalist class scheduled.

She knew her mother's power, her mother's strength. She depended on it. How much strength and will had it taken for Lana Bingham, a child in her belly, grief in her heart, to leave New Hope and that circle? To leave it to save the child and everyone, everything she'd left behind?

More than anyone she knew, Fallon decided.

She thought of the other women—she knew their stories.

Katie, who'd lost her husband, her parents, her entire family but for the twins inside her. It had taken strength to survive, more strength, and such compassion, to take another infant whose mother hadn't survived as her own.

With Jonah's and Rachel's help and friendship, Katie had escaped New York with her three infants.

Arlys Reid, intrepid reporter, had watched her colleagues sicken and die of the Doom, had watched her city fall, the world crumble. But she, along with a few brave souls, including Fred, had continued to broadcast for as long as possible.

With Chuck, hacker and IT guru, as her source, Arlys uncovered the truth and the lies. How many lives had she saved by telling the truth? Fallon wondered.

What had it been like for Fred to discover the magick inside her, to sprout wings? For some the emergence of powers brought madness or turned them dark.

For Fred it brought joy, a passion for spreading that joy, and a devotion to defend and protect all.

Her mother had chosen her circle well. Without them, without the sacrifices they'd made, the will not just to survive but to rebuild, there would be no New Hope.

Without New Hope and communities like it, the light would dim, and dark prevail.

She'd intended to ride through town to the police station in hopes of finding Will Anderson. But she saw him standing on the sidewalk talking to a couple—Anne and Marla, she remembered, weavers who raised llamas. Will crouched down to the level of the little boy they'd taken in. After Petra had killed his mother. He'd be about five, Fallon calculated, and chattered happily at Will as they examined a little toy horse.

But as she approached on Laoch, the little boy huddled behind his mother, peeked out at her.

"It's all right, honey." Anne stroked his curly cap of hair. "This is Fallon. You remember her. He's shy until he gets to know you," she told Fallon.

"That's okay. I don't mean to interrupt."

"We just came into town to deliver some socks," Marla said. "And stopped into Bygones. Elijah said his alphabet for Mr. Anderson and got a prize."

"That's a nice horse." As Will had done, she crouched down, but didn't move closer. "My dad made me a wooden horse when I was little. I still have it. And now I have this big guy, too."

Because she'd looked into the boy, she smiled, then murmured to Laoch in Irish.

He spread his wings.

"Like yours, Elijah. I see the light in you."

He dipped his head, but she saw his smile, shy and sweet. And his wings, a quick flutter of blue.

Anne pressed her fingers to her lips as her eyes filled. "He never—We had no idea. Oh, Elijah, look how pretty your wings are."

"We wondered." Marla leaned down to kiss the top of Elijah's head. "But he never showed any signs."

"It takes time for some, especially . . ." Fallon let that go as Anne lifted him, settled him on her hip.

"Yes, especially. I think tonight, after dinner, we're going to have an ice-cream party with Clarence and Miranda."

"Ice cream!" Elijah threw back his head and laughed. "Tawbewwy!"

"Yes, strawberry. We'll work on those *r*'s later. Come on, Marla, let's get our little man home. It's good to see you Fallon, Will."

They settled Elijah in a carrier seat on a bike. Marla got on it, Anna on another. With a wave they rode off, with Elijah's wings still fluttering.

"They're good people," Will commented. "Taking in three damaged kids and making a family. Three magickal kids, as it turns out. You could see he was a faerie?"

"His light's quiet and shy. And sweet," she added. "Very sweet."

"His mother was one of the rescues from the anti-magick cult. Indoctrinated and brainwashed to believe magick was evil. She'd have taught him that, tried to repress what he was."

"I remember. Petra pretended to come from the same cult and lived with them here. God knows what she tried to teach him. They are good people, his mothers now. If they'd reacted differently—too strongly, not strongly enough—he might have tried to hide his nature again instead of embracing it."

"Strawberry ice cream never hurts. You've got something on your mind," he added.

"I came into town to talk to you."

"Okay. We can head up to the station, or just head up to the house. I was just coming from the house, going to check in with Chuck. Trying to find my wife."

"Oh, she's at our place. Having a . . . meeting with Mom and Fred, Katie. Could we go ahead into Chuck's den? He could add to this."

"Sure."

She turned to Laoch, stroked him. He rose up on his wings, soared off.

"Never gets old." Shading his eyes with the flat of his hand, Will watched Laoch fly. "Where's he going?"

"Where he likes. He'll come when I need him." As would her wolf, her owl. "Can you tell me if the rescues are acclimating? That's the wrong word," she realized. "That sounds cult-like, doesn't it?"

"Not when I know what you mean. The medicals have set up therapy—group and individual. Physically some of them still need some time to heal. Emotionally's going to take longer for a lot of them. You know Marlene, right?"

"Town planner."

"Yeah. She's playing den mother in one of the group houses. Plus, one of the rescues was a therapist before the Doom. He's a little shaky yet himself, but it seems like a good idea to have one of their own working with them."

"It does." Resilience, she thought, was a light of its own. "How many have left New Hope?"

"Three so far."

"A smaller number than I figured. And the baby, his mother?"

"Both doing okay, according to Jonah. I saw him earlier."

They walked around the back of the house where Rachel and Jonah lived with their boys, and to Chuck's basement entrance.

She smelled freshly mown grass, sun-soaked herbs before they went inside and down.

There she smelled salt, something sugary.

Chuck sat in front of monitors and keyboards and odd electronic boxes, switches, and joysticks.

Fallon could speak countless languages, had within her every spell ever written, but the world of computers posed a thorny mystery for her.

She'd gained a little skill—with Chuck's help—since coming to New Hope, but for her entire life before they'd left the farm for New Hope, she'd been IT-free.

"Who enters the master's den?" Chuck slurped at the something sugary in his glass. "Hi, guys."

"No minions today?" Will asked, as Chuck had a variety of IT apprentices.

"Class dismissed. It's summer, dude. And my top guys and gals are working on their own with some of the goodies you brought me back from the dungeons. You fried a bunch of it."

"We were a little fixed on life and death," Fallon reminded him.

"Yeah, yeah. Well, components are people, too. Anyway, I got Hester seeing if she can revive some of it with the woo-woo." He reached a hand into a bowl of chips. "Want? Got more. Fixed this old PlayStation out at Fred's yesterday and scored the chips of potato."

"I'll pass on the chips," Will told him, "but I could use something cold if you got it."

"Brew?"

"I'm still on duty."

"Lemonade."

"Sold."

Will went over to Chuck's cold box, took out the jug. "What are you monitoring?"

"I've got a PW base in Utah—that's a new one. They're just setting up."

"Branching out," Will added.

"What I'm getting is that our favorite lunatic, Jeremiah

White, sent about twenty from Michigan, had them
meet up with a group from Kansas, then pull together
with some new recruits in Utah to set this up. They lost
about fifteen percent getting there. But they rounded up
most of a community in Nebraska—farming settlement,
magickals and nons. They're estimating to have the base
secured—the housing, the weaponry, the supplies, and
all that—by the end of the week. So they can have their
first round of executions on Sunday."

He shoved the bowl of chips aside. "Fuckers."

"We've never attempted any rescues that far out,"
Will said to Fallon. "They're not secure yet, but—"

"Now's the time. They won't have any Dark Uncanny
with them."

"If they did," Chuck put in, "it wouldn't take them
days to secure. So, no DUs."

She shifted Arlington out of her mind for the moment.
"Can you get exact coordinates?"

"I'm working on it."

"How confident are you in your numbers?"

"I'm confident that's what they're reporting back to
Arlington. I've been catching bits of chatter off and on
for a while, but it didn't amount to much before this
morning. And like Will said, they're a hell of a lot farther away than anything we've tried. I've been banking
it, keeping track when I could."

A new plan, even more ambitious, began to form in
Fallon's mind. "We need everything you have. We'll get
it to Mallick and Duncan. Both have flashed farther than
Utah before, and they'll know who at their base can handle the tagalong."

She took the lemonade from Will but set it down again
as she paced the big room crowded with electronics, with
monitors and screens, with shelves stacked with wound-
up cables, components, spare parts.

And the scavenged dolls Chuck haughtily called action figures.

"Duncan takes two to scout, get the lay of the land, the setup, the security in place."

"Elves and shifters are usually best for that," Will said.

"Yeah. He'll know. Relay the intel. By the end of the week, you said."

"They're reporting they'll be fully up and operational by Friday," Chuck confirmed.

"That gives them three days. But it can be done. The prisoners will fight back. They've formed a community, so they'll fight back once they're able to. And once they hit it . . ."

Yes, yes, she could see it. See how it could be done. Fate had just dropped an opportunity in her lap.

"We don't take out their communications."

"Yippee." Chuck pumped a fist in the air. "More toys for me."

"We don't take them out. Let them signal the attack— back to Arlington. And when they do, when Arlington's dealing with that, we hit Arlington."

Will lowered his glass. "Sorry, what? Did you just say we hit Arlington?"

"Yes. It's what I wanted to talk to you about. I'd thought next week, but this is the time." She considered a minute. "And one more. There's the base in South Carolina we've been monitoring."

"Yeah, near Myrtle Beach, but it's more an outpost, almost a vacation spot for good PWs," Chuck added.

"We haven't gone that far afield, either, and it hasn't been high on the list, as it is more an outpost. But now." She circled the room again. "We hit all three, simultaneously."

"Holy shit, Fallon." Will, a man who'd survived the Doom and all its horrors, who'd fought DUs, PWs,

Raiders, commanded troops, served as the town's law, sat down. Hard.

"They'd never expect it. They're getting reports on attacks on two far-flung bases. There's a scramble, distraction. Add it's a walled base—a fancy gated community they've fortified."

"They've got DUs," Chuck reminded her, thoughtfully tugging on the little goatee he'd dyed magenta. "You've helped me take down the shields their DUs put up so I could get some intel, but they've got DUs, Raiders and, from that intel, experienced ex-military. Ex-cops. It's their main conduit to the war in D.C. I know we've kicked this around—"

"You kicked it around?" Will interrupted.

"Theoretically," Fallon told him. "And I talked to my dad about it last night. I'd plotted it out differently, but this is better. It's more than a rescue, and yes, getting people out is always the priority. But this is more. Three bases, the weapons, equipment, supplies—and the damage done to White's organization. To his reputation. His power grid.

"Duncan and Mallick to Utah, Thomas and Minh," she decided, thinking of the elf community, and the base established near Mallick's cottage, "to South Carolina. And we hit the main target. We take Arlington."

She looked around. "I need a map."

"I've got one . . . somewhere."

Rather than wait for Chuck to find anything that wasn't electronic or edible, she flashed back to her room, flashed back with a map.

"Let me show you how I see it. Then you can show me how it can be better."

CHAPTER FOUR

With time so short, the goal so ambitious, Fallon called for a meeting that night, asked the key members to gather at her home.

As her mother, being her mother, would never consider holding any sort of gathering without food, Lana organized a menu. When Fallon finished her own preparations, she went out to find her mother making her own in her outdoor summer kitchen.

"Deserted by the men? I'll give you a hand."

"Cucumbers, thin, curled," Lana told her.

"Got it." As she worked, Fallon felt the mood. "You're worried about the scope of these missions, the timing, but—"

"Of course I am." Hands busy, Lana selected vegetables she'd already turned into art. "Three of my children, my husband, my friends, are going to war in a matter of days." While the anxiety leaked through, Lana continued to layer crackers she'd baked, herbed with rosemary or seasoned with garlic, with various toppings.

"I can't hold Travis back, not this time. He's—"

"I know that, Fallon. I've known this was coming

since he started training for it back at the farm. What I
don't know, what I don't understand is why you talked to
your father about this, to Will, to Chuck, to everyone, it
seems, but me."

"I only talked to Dad, seriously about Arlington, last
night after I'd worked on the details. I asked him not to
say anything until I'd talked to—"

"Everyone else."

"Mom." Fallon put down the kitchen tool, turned. "I
needed to talk to Travis, to Tonia about the recruits, get a
sense if we could use any of them, or if any of them were
ready to . . . move up if we lost people on this mission."

"And still, you didn't—"

"Wait, please."

A bee buzzed in, hovered over the crackers. Fallon
merely gave it a warning look to send it zipping away.

"I came back home after I'd talked to them, had a
look for myself. I knew you had a meeting with Arlys
and Katie and Fred about establishing permanent homes
for the new rescues. I wanted to talk to all four of you
about Arlington, but you were having a little fun. The
four of you were just having a little fun, and I didn't want
to ruin it."

Lana stopped what she was doing, turned to Fallon.
"I'm sorry. I should've known better."

"You looked so happy, all of you, buzzed on wine and
friendship. I really wanted you to have that. I wanted
some of it, too. I took it with you."

"You did." Lana drew her in. "I'm glad you did, and
I'm sorry."

"Don't be sorry. All this is hard and ugly, and . . . I
thought of the four of you when I left. I thought of all
you've done, what you faced, overcame, what you've
made. Your circle—not quite the full one, as Rachel and
Kim couldn't be there—they're all heroes to me."

"One day." Lana brushed a hand through Fallon's hair. "One day my circle and yours are going to get buzzed on wine and friendship and talk about men and sex."

"I hope I have some experience with the last two by then so I can add to the conversation."

"You will. But tonight, we'll do what we have to do."

"Starting with food."

Lana laughed. "Always."

So on a sultry summer night with the younger children with sitters or older siblings, the New Hope Originals gathered on the patio. Members of the next generation gathered with them for food and drink, and talk of war.

Across the field, green with summer, cows lowed as the first stars began to blink awake. Growing fuzzy again after their shearing, sheep dotted the gently rolling hills like small clouds. In the coop chickens hummed as they bedded down.

She saw Faol Ban slide like white smoke through the trees beyond where Taibhse sat wise and silent on a branch. Over the western hills, the sun slowly simmered its way down toward the rounded peaks.

She watched their Jem and Scout romp with Eddie's dog Hobo while old Joe, ever faithful, snoozed at his feet.

Not like her mother's little private party that afternoon, she thought, but still a circle of friends.

"I should start by telling you I spoke with Mallick and with Thomas."

"By radio?" Katie asked.

"No, I flashed. I wanted to speak face-to-face."

"Did you see Duncan?"

"No, sorry. He was out on maneuvers. I laid it out for both of them, and they agree it can be done. They'll work on tactics, logistics, do the scouting, and we'll continue to coordinate. Not by radio or computer," she added. "I know Chuck's got those covered, and we've added shields. But if any of our communications leak, well, it all goes to hell."

"Not insulted." Chuck popped a fat strawberry in his mouth. He wore sandals of braided rope with soles made from strips of old tires. "They've got some good hackers," he added. "I'm better, but they've got some good ones. I'll keep monitoring all three bases. Can't get much direct out of Arlington itself, but I got a clear line to the others, and it leads back. Any changes, champ, you'll hear about it."

"And we'll adjust to them," Fallon confirmed. "Right up until we strike. Will and I worked out the broad strokes, and some of the finer ones earlier. To start."

She held up her hands, drew the power up, out as she spread her hands over the air.

The map she'd drawn appeared, standing as if pinned to a wall.

"Excellent," Eddie said, and crunched into a cracker.

"Tonia and I worked on it. Target bases in red, ours in blue. I'll have more detailed maps after the targets are scouted."

"What's the green?" Flynn asked. No sandals for him, Fallon noted, but sturdy boots he likely made himself.

"Locations where we can potentially relocate the rescues. We're about at capacity in New Hope, considering housing, supplies, medical. And we need to start establishing bases farther south, west, north. Colin, you and Dad need to pull out some of our experienced troops, ask for volunteers to relocate. We'll also need the town council to talk to skilled, experienced people—who we can spare—to help with that. Tonia and I will speak to some of the rescues, and Hannah, Rachel, Jonah need to work out who we can spare with medical experience, and if we can spare any supplies. If we can't, we'll scavenge as we go."

She turned back to the map. "The group in Utah taken by the PWs had settled in Nebraska—farming community, and from what we've gathered, poor security and defense. We can get them back to Nebraska, but we'll establish a base."

"It's a long way," Rachel chimed in. She held a glass of wine, but had yet to drink. At her feet sat a small medical kit the doctor carried everywhere.

"We can rotate volunteers, but we need a solid contingent to build and secure not just a community, but a base, one that can defend itself against PWs, Raiders, and the government forces still hunting magickals. We need the same in South Carolina. There's a forest here." She gestured to the map. "And access to the ocean. We can set up to mine salt."

"Roads have to be cleared." Arlys paused in her note taking, frowned at the map.

"And repaired," Poe added. "Likely bridges, too. You need water, power, sewer or septic—your basics."

"Fuel," Kim put in, "lumber, tools."

"We transport what we can, scavenge. We build. There should be plenty of game in both locations, and it's good farmland in the west. We'd clear for farmland, if necessary, in the south. We plan for this, or taking the targets, getting people out . . . we've got nowhere to put them safely. And we need to start adding locations. Once we have these bases, they can scout, scavenge, rescue where we haven't."

"You're talking about doing a lot in a really short time." Will adjusted the cap Fallon knew his daughter had made in crafting class. Across the forest green it read LAWMAN in precisely embroidered white.

"I know. The new bases would be rudimentary, initially, but we'd claim our ground, then build. Just the way you, all of you, did right here. We need more like you. We have to find more like you, more people like my father, like Thomas, Troy, and others my family and I found on the way here. You don't know Thomas or Troy or those others yet, but they built communities, societies, and they'll fight to protect them because, like you, they know survival comes first, but it isn't enough."

"We don't know the world you knew." Tonia got to her feet. "We only know it through books, DVDs, what you tell us. We were babies, or not even born in those first years where every day was life-and-death, when everything you knew was gone. But we know this world, what it takes to live in it."

"We've seen what you've done." Now Travis got to his feet. "At the farm, Dad, the cooperative, the village back home. Here in New Hope, and all the places we found people fighting to build a life. Here we are sitting together, feeling safe on a really nice night with Eddie's farm over there and the barracks over there. You can't have one," he said, gesturing toward the farm, "without the other," and to the barracks.

"Like Tonia said," he continued, "we know this world and what it takes to live in it, because you gave it to us, you fought for it, built it, and taught us how to live in it. But the world goes beyond the farm back home, New Hope, and the places from here to there. If we don't take it for the light, they'll take it for the dark."

"They're right." Hannah let out a sigh. "Sometimes I imagine what it would be like if New Hope was the world. If this was all there was. Our homes, our neighbors, working at the clinic, learning to be a doctor, spending time with friends, music in the gardens on a night like this. Then I remember another night like this in the gardens. I remember when someone I thought was a friend tore through our home. I think of Denzel and Carlee and everyone she killed. I think of what we do, Rachel, Jonah, in the clinic after a mission. You taught me what to do.

"I don't have magick like Fallon, Tonia, Travis. I'm not a soldier like Colin. But I know what to do, and what needs to be done, because you all taught me."

"Basically," Colin said after a pause, "we're saying it's time we kicked some ass."

That got a laugh, reluctant in some corners, but a laugh.

"You're not wrong," Fallon told him. "Ass kicking's on the list. So's rescuing, training, staking claims, building, expanding."

"Okay." Katie lifted her hands in what struck them as a gesture of surrender. Her eyes, Duncan's eyes, Fallon thought, scanned the group. "First I'm going to say I'm proud of all of you. Next, I'm going to say it sounds like you're telling us it's time to pass the torch."

"No. I don't want you to pass the torch," Fallon said quickly. "I hope like hell you won't pass it."

"But we need more torches," Simon finished, and had her releasing a relieved breath.

"Yes. We need more torches. They bring the light."

"The light will grow," Lana said.

Fallon felt the vision take her mother even as it took her. "From the source to The One and beyond." It rose in Fallon, spread with the words she spoke. "The end is done, the beginning begun. The five links joined, for good or ill."

"The dark will come, with blood and death, in madness and guile. It lives to extinguish the light. On a dark beast it rides to bring grief and loss. You will weep, daughter, child of the Tuatha de Danann, and the dark will drink your tears. You will despair, and the dark will feed on your heart. This is your mother's sorrow."

"Light against dark, life against death, blood against blood. We will rise up, rise up, rise up, and when the storm passes, if the light holds, five will stand together."

"The five links joined," they said together, "never again to break. Who rides through the storm and stands brings good or ill for all."

With the visions fading, Fallon gripped Lana's hand. "I won't fail. I can't."

"The dark beast is real. A black horse. No, a dragon."

"With a red inverted pentagram." Fallon ran a finger down the center of her forehead. "I saw it. I can't tell you not to worry, because that would be stupid. But I'm asking you to believe in me."

"If I didn't, I'd have defied the gods and kept you on the farm."

"What's up with the five links?" Eddie asked.

"Fallon's symbol. Well, the fivefold symbol," Fred corrected. "I think of it as Fallon's because it's on her sword."

"The four elements," Fallon explained, "linked by magick. So, whoever wins this, those links are for good or for ill."

"So, we win," Colin said simply.

"You got that right. We're going to start lighting those torches. Tonia, Flynn, and I will scout Arlington tonight."

"Tonight?" Katie jolted in her seat. "We haven't begun to organize."

"It's a lot to accomplish in a short time. We can flash Flynn—it's always easier with another magickal. Duncan, Mallick, and another of their choosing scout the Utah base, Thomas and two of his people the one in

South Carolina. Then we coordinate, work out plans of action."

She looked back at Katie. "Organize. Meanwhile, we've got a—I'll go with rudimentary again—idea of the layout in Arlington from what Chuck's pieced together, and what I've pieced together through a series of looking spells."

"I would have helped you with those."

She glanced at her mother. "I know. I started doing them when I couldn't sleep, then realized needing to do them was *why* I couldn't sleep."

Fallon put up another map. "The problems are the distance for the looking, and their DU shields, so there are areas where it's more best guess and logic than actual seeing. The DUs working with them are highly skilled, so I didn't want to push it, risk leaving a trace they'd pick up."

"It's bigger than I thought." Will rose to walk closer to the map.

"Thirty-five acres, walled and shielded. I've marked the guard posts, and they have sentries patrolling twenty-four-seven. Additional security with the black magick shields. I watched a couple of deer drop when they got about three feet from the wall. When we're ready, we won't worry about traces or alerts, and take them down."

"Can we?" Kim, a woman with courage and brains Fallon respected, stood as well, walked closer to the maps. "There's no point losing people before we get through the wall."

"We'll take it down. Not all the buildings are going to be fortified or shielded. That takes too much power, and too many supplies. But we can count on the prisons— they have two—the armory, and other key buildings having their shields and fortifications."

She went over the layout section by section, asked Chuck to fill in with his bits of intel.

"So, we think they have somewhere between four and five hundred troops in the base at any given time. And possibly another fifty Raiders who use the base between raids by virtue of an alliance."

She nodded at Poe. "They rotate them out, do some training there, have designated squads for raids and Uncanny sweeps. As far as we can tell, Raiders don't serve on security, as guards, or the basic workforce."

"They keep some animals," Chuck put in. "Fresh eggs, fresh milk to supplement their hunting parties. And they grow some crops—all of that's taken care of by slaves. It's a lot of mouths to feed, clothe, and like that. Raiders bring in supplies, and get use of the base."

"We calculate they hold at least a hundred as slaves," Fallon continued. "It looks like they rotate them, too. When they need more in another location, they transport them. We can't really estimate prisoners at this point. While they hold weekly executions according to their fucked-up tradition—" She caught herself, looked at her mother. "Sorry."

"Considering the subject matter, it's hard for me to comment on your language."

"Ah. They hold their public executions every Sunday, but our best information is they keep it at one prisoner. The base serves as a kind of holding center for anybody they grab between—most likely—Virginia, down to North Carolina, and over to West Virginia, possibly eastern Tennessee."

"See, they pull them in," Chuck explained, "then if some of their other bases are running low for that Sunday picnic, they send some out."

"Add to that anyone—civilian, magickal—they pull in

from a mission into D.C. What passes for the government still holds the city. James Hargrove stands as president."

"Fucker." Chuck shot up a middle finger for emphasis. "And I'm not sorry."

"It's no democracy," Fallon continued. "Basically, he's an autocrat, running the show with the military."

"We can't get much from inside the White House," Chuck added. "But rumors fly. Executions again, but not public."

"A veneer of the civilized," Arlys put in. "But it's clear he's shredded the Constitution, and his agenda is removing magickals by any means."

"Experiments, containment centers," Chuck went on. "Vaults full of treasures—that's a rumor, so who knows. But it's pretty clear he's living in the lap, and likes it."

"He holds the power center in a dead city." Fallon had been there, felt it. "The resistance keeps fighting, has had some victories. And the Dark Uncanny prey on both."

"White wants D.C.," Simon commented. "There are plenty of locations, like theirs in Arlington, more removed from that war zone—twenty years now. He chose strategically, allied with Raiders so he doesn't have to worry about them. Allied with DUs for their power and again, so they don't go after him."

"I agree. He's wrong because they will go after him when they don't find him useful, but I agree. White wants the city."

"Symbolism, a seat of power. If he can take it, and publicly execute Hargrove, some generals, that's a statement."

"Hargrove goes by CIC more than president," Travis told him. "Commander in chief. It's more military."

"He was military," Fallon put in. "Served during the

Doom, and commanded the forces that swept New York, Chicago, and Baltimore."

She knew more of him, much more, but left it at that.

"They want the city, Hargrove, and as many key officials as they could take. But equally, they want the magickals, dark and light, in containment there. They want the locations of other containment camps. However much White wants D.C., its symbols, its structure, and whatever's left of its resources, his reason for being is still to destroy us."

"He's going to die disappointed."

She smiled at her father. "Yeah, he is. Because he's not going to take D.C. We are."

"Whoa." Jonah picked up the beer he'd set aside. "Even if we managed to hook up with the resistance there, we'd be outnumbered a hundred to one. We've treated escapees from D.C. in the clinic. It's a daily bloodbath."

"Today we'd be outnumbered. We won't be when we take it, and we *will* take it. It starts here." She turned back to the first map. "With Utah, South Carolina. And Arlington."

Fallon waited until full dark before she walked away from the house with Tonia and Flynn. Lupa walked by Flynn's side.

"I wanted to leave him with Joe and Eddie, but . . ." He laid a hand on Lupa's head. "He wouldn't have it."

"He's welcome."

Flynn had a rifle strapped over his shoulder, a knife on his belt. Tonia had her bow and quiver, her knife, and Fallon her sword and shield.

When she lifted her arm, the white owl glided out of the dark to land on it.

"Okay. Who's better at scouting than an owl?" Tonia

decided. "You know, we shook them pretty good tonight."

"I wish we had more time, but we don't. Flynn, you've been with them from the beginning."

"And younger than either of you when we started. They'll handle it. It's hard, you're their children, but they'll handle it."

He'd never taken a mate, Fallon thought, though she knew he'd taken lovers here and there. She wondered why.

Nobody's rung the bell, he said in her mind, and added a half smile when she winced.

Sorry. "Then let's get started," she said out loud. "Before we do, I'm aiming for a spot about a half mile from the base. I'm estimating, as I couldn't risk going into the crystal, leaving a trace to pinpoint it more exactly."

"Won't we leave that trace tonight?" Tonia asked.

"I'm going to use a cloaking spell." She took charm pouches out of her pocket. "Keep them on you," she said, then laid her hands on their arms.

"From friend and foe alike, we are hidden from their sight. Though within us burns the light, it leaves no trace upon the night. They may look but will not see. As I will, so mote it be."

"We're going to be invisible?" Tonia slipped the pouch into her pocket, patted it. "So, so cool."

"Not invisible—though very cool. More like shadows, shapes. Magickal searching spells should pass right over us."

"Should?"

"There are spells to counteract cloaking spells. We have to risk it. Any trouble, we flash out. We can't risk the whole mission. Ready?"

They flashed onto a deserted road that cut through a stretch of empty houses. Some had been burned to the ground—a waste of resources and shelter. Someone more enterprising and practical had dismantled others to the foundation, and a handful more still stood, window glass smashed, doors removed or hanging open.

As she scanned what had been a neighborhood before her birth, she felt it.

"They left the dead," Fallon stated.

"Where?" Hand on her knife hilt, Tonia scanned the area.

"In the houses. There are still remains from the Doom in some of the houses. Children would have played here once. Friends would have gathered on patios, like we did tonight. Now there are rats."

She watched one tunnel through the high weedy lawn as they walked.

"A half mile," Flynn said. "And still some housing, easily repaired. When we take the base, we could use this as an outpost, a checkpoint."

They followed the road, then into what had been a small park. Now the trees had thickened and wild things grew in a kind of mad splendor.

"Probably snakes," Tonia said.

"Probably."

They saw deer, a red fox, a lumbering possum, crossed a thin stream clogged with debris.

Both Fallon and Flynn stopped, heads cocked.

"Elf ears," Tonia muttered. "Both of you. What do you hear?"

"An engine." Flynn glanced at Fallon, nodded. Lupa stayed by her side as Flynn blurred away in the dark.

"He's going to look. The base should be just a couple hundred yards to the east, and the engine's coming from the road that leads to it."

They moved ahead, keeping to shadows as security lights from the compound glowed through the dark.

Flynn slipped back to them. "Single cargo truck, cleared through the main gates. Guard posts coordinate with your map. The walls are a good fifteen feet high. We're not going to be able to see over them from this vantage point, and we'll be in the open if we go another twenty feet. I can scout the perimeter, see if there's a better angle, higher ground."

"We need to go higher, but not on the ground. We separate. Flynn scouts the east side, Tonia the west. You'll meet up on the north side. We need to know the terrain, any additional sentry positions or security measures, potential weak spots. You know the drill. Tonia will flash you both back here."

"And you?" Tonia asked.

"I'll go up."

"You can fly now?"

"Taibhse can, and I'll see through his eyes."

"You mean to merge with him," Flynn began as Tonia shook her head.

"Then Flynn and I should stay with you. You'd be vulnerable—body here, spirit there. And you told me you were still working on a true merge."

"The owl god's mine for a reason. And Faol Ban will guard me."

"Lupa stays, too," Flynn insisted.

"All right." She held up her arm so Taibhse glided down from the tree branch where he'd perched, landed softly. "Move out. We'll rendezvous back here. What we take back with us tonight is going to be the difference between success and failure."

"You can mind-speak to both of us," Tonia said. "Any trouble, you signal."

"And the same goes."

Fallon waited, and when she stood alone with the owl,

looked into his eyes. "I'm yours; you're mine. You are wisdom and patience. You are the hunter. My heart beats with yours; my blood flows with yours. Be my eyes."

As she looked into his, she saw herself, a shadow in shadows.

"Be my ears."

She heard all the whispers of the night. A mouse breathing, the crawl of a spider over a leaf, a fox slinking through the grass.

"Taibhse the wise, my spirit joins with yours. Now be my wings."

She rose up in him, through him, and with the great spread of his wings glided up, up, above the trees. She felt the air swim by her, scented the mouse, the spider, the fox below.

For a moment, the thrill took her, the freedom of flight, the power of sight that picked out a squirrel nesting in a tree, and the union that allowed her to soar.

The sting of fuel, the stench of dark magicks, the smell of man.

She saw the elf to the east, the witch to the west, moving shadows in shadows.

She circled above the houses, the streets connecting them. A garden surrounded by fencing, penned livestock. She noted the guards posted outside of buildings, drew the map in her head.

Four men unloaded the truck Flynn had seen—of prisoners. She caught the smell of fresh blood, watched as they were dragged to a guarded building. Someone drove the truck across the compound. Another guarded area, another gate.

She counted the vehicles inside the fence, and the fuel tanks.

A group of Raiders—four, five, six, seven—sat outside, in the rear of a big house with a peaked roof. Two of them smoked something that clogged the air. The others drank . . . whiskey?

With Taibhse's ears she heard their voices, rough and drunk. Celebrating a successful raid that day, she realized. Two dead, three slaves to trade to the PWs.

Another pulled a woman on a leash. Fallon saw the mark of a slave on her wrist, the bruises on her naked body. One of the female Raiders got up, walked over, plowed a fist into the slave's belly that would have doubled her over if the leash hadn't snapped her back.

"You flirting with my man, bitch."

That brought on uproarious laughter, calls for a catfight.

The woman punched her again.

"Don't damage her too much, Sadie," one of the men warned as he puffed out smoke. "We gotta turn her back in in the morning."

"She was giving you the eye." Sadie drew a knife. "Maybe I'll cut hers out."

"We only rented her for the night. No point paying for a buy. Come on and bring that hot ass of yours back over here. Who won the first taste?"

One of the others stood up, rubbed his crotch.

"Well, take her on inside, start getting what we paid for."

Sadie turned the knife in front of the slave's face, then spat in it before she turned away.

Fallon's spirit burned. She could help the slave. But in helping her, she risked all the others they could save. Heartsick, she glided away.

She'd remember them, she vowed. Sadie and the others, she'd remember them. And hoped with all she was they remained on the base when she led the attack.

She saw a man in black step out of a building, and felt the power from him, the ugly edge of power. Even as she understood he could feel hers, as he hesitated, began to lift his face to the sky, Taibhse winged away.

She separated from him with the wolves beside her, and Flynn, Tonia standing by.

"You were gone a long time," Tonia began.

"There was a lot to see. Not here," Fallon said quickly. "They have at least one powerful DU, and he might have caught a whiff of me. If he did, he'll push out. We go back now."

She gripped Flynn's hand, called Taibhse to her arm, and, with Tonia, flashed home.

CHAPTER FIVE

Duncan had never seen anything like Utah.

He'd flashed west before when he, Tonia, and Fallon had searched out warheads to transform and destroy. But the time they'd spent had been inside, deep inside, those bases and compounds.

He hadn't seen the strange, endless land, the jagged rise of mountains, the fascinating sculptures of rock or deep canyons with twisting rivers.

He hadn't felt the breathless, baking heat or witnessed the eerie beauty of the star-drenched desert sky at night.

They'd come, he and Mallick, to scout the enemy base—what there was of it. But he took back so much more than battle plans, logistics. He brought back a kind of wonder.

Even as he asked himself what drove people to settle in a land so inhospitable, he understood it.

Eerie or not, there was beauty, and the sheer scope of space. He wanted to come back in the daylight, see what colors the light teased out of the baked earth, the towers and coils of rock, the rough peaks.

Something had driven and pushed people to leave the

green of the east and travel so far, in such hostile condi-
tions, to the browns and burned golds of the West. To
build scrubby little desert towns like the one the PWs
now used.

With Mallick, he studied the target—a huddle of
buildings, half in serious disrepair. Trucks, bikes, a paddock holding half a dozen horses, a single milk cow, a
scatter of chickens.

And one sentry, asleep on duty.

They didn't speak much as they quietly circled the target. Sound carried on the desert air. Duncan heard the
echoing calls of coyote, wolf, and the bored conversation
of a trio of men sitting out at a picnic table playing cards.

He felt magicks on the air, dim, struggling, from the
building behind the card game. Prisoners, he thought,
drugged or injured, or both.

Fury eked through the wonder.

"We could take them out tonight, ourselves," he whispered to Mallick. "They're idiots."

Mallick nodded. "No doubt, but it's not for us, not tonight."

"I get it, but, man, it's hard to walk away. I'm going to
get a closer look, back of the building where they've got
the magickals."

"Be quick, and quiet."

He could flash, but that wouldn't give him as many lay-
of-the-land details. So he moved swiftly over the hard-
baked ground, keeping out of the range of the battery-run
security lights.

As he got closer, he realized the building had been—
and was—an actual jail, with barred windows, no rear
door.

He peeked in, saw a trio of small cells, a locked interior door separating it from the rest of the building.

Twenty-six by his count, including kids, all sprawled out in a stupor. He saw fresh brands on foreheads, fresh bruises, old bruises, dried blood. Bare feet—torn up from being forced to walk Christ knew how far. Hair shorn so close and rough that scalps showed raw gashes.

He spotted two dirty jars on the floor outside one cell, and the weak lights inside it.

He heard the locks on the interior door slide, ducked down from the window.

"Told you they were all out."

"We got orders to check every four hours, we check every four hours. Now get over and do the same on the slave quarters. And keep your dick in your pants this time."

"What's the point having slaves if we can't have some fun with them?"

"Command put me in charge, and slaves are for work, not recreation. You want to fuck something, you fuck one of the bitches in here before we hang them. Now go do the goddamn check on the slave quarters."

"Yeah, yeah."

Duncan heard one leave, the other move deeper into the room. "Dream of hell," the man muttered. "Because you're going back there soon. We're going to send every one of you sons and daughters of demons back to hell. We're going to take back our world."

He stood there in silence a full minute. "We're going to start building the scaffold tomorrow—right out there."

He walked to the window where Duncan crouched below, looked out. "Right out where you can see it every damn day and know what's coming for you. We're going to wipe the abomination of you off the face of the earth, one noose at a time."

He went out, locked the door.

When they finished the mission, flashed back to the cabin, Duncan pulled a beer out of the cold box, poured wine for Mallick.

"I'll draw it up. If they don't get reinforcements before we go, we can take them with fifty troops, max."

"I agree. We close off their access to their weapons. They're poorly organized as yet, and not yet fortified."

"They think they're off the radar—that's the term, right? They don't figure we know about them, think they have plenty of time to set up. They're taking a break, more or less, after the trip out there."

He took a long drink. "Twenty-six prisoners, drugged, most injured. I couldn't tell how seriously. At least one of the PWs in charge is a true believer."

Calm as a lake, Mallick sipped wine. "You're angry, and anger clouds judgment."

"They had pixies in fucking jars on the floor. One of the kids in the cells couldn't have been more than three or four years old. Damn right I'm angry. You and I could've ended it tonight."

He threw up a hand before Mallick could respond. "I get why we didn't. Get why we couldn't. It's a freaking brilliant plan, and it could net us Arlington. That doesn't mean it wasn't hard to walk away from what we saw there."

His thoughts as rough as the scruff on his face, Duncan dropped down in a chair. "They're going to start building the scaffold tomorrow. They might use it before we hit."

"Think strategically," Mallick advised.

"I will. There's no law saying I can't bitch about it first. I know we can't save everybody. I learned that early on."

But it ate at him, always.

Mallick sat, sipped his wine. "Let me know when

you've finished bitching so we can begin the work needed to save who we can."

Duncan studied the sorcerer, the white-streaked beard, the dark eyes, the unflappable dignity. "You're a hard-ass, Mallick. I've got to admire that. They've got fifty-two troops by my count."

"Your count's incorrect. They have fifty-four."

Duncan might have argued, but he knew Mallick missed nothing. Ever. "Okay, fifty-four. Most of them carry sidearms or long guns. Every one I saw had a knife. I didn't see any swords."

"They have three stored in the building they use to house weapons."

Duncan's eyes narrowed. "How do you know that?"

"I looked. While you checked the prisoners, I went inside. I have count of their stored weapons."

"You said no going inside the buildings."

"I said you weren't to go inside," Mallick corrected— unflappably. "I had an opportunity, and took it. And we now know they have three swords, ten more of the long guns, twelve more of the handguns, and ammunition. Not enough ammunition for all the weapons."

Duncan pushed resentment aside for later. "They're low on ammo. Good to know."

"It's possible they have weapons and ammunition for them in other locations."

"I would," Duncan agreed. "I'd have at least one more weapon than the one I carry where I sleep, so there's that. I might keep one or two in some of the vehicles. But the point is, they're not particularly well armed and, like you said, not all that well organized as yet."

"And how would you take the base?"

"Depends. We're coordinating with the other two attacks. She'll hit Arlington after dark, but it could still be light in Utah. That matters."

"She'll have factored that into her timing. Assume we strike at night."

Yeah, she'd factor it, Duncan had to agree. Fallon was another who rarely missed a thing. "Okay. We take out the crap sentry—or sentries if they post more. Quick, quiet, so archers or elves with blades. Move in from the west and east, cover the prison, slave quarters, and armory first. Secure the prisoners—get them out. Secure the weapons and vehicles. Neutralize any enemy forces necessary to achieve that."

"Do you wish the enemy dead, or the prisoners freed?"

"Trick question?"

At Mallick's arched brows, his silence, Duncan huffed out a breath. "Okay, all right. They've got no DUs, not unless they have any passing as civilians. So we can overwhelm them with power, neutralize them that way, and cut down on body count. Take out the sentry or sentries with a power punch. Give them a zap, secure them, move in. Fallon wants us to give them time to send out an SOS, and that's part of the smart here. We let them do that, then take down the comms."

He took another swig of beer. "But I'm not risking anyone to spare that enemy body count. If it comes to it, we take them out."

"Then we're agreed. Make your map. We'll plot out the strategy, select our troops. We'll take the map and the plan to Fallon in the morning."

Now Duncan studied his beer. "She doesn't need both of us. You take the meeting. I'll stay here and work with the team we put together."

"That might be wise."

Mallick might have been too dignified to smirk, but Duncan heard it in the tone. "There'll come a time, old man. It's just not now. I'll fight for her, fight with her. I'll fight for the light with my last goddamn breath. But I'm damned if I'll hook up with a woman because the gods freaking deem it. I choose who and when and where."

"It's all a choice, boy."

"Is it?" Pushing up, he paced. "Who puts these dreams of her in my head, these feelings for her in me?"

"How is it you don't know the answer?"

He gestured with the beer. "You're saying I do it to myself. That's bullshit. My mom says I got worked up and happy when Lana came around, before Fallon was born. And the bitch of it is, I half remember."

"Recognition. Light to light, blood to blood. The rest, if the rest is to be, is for you, for her."

"Yeah? And what if I decide, hey, you know, I'm more into that blonde or that redhead than The One? Do we lose that connection? Because the connection matters, it's a key to ending this. I know it. She knows it. And I'm pretty damn sure it pisses her off as much as it does me."

"Then she'd be as foolish and shortsighted as you."

So much to learn yet, Mallick thought. Still so much.

"Your connection is your blood, your light, your ancestry, and it isn't sex that joins you together. Or do you perceive Tonia and Fallon must be fated to join in that way as well? Or the three of you—"

"Whoa." Sincerely appalled, Duncan shoved out a hand like a stop sign. Snaps of light shimmered from the fingertips. "That's my sister."

"Your twin. As close to you as any could be. Her light connects with yours, as does her blood. Nothing can sever that. Your light, Fallon's. Her blood, yours. It's a bond unbroken. You'll bed who you choose, as will she."

Duncan sat again. "It's not ordained? Because thinking maybe it is bugs the shit out of me."

"The gods don't bind you, Duncan."

"Aren't you bound?"

"I took an oath. I chose to take it. So the binding is my own. I'll never break it."

Duncan contemplated his beer before polishing it off. If he knew one thing, absolutely, about Mallick, it was the man never lied. "Okay then. So when I go back for her, and I will, it's because it's what I want."

"Keep in mind, boy, she also has a choice. Now, keep your blood cool and draw the map. We still have work ahead of us."

Duncan drew maps, and with Mallick plotted out their plan of attack. Timing, directions, numbers.

They hand-selected the troops, a mix of magickals and NMs, pinpointed a safe zone they'd secure to move the prisoners, any wounded, and a system for transporting them east while leaving a contingent in Utah.

They'd establish their first base in the West.

Long after Mallick went to bed, Duncan couldn't sleep. Instead he sat at his desk sketching the land he'd seen, that desert sky, those fanciful, to his eye, buttes and mesas.

He didn't feel the vision take him, but caught in it, his hand chose pencils, moved over the page, drawing, shading, detailing what formed in his mind.

He more than saw those images. He heard, he scented, he felt.

When he came out of it, his fingers cramped, his arm ached. He'd worn one of his precious pencils to a stub, had sharpened and used a second.

The drawing—and he knew he'd never done anything to match it—lay complete. The great towers rising, the rubble, the smoke, the circling crows in air thick with it. Streets, the vehicles jammed over them. The bodies, some torn to pieces, on sidewalks or sprawled out of the broken glass of windows, of doorways.

He'd drawn a dog feasting on what had been a man, its muzzle filthy with blood and gore, as he'd caught it in a snarl.

Something larger, even darker than the crows, winged overhead, and the forks of lightning cracked the sky.

He stood there, his sword drawn, stained with blood. She stood beside him. Fallon Swift, her sword in hand, stained like his.

They stood together in the carnage, in the smoke and the storm. And looked at each other.

"New York City," he murmured. He only knew because the vision brought him the knowledge. He'd been only one day old when his mother had fled the city with him and his sisters.

But now he knew he would go there, fight there. And he would stand with Fallon there.

He put the sketch away. Suddenly weary to the bone, he sprawled on his bed. He dreamed of her, but the dreams faded with morning.

Considering its space and location, Fallon set up the lower level of her family's home as the war room. Until she could build or scavenge better, she used a reclaimed sheet of plywood on sawhorses as a table. With Ethan's help, she hauled in a motley variety of extra chairs.

Since school was out for summer, she borrowed a blackboard, bartered for chalk made from crushed eggshells and flour.

On the board, she wrote the three targets, and under Arlington listed the fighting troops from New Hope, by name and designation, that she, her father, and Will— with some input from Colin—had chosen. Then the support troops—straight rescuers, medicals, transportation.

With them she listed the enemy's known numbers and resources, the number of magickal prisoners, the number of slaves according to their best intel and estimations.

On the table, she pinned her map of the base, and used chess pieces borrowed from Poe and Kim—black for the enemy, white for her forces—to designate troop positions.

When her father came down, a mug of coffee in each hand, he studied her work. "You've been at this awhile, and it's barely dawn. I'd have helped you with it."

"It helped me focus. So will that coffee, thanks."

"It's a good job."

"I had good teachers. I got the chess pieces from Kim, but I don't have enough for three targets. I got these from Bill at Bygones. He wouldn't take anything for them."

She showed Simon a container of plastic soldiers and jungle animals. "I figured we're the soldiers, they're the animals. Not very dignified, but—"

"It works. Nervous?"

"I thought I would be, but it's more anxious to get started. They'll be here soon—Mallick, Thomas, Troy, Mae Pickett, Boris, Charlie from back home, along with the New Hope Originals. It's the first time all of them will have been in the same place, the same time."

"And most of them are used to, more or less, running their own show."

"There's that."

"We picked good people to lead, Fallon. Now it's time for you to use their strengths, balance any weaknesses, and move forward for the whole."

Will and Arlys arrived first, then others trickled in. She'd wait until leaders from every base came, begin with introductions, she thought. Acknowledgments. Some would fight together for the first time, or send those under their command to fight under another leader.

Acknowledgment mattered.

She stepped outside, thinking to gather herself and prepare for the diplomacy portion. Something her father was so much better at.

As she stood with the voices floating out through the open windows behind her, the first from outside New Hope flashed.

Thomas and Minh, with Sabine and Vick—two of the witches she'd asked to join the elf colony. And one more.

The last time she'd seen Mick he'd stood at the edge of the woods surrounding Mallick's cottage, his hand lifted in farewell as she'd left for home.

He'd been her first friend away from home, the first elf she'd formed a bond with. He'd been her first kiss.

He grinned at her now, those leaf-green eyes alight. He'd grown his bronze-colored hair longer, had trios of thin braids on either side of his head to hold it back. His face had fined down, and he sported a triangle of beard on his chin.

But he looked so much the same.

"Mick!" She leaped forward to throw her arms around him. He swung her, laughing.

Stronger, she realized, and more solid. A soldier now who still wore the braided bracelet with the charms she'd made him as a parting gift.

"Fallon Swift." He eased her back to study her face. "You look good."

"You, too," she said even as she tugged on the beard.

"Thomas, Minh." She embraced them in turn, shook hands with the others. "You're well? And everyone?"

"We are," Thomas told her. "And prepared."

"Let me take you inside. I want you to meet my parents, and the others." She gripped Mick's hand. "We need to catch up."

Others arrived, and she did her best to greet each personally, to make those introductions. And gauge reactions, moods.

Then Mallick stepped in, alone.

She moved to him.

"Mallick the Sorcerer."

"Fallon Swift."

She kissed his cheek, stepped back. "You're alone."

"I am. I have the map of the base in Utah, and its surroundings."

"All right." She turned, took the map to the table to pin it with her own and the one Thomas had brought.

She looked at those gathered. Elves, faeries, witches, shifters, farmers, teachers, mothers, fathers, sons, daughters.

Soldiers all.

"We begin. Here, we work together to coordinate three simultaneous attacks on enemy bases. We will take those bases, free all prisoners, secure and fortify those bases and all assets within as our own. We will send a message to Jeremiah White and all who follow him that we will end their reign of fear and brutality. And that message will reach all who threaten the light and the lives of others. We stand here today, magickals and non-magickals, together for one purpose. To push back the dark."

She paused. "Thomas," she continued. "Will you report the results of your scouting mission?"

She listened to the details, watched as he pointed out areas on the map, gave his estimation on enemy numbers, prisoners.

Nodding, she added the information to the board.

"How many troops, and support forces, will you need to take the base?"

To her surprise, Thomas looked at Mick, who took over.

"We can take it with sixty. Seventy would be better because it's spread out. See, we'd . . ." He moved to the map, picked up one of the toy soldiers—grinned his Mick grin at it. "Cool. They've got sentry posts here, here, here."

She didn't comment that he'd used the soldier toys for the enemy. No doubt Mick preferred to be represented by a lion or tiger.

But his strategy rang clear as he moved pieces.

"They've got four boats—two sail powered. We could cut off any escape attempts by water if we had, say, three to five merpeople."

"We'll get them," Fallon told him.

"That cuts them off to the east," he continued. "They keep the prisoners here—it's basically a fortified hut on the beach. One guard. Slaves are on this level of the main base."

"It was a hotel."

"Lots of rooms," he agreed. "The top PWs have the top floor."

"For the views," Poe put in. "And the status."

"I guess."

Mick went over the compound, point by point.

"How do they get power?" Fallon asked.

Sabine answered. "They have three generators, powered by battery and magicks."

"They have DUs?"

"No." She had golden skin and deep, dark eyes, wore her hair, black as a raven's wing, in a straight fall to her waist. "It may be they tortured witches into helping them gain power, or used DUs at one time."

"We cut the power. Can you do it?"

"I can countermand the magicks. I need one other witch to do it. But Minh says if the batteries are charged, they'd still operate. I don't know how to deactivate them."

"We'll get someone who does to work with you." Fallon wrote it down. "With the power down, *after* the initial attack, after they have time to send out the alarm, the leaders will have to get to the battle by the stairs."

When Mick finished the report and plan, she moved back to the board.

"Seventy troops, including four of the mers, twelve support for medical and rescue transport. How many do you have ready for the mission?"

"Fifty," Thomas told her. "We have the additional twelve, but only fifty seasoned enough for this kind of mission."

"Another twenty needed. Mallick?"

She listened without comment as he reported. She didn't allow herself to wonder for more than a moment why Duncan hadn't come with him.

When he'd finished, she turned to the board. "You need fifty. How many do you have?"

"We have the fifty."

"And the eight support?"

"We have them."

"Good." She drew a breath. "Arlington."

Now she felt those doubts, a shift in mood from several corners.

"I gotta say." John Little, a big man she'd recruited largely by kicking him in the balls, cleared his throat. "Hitting those two bases makes sense. One-two punch. And holding them gives us more room to spread out. But Arlington." He shook his head. "It's hard to see it, to tell the truth. Nobody's put a dent in that base. The government's tried, from what I hear."

"We're not the government," she said over a few murmurs agreeing with Little. "Beyond freeing prisoners, Arlington is the purpose. It may not break the back of the Purity Warriors, but it cuts off an arm."

"We get our asses killed trying, and lose? It cuts off both our arms. And legs."

She'd expected objections, half hoped her father would take up the debate. But he remained silent, kept his gaze on hers.

Okay then, she thought.

"As long as Arlington remains in their hands, they hold an advantage. The strategic position, the sheer size of the base and its resources, its training ground. We need it in our hands. And we'll have it."

"Well." Mae Pickett shifted in her seat, pushed back her long gray hair. "I get why you want it, but it seems to me you're going after a hell of a lot, and you haven't been at this very long. A lot of the rest of us have been at it less. Maybe we ought to take smaller bites for a while yet."

"I'm looking at the numbers up there," Little added. "The ones you got under Arlington. That's a high number. And that ain't talking about how we hear they have freaking rocket launchers, and got Uncannys working with them who can fry a man with a look. And some of them fly around like bats. Now, I like a good fight as much as the next, but we've already got our hands full. Maybe we study on this awhile, take a few months to train more men, get a better lay of the land. We can look at it again later on."

"We strike, all three, tomorrow night."

"Tomorrow?" That not only brought Little out of his

seat, but started a roll of those murmurs and mutters. "Listen, girlie—"

"Here is the light." She drew her sword, and it flamed. "Here is the storm." The air in the room trembled at her words. "You are not bound, and so you will choose. Fight or flight, courage or caution. You think this is the beginning? The beginning was long ago, long ago when men turned from magicks. When faith lost turned to hate and fear. When the dark crept over and through."

"Okay now." Little patted a hand at the whirling air. "Just bank that down."

She stopped him with a look from gray eyes gone to smoke. "The shields are seven, and one is open. What poured through killed your mothers, your children, and still you doubt. They feed on your fear in feasts, and still you question courage. Look and see, look and see what comes if the next opens."

She flung out a hand. Where the blackboard had been stood a window, and through it, madness.

Men striking down men in fields where crops lay dead and dying. Children huddled with the glassy eyes and distended bellies of the starving. A sky ripped with lightning, red and black.

And the crows, always the crows, screaming in triumph as the world burned and bled.

"I will strike the light against the dark, and I will cleave it until its blood runs black on the ground. I will burn the blood, bring a storm to whirl away the smoke.

"We will strike this blow, one, two, three, on the desert, by the sea, near the battle cries of the dead city. Before the dawn breaks, the standard of The One flies."

As she felt the power ebb, she sheathed her sword.

"Okay then." Eddie gave Fred's hand a rub. "Arlington."

Giving Eddie a nod of approval, Mick echoed him. "Arlington."

Colin stepped up beside her. "Arlington."

As others did the same, Little rubbed his jaw. "You punched my lights out once before. I guess you did it again. Arlington."

PURPOSE

Necessity's sharp pinch!

—William Shakespeare

CHAPTER SIX

With the plan in place, Fallon addressed the numbers again.

"We have ten from Mae, ten from Troy added to Thomas's troops. Boris, Charlie add the rest to New Hope's. We'll need volunteers willing to relocate, to secure and hold those bases, to recruit from those locations, and train."

"We have fifteen who've agreed to go to South Carolina," Thomas told her.

"You'll need that many more to start, and at least one with tech knowledge, two medicals."

"Ray would go," Rachel said. "We'll miss him here, but he came to me, told me he'd like to go. He was born not far from there."

"We can send a healer." Troy folded her hands. "In that way, they'd have a witch as well. Mae, you have Benny."

"Yeah. He's hardly more than a kid, but he gets all that computer stuff and so on. He'd go."

"Who would you put in charge, Thomas?"

"Mick."

She started to object. In part of her mind he was still the goofy boy who'd flipped out of trees and run races through the woods. But he was more, she thought as she looked at him. Much more.

"Good. Mallick?"

"Forty. We have them, and the medicals, the technicians. We would need building supplies. There's much disrepair."

"We'll work on it. Who will you put in charge?"

"Duncan. For the next six months, we estimate."

She'd known it, already known. But she heard Katie's quick sound of distress.

"It seems far." Fallon went to her, took her hand as Hannah had taken the other. "But he can be with you just as quickly from there. Tonia can take you to see him, to see where he is. Both of you," she added for Hannah.

"Is he ready, and willing?" Katie asked Mallick.

"He's both. You can be proud of the son you made."

"I am. I would—Hannah and I would like to go, see where he is, when we can."

"We'll make sure of it. We'll need two hundred, minimum, for Arlington," Fallon continued. "I'd like some from every base. Even green recruits, as we'll have the training ground. Four medicals to begin, at least one of them a witch with healing experience and skills. Three techs."

With the numbers satisfied, she turned back. Some still had doubts, she knew, but they'd fight. "Three a.m. for South Carolina and Arlington. One a.m. for Utah. We'll take the dark to defeat the dark. What you need—troops, weapons, support—will be sent to you by nightfall. Thank you for what you've done, what you do, what you will do."

Lana, who hadn't spoken throughout, stood. "And

please, come upstairs. There's food and drink before you travel home again."

Of course there is, Fallon thought, but touched Mallick's arm. "A moment first?"

When he stepped outside, he took part of that moment to glance around. Smiled at the beehive.

He listened to the bees hum, smelled the green, the sweetness of flowers, herbs, the scents of food ripening in and above the ground, on branches.

He watched with easy amusement as a large woodpecker with its red crown pecked manically at a cake in a feeder.

"Suet," Fallon told him. "Dad built the feeder, Mom makes the suet. The birds go nuts for it."

"It's not your farm, but still a strong place. And you've done well here." He gestured toward the barracks. "I'd like to see your training grounds before I leave."

"I'll take you, and anyone who wants to see. We have strong, skilled soldiers. We're ready for Arlington."

"I have no doubt."

"But you knew John Little had doubts."

"Yes, as others would." He turned back to her. "If you can't alleviate doubts, or convince those who have them to follow you despite them, how can you lead?"

"Did I? Alleviate or convince? Enough for those who doubt to keep following me even when we bury our dead? Because we will bury dead after Arlington. And there are harder battles to come."

"War is loss, girl." He gripped her shoulder when she started to shake her head. "Not fighting this war means the loss of all. Lose sight of that, we've already lost. Lose faith in yourself, no one else will keep faith with you. You know this."

"Knowing it at thirteen, fourteen when you trained

me, when I picked up the sword and shield is almost a picture in a book, or words on a page. Using my sword, as I have, my powers, as I have, to spill blood, to take lives, is no small matter, Mallick."

"War should never be a small matter."

"I'll use my sword, my powers, in this war. I'll lead men to battle, and some to their deaths. And I will never, never consider a single death by my hand, a single death by my order, a tactic. If I don't feel the weight of each life lost, what have we won? Who will we be at the end of it?"

The hand on her shoulder gentled. "You learned well. Accept the weight and fight on."

"Why didn't Duncan come?" She hadn't meant to ask, but the words slipped out. "His mother misses him. And Hannah. Tonia, at least, sees him now and then."

"He felt he'd better serve by staying behind, working with those we've chosen for the mission."

"Like he feels he'd better serve by staying in Utah for six months?"

"Yes."

"You agree?"

"Yes. Those under his training and his command trust and respect him. And what he learned in New Hope he takes with him to build there. The West is vast, and much of it empty. You'll find uses for it. He'll find them for you."

"Then we'll see what he can do in six months. Go, eat. I've kept you from my mother's cooking long enough. I'll take you to the barracks before you leave."

"Will you eat?"

"Let them enjoy a little hospitality without The One hovering."

She walked toward the hive. They'd built these here, another at the barracks. Enough, as Fred had four at the farm next door, and others had their own.

She thought of how her father had taught her to build the hives, how she'd learned from what pulsed inside her how to call the queen and the swarm.

She'd taught Mallick how to build a hive, called the swarm for him, taught him how to tend it, gather the honey, the propolis.

They'd need hives at the new bases. Did Duncan know how to build a hive, how to call the queen, how to tend and gather?

She held out a hand. Dozens of bees flew out to cover her hand, her wrist.

"That always creeped me out," Mick said from behind her.

"We need them more than they need us." She sent the bees flowing back. "It's really good to see you, Mick. The couple of times I went back to check in with Thomas, you were off hunting or scouting or scavenging."

"Bad timing. But now it's good to see you, too. And all this. I was hoping to see the whole community, the town and all, but, well, next time."

"Next time."

"You always used to tell me what a great cook your mom is. Man, you got that right." He patted his belly, then held out a cookie. "Brought you a cookie."

"Thanks."

"I like your dad, and your brothers. You've got one more brother, right?"

"Ethan, the youngest. We sent him and Fred's kids into town for the meeting. They're still too young to fight." But not for much longer, she thought. "They train, but today, they're helping in the community gardens."

She gestured with the cookie, started to walk toward the barracks. "How are Twila and Jojo and Bagger and, well, everybody?"

"We're good. We've been taking care of the cottage,

the gardens, and all that. The faerie tribe and the shifters, too. There are more of us now, and some regulars."

"Regulars?"

"You know, like your dad and Colin."

"Non-magickals."

"Right. Hey, there's Taibhse."

The owl stood on his branch, sent Mick a stony stare.

"He's still pissed off I tried to shoot the apple. Man,
that was years back."

She remembered, too, the faerie glade with its lovely
green light, the pool, the great white owl and his golden
apple. And her horror when she thought the young elf
meant to put an arrow in the owl. She'd leaped up, the
first time her powers had taken her so high. In deflect-
ing the arrow, shedding her own blood, the owl bound
himself to her.

And oddly, that had begun her friendship with Mick.

"Where are Faol Ban and Laoch?"

"They're here. They'll go with me to Arlington." She
turned to him then. "We will take Arlington."

"I know it. I believed it before we came here. I only
believe it more now."

His simple faith warmed her. "And you want Carolina? To leave the elf camp, build our base there?"

"I've never seen the ocean. Sabine's taken us higher
in the hills, down in valleys, but the ocean? I mean, man,
it's the ocean. Sabine and my father have cozied up."

"I— What?"

"Yeah, they, you know, got together. I'm good with
it. She makes him happy. And she's smart, sort of calm,
like him. They work, I guess."

"I'm glad."

"Anyway, this is the farthest she's ever flashed me
so far, and what a ride. I'd like to see the ocean. I've
learned a lot," he told her, looking away from the groups

working on the training grounds. "We train, like that. Minh whips us pretty hard. We build. Like I said, there are more of us now. Minh had first choice, but he and Orelana don't want to uproot their kids from the life they know. Not yet. I'm second choice, but—"

"Not for me." She put a hand on his arm. "Even when we were kids, the others followed your lead. When your camp took sick, you, sick yourself, were the one who managed to get to us for help."

"I wasn't sure how you'd feel about me commanding a base."

"Then I'll tell you I know that base and the people on it will be in good hands."

"That means a lot. I've missed you, Fallon." He put a hand on hers, and she felt it, saw it in his eyes.

What he'd felt for her as a boy, what he'd felt with that first kiss, still beat inside him. She wished she could give it back to him, feel it for him, want him as he wanted her.

Because she couldn't, she turned her hand under his, gave his a strong squeeze. Of friendship. "I've missed you."

And though she knew it hurt him, turned to walk back toward the house, and spoke—as a friend—of their childhood adventures.

After they'd left, after she'd walked Mallick through the barracks, she sat with her parents, ate the cold pasta salad her mother put in front of her.

"I thought everything went very well."

Fallon eyed her mother between forkfuls. "You didn't say much."

"I had nothing to add. You knew what to say and how to say it. You knew what to show them when they needed to be shown." As she spoke, sitting at the outdoor table in the summer heat, Lana snapped beans she'd make for dinner. "I've seen what you showed them, and worse, in visions of my own."

"You never said."

"I want you to know I understand what's at stake. I don't go into battle like you do—"

"You battle every day."

"Not like you do, not in a long time. But I know how to defend myself and others. That's why I'm going to Arlington. Wait," she said before Fallon could object. "Your father and I already went a few rounds on this, and I won."

"I'm calling it a TKO," Simon added.

"A win's a win. Rachel, Hannah, and I will set up the mobile medical stations. We know how to fight if the fight comes to us, but more, there are going to be a lot of casualties on both sides. You need us."

She couldn't stand it, couldn't stand it. Her mother was snapping beans she'd steam for dinner, and talking about going to war.

"I'm taking your husband, two of your sons. I'm sending two of Katie's children into the fight already. Jonah and Rachel have three kids, still young. One of them should stay in New Hope."

"We're needed. Jonah and Rachel have made arrangements for their boys if anything should happen to them. So have Poe and Kim for their kids. It took considerable arguing to convince Fred and Arlys to stay behind—and the children helped tip that scale.

"We were the first wave," she added. "You won't leave us out of this."

"Hannah's not a warrior."

"She's a medic. Medics go to war because soldiers go to war. My power doesn't reach yours, Fallon, but it's not inconsiderable. Trust it, and me."

"You won't budge her," Simon warned. "Let's talk

about what you left out of the meeting. You didn't say who you've got in mind to command Arlington."

"We need a team of leaders there, considering its size and its location. My first choice would have been you." She took her mother's hand when the knuckles went white. "But you're needed here. So I've asked Mallick if he would go, and, since Duncan's staying in Utah, who he'd put in charge of that base. He surprised me by naming John Little. So . . . I'm going to trust him on that. He'll go to Arlington, along with—if they agree—Aaron and Bryar. We'll need instructors, teachers. There's an elf, Jojo, the best scavenger and scout I've ever seen. Thomas will ask her. And . . . I want to ask Colin."

She heard her mother's sigh—resignation, not surprise—as Simon reached for Lana's hand. "We expected it."

"I want to say he's too young to lead," Lana began, "but he's not. So, once again, I send one of my children to Mallick."

"Everything you both taught him, everything he learned since coming here, he'll take with him. If you ask me to pick someone else, I will."

"He'd want this," Lana said. "He'll want it. I asked you to trust me. I trust you. Go talk to him."

"I will." She rose to take her plate to the sink. "Then I'll go talk to Aaron and Bryar before I stop by the clinic and talk to Rachel and Hannah about the mobile medical."

She saddled Grace for the trip to town, then rode first to the barracks.

Colin, hands fisted on his hips, disgust on his face, berated two recruits on a poor showing in hand-to-hand.

She let him run through the insults—lead-assed, shit-for-brains, mama's babies, and so on—then signaled him over.

"Clipper, take over here. And if one of these dance-arounds doesn't land a punch, punch both of them."

He strode to her. "Make it fast, okay? I'm still behind because of this morning, and I've got to drill with the Arlington platoon."

"It's about Arlington—or after Arlington. I'm asking Mallick to relocate there."

"Good choice," he agreed.

"And some others," she continued, "including Aaron and Bryar."

"Huh." He considered it as he watched the—obviously by his standards—pitiful show of hand-to-hand. "Yeah, I see that. They've got a couple of kids, but they'd do all right. Both of them are smart, good teachers, resourceful."

"I'd like you to go. Help secure, hold the base, train. Lead."

He turned to her slowly. The old Colin would have leaped with a: Hell, yeah! And she could still see that in him. But over it the man he'd become studied her, took his time.

"Why?"

"Because you're smart, a good trainer, resourceful. You're a damn good solider, you even know some of the IT stuff. Because holding Arlington is as important as taking it. And I trust you can do it."

"What about Travis?"

"I need him here, for now at least. I need you there."

"Then I guess I need to pack. Except . . ." He rubbed his jaw. "Mom and Dad may be a problem."

"No, they won't. We've talked, and it's your choice."

He took another minute, looked around. "I like this place," he told her. "I like the people. I even like the candy-ass recruits. I love the farm, you know? But I'm never going to be a real farmer."

"You're never going to be president, either," she said, and made him laugh. "You're a soldier, Colin."

"Hey, soldiers can be president. I'll hold Arlington for you. But one thing. What's my rank?"

"Since when do we do ranks?"

"Since now. What's mine?"

"How about Five-Star Dickhead?"

He gave her a light punch in the arm. "I like ME Commander."

"ME?"

"Most Excellent."

She just rolled her eyes. "Pick ten recruits, willing and able to go with you. If they have families, the families have to be willing to let them go or relocate with them."

"Got it. Jesus, do you see those two? I've got to get back to this." He strode away, glanced back. "I won't let you down."

"I know it."

Still watching him, she mounted Grace. Then she turned the horse and rode toward New Hope.

When she rode past the community gardens, she saw groups of volunteers hoeing weeds, others harvesting vegetables and fruit into baskets woven by other volunteers and craftspeople.

Kids too young to help, or to help for long, played on swings and slides, seesaws and jungle gyms, all scavenged and repaired or built from scavenged parts. Members of what New Hope dubbed the Triple Cs—Community Child Care—kept a watchful eye.

Parents, she knew, bartered for the babysitting with other services, food, crafts. She watched a faerie, no more than three, try out her wings. One of the watchers scooped her up before she went too high or too far.

The system worked, she thought as she continued on to the clinic. Just as the bartering for medical services worked, or for the milk and eggs and butter and so on produced on farms, the wool sheared, the fabrics woven.

She'd seen it work in other communities, just as she'd seen in some the lack of center, of leadership, of structure. And in others still a subtle segregation and lack of trust between magickals and NMs.

Winning the war wouldn't be the only challenge. Establishing that center, that structure, that trust would be its own kind of battle.

After tethering Grace, she walked into the clinic, past the waiting area—only a handful of people today—and turned to the desk.

"I need to talk to Rachel when she's free. Hannah, too, if it's possible."

"Rachel's with a patient. I think Hannah's doing a round in maternity and peeds." April gestured. "All the way down, turn right."

"Thanks."

She moved down, past exam and treatment rooms, beyond a ward—only three beds taken, a good sign. When she turned right, she heard the fretful cry of an infant, and Hannah's soothing voice.

"Somebody wants her mama. It's feeding time, isn't it, sweetie?"

She turned into what had been a classroom, saw Hannah pick up a swaddled infant from one of the clear baby beds. In another, one wearing a little blue knitted cap slept on.

Across the room a woman sat in a rocking chair with a tiny baby at her breast.

Hannah cuddled the crying baby, rubbed her back as she smiled at Fallon. "Welcome to the happiest spot in the clinic. Are you looking for Rachel?"

"And you."

"I just need to get this little darling to her mother.

We're giving our moms a rest, but somebody's hungry. If you give me a couple minutes, I'll track down Rachel once I get Jasmine settled."

"Sure. I'll walk with you."

"Fallon Swift." In the rocking chair, Lissandra Ye carefully shifted the baby to her other breast. "Could I speak with you?"

"All right."

"I won't be long," Hannah said, and carried the baby out.

"He can only be out for short times," Lissandra said, and glanced at the incubator. "He's still very small. My milk wasn't enough to help him grow, but your mother helped me, and now . . . he's nearly five pounds. Rachel says he won't need the incubator when he's just a little bigger."

"That's good." She moved closer. "He's really pretty."

At her words, Lissandra's eyes filled. Tears spilled.

"I'm sorry." Fallon pulled over a second chair, laid a hand on Lissandra's arm. "You're worried, but he's in good hands here."

"I know that. I trust that. At first, I didn't believe he'd live. He was so tiny. I wasn't sure I wanted him to. I'm ashamed of that."

"You shouldn't be."

"He's mine, you see? He's mine, but . . . It wasn't only one who raped me, and it wasn't only once. I couldn't fight back. They gave us drugs so we couldn't fight, but I could feel, and see. They let the guards have us when they wanted."

Fallon had heard similar stories before, too many times before. But those stories never lost the ability to shock and enrage.

"You're safe now. Do you talk to the counselors here?"

"Yes, yes. It wasn't just the guards. The Torturer. The Dark Uncanny in the lab. He . . ."

Understanding now, Fallon sat back. "You're worried he might be the one, that his blood is in your son."

"He's mine." Even through the tears she said it fiercely. "I named him for the man who died trying to save me. Brennan. He's my child, and no matter what, I love him. I thought I wouldn't, I couldn't, but he's my son. But I have to know. If he carries the dark in him, I have to know so I can help him fight it. Please, you can see. You can see and know, and tell me."

"The dark's a choice, Lissandra, just as the light's a choice."

"Please." The child lay quiet, his mouth slack as the milk and warmth lulled him to sleep. With eyes filled with hope and tears, Lissandra held him out to Fallon. "Please."

What torment had the woman endured already? And how much more would she endure without answers, without the comfort of them?

So Fallon took the child. Her brothers, she recalled, had seemed so tiny to her at their births. But compared to Lissandra's son, they'd been robust.

"Brennan," she whispered, "son of Lissandra. I see you."

She looked at him, looked into him, laid a hand on his chest where his heart beat under her palm.

"I see the light in you." Lowering her head, she brushed her lips over his downy head. "I see you."

With a smile, she looked back at Lissandra. "This is your son, and he holds light."

"Do you swear it?"

"I swear it. He's innocent, as you are. Innocent, and he's your son. He's your cub."

Now joy glimmered through the tears. "He's . . . like me?"

"Yes."

"Would you bless him?"

"I don't—"

"Please."

"Ah . . ." Following instinct, Fallon touched her fingers to the baby's head, his lips, and again his heart. "Bright blessings on you, Brennan, son of Lissandra." She repeated the words in Mandarin.

Now Lissandra smiled. "I haven't heard anyone speak Mandarin since my grandmother died. Thank you, more than I can say." Lissandra took the child back, rocked. "More than I can say. You've been blessed by The One," she murmured.

As Fallon rose, Rachel stepped in. "Give him a little skin-to-skin time, Lissandra, then you can change him before we put him back."

"He nursed really well."

"We'll weigh him a little later, but I think maybe tomorrow he can go into a regular crib."

"Did you hear that, baby? You're going to graduate."

"One of the nurses will be in to help you."

Lissandra nodded, but looked at Fallon. "I can fight. I'll fight for you. I'll fight for him."

"I'll fight for him," Fallon told her. "He needs you to tend to him. I'll see you both again."

She walked out with Rachel to where Hannah waited in the doorway.

"That mattered as much as any care we've been able to give them."

"She's strong," Fallon stated.

"And she'll be stronger now. You needed to see me?"

"I wanted to talk to you and Hannah about the mobile medicals. It's a big lift to flash your teams and your equipment to the safe zone at Arlington."

"Lana's talked to us already, but we can take this into my office. I want to show you the plans we just got."

"Plans?"

"For expanding the clinic." Rachel, a soft cloud of curls around her face, worn sneakers on her feet, led the way. "I know it's not top of your mind right now, but it's got to be pretty close to the top of ours."

"I didn't realize you wanted to expand."

"Need to even more than want to. We talked to Roger Unger weeks ago. He was an architect before the Doom—just starting out. He's been tutoring a few students with an interest."

"We need people who know how to design and build."

"Jonah and I like his plans. Maybe we want a few changes, but it hits the right notes. We're looking—might as well go for the gold—at making this a medical complex, bringing in the dental, the basics we've been able to put together on ophthalmology.

"A long way to go there," she added, tapping the reading glasses hooked to her chest pocket, "but we've got a start. The herbalists—and Kim's on board—the chemists. The healers. Everything in one place," she continued, "instead of spread around town. We'll need more equipment, more beds, more staff, but we can't go there until we have the space."

"It sounds . . . ambitious."

"So does taking Arlington."

Fallon managed a half laugh. "You're right. Let's talk through Arlington, one more time. Then I'd like to see the plans."

Plans, Fallon thought later as she rode home, spoke of hope, of optimism, and of determination. They'd need all of that to win, to survive, and to build those centers.

She intended to take all of it to Arlington, and beyond.

CHAPTER SEVEN

A half-moon rose over the base as she stood with the men and women she'd lead into battle. With sword, with arrow, with bullet, with tooth and claw and fist, they'd fight with her on a night so hot, so close the air had weight.

In the south on the beach, they'd fight. And more than two thousand miles to the west in the desert, they'd fight.

They'd fight and take the next step on the journey begun centuries before.

"Now," she murmured, and so the order passed from place to place, to the south, to the west.

Lifting her hands, she thought of the lessons Mallick had taught her at a deserted prison. Patience, quiet, control.

She slid her power along the dark magicks circling the base like a deadly moat. Strong, drenched in blood sacrifice, thriving on the flesh and bone of whatever creature might cross into its open jaws, it floated into her mind's eye.

Black and bubbling.

"On the blood of the innocents slain I call. Hear their cries, taste their tears."

She heard them; she tasted them.

Mournful. Bitter.

"I am your sword. We are your justice."

The black magicks clawed, scraped, snarled as she pushed against them. Bubbling dark, pulsing with heat.

"Let the light of those cut down flicker, shine, rise into flames, and burn bright to break the chains. Bodies sacrificed for ill, let the light into your spirits spill."

She heard them calling out, felt that rising as her muscles trembled to hold it, embrace it.

And felt her father's hand on her back, drew from that strength, that faith. .

"On this night, at this hour, I call upon the power of those slain. Hear me, join me to wipe away the bloody stain.

"Your light, my light, our light unwinds the spell. And so in silence it falls to hell."

With sweat running down her back from the effort, she nodded. "It's down. Troy."

The witch and her coven bespelled the security cameras. Even those few minutes would add advantage.

"Archers."

Arrows winged their quiet death to those manning the towers.

"First wave, go."

As elves swarmed out of the dark to scale the walls, she pushed power against the gates. She felt the locks give, turned to meet her father's eyes. "Gates down. Second wave, go."

And she flew up on Laoch, dived toward the base. As her forces poured toward the gates, she called for the third wave. Faeries swooped toward the prison, the slave quarters.

No alarm sounded—not yet—as she touched down. A team of elves surged toward the HQ and communications.

Shifters streaked toward the armory. Since she hoped to save the fuel tanks rather than destroy them, she ringed them in cold fire.

As the first shouts sounded, the first clash of battle rang, the first bullets flew, she drew her sword, pivoted on Laoch. She rode toward the enemy charge, sword singing, striking, her blood as cold as the fire she'd conjured.

Screams ripped the air. As bullets struck her shield, she flung out power to engulf guns in flame. Each one rendered useless was one less that could be used against her people.

She heard the raging, rapid report of automatic fire, rode straight toward it and the man who sprayed the air with bullets. Even as he swung toward her, Laoch impaled him.

She heard the screams of women, the shrieks of children as faeries risked their lives to lift them to safety. She heard the moans of the wounded, leaped off Laoch to strike down an enemy before he could slice the throat of one of her people who lay bleeding.

She saw a shifter take a bullet in mid leap, fought her way to him as she mind-spoke to Travis.

We need more medical transport.

Working on it.

Work faster.

She raced toward more gunfire, a barrage of it, coming from one of the fortified buildings. Bullets pinged off her shield as she pushed her way toward it. With a sweep of power she took down the door, then rose up as she once had as a child in a faerie glade.

But this time she rose up with a flaming sword, shot a stream of fire into the sniper's nest. She flipped back through the air as Mick had taught her, landed. Five came at her at once.

She took the first out with a sweep of her sword at his legs before she leaped up. Sent another flying back with a vicious strike of her shield. She blocked a sword, spun, pumped up and back to kick out with both feet.

Blows landed, but she'd been trained to fight with pain. She struck back a sword, danced away from the swipe of a knife. With a slash of her blade, she cleaved the arm from one, and with his screams ringing in her ears, drove the point of her sword through the heart of the other.

Through the stench, the smoke, the screams, they fought. Bodies, so many bodies, littered the ground. She pushed away any thought of the carnage and the cost because she felt, she *knew* the tide had turned hard in their favor.

Some of the enemy ran for the gates, deserting the field. They would meet another line, she thought, be given the choice to surrender.

All prisoners and slaves secured, Travis said in her mind.

She caught an arrow in her shield inches from her heart, drew it out, flung it with a whip of power at the bowman.

Colin charged up to her. "We've got fifty secured in the prison. A few deserters got through, but we've got about a dozen of them. They're done."

Once again her shield blocked an arrow, this one before it cut her brother down. "Not quite."

"Just mop-up now."

Even as he grinned, she felt it.

"Get behind me."

"Bullshit on that."

"Don't argue."

She swung around to face the dark.

He stood tall, well over six feet. He dressed in black,

and the air around him rippled with it. He flung a bolt of lightning toward her, easily blocked.

And he smiled.

She saw him, clearly, pouring the blood of the sacrificed onto the ground, burning the black fire, chanting the foul words to create the moat.

"These are nothing." He spread his arms to take in the fallen. "Tools and dupes to be used and discarded."

An arrow sang out, dropping with a hit that rippled air. He bent to retrieve it, glanced up at where Tonia stood on a rooftop. He shot it back at her with a strike of his arm.

Fallon swept out with her own power, broke it to pieces. He laughed.

"She knew you'd come, would have to come to try to save these pitiful creatures. She knew you'd bleed for them. Your cousin sends her best."

He flung out power that rattled her bones when it struck her shield.

"Get clear," she ordered Colin.

"I'm not leaving you to—"

"Get clear. And mop the hell up. That's an order."

The brother in him nearly snapped back, but the soldier obeyed orders.

"You're what she sent?" Fallon kept her tone mildly interested.

"I am Raoul, the Black Wizard. I am bound to Petra by blood, imbued with powers dark and glorious by what lives in her. I am the slayer of The One, in her name."

"Raoul, the Black Wizard?" Now she added contempt. "You've got to be kidding."

"Burn, burn, burn." He circled his hands as he shouted the spell. "Now the fires and hungers of hell."

Black fire struck her shield, circled her. She felt the

pulse of heat, of dark joy. Some of her people rushed to defend her. As she shouted them back, Raoul snapped out a whip of lightning. It streaked toward Flynn, fast and deadly. Before it struck, Lupa leaped to shield him.

And fell bloodied and burned to the ground.

She heard Flynn's cry of grief like a heart breaking inside her head. With rage, she flung power at the fire around her, beat at it with furious fists of light.

His laughter rang as he pulled lightning from the sky, pummeling the ground with it like rain. She pushed through the dying fire, striking at bolts with her sword, flinging them upward with her shield.

He chanted, drawing up smoke from the ground that hissed and snapped like snakes.

"Your light dims and dies," he shouted. "And the shell that's left of you I'll spread at Petra's feet."

Drawing in, drawing up her power, pulling it as she charged across the bloodied field. She swore she heard the sword in her hand sing.

"By the blood of my blood." Heat soaked her, but she fought forward. "By the flesh of my flesh, the bone of my bone. By the light of my light, be damned."

When she struck him down, when his laughter became a shriek, she felt the jolt shake through her, all but steal her breath.

He lay, breath gurgling. "She will be your doom."

"No. I'll be hers. As I'm yours."

She plunged the sword into him, ended it.

She lifted her sword high, called on the cool light of the moon to cleanse it. Once cleansed, she drove the point into the ground. So the ground shook, and light burst like noon before it faded to starlight.

"This place is now the place of the light. We claim this place. Light for life."

There were cheers, but she walked through them with tears on her cheeks toward Flynn.

He stood, holding the wolf who'd given his life to save him. She saw his broken heart in his eyes.

"I'm sorry. I'm so sorry."

"He died a warrior, a hero. He died in—" When his voice broke, Flynn pressed his face to Lupa's bloody fur.

"He died in service to The One." Starr stepped up beside Flynn, and though her voice shook, she continued. "To the light she stands for. To the light we fight for.

"Come." She who rarely touched or allowed herself to be touched, laid an arm around Flynn's shoulders. "We'll take him home."

At another shout, Fallon turned, looked with eyes blurred with tears as Colin fixed a cloth with the fivefold symbol shining silver on a field of white onto a flagpole.

The PW brand lay trampled in the dirt. And they raised the standard of The One over Arlington.

Faeries flew in to transport wounded even as, now with the base under their control, more healers rushed in to treat some where they lay.

Fallon ordered sentries to take their posts, and teams to sweep through every house and building, every shed and structure to make certain they missed no enemy, no wounded.

No dead.

She searched for her father as she did her own sweeps until her heart began to pulse in her throat.

When she saw Will leading a team out of a fortified house, giving the all clear so one of the witches could shimmer a fivefold symbol on the door, she hurried to him.

"I haven't seen my father. I need to—"

"He's okay. He took a hit, but—"

"Where is he? How bad? My mother—"

"Breathe," he told her. "I swear to you he's okay. We had him, you know, airlifted to the mobile. Your mother treated him herself. A through and through, right side, mostly caught meat."

"No one told me."

"He made me swear not to, and I agreed with him. I just got word from one of the medics he's on his feet, and already on his way back here." He added a smile and a shoulder rub. "Your mother cleared him."

"Okay." She did as Will suggested and breathed. "Eddie, Aaron," she began.

"They're okay. We lost people, Fallon, and it's going to be hard to take those losses back to New Hope."

The weight already lay in her belly like stones. "I need names and numbers, casualties and wounded, as soon as it's possible."

"You'll have them. Are we going to count you among the wounded? You're bleeding here and there, and you've got some burns."

"I'll take care of it when the rest are treated. We need to—" She broke off, managed a shaky "Dad," and ran to Simon.

He caught her, his grip on her as tight as hers on him. "I'm okay. But you—" He pulled her back. "You need a medic."

"When everyone's treated. It's nothing. You're pale. Let me see."

She yanked up his shirt before he could object, studied the healing wound in his right side. Laid her hand over it. "It's clean, and healing. You're pale from the blood loss. You should rest until—"

"I'm good enough, and your mom agreed."

She studied his face, saw a little pain. "After how big an argument?"

"I won. Word's already traveling back at how you

ended this, and I want to hear all about it later, from you. I'm going to tell you now your mom, Travis, everyone on medical and support are okay."

Her blood went cold. "What does that mean? What happened?"

"A handful of deserters got through the lines. They figured they'd take one of the mobile units and escape. They didn't, but there was a skirmish. Your mom, Travis, Rachel, Hannah, Jonah, some of the others? Kicked some serious ass."

"Was she hurt?"

"Not only not hurt, but she, and the rest of them, protected the wounded, the mobiles, and ended up with seven prisoners. Take your victory, baby."

"The Dark Uncanny killed Lupa. He— I couldn't stop him in time."

Simon lowered his brow to hers. "I'm sorry. I'm damn sorry. Flynn?"

"He and Starr will take him home. We'll take our dead home. We'll cremate the enemy dead. There are too many to bury, and we'll take ours home."

She looked around, saw Taibhse perched on the pole above the flag. She sent her mind to Faol Ban, found him where she'd asked him to be, helping guard the wounded. And Laoch returning to her from taking the last injured to medical.

All of hers, she thought, alive and well. But others . . .

"Their blood sanctifies the ground."

With his hand still gripping hers, Simon felt the rise of her power, saw others who worked to clear, to gather the dead stop. Her voice rang, lifted, carried to every ear.

"In this place where once dark ruled with cruelty and bigotry for a false and twisted god, I will bring a white stone, pure and polished. On this stone I will carve the names of all who died in the name of light and right, for the sake of the innocent. They will be mourned. They will be honored. They will be remembered."

Sighing, she turned back to Simon. "Can you help gather the names?"

"Of course."

She stood in the smoke, and remembering her own vision, swept up her arms to clear the air of the stink of it.

"I need to bring Chuck in to check out the tech, and I need a report from Thomas, one from Mallick. Troy and some of the others can add layers of magickal security to keep out enemies. We need an inventory of weapons, of supplies, equipment, medicines."

"What you need is a temporary HQ. Take theirs for now. Colin's already on the weapon inventory. I saw him on my way in."

Just do the next thing, she told herself. Do the next thing, and when that was done, do the next.

"If they can spare Jonah or Hannah back at the mobiles, I'd like one of them taking charge of doing the inventory of medical equipment and supplies."

"I'll send a runner. We'll get teams on the rest of the inventory. Baby, do your dad a favor and let one of the medics treat you."

"I can do it. I'll set up in the HQ. I could use Chuck."

"I'll have him brought in. Fallon? You've done what no one has been able to do in the decade or more since White and his PWs took this place."

"We did," she corrected.

"You're right. And you were right about fighting for it. We won't forget the dead, but don't you forget that. You were right."

He gestured to where a team had already begun dismantling the scaffold. "Put your stone there. Put it there where the bastards held their fucking public executions."

"Yes." Thank God for him, she thought. Thank God

for the man who could see and feel and know. "Yes, I'll put it there."

As she started across the base, Tonia fell into step beside her. "Thanks for the save."

"Anytime."

"He was stronger than I anticipated—my mistake. Goddamn Petra."

"His death won't mean anything to her. She'll just find another. She already has others."

With Tonia she crossed a sidewalk, went up a trio of steps to a paved walkway toward a wide, covered porch.

"I talked to Duncan." Tonia tapped her temple. "We have Utah."

Fallon felt twin tugs of jubilation and trepidation. "How many casualties?"

"Zip, zero. Not a single one. Some injuries, but not a single casualty on our side. He said their security was a joke, and half the enemy was drunk or stoned on peyote—which is a big no-no for PWs. I don't think White sent his best. I think Dunc's actually a little disappointed it was so easy."

"The next won't be." Fallon paused on the porch. "I'll need a full report, and details of what they've done and are doing for our security there. The supplies, the prisoners, the rescued, all of it."

"He knows. Once they've done the inventory, got their numbers, and all that, Mallick's coming back to report to you directly."

"Good. I'll check in with Mick, and we can hope the news there is as positive. Meanwhile, we're going to set up our HQ here."

She opened the door.

As they stepped in, Tonia gaped. "Holy . . . Wow!"

The entrance spread over gleaming floors, towered up three open stories. An elaborate staircase split and veered off right and left on the second floor. Overhead, an enormous light showered with crystals.

Art in ornate frames covered the walls.

As Fallon wandered farther, she saw some sort of open sitting room to her left with twin sofas covered with silky fabric, chairs with curved legs, tables of polished wood, lamps with more crystals sparkling.

"I've never seen anything like this," Tonia said as she shifted right.

A fireplace framed with white stone shot through with silvery gray stood between tall white pillars. The room held a piano painted gold, more sofas, more chairs and tables and lamps, more art.

A few pieces had been smashed or broken during the battle. The steel shutter over the big front window, compromised during the fight, hung crooked. Blood stained the colorful rug. Some had spilled on the polished floors.

"Luxury," Fallon said. "The leaders lived in luxury, stealing whatever they wanted, decorating their nests. And you see?" She moved to the window. "They could sit here, stand here in their stolen palace, and watch the crowds cheer as they hanged those like us."

"Not anymore."

"No, not anymore. We'll leave what's needed, take what isn't to distribute where it is needed, or store until it is."

She roamed on, amazed at the space and furnishing of a dining room—another fireplace, this in a green stone she knew as malachite, a long, glossy table large enough to sit twenty surrounded by chairs with high backs and fancy seats. Sideboards holding silver candles and bowls.

A kitchen that would surely have made her mother weep with joy, despite the blood on the floors, the broken doors of glass that led out to a stone patio, a pool, a garden, a fountain.

A kitchen, she thought, where slaves had cooked and served.

She opened a door. "A pantry—a big one, and with enough supplies to feed fifty for a week."

"Same with this fridge." Tonia opened another door. "It's a kind of laundry room. There's a cot in here, shackles. They kept a personal slave."

"Not anymore," Fallon said again, and opened another door. "Leads downstairs." Though she knew the house had been cleared, she laid a hand on the hilt of her sword as they started down.

"Communication center. Bless the goddess," Tonia said with a wild grin. "Chuck is going to lose his shit. Man, oh fuck, Fallon, it's as full of toys as anything I've seen outside of the nuke plants we hit."

"They worked hard putting this together." Fallon studied the controls, monitors, radios, components. "Now we'll use it against them."

"It's got to be full of data, records, locations, everything. Chuck will dig it out."

"That's his magick."

The battle had come here, she saw, in blood and gore, overturned chairs, bullet holes in walls.

She walked to the broken door, stepped out into the steamy night. Closing her eyes, she reached out to Mick.

Man, we've been waiting to hear from you. You're okay?

We have Arlington.

Hot damn! What did you—

Later. I need a sitrep.

Well, we've got Carolina—or this part of it. Utah?

Yes.

We freaking did it!

Casualties?

She felt his hesitation, prepared for the worst.

Eight. Sixteen wounded. We lost eight, Fallon. We lost Bagger.

She grieved for the elf she'd known as a child, for the boy who had a love for jokes. *I'm sorry, Mick.*

They lost more, I can tell you that. A hell of a lot more.

She glanced back when she heard Chuck's voice.

"Oh, my hot, sexy mama, come to Papa!"

I need Thomas or whoever you can spare to come in, give me full reports.

Once we're fully secured. The standard of The One flies here now.

Do you have control of their comms?

Yeah, we do, and the IT guy's all over them.

I need you to send a message on my signal.

What and where?

She told him, then went back in to relay the same to Tonia to give to Duncan.

"Can you set it up so I can send out a message?" she asked Chuck.

"You bet your fine ass I can. No offense."

"None taken. Can you send it so it goes out to whoever can listen? Whoever has communication abilities?"

"With what I've got here, I've got a pretty long reach. You and Tonia could boost that. You probably don't remember how you and Duncan boosted our first broadcast from New Hope."

"I actually do, at least a little."

"Tell Duncan to do the same on his end," Fallon said as she communicated the idea to Mick. "How long do you need, Chuck?"

He was already working controls. "Just a second. Do you want visual or just audio?"

"All. Wait." She held her hands to her face, did a glamour to mask blood, bruising, burns. "Not vanity," she began.

"You're unhurt," Tonia said. "Untouched. Any blood on The One is enemy blood. That's good tactics."

"Ten seconds from my mark," she told Tonia, Chuck, and Mick. "Boost it."

As controls lit up, monitors flashed, Chuck laughed. "Don't get too crazy, girls. We're up when you are."

"Mark," she said.

"Ten, nine, eight," Chuck counted it off, then opened the channels.

"To all who gather together in peace, to all who wish for peace, who protect, defend, who have suffered or shed blood to protect or defend, hear my voice and know there is hope. Know the light is with you, all of you, magickal and non. To the farmers, the builders, the teachers, the soldiers, the mothers, the sons, the fathers and daughters, know the light stands for you, fights for you. Rise up, rise up against those who oppress, against those who persecute and enslave. Know that for every one who seeks to destroy, we send twenty to stop them.

"Hear my voice, persecutors, oppressors. Hear and know, Purity Warriors, Dark Uncanny, bounty hunters, Raiders, any who hunt and imprison, who torture and kill, your time is ending. What comes from the dark will die in the dark."

She drew her sword, filled it with light. "The light will burn you out. Tonight, the light has broken the chains of those held on the beaches of Carolina, in the desert of Utah, driven out the dark to claim those places in its name. Tonight, the light burned bright through the dark of Arlington, and it is ours. Fear me, all who shed innocent blood, all who seek to live on the fat, on the backs of slaves, fear me, all who have chosen the dark. Fear me and all who follow the light, for we will end you."

She held up her free hand, and in her palm a ball of fire blazed. "Here is the fire to burn through the dark, and all who follow it." She closed her hand around the flames, opened it again. She held a white dove. "And here is the hope offered to all the rest.

"I pledge both, the flame and the dove.

"I am Fallon Swift. I am The One."

She nodded to Chuck. His hand shook a little as he ended the broadcast.

"Some speech," he managed.

"Yeah. Some trick." Tonia touched a fingertip to the dove's breast.

"It just came to me." Fallon released the dove, waved it to freedom through the broken door. "Too much?"

"I can tell you, if I was one of the bad guys?" Chuck let out a laugh. "I'd have shit my pants."

"Good." Fallon laid a hand on his shoulder. "That's what I was aiming for."

"Direct hit."

CHAPTER EIGHT

While Fallon set up a headquarters at Arlington, Duncan did the same in Utah. He didn't have the fine things, as she did, and had already started a list of what he'd need to build and maintain a viable base of operations.

They'd need supplies to build better shelters, an agrodome for growing fruit. More chickens, cows, some goats, pigs, which meant pens and paddocks, some sort of barn. While he knew how to deal with livestock, there had to be somebody on base who'd have a better handle on that.

He'd delegate faeries to start growing vegetables, herbs, and grains wherever it made sense, send scouts to find what they could find, possibly barter with communities, when and if they found any.

Flour, sugar, salt—basics they'd have to flash in from New Hope until they found a better way. He was, he thought, essentially starting out like his mother and the New Hope Originals had.

At least he had their template to work from, and experienced troops.

The armory would serve for now, he calculated, but they'd want to add to that, too.

He sat in what was essentially a shack with his lists and maps. The most secure structure—which he'd added layers to—now served as a prison, not for slaves or tortured magickals but for captured enemy.

He needed them off his base as soon as possible and wrote down suggestions for prison camps.

He glanced up when Mallick came in.

"I'm sending out hunting, scouting, and scavenging parties at first light. I figure the faeries we've got with us can get started on growing food, for us and for livestock, but maybe we need some sort of agrodome for fruit trees."

"I'll ask about that when I get to New Hope." Mallick glanced over to where Duncan had stacked bottles of whiskey, gin, beer, wine.

"I figured it was safer in here with me. We'll keep some. Soldiers need a little recreation, and some can be used medicinally. And we can barter with the rest."

With a nod, Mallick selected a bottle of wine, opened it, sniffed. "Barely palatable. Still." He found cups, lifted a brow at Duncan.

"Yeah, why not? I'm sending a list of need now with you, and a list of need eventually."

"All right. You did well tonight."

Duncan took the cup of wine, tapped it to Mallick's with the *clink* of tin to tin. "You, too. Then again, it wasn't much of a fight."

"Because we'd prepared and planned and followed through on the plan."

"And because the enemy was mostly drunk assholes."

"Yes, but even drunk assholes can kill. We lost no one." He sat with his wine. "South Carolina lost eight."

Looked into his cup before he drank. "Arlington lost sixty-three, with another ninety-eight wounded."

Duncan set down the cup, rose to walk to the window. "Tonia said it was bad. She said Flynn lost Lupa. I know Lupa and Eddie's Joe have lived longer than they would have because of magickal treatments and healing, but still . . . I can't imagine New Hope without Flynn's wolf."

He turned back. "Do you have the names of the dead, the wounded?"

Mallick laid a paper on the table, so Duncan came back.

As he read, he picked up the cup, drained the wine.

"You'd know them," Mallick began.

"I went to school with two of them. Len and I used to play basketball, pickup games. I dated Marly a couple of times. Ben Stikes used to play this thing—ukulele—on his front porch. Margie Frost taught me and Tonia chemistry in the academy. I knew them. I knew all of them."

And he could see them, hear them. He knew their families, their friends. He remembered he'd dated Marly primarily because she'd caught him with her quick, infectious laugh.

"It grieves her."

Duncan pressed his fingers to his eyes, dropped them. "It has to. It should never be easy."

"Correct."

"I don't mean she deserves—"

"I know what you mean, boy. I trained her, I watched her become. And though I had devoted my life to just that, when the time came, I grieved for her, for the weight she'd carry."

"You came to love her."

"I did. An unexpected development." Mallick drank

again. "And tonight, though it's another beginning and not the end, she showed what she is."

"She invited an attack. Not here. We're not worth it at this point." Though he'd make damn certain they would be. "Probably not South Carolina. But Arlington."

"She meant to. She'll hold what she took."

"I know it. I have issues with her apart from this, but I believe in her, absolutely."

"I know that as well. You're a credit to your blood, Duncan."

"Wow." Sincerely surprised, Duncan searched for words. "That calls for another drink."

With a laugh, Mallick poured them both more wine.

"I'll build this place into a stronghold, and from here, we'll expand the West. Tell her . . . Shit, I don't know what I want to tell her."

"You will, when you see her again."

"I don't know. Maybe." Right now, he thought, he had to focus everything on making that stronghold, feeding, clothing, drilling the troops who'd hold it.

"What I do know?" Duncan said with a shrug. "Unexpected development—I'm going to miss you."

"And I, also unexpected, you."

Mallick lifted his cup. "To the light, and to the unexpected."

Duncan tapped his cup to Mallick's again, and drank.

Fallon stayed in Arlington for two weeks, helping to organize and arrange housing, training, overseeing the transfer of prisoners, and working to relocate any former slaves and captured magickals who chose to leave.

As more opted to remain—to live, work, train there—she supervised the redistribution of supplies and furnishings within the base.

Volunteers cleared the houses in the outlying neighborhood of the remains of the dead, banished rats, cleaned, repaired.

She used Katie's blueprint from New Hope for assigning jobs—skills, experience, or interest in gaining both—for creating volunteer sign-ups.

The attack came on the dawn of the third day after her broadcast. Prepared for it, forces who now called themselves Light for Life repelled the PWs in under an hour. It had been, in Fallon's estimation, more an angry, arrogant barrage than a structured attack.

There would be others, but at the end of two weeks, she trusted Colin and his troops to defend the base and any who settled on its outskirts.

She stood with him by the white memorial stone she'd placed. She'd shaped it like a tower to symbolize a rising, and with her light, had carved the names of everyone who'd given their life to take this ground.

Below the names, she'd etched the fivefold symbol, and had added LIGHT FOR LIFE.

Already someone had planted flowers at its base, and they bloomed as white as the stone.

"Mallick will be on and off base for the next couple weeks. You know how to send for him or for me if you need to. And I need those weekly reports, detailed."

"We've been over it, Fallon. Detailed weekly reports. Anything unusual or noteworthy that comes out of scouting missions, you hear asap."

"They'll attack again. The PWs, and very likely government or military out of D.C. Watch the skies, Colin."

She let out a breath. She had to trust he was ready. She'd already sent Taibhse and Faol Ban back to New Hope. Now it was time for her to join them.

So she turned to him. "Listen to Mallick. Learn from him. You're in command—but you're not president."

He grinned at her. "I like fighting better than politics."

"Clearly, but don't forget the politics. Train them hard, Colin."

She looked around the base, at the soldiers and recruits on the training grounds, the volunteers working the gardens, tending the livestock. Laughter filtered out of the house they'd outfitted as a school, and the scent of fresh bread wafted out of another they'd designated as a base kitchen.

More than a base, already more, she thought. A community in the making.

"Train them hard," she repeated. "Within the year, we take D.C."

"We'll be ready."

She turned to him, hugged him hard. "Keep them safe," she said, then swung onto Laoch. "You're still at least a little bit of a jerk, but I love you anyway."

"Same goes."

Laoch spread his wings. She flew up over Arlington, circled once, then soared toward New Hope.

She wanted the flight rather than the flash, and used it to make maps in her head of the land below. Too many roads not yet cleared or in impassable disrepair. What had been cities, what they'd called suburbs, developments of houses, centers for shopping remained largely deserted. The land itself had taken over in the two decades since the Doom so grasses grew thick and high, trees spread like weeds. Over them, through them, wildlife roamed in herds and packs, and she imagined the rivers and streams below busy with fish and waterfowl.

With their mad mission to eradicate magickals, to enslave, the Purity Warriors had done little to nothing to tend the land, to build. Raiders raided, and left destruction in their wake. What government there was seemed focused on rules and the battles in the major cities, and still, she knew, on their work to contain and restrain those with powers they refused to understand.

She wouldn't make the same mistakes, and wouldn't aim her focus so narrowly.

She veered west, studied the hills, the forests, waterways, fallow, overgrown fields, and the buildings—houses, vast shopping areas, and service centers.

Twice she took Laoch down for a closer look when she saw signs someone had settled. A broken trail, a few houses in good repair, a cow in a pen.

She marked the locations in her mind, continued home.

When she landed, Ethan gave a shout, and with Max, his closest companion, and a pack of dogs, raced over from the farm.

Under a tattered, faded ball cap, Ethan's hair was damp with sweat. Both boys smelled of horses and dogs and dirt. Max, gangly like his father, waded through the dogs to lay a hand on Laoch's neck.

"We were watching for you," Ethan told her. "Mom said you'd be back today."

"We've been helping Dad and Simon with the haying." Max gestured out to the field and the oft-repaired baler. "But they said we could come when we saw you up there. Your mom made cherry pies, and mine's going to pick sweet corn."

"We're going to have a cookout." Already Ethan hefted her saddlebags. "Because you're back."

"Sweet corn and cherry pies?" Fallon dismounted. "When do we eat?"

Because nothing pleased them more, she turned Laoch over to them. They'd cool him down, groom him like a king.

She hauled her bags in through the kitchen.

Pies with glossy cherry filling, bold red through the

golden latticework crusts, bread, fresh and scenting the air, wrapped in cloth on the counter. Wildflowers in a jug, peaches ripening in a bowl, potted herbs thriving on the windowsill.

After the battle and the blood, the work and the worry, here was home.

And here, she realized, was what she needed to bring to the world as much as peace.

She dumped her bags—they could wait. Now she opened the fridge, found another jug. And grateful, filled a glass with her mother's lemonade to wash away the heat and thirst of the journey.

Travis came in, nearly as sweaty as Ethan.

"Saw you coming in." He grabbed another glass. "Had to finish something up, but I wanted to come by. Is everything okay with Colin, with Arlington?"

"He's good. The base is secure."

"Haven't had a chance to talk to you really." He glugged down lemonade. "We've made good use of some of the stuff you sent back—got a couple houses furnished and supplied already. The mayor and council and committees are working to help the people who wanted to come here settle in."

He grabbed a peach—just underripe as he preferred. "We had the funerals last week. It was rough."

"I should've been here."

"Everyone knew why you weren't. We're going to have a memorial. The council voted on it, since we always have the annual on the morning of the Fourth, but we're going to hold one for the placing of the stars. Now that you're back."

"It's good. It's right."

"The last of the wounded were discharged a couple days ago. Most are already back in training. It was rough," he repeated, talking quickly through it as he bit into the peach. "But taking three bases—and, Jesus, Arlington—then your broadcast after?"

With a satisfied head shake, Travis gestured with the peach. "Arlys printed it out, word for word, and posted it. Anyway, the mood around here is strong. In the last week, we've gotten fourteen more recruits from the outside. Mick just sent word they've pulled in eighteen. Eighteen."

"Duncan?"

"He's pretty remote, but Tonia told me—and she's going to meet up with you as soon as she can get away—he had seven last count. And one's a doctor, or was a—what's it—intern when the Doom hit."

"That's good news, and we'll need to go over all this. But now—"

"Here it comes." He held up his hands, one holding the half-eaten peach. "First, we were a little busy dealing with the deserters, and keeping the wounded and medicals from getting overrun."

"Which is why you should have let me know."

"Busy," he repeated, "and pretty much under control. Plus, in the thick of it?" On a shrug, he bit into the peach again, the underripe fruit snapping crisp as an apple. "Mom was like—wow, just wow. I've never seen her in full battle mode, you know? The thing was, she had Dad out, like in a trance so she could treat the bullet wound. These PWs break through the lines to try to get to the mobiles and escape, and Mom's *zap! Zap, pow!*"

To demonstrate, he jabbed one fist, then the other. "Seriously, she took out three of them before you could fucking blink. And I've gotta say, Rachel's no slouch. Grabs a scalpel with one hand, smashes this dude with an elbow, then slices him open. Then Hannah?"

He tossed the peach pit in the kitchen composter, turned to rinse off his hands. "You know, I've worked

with her on combat training, self-defense. Let's just say
it hasn't been her strength, right? She was moving from
one mobile to the other when they hit us, and I'm yelling
at her to get inside, barricade herself and the wounded.
But she swings right around. *Pow, pow, wham, bam.*
Man, she is fierce when she's cornered. A ball-kicker. A
fierce ball-kicker."

"Hannah?" Fallon sincerely couldn't imagine her loving, openhearted friend kicking balls.

"You bet your ass. It couldn't have taken us more than
a minute, two tops, to subdue them. Hannah's bleeding
a little—the guy whose balls are probably still bruised
managed to punch her in the face. So Jonah and I are
securing the deserters, and Mom tells me not to let you
know, not then. Rachel's checking out Hannah, and seconds that. Hannah chimes in, all cheerful, how we're all
fine, and not to distract you, and Jonah says the same.
Mom gives me that look. You know, the one that says
don't screw with me, and goes back to fixing Dad up."

"I was outvoted, and they were right."

"Maybe." Because with words and gestures, Travis
had taken her into the thick of it, she understood the decision. She leaned back against the counter. "Maybe, but
the enemy shouldn't have broken through, and that's a
weakness we'll fix."

"They were scared shitless, Fallon. Every one of
them. Even if I couldn't see it, and I could, I could feel it.
And hey, we won. I gotta get back, but welcome home.
Big feast tonight."

He eyed the pies.

"Don't even think about it."

"Too late, but I'm not stupid enough to risk the mighty
wrath of Mom."

He opened the door, turned back. "But if we'd needed

you, even the mighty wrath of Mom wouldn't have stopped me from calling you."

Satisfied with that, she washed out her glass—and his—then took her bags to her room to unpack.

When Lana came home, carrying supplies, Fallon hopped up from the kitchen counter where she'd set up to draw her new maps.

"My baby."

Before Fallon could take the cloth bags, Lana set them down, enfolded her.

"I'd hoped to be back before you got here, but Rachel needed some help in the clinic."

"What happened?"

"No, no, nothing like that." Lana eased back, cupped Fallon's face to study it. "School's starting soon, and they're doing wellness checks. And she wanted to show me some changes they've made in the plans for the expansion. Sit while I put these things away and tell me how your brother is."

"You sit while I put them away."

Fallon nudged her mother to a counter stool, found olives from the Tropics, oil from the press her father had helped build, peppercorns, coffee beans, a bag of salt.

"Colin's in his element," she began. "The troops respect him, which is vital, but they also like him. We turned that fucking palace—" She caught herself, winced. "Sorry."

"I think we're beyond me scolding you over language."

Still, Fallon thought. "That palace of an HQ? We cleared out the unnecessary."

"And much of it's been put to use here and elsewhere."

"It had seven bedrooms, and other rooms that we

turned into bedrooms. We've got troops housed there. Mallick will have a room there, one with a kind of parlor for his workshop. Colin has a room to himself, it's the smallest of them. It works. We set up other barracks, and civilian housing."

She went through the broad details as she put away the supplies, then sat.

Impressed, approving, Lana nodded. "You're combining the templates from New Hope and our own cooperative back home."

"I know how they work, and that they work. We need those fortified structures in locations like Arlington especially for training and to keep people safe. When Mallick gets back there—"

"He's not there now?"

"I asked him to help Mick for a few days, then visit our other bases before he comes here, briefs me. Then he'll go to Arlington. Colin's solid, Mom."

"I know it. I do. But I think he could use some of Mallick's discipline and worldview."

"Trust me, he'll get it."

"I resented him so much when he took you away. And now I'm depending on him to help another of my children. Life is damn twisty and strange."

"I need him with Colin, but I need his perspective on our other bases, and future ones."

Lana looked down at the maps in progress. "You've picked locations for others."

"For bases, for fortifications, for communities they can protect—and who will have to protect themselves. Once Duncan has the Utah base fully secured and running, we'll need to expand there. The same for Mick in the South. And from here to Arlington."

Fallon traced a finger over the map. "There're so

many untapped resources, so much land that should be cultivated and put to use. Too many roads, and a lot of them useless. Buildings that need to be dismantled for supplies so we can build those bases and communities. Too many people still hunted and hiding. We need to rally them."

"You've made a good start on that."

"Not enough." Fallon pushed up to pace. "Not nearly. I need to double our fighting troops, at least double them to take D.C. I need to—"

She stopped herself, turned back. "We don't need to get into all this now. I just got home. Let me tell you how it felt to walk into this room and see pies on the counter, fresh bread and lemonade, flowers."

She walked back, took Lana's hands. "It reminded me it's not all battles and wars and beating back the dark. Because there are places like this where the dark is beaten back. Where people live, and kids go to school, and neighbors have cookouts. I need to remember that. I need you to remind me of that when I forget why I took the sword from the fire. Sometimes I'm afraid I'll forget."

"No, you won't. But sometimes I worry you'll forget if you don't give yourself a life, if you don't eat the pie, dance to the music, laugh with friends, and, God, make love with a man you care for, you'll forget what it means to live. Just live, Fallon."

Fallon brought her mother's hand to her cheek. "I could probably choke down some pie now."

Lana's bluebell eyes danced with amusement. "That was tricky of you."

"Did it work?"

"Put on the kettle for tea," Lana decided. "We'll both have pie."

Later, she feasted with neighbors, laughed with friends, danced to the music. And just lived.

The next day, she visited everyone who'd lost someone in the battle of Arlington. Their grief tore through her even as their strength humbled her. These, too, she knew, she must remember. The day would come when there would be too many lost for her to visit all, to console.

She attended the memorial for the fallen, didn't hide her tears. When she watched Flynn hang Lupa's star, she wondered her heart didn't break to pieces.

When he asked, she walked with him into the woods, wandered with him in the quiet with Faol Ban hunting in the shadows, with Taibhse sweeping through the trees.

"I wanted to tell you," Flynn began, "I thought about leaving, maybe going out to Utah with Duncan. Somewhere so different I wouldn't see Lupa in every turn of a trail."

"Wherever you want to go—"

"I'm here," he said simply. "This is my place. Max, your mother, Eddie, Poe, Kim, they helped bring me and mine here. Helped make this place. It's my place. I had no family left, and made family, then they gave me family and this home. I waited for you, and I'll fight for you. But . . . part of me died with him. You understand."

She watched her wolf slide through the shadows like white smoke, felt his heartbeat, knew his spirit. "Yes, I do."

"Your mother gave Lupa these last years. Kept him alive, vital, when his time had come and gone. I'll always be grateful. He died to save me. I'll use the life he saved to fight. Give me a mission."

Was it fate, she thought, that laid that request at her feet?

"Pick a dozen, not only skilled in battle but who understand what's needed to form a secure community. You'll need to scavenge and scout and recruit along the way. Just the way you did twenty years ago on your way to New Hope."

"Where?" was all he asked.

"I have a map, and I'll show you where you need to go. You'll need horses, because too many of the roads won't be passable in trucks and you can't count on fuel. I've gone over all this with my father, so when you have your twelve, bring them to us. It'll take weeks, Flynn, longer."

"That doesn't matter."

"Once you've begun what needs to begin, you'll come back."

Something shifted inside her, lifted a weight as she looked at him. "You won't come back alone."

Before she sent men off on a mission, a journey of nearly three hundred miles, she wanted to refine her map and take another firsthand look at the location, the terrain, the positioning.

She rode Grace back home to gather what she needed. An hour, she thought as she packed the map and supplies to draw more. Two at the most if she scouted out the second location she'd already considered.

Fly there, she decided, then to the second. Flash back.

For this she'd take the owl, the wolf as well as Laoch. What she didn't see, sense, hear, they would.

As she stepped outside to call them to her, Tonia flashed beside her.

"I had a feeling," Tonia said.

"About?"

"I heard Flynn talking to Starr and a couple of others.

You're sending him out to build another base. I figured you'd probably take another run at it before you sent him."

"You figured right."

"I'll go with you. Two pairs of eyes. Well," she added when Taibhse landed on Fallon's arm, the alicorn trotted up with the wolf at his side. "One more pair."

"I'm going to two places, the one for Flynn and his team, and another I hope to use."

"I'm up for it." Tonia drew up the hat hanging from a strap down her back, set it, with its wide, flat brim, over her head. "And the thing is, after the memorial, I could use something."

"All right. I could use your take anyway."

Fallon signaled Faol Ban so the wolf leaped nimbly onto Laoch's back before she mounted. Tonia swung on behind her.

As they rose up, Tonia lifted her face to the wind. "And this never gets old. So what's the plan?"

Fallon released Taibhse so he could soar. "The first, where I want Flynn, was a small town. Smaller than New Hope. In the foothills, so the land's hilly and rough. There's a river, and the bridge over it is broken, impassable. Some of the land's wooded, and some, though it's rocky, is farmable. And when I passed over and marked it, I saw no signs of people. There are houses and buildings—some are beyond repair, but a lot of them are stone or brick. Narrow streets, and some burned-out or abandoned vehicles."

"Raiders?"

"Probably. At this point it's only accessible by horse or bike. Or crossing the river—small boat or swimming it."

"So some defenses built in."

"Yeah. And land to plant, woods to hunt, housing. It's remote, but only about sixty miles from D.C."

"Excellent. Where's the second place?"

"East of D.C. It's good land, a lot of it flat, some bogs. Waterways. Rivers, bays, inlets, some beaches. Cabins, old houses, and other buildings. I saw some pockets of people, but their defenses are limited. Nomads more than settlers, I think. Hiding."

"Okay." Tonia looked down as they flew. "So much space. All those roads—I can't imagine what it was like when they were packed with people driving somewhere. Like them."

"Military convoy." Fallon studied the three trucks heading east. "Armored. Probably carrying troops into D.C."

"Conscripted. That's the way it's going now. They sweep up the able-bodied when they find them, and hunt people like us. It doesn't make any sense. If they merged forces with us instead of hunting us down, we could fight the DUs together."

"All magickals, dark or light, are the same to them. We have power. They fear it, and they want it."

"One of the new recruits got swept up last spring. He and the group he'd traveled with got caught in a flash flood, separated. He broke his ankle. A military squad found him, and gave him a choice. Sign up or die. A non-magickal, about sixteen. Who does that, Fallon?"

"They do."

"Yeah, they do. And we're hearing more about some of the ones they catch, sweep up, force to fight. They lock up their families, threaten them. Anyway, he signed up, they treated his ankle, put him into training. They make them watch those films, right? Films of DUs slaughtering people, and old footage of the Doom."

"Brainwashing."

"His wasn't washed, but he was smart enough to play the good soldier. First chance he got, he escaped. One of our scouting parties found him, alone, half-starved, and brought him in. Kim was with them, said he was scared to death, thought they were going to take him back. Then we gave him a choice."

"Stay, join the community," Fallon said, "or we'll give you the supplies you need to move on."

"He stayed."

"More will. And we need secure places for them. This'll be one."

CHAPTER NINE

Tonia looked down again as Fallon circled. She saw the river, wide and brown as tea, the rising land, the narrow streets and houses stepped up from it. Thick woods grew close with some leaves tinted with the first hints of fall. She saw the leggy form of a coyote slink back into the trees, and a small herd of deer cropping its way across rough, rocky ground.

"Farming's going to be a challenge," Tonia decided. "Then again I'm better at pretty much anything than farming. But yeah, some built-in defenses that could be well fortified."

When they landed, the wolf leaped off, began to explore. The great owl swooped toward the trees.

"Did you see how the road winds and winds down? Switchbacking. From here, a sentry would see anyone advancing." Fallon hopped off. "That building, an old church?" She gestured to the faded brick structure with its tall steeple, dingy gray from weather and neglect. "The highest point, and a perfect sentry post."

"And a lot of the road's eroded away in the low-lying

areas." As Fallon did, Tonia looked at the land for defense, offense. "Add a barricade. Access and cover for
an advancing force through the woods, but that could be
tightened up."

"And the fields are wide open. You couldn't cross
without being seen." Plant wheat, grains, Fallon thought,
build a mill on the river.

She climbed up to the church. The doors, like the
steeple, had been white once. Someone, long ago, had
written DOOM over them. Now the despairing red paint
faded into the gray.

Hinges protested with rusty shrieks when she opened
the doors.

More gray, she thought. The air, the walls, the windows. Someone had tried without much success to set
fire to the pews, so a few stood crackled and charred.

Above the altar hung desiccated remains.

"Not Raiders." Tonia's voice echoed in the musky air.
"Not enough damage for Raiders."

"No, not Raiders. He's been there a very long time."

She moved closer, opened herself.

"A nightmare, God's punishment, some thought. But
whose god? It took all, every soul, through the sickness or the madness that came with it. Crows circling,
smoke rising. Oh, the screams, the terrible laughter that
no prayer could overcome. Even here in this place of worship, Doom crept and clawed. Too many to bury, and the
stench of burning flesh rises with the smoke, rises to the
crows as they call me. It calls me, it promises, it lies.
There is no salvation. Only death."

"Don't." Tonia touched a hand to Fallon's arm to bring
her back. "Don't look anymore. It doesn't help."

"He was one of us, and the power that woke inside
him terrified him. What pulled at him terrified him because he wanted to answer. He tried to burn the church.

Fire's the first skill to come for most, but he was afraid, and he was the last, the only one who survived. He hanged himself in fear and despair."

"We'll take him down. We'll bury him."

"Yeah. There's no one here, and hasn't been since he did this. Maybe whatever he did, or tried to do before he took his own life, kept the dark away."

Tonia raised a hand, pushed power at a window so the sun struggled through. "We'll bring back the light."

They buried him in the stony ground behind the church, and when it was done, walked down to the river.

"I'm glad you came," Fallon said.

"I've got your back. Not just because of what you are, or because we share a bloodline. Because we're friends."

"You and Hannah are the first friends—girls—I've had. I used to wish for a sister, kept getting brothers." She found she could smile again. "There were some girls on other farms, or in the village, but . . ."

"Your parents had to be careful."

"That, yes, that, and I never made a real connection with the other girls. Too used to boys, I guess."

She watched a dragonfly, iridescent in the sun, swoop over the river's surface, sending out ripples. From somewhere in the trees, a woodpecker hammered madly.

The sound echoed forever in the empty.

"Then I went with Mallick. Mick was the first real friend—outside my family. Looking back, I don't know what I'd have done without him. Always outnumbered by boys."

"Duncan likes to bitch about being outnumbered by girls. And we did—and do—enjoy tormenting him. You know you can count on me, right? Not just in battle."

"I do. You and Hannah. Kick Balls Hannah."

As she shoved her hat back, Tonia laughed. "She is so digging on that status right now. How about the three of us score a bottle of wine tonight, stake out a place without boys around, and hang out?"

Fallon bent down, plucked a tiny flower, yellow as butter, from the weedy verge. Dragonflies, woodpeckers, wildflowers, she thought. There was life and beauty even in the empty.

"Oh yeah. Let's do that."

They took the time to scout more of the town, to add to Fallon's maps before heading north and east.

She skirted D.C., the smoke, the circling crows.

The time was coming, she thought, when she would meet the forces there, all of them. They'd come from the south, the west, the north, the east, ten thousand strong.

And when they freed those held in cages and labs and camps, the army would swell.

"Your mind's busy," Tonia commented. "It's buzzing all over."

"They fight for nothing there. They can't stop. The city's dead, a rubble on charred bones, but they won't stop. Once we take it, all that'll be left are ghosts and the hollow ring of false power."

She left it behind, winged south. "See, a few camps scattered through the hills. Nothing permanent or structured."

"Good hiding places," Tonia said. "Bad roads, and the winters would be hard. A couple feet of snow, what roads there are would be rough going without a good horse or enough fuel to run a Humvee like Chuck's, or a tank or snowplow."

"Plenty of game, wood, water." Fallon circled.

"Lots of water—lots of fish, probably mussels, crabs, clams. Get some boats seaworthy, and it's seafood time."

"Merpeople," Fallon pointed out, and watched the jeweled tails flash as they dived. "Good warriors."

They circled up, over a bluff. Good, high ground, to Fallon's mind.

"No power," she noted, "but those cabins look sturdy. There's a clearing. I'm going down."

The air sparkled, fresh, clean, and cooler than it had been. She smelled pine, and water from a stream, a hint of smoke from a camp a few miles west.

She walked toward a cabin that reminded her of the one she'd spent her first night in with Mallick on the way to his cottage.

"A hunting cabin most likely, or a vacation place. Log, well built. No power, but we can restore it."

She saw the red flash of a fox, deer scat, tracks from bear.

"This is nice." Tonia turned a circle. "I'm not especially a nature girl, but this is nice."

Fallon flicked a hand at the door, opening it as she approached.

"Scavengers picked it clean," she noted. "Nomads, probably, since they left the heavier furniture and there's no sign anyone settled in for long. Ashes in the fireplace, old and cold."

"The other cabins around here are likely the same. No supplies, but solid walls, roof, fireplace for heat. Tiny kitchen." Tonia turned the rusted tap on a shallow sink. "No running water, but yeah, we can fix that, too."

"One bath, toilet and shower. Serviceable, and more than I had for a year with Mallick."

Tonia's mouth dropped open. "Seriously? A *year*?"

"Deadly. This is better than I thought," she decided as she walked out, pushed her way along an overgrown track to another cabin. "Secluded but strategic. Get the basics up and running, add security, sentry posts, communications. Clear some of the land for a decent garden, a greenhouse, beehives, fortify the cabins, and use one as an armory. Get those boats on the waterways. Flash or fly in supplies. There's plenty of wood to build more cabins, for fuel. Let's see how many . . ." She trailed off, looked at Tonia.

I hear them, Tonia said in her mind. *North and south. About three dozen. Hold on.*

Not wanting to frighten off, but ready to defend, Fallon spoke clearly. "We're not here to harm, or take. You have nothing to fear from us unless you attack. Then you have everything to fear."

"Big talk from little girls."

The man who stepped into the clearing made John Little look spindly. He reached seven feet, with a burly, muscled body clad in a scarred leather vest and boots, and denim pants worn to holes at the knees.

He had a face like carved ebony, a black beard that hung to his chest, black hair in a grungy series of braids.

And an arrow nocked in his bow.

Some of the handful behind him held wooden spears or bows. One held a sword in a way that told Fallon he didn't actually know how to use it.

"Anyone would be little measured against you," Fallon said easily, and kept her hands at her sides. "Is this your land?"

"We're standing on it."

"And so are we. If it's your land, you haven't made much use of it. Still, you've got no need to defend it from us. We're not here to fight you."

He smiled wide, showed the gap of a missing tooth. "Why would you? You're outnumbered. Skinny girl with a big sword, best go back the way you came before we have to hurt you."

"You know what?" Tonia cocked a hip, set a hand on

it in a gesture of defiance. "I don't like being threatened for walking in the woods. You?" she said to Fallon.

"No."

Faol Ban slipped out of the trees, growled low in his throat. As the big man pivoted, drew back on the bow, Taibhse swooped down, gripped the arrow in his talons.

"If any of you threaten what's mine, you'll regret it." She spoke to her spirit animals quietly in Irish. The wolf slipped into the shadows; the owl perched on a high branch. "Is this how you treat strangers who cross your path?"

"Strangers who try to take what we have, sell us into slavery."

"We don't steal, and we free slaves."

His lip curled over the missing tooth. "Skinny girls with a wolf and trained owl free slaves?"

"Are there magickals among you?"

His face hardened, and despite the owl, the wolf, he drew another arrow out of his quiver. "Go. While you can still walk."

Fallon pushed out power, just a leading edge. As she did, as the big man and the people behind him stepped back, she heard a baby's quick cry.

She pulled back quickly. "You have children with you."

Face fierce, he grabbed a spear from the man beside him. "You'll never take them."

"Oh, for the sake of all the gods. We don't harm children, or take them. Wait." She held up a hand, rippled the air between them, and drew her sword. She thrust it up, filled it with light so it gleamed silver.

"I am Fallon Swift. I am pledged to defend the light, to protect the innocent. I come to destroy the dark, to tear down all who seek to harm those who seek peace. With this sword, I will lead into battle those who choose to follow me. And we will cut down all who stand against us."

"She's damn good at it, too," Tonia commented. "Come on, people. You've never heard of The One?"

"Just a story. A tale told to children around the campfire."

"No." A woman, a child gripping her hand, a baby in a sling at her breasts, pushed through.

"Liana, get back!"

"No." She laid a hand on the big man's arm. "I told you it wasn't a story. Kilo, why won't you listen? You're The One."

"Yes. And I see the light in you, your elfin blood."

The woman had eyes as dark as night. Her dusky face bore a long scar down her left cheek.

"And in you." Fallon crouched down to the level of the little boy with hair as dense and soft as a black cloud. "Do you see me? Do you see the light in me?"

The boy giggled, then pressed his face shyly to his mother's leg, peeked out.

"He's hungry." She called Laoch. When the alicorn landed in the clearing, people gasped and murmured, drew closer together.

"We bring no harm, no threat. Tonia, there's a peach in my saddlebag."

Tonia brought it to her, kept her gaze, cool and even, on Kilo's face.

"Is it all right?" Fallon asked Liana.

"Yes, yes, of course. Thank you. Say thank you, Eli."

He whispered it, still shyly clinging to his mother. But he reached out to take the peach after Fallon mimed biting into it.

When he bit into it himself, his wide eyes and the long *mmm* as juice dripped down his chin made Fallon laugh.

"It's all I have, but we can bring you more."

"Why?" Kilo demanded.

Still crouched, she shot him a look of sheer annoyance. "Because your boy doesn't have to be hungry, your people don't have to be afraid. Because we're not your enemy." She straightened. "I'll ask again. Is this your land?"

"We're camped here, until we move on and camp somewhere else."

"How many are you?"

When he folded his arms, Liana sighed. "Kilo, if you won't trust her, trust me. I see who and what she is. What they are."

"Thirty-six," he muttered.

"Eight are children," Liana added. "And one will bring another into the world soon."

"Do you have medicals with you, healers?"

"I do what I can," Liana said. "But I'm not skilled enough. The one who's pregnant needs to rest. So we stopped here, only a few hours ago. Don't you see the miracle, Kilo? Only a few hours ago."

"There are no miracles."

Fallon lifted an arm, and the owl landed on it. Faol Ban walked out of the woods to stand at her side. She gestured to Laoch. "A leader, even a stubborn one, should believe his own eyes. Would you stay if you had supplies, defenses, more people and weapons? If the shelters here could be made to serve?"

"A moving target's harder to hit."

"How long do you want to be a target?" she retorted. "How long do you want your children to be targets? If you stay, I can and will send supplies, weapons, more people who can train yours how to fight, how to plant, how to fish, how to build a community, and one with security. Milk," she said to Liana. "Fruit, vegetables, blankets, clothing."

"What do you want for all this you'll bring?" Kilo demanded.

"An army. War's coming. I'll build that army whether you go or stay. I'll bring supplies whether you go or stay, because your people need them. Whether you go or stay I'll build here, in this place, because it serves my cause. And if you stay, or wherever you go, I'll fight for you. She'll fight for you," she said, laying a hand on Tonia's shoulder. "The army we raise will fight for you."

"In other words, lead, follow, or get out of the way." Tonia shrugged. "To keep it simple." When he gave her a curled lip, she pushed forward, slapped a fist on the brick wall of his chest.

"Let me tell you something else, asshole—"

"Tonia—"

"No, fuck diplomacy. Skinny girls, my ass. That skinny girl led this skinny girl and an army of people who aren't big, giant dicks to Arlington, and won."

"Bullshit" was Kilo's response as others muttered and murmured.

But someone else shoved through. He, too, bore scars, and limped as he leaned on a staff. But the hand that gripped Fallon's arm had strength.

"Arlington? They took my sister. They left me for dead, and took her. The PWs. They took her to Arlington."

"When?"

"We found Sam last winter," Liana said. "He was badly hurt. We didn't think he'd live."

"But you didn't leave him behind. You helped him."

"Maybe not a complete asshole," Tonia mumbled.

"Your sister? Is she magickal?"

"No. Please. She's Aggie. Agnes Haver. Please, they took her."

"If she was there, we freed all the slaves. I'll find her, and I'll bring her to you. I have the names of everyone we got out. We took Arlington," she said to Kilo. "And more than sixty who fought with me died to free those like his sister. They fought and died to take a place of torment and cruelty and bring the light. Do not dishonor the dead. If you can stand here and do that, you're not worthy to lead or follow. So you can get out of the way."

She stepped back, drew her spirit animals to her. "I'll send supplies, and if they held Aggie in Arlington, I'll bring her."

She nodded to Tonia. They flashed.

"The man's a freaking giant," Tonia said the minute they stood behind Fallon's house. "And a total dick."

"Still, he's kept over thirty people alive, including kids, and when he came across a half-dead stranger, didn't just move on. One way or the other, the location works. We're going to start building it a lot sooner than I'd thought. Gotta follow the signs when they smack you in the face."

"Who do you figure to send up there?"

"Poe and Kim. Their kids are old enough to go, or to stay in the barracks for a few weeks. Or months, depending. Poe and Kim? They're tough, smart, experienced, and they won't take any crap."

"You got that. Plus, Poe?" Tonia shot out a grin. "He's not a freaking giant like that Kilo, but, man, he's totally ripped. That gets respect from dicks. And Kim's logic-genius brain will do the rest. So. I'll talk to them."

"If they don't want to go—"

"I have a feeling they will. It's just the kind of challenge they'd go for."

She thought the same, and since Tonia's connection with the couple went all the way back, she'd leave the approach to her friend. "We'll need to send a healer and at least twelve skilled in fighting and building. Three to help establish plantings, a greenhouse."

"Let me talk to my mom. She'll know."

"They don't all have to come from New Hope. I can pull some in from other bases. But yeah, ask her who she thinks would work best in that kind of situation. I need to go check my names for Agnes Haver."

"You'll find her. Trust the signs. Hell of a trip, Fallon. Thanks for the lift."

The setting sun burned red through the trees when Fallon came back to the clearing. This time she came with four other magickals, a former slave, and supplies.

Kilo rose from his seat around a campfire, spear in hand.

He said nothing when Sam let out a cry, stumbled forward to embrace his sister. "Aggie. Oh God, Aggie."

"You're alive. I thought they'd killed you. Sam. Sam."

"She should sit, have water," Fallon told them. "Flashing, even with the tonic, can leave NMs—non-magickals—a little dizzy and shaky."

"Take her in the cabin, Sam." Liana rose as well. "Let's get her inside."

With tears streaming, Sam turned to Fallon. "I'll fight for you."

"Take care of your sister for now."

Kilo watched them help Aggie into the cabin. "You keep your word."

"I do. I've brought you some basic supplies as well as a healer. Magda's also a skilled soldier. You have three other skilled soldiers. Buck can help you build a greenhouse and plant if you choose to stay. Carolyn and Fritz can help begin to fortify your shelters. More are coming, but it's going to take several days, more likely a couple of weeks for them to get here."

"They can't just—" He snapped his fingers, made her smile.

"Poe and Kim will be in charge. They survived the Doom, are fierce warriors, and helped build a community. They'll build one here. Their sons are coming with them—good soldiers. Young, but good soldiers. They'll help train any who stay. They're bringing horses, a milk cow, chickens, more medicines. Kim's also an herbalist."

She looked around. "In time, if you don't already have them among you, you'll have teachers, weavers, farmers, technicians, fishermen. Until you can self-sustain, we'll bring what you need. And in time, instead of being the target, you'll be the arrow."

Liana came to the cabin door. "Could we have the healer? Kara's water broke. I've helped deliver before, but—"

"Be right there." Magda tapped the kit she carried. "New life. The best part of the job. Bright blessings on you, Fallon."

"And on you, and the new life you help bring. Carolyn, why don't you take a couple of the blankets in there, and some of the tea and honey. Where would you like the rest?" she asked Kilo.

"The rest?"

"Bread, butter, cheese, eggs, some grains, vegetables, and so on. More blankets, socks, sweaters, some cooking gear, knives, swords, arrows. Basics," she repeated.

"You might want to, for now, designate one cabin for the foodstuffs and the other supplies, and another for weapons."

"You bring all this, say take it whether we fight with you or not."

"Fighting's a choice. Food, shelter, clothing are necessary for life. The weapons? If you go, they stay, but the rest? You can take whatever you can carry."

"If we stay, if we fight, this is our land? Our place, one you'll help us build and defend?"

"Yes."

He stepped to her, held out a huge hand. "Deal."

She helped organize the supplies, stayed for a meal of stew holding some of the vegetables and herbs she'd brought with her.

Recognizing the accent of the old man beside her, she spoke with him in Spanish as they ate.

When she offered a bottle of wine, the bottle passed from hand to hand around the fire. She supposed they'd make use of the cups she'd brought later.

The cry of a newborn carried from the cabin, so the bottle passed around again.

Liana came to the door, called out, "A girl. A beautiful, healthy girl! She'll be called Saol, in honor of the light."

"Light for life," Fallon murmured, and took the bottle Kilo passed her. "To new life," she said, lifting the bottle in toast. "To the light in her."

And drank.

CHAPTER TEN

With fall riding chilly winds, Fallon traveled to both emerging bases. When needed, she brought supplies and personnel, drawing from New Hope, Arlington, even what Mick had dubbed The Beach.

With Poe, Kim, and Kilo's people, she set up Bayview. With Flynn and Starr, Forestville. As October waned, she had bases on three sides of D.C., and plans to cover the fourth.

"Rock Creek Forest." She showed her father on the map.

"Close, and without the river as a natural boundary. D.C. gets wind you're moving in there . . ."

"It has to be a covert operation. It's forested, mostly uninhabited. Most who escaped D.C. kept going. There's game, a strong creek, nearby houses. This? Was a school, a good-sized campus, with its buildings largely intact."

"You've scouted?"

"A few times now. Strategically, it's tailor-made for a scouting base. Here?" She moved her finger over the map. "A small city, deserted, wasted, borders D.C. We'll leave it for now, but it'll be useful after."

"After we take D.C."

Not if, she thought, not from her father. "Right. Thomas has nearly a hundred and fifty at his camp now, the faerie bower more than sixty, the shifter's den nearly the same. I've asked for who they can spare, and we could put a hundred. A hundred," she repeated, "skilled at blending into forests, living in and from them in Rock Creek. Nobody moves faster than an elf, and shifters and faeries aren't far behind."

"When we're ready, we attack from all directions."

"All." She pulled out her map of D.C. and went over the tactics and timing, the troop movements with him.

Then she drew in a breath. "And with Duncan's forces, less those who'll stay back to defend Utah, Troy's, and forces from New Hope, we hit here."

Simon stared at her when she jabbed a finger at the map. "Jesus, Fallon, from inside? Pennsylvania Avenue?"

"We flash. Five thousand soldiers."

He had to sit back. "You can do that? Five thousand?"

She smiled. "It'll take a lot of tonic for the NMs, but yes, we can do it. Five thousand from inside the lines, another five thousand breaking the lines from all directions."

"We'd have them outnumbered, when you add in whatever resistance forces are in or around the city." As he considered, Simon rose to wander the kitchen. "Still, it's their turf, the structures, the roadways. They've got tanks and armored vehicles, and access to some serious weapons. But . . ."

He stopped. "A coordinated surprise attack? It's bold, baby. It could work."

"We need it to work. It'll take more than ten thousand to take New York, to take the West, to cross oceans. Taking Arlington added to our numbers, our assets. It inspired. Taking D.C., defeating the seat of a government that hunts its own people? Pays bounties on children

because they're different? It strikes a blow to the heart
of the enemy."

"When?"

"We've got more to do, but . . . Even though it took
longer than I'd hoped, I'd started to worry it would
take longer yet. Arlington changed that. January second."

Understanding, he nodded. "The day the first died.
The day Katie's father died of the Doom."

"And the day I was conceived. Magicks began their
rise, both the light and the dark. Another symbol, I
guess."

She knew it in her head, her gut, in her blood.

"January second."

Duncan held the Samhain ritual—you had to respect
rites and traditions—and made it optional. You also had
to respect some of the base, and plenty of the NMs on it,
didn't want to get into calling on gods and dead ancestors.

But when he cast the circle, lit the candles, brought
food and flowers to the altar, it surprised him how many
came out, either to participate or to watch.

He decided they figured, as he did, a band of eighty-
three on a base in the desert could use all the power it
could get.

So he said the words, called the elements, let the power
roll through him, from him. He thought of his grandparents, the father he'd never known, the man who'd stood—
too briefly—as a father to him. Of Denzel, who'd been
a brother. Of Marly and Len, of all who'd fallen in the
fight.

The wind sighed and stirred in that vast space, the
voices rose up like the buttes into a sky gone bloodred
with the setting sun.

And he felt her, for the first time in weeks felt her in the sigh and stir, heard her in the rise of voices. She, too, would have cast the circle, lit the candles, brought the food and flowers. As he knew his own thoughts, he knew she thought of the father she'd never known, of the lost and the fallen.

So for a moment, almost painfully, he was linked to her, as if he gripped her hand. For that moment, almost painful, they joined in prayer and purpose.

Then she was gone.

Out of habit he patrolled the base after nightfall. The eighty-two with him knew their jobs, but he patrolled because it kept him busy, kept the troops sharp. He had armed sentries on six-hour shifts, had transformed the half-assed PW base into a secure and fortified one, a self-sustaining one with gardens, livestock, wind and solar power, a supply hut, an armory, infirmary, disciplined troops.

Some still green, he thought, but the hours of training, the rotations of scouting, scavenging, cooking, drilling had sharpened them up.

Still, some of them were green, and he'd need every one of them seasoned, well seasoned, by January second.

He'd heard that on the wind. She'd probably send word to him, though she had to have felt him just as tangibly as he had her. But Fallon would send word, one way or the other, and he'd prepare those troops for the onslaught on D.C.

Not yet enough of them, and that worried him. Not all they'd freed had stayed. Most, but not all, and the scouting had only gathered in a handful.

He knew there were more, he'd felt that, too. Watching. Waiting for who knew what.

Restless, edgy, mildly pissed off for reasons he couldn't pinpoint, he got his bike. He'd ride out a few miles, take a little solo time, let the wind and speed blow away the mood.

He went out through a checkpoint, then opened the bike up on the long, flat road. From the first, he appreciated the sights, scents, sounds of the West. The echoing canyons, the fast rivers with their wild rapids tumbling, the sheer brilliance of the stars. But tonight, he yearned for home, the fields and forests, the roll of hills, his family, his friends. All the familiar.

When he'd worked with Mallick, he'd been able to take an hour or two now and again to flash home. But here, fully in charge, he couldn't afford the luxury.

The agrodome had just begun—ha-ha—to bear fruit. Coyotes and wildcats meant constant vigilance with the livestock. Scavenging alone could equal a full-time job.

He shouldn't, he knew, even be out like this, but, God, he needed it.

He needed to kick up the hand-to-hand training. D.C. meant street fighting, of the ugly and bloody. He wondered if he could devise a way to conjure the illusion of streets, buildings, rubble. It would help if he had a clear idea what D.C. looked like. It sure as hell wouldn't look like the old pictures and DVDs.

Brooding, he nearly missed it, that shimmer of power on the air. Instinct kicked in. He slowed the bike, reached out.

Watching, he thought. Waiting.

Well, screw that.

He stopped the bike, got off. Put a hand on the hilt of his sword.

"If you need help, I can offer it. If you want a fight, I can oblige. Either way, grow some balls and come out."

"I'm not interested in growing balls." She rode a painted horse out of the dark as if she'd parted a curtain. "I've no problem slicing them off a man, if necessary."

"I think I'll keep mine."

Late twenties, he thought, and striking enough he wanted to sketch those sharp cheekbones, the deep eyes, the long black braid that trailed to her waist. She carried a bow and quiver and sat the horse bareback.

"I might let you keep them, and just take the bike."

"Nope." He felt the movement behind him, tossed power back, heard the *whoosh* of stolen breath.

"Good reflexes," she said. "But small brains to ride out so far alone."

Another dozen riders walked through the curtain to flank her. In a finger snap he had his sword in his hand, laid down a line of fire between them.

Most of the horses shied, but not hers. Both she and her mount stayed steady.

"Is it worth your life?" she asked.

"Is it worth yours?" He started to scan the faces, stopped on one, a girl of about fifteen. "You were with the PWs. They made you a slave. Kerry—no. Sherry. They hurt you. They hurt her." He looked back at the leader. "They branded her and . . . worse. Is she one of yours?"

"She rides with us."

"Then you know we didn't hurt her, and dealt with those who did. Our medic treated her, but she took a horse, slipped out of camp before morning. We looked for you," he said to the girl, "to help, to give you supplies if you wanted to go, but we couldn't find you."

"Why would she stay? You may have done the same as the others."

Heated now, Duncan's gaze whipped back to the leader. "You know better. What kind of bullshit is this? Is this how you treat people who rescue others from PWs?"

She studied him, straight as one of the arrows in her quiver on the horse. "You didn't kill them all. Why?"

"The ones we didn't surrendered or were no longer a threat. Now they're in prison."

"Where?"

"In the East. They won't hurt you again," he said to the girl.

"Why do you care? She's not one of you."

"You don't look like an idiot," he shot back, "but that's a stupid, ignorant question."

Her eyebrows arched over those intense, dark eyes. "Your ancestors slaughtered mine, stole their land, brought them disease and starvation."

"Maybe. My mother's people came from Scotland. The English slaughtered our people, stole their land, burned their homes. But if some English dude's ready to fight with me against the PWs, the DUs, and the rest of the fuckers, I don't give a rat's ass about what his ancestors did to mine. This is now."

He looked back at the girl. "I'm glad you're okay, and from the looks of it, you'll be safe with her."

"What do you fight for?" the leader demanded. "Who do you fight for?"

Duncan muttered, "Shit," when he felt the vision fall into him. Resigned, he let it take him.

He raised his sword, shot a bolt of light into the sky before his blade flamed.

This time her horse shied, and she controlled it with a murmur, a squeeze of her knees.

"I am Duncan of the MacLeods, child of the Tuatha de Danann. I am the sword that slashes through the dark, brother to the arrow that pierces it. I am blood to blood with The One, and am pledged to her. I fight with her, I fight for her. My light for life. My life for her, and all who stand with her against the dark."

Lowering the sword, he passed a hand down its length to extinguish the flame. "Got it?"

She dismounted, walked to the low wall of flame. "Then, Duncan of the MacLeods, you're the one I've been looking for." She held out a hand. "I'm Meda of the First Tribe. We'll fight with you. We'll fight with The One."

Once again he trusted instinct. He let the flames between them die, shook her hand. "Welcome to the war."

Fallon had felt him, and it left her unsettled. She felt Duncan's sorrow for those lost twine with hers. A kind of grieving intimacy she hadn't been prepared for.

Like him, after the ritual she felt unsettled. She'd hoped, as she'd hoped every year since he'd come to her, her birth father would come to her again. But she knew it wasn't to be.

Not yet.

She made excuses, slipped away from the festivities in town, the bonfires, the carved pumpkins, the treats made for costumed children, the music in the gardens.

She told herself she needed to go back to her maps, her plans, refine all her battle tactics. But she knew she lied, even to herself.

It was time, she thought, to do more than plan. Time to see, time to be, time to take the next step.

Risky but worth it, she decided. And she'd look into the crystal first, judge if the way was clear.

At home, she lit the candle Mallick had given her when she'd been an infant. In the quiet, with only that light, she laid her hands on the crystal.

"Open now and clear for me. Let me see what I must see."

Like clouds rolling, then a wind blowing to part them. And now colors, shapes, space.

"More," she urged, sliding a hand right, watching,

THE RISE OF MAGICKS 171

watching, before sliding a hand left. Drawing one up, waiting, studying, then drawing it down.

She spent nearly an hour with the crystal, once again sketching a detailed map until, satisfied, she went to her closet.

Inside she kept the Book of Spells, potions, charms, tools. Though on the day she became, every spell in the book lived inside her, she deemed this one important enough to validate.

She passed a hand over the book so that it opened to the spell in her mind. With the care and precision she'd learned from her mother, from Mallick, she gathered what she needed. Floating a small cauldron over her desk, lighting the fire beneath it, she added ingredients, measured others, said the words.

Here the power ran through her, warm and liquid. Here a pouring into as the spell coalesced with a pulsing beat, as a tower of pale blue smoke rose, thin and straight as a needle.

She put out the fire, cooled the cauldron, placed what she'd created inside it into a pouch.

"It'll work," she said aloud, tying the pouch to her belt.

Once again, she checked the crystal. Focused, focused.

Time, she thought again. It was time.

"There I go as powers flow, through you, in you, so I pass through the glass. Through you, in you, beyond the shields both dark and light, beyond the locks I take this flight. Take me where you let me see. As I will, so mote it be."

As she spoke the last words, as she threw out her power, Tonia and Hannah stepped into her room.

Tonia said, "Holy—"

Then the mad pull Fallon unleashed took all three of them.

"Shit," Tonia finished as the pull released, dropped them. "What—" She broke off, dropped down as Hannah slid bonelessly to the floor.

"Damn it. Be still, be quiet," Fallon ordered. "I'll be right back."

On a snap of wind, she vanished. Ten seconds later, while Tonia tapped Hannah's pale cheeks, she snapped back again.

"She's out cold. Jesus. That wasn't a flash we got caught up in. It was different, and more."

"We need to bring her around first, then you're going to get this tonic into her. All of it. Quick."

Fallon pushed the small bottle at Tonia, then laid a hand on Hannah's heart, another on her forehead.

When Hannah's lashes fluttered, when she moaned, Fallon snapped, "Get it into her."

Hannah swallowed reflexively, choked a little, sputtered, then managed, "What the hell happened?"

"I pulled you through with me, through the crystal. It's stronger than a flash, and you weren't prepared."

And not steady yet, Fallon determined, as Hannah's pupils turned her eyes to dark moons.

"Stay down for another minute. I couldn't risk a flash," Fallon continued. "They'll have shields either conjured by DUs or magickals they forced or coerced. I needed to get through them without setting off any alerts or leaving any trace."

She sat back on her heels. "We're going to have to hope that covers both of you."

As she helped Hannah sit up, kept an arm cradled around her, Tonia looked around the room. "Jesus. Are we where I think we are?"

"The White House. Oval Office."

"In the now?"

"In the right now. They lost the Capitol, but they've

fortified and shielded the White House. They're running nearly everything out of this location, according to Chuck's intel."

"Where's that pissant bastard Hargrove?"

"In the Residence. They've got easily a thousand military and civilian guards in and around the building, from what I've seen through the crystal. They've built a military base in what I think used to be the Rose Garden. Everything magickally shielded. From the outside."

Tonia stopped gawking, shifted her gaze to Fallon. "And we're inside."

"That's right."

"Are we going to take Hargrove?"

"Not this time. No trace," she repeated before Tonia could argue. "But before we take him, take D.C., we're going to know their moves, their plans, their numbers, and if the goddess shines, the locations of all their containment centers. I conjured listening devices."

"Bugs. No, I'm okay." Hannah patted Tonia aside. "Maybe just feel a little buzzed, but okay. Bugs," she repeated. "Wouldn't they sweep for those, routinely?"

"They won't find these. I've picked what I feel are the most strategic locations for them, starting here."

"The Oval freaking Office," Hannah said in amazement. "It looks more like a throne room than an office."

Buzzed or not, Fallon thought, Hannah's observation hit the mark. She turned, looked at the luxurious gold drapes—enough material to make clothes, blankets for a dozen people—the rug bearing the presidential seal for a man no one had elected. All the furnishings of glossy, polished wood, silky fabrics. The art in ornate frames.

No different in her mind from the hoarding of beauty and luxury she'd found in Arlington. Only more of the same, and for one man's ego and ambition.

He wouldn't hold it, she vowed. Not after January second.

"We're going to move fast, and quiet. If there's any trouble, any, Tonia, you flash back with Hannah."

"We don't leave you," Hannah said.

"I'll go back the way we came, through the glass. Take all of us if possible. We don't risk January second."

"I see cameras," Tonia pointed out. "They've got security in here."

"I took care of those," Fallon told her. "We focus on one area at a time. Plant the device, move to the next."

She opened her pouch, took out a long, slender leaf.

Tonia eyed it. "Seriously?"

"He keeps two plants, see there? Flanking that door."

She walked to one, slid the device among the leaves. As she spoke the words, it attached.

"Nice. Very nice. What language was that?"

"Ancient Aramaic. It's a date palm." She shrugged. "It fits, and it helps shield it from those sweeps, as it's unlikely they can break a spell sealed in Aramaic."

Hannah peered closer. "It's organic."

"That helps, too. It'll pick up whatever's said in this room. If I did everything right, Chuck can listen in."

"He's going to have an orgasm," Tonia decided. "Where next?"

"It used to be called the Situation Room. They call it the War Room." She took out a piece of carved wood painted gold. "There's a portrait of Hargrove on the back wall, framed."

"What language for this?" Hannah wondered.

"Hargrove's an Old English place name, so—"

"Channel Chaucer."

"That's the idea. If we manage only those two, it's a big one. I have another, for the office of his chief of staff, something for the Residence, if possible, another for the kitchen."

"The kitchen?"

"Staff gossip. They hear things, and gossip." Taking too much time, Fallon thought. Already taking too much time. "You should flash back, and I'll get this done."

"Not only aren't we leaving you, but you don't get to have all the fun. Hannah?"

The potion had put color back in her cheeks. Now her eyes glittered. "All in."

"Arguing wastes time, so we move, and we move by priority."

"If you taught me the spell, we could split up, cover more ground in less time."

"No, we stick together, get planted what we can with as little movement as possible. The more movement, the more chance of hitting some alarm I didn't see, or running into a guard. So we flash, flash. It'll be a little rough on you, Hannah, but I can't risk leaving you here."

"I can deal."

"Going to have to." She took Hannah's hand, nodded.

Twenty minutes later, Hannah sat down heavily on Fallon's bed. Then she gave up, lay back on it. "I'm okay. A little shaky. And that was amazing. All of it. I've been inside the White House and helped plant magickal bugs. Can we have a whole bunch of wine now?"

"Which is why we came over in the first place," Tonia remembered. "Look, Fallon, I know you probably want to get all this to Chuck, but the fact is, Hargrove and whoever's sharing his bed were tucked in for the night, the rest of the rooms we hit were empty and locked up. They even secure the kitchen at night. Let's have a drink to stealthy girls who just infiltrated the freaking White House."

All good points, Fallon conceded. "Okay. First thing in the morning's soon enough." She led the way out to her own war room, got a bottle of wine from storage, some glasses. "It doesn't feel as if anyone's home yet."

"They wouldn't be," Hannah told her. "Your parents were going over to our place, a bunch of them were. Your mom said we should come over here, talk you out of working tonight."

On a laugh, Tonia took the bottle, poured liberally. "Didn't manage that, did we? Is it always like that when you go somewhere through the crystal?"

"No. It's usually more like sliding into a pool—a really deep pool. But with this, I needed a big punch to get through the barriers there."

"Definitely a big punch." Hannah drank deep.

"Your eyes rolled back, then . . ." Grinning, Tonia drew her hand down in a slow curve. "Actually, you even faint gracefully. It's annoying."

"It's class. All class." Dropping down in a chair, Hannah sighed, drank again. "I've never been a part of anything like what we did tonight. It's exciting."

"You've been in battle," Fallon pointed out. "Treating wounded. And kicking PWs in the balls."

"It's different. You don't think, you just act. You do what you've trained to do. But this? You have to think, every second, about what you're doing, what's around you instead of how to stop the bleeding or set a bone. And the magicks. I'm around it all the time, obviously, but I've never been *in* it, not so, you know, intimately. It's the only time, other than now and then when I watch what the healers can do, I've wished I had some of that."

"You're a doctor," Tonia said. "Saving lives, easing pain, that's your magick. And it's awesome."

"I saw you." Fallon spoke quietly. "On the night Petra attacked, when her twisted parents attacked. I saw you below, covering someone with your own body. You're a doctor, and a warrior."

"Ball-kicking warrior."

"I didn't have a sword on me at the time. Thanks. Anyway, I didn't mean it to sound like I'm jealous. Maybe I had some moments when we were kids—"

"Mommy! Boo-hoo! Tonia's making the puppy fly again."

On a huff, Hannah rolled her eyes. "I was six."

"Seven."

"Whatever. And you weren't supposed to fly the puppy."

"He liked it."

"So you say. Anyway." Hannah exaggerated the word as she gestured with her glass. "As an NM, I can tell you I've observed that magick's fun, and powerful, and important. But it's also a heavy responsibility. I'm happy not to carry it. The two of you were born to carry it. I think—no, I absolutely know—I was born to be a doctor. I think about my birth mother sometimes. You must think of Max sometimes, Fallon."

"Yes. I thought of him tonight."

"Like Duncan and Tonia, and their father. Maybe tonight especially. When I think of her, I feel sure she was meant to survive long enough to bring me into the world. It had to be terrible for her, for all of them, but she survived until I could live. And Mom was there, right there, Rachel and Jonah, all right there, and I believe that was meant, too."

Tonia reached over to squeeze her hand. "We were meant."

"Yeah, we were. They'd never have left a helpless baby behind, but they did more. Mom did so much more. She made me hers, and not only kept me alive, but loved me. She gave me a life, and I was meant to use it to save others. We're all here for that."

Hannah picked up the bottle, poured another round for all. "And tonight? We—stealthily—kicked ass."

"She talks a lot when she's drinking," Tonia pointed out.

"I've noticed that."

"I really do. But, crap, did you *see* all that stuff? In the office, in the—what is it—Residence? Who the fucking fuck are they, living like princes while people, so many people, still struggle to feed their children?"

"And Mouthy Hannah throws the F word around, liberally."

"Well, fuck them!"

"Oh, we will," Fallon assured her, enjoying Mouthy Hannah.

"Good. Do you think there's any pizza? We could have some pizza and talk about men."

"Like how Justin makes non-flying puppy eyes at you."

Hannah gave her sister a cool stare. "He's still a boy. I said men. Not like Garrett, who still makes those puppy eyes at you, but more like Roland, who I clearly saw you making out with a few nights ago."

"Forget Roland. He's a sloppy kisser. I just don't go for the sloppy kisser. We could talk about all the guys who make the puppy eyes at Fallon."

"Me?" The grin that had started while listening to the sisters turned into shock. "What?"

"I could name half a dozen who'd slurp you up like Fred's rainbow ice cream."

"That's ridiculous, and I don't have time for that anyway." But now she wondered. "We've got pizza." She rose, grabbed the bottle to go with it. "We'll go up and eat—we earned it."

She paused at the base of the stairs. "Maybe you should make me a list of those guys."

Tonia laughed, slung an arm around Fallon's shoulders. "It'll be a long one."

BATTLE AND BLOOD

The brazen throat of war.

—John Milton

CHAPTER ELEVEN

Fallon had expected to take some heat from her parents over her mission to D.C. She hadn't expected to feel that heat scorch over her from all directions.

"You could've gotten caught, or worse. We wouldn't have known where you were, or what happened."

"I didn't," Fallon pointed out to her mother. "I took precautions."

"One precaution," Simon tossed back, "was not telling us."

She'd hoped to appeal to him as a soldier, but he was, currently, all Dad. "It needed to be done. I was prepared. I was careful."

"So careful you ended up pulling Tonia and Hannah in with you."

Maybe her mother had her there, but—"They walked in on it. I adjusted. The intel we'll gain from this is invaluable."

"So are you. Not just to me and your father. To everyone."

How was it, she wondered, her parents could wipe

away years, training, freaking destiny, and make her feel like an eight-year-old in dire need of a lecture?

"I did what I knew had to be done, to take D.C. and minimize our casualties. I'm going to do other things that worry and upset you. You need to trust me."

"Two-way street, Fallon. You did what you felt you had to do, but you didn't trust us." Simon kept his gaze steady on his daughter, laid a hand on his wife's shoulder. A united front. "We don't deserve that."

That was bad enough, but she had to suffer through the same reaction from nearly every New Hope Original, from Fred's sad eyes, to Arlys's cool insult, Katie's—okay, justified—anger at having her two daughters involved without her knowledge.

Even, crushingly, from Chuck.

"You know a sure way to demoralize and damage an opposing force? Any video game proves it—and, well, history. You take out the head, the leader. You risked that, kid."

"Jesus, not you, too. My parents are down on me, I'm still raw from a Will lecture. I figured you, at least, would be on my side."

"Everybody's on your side. You oughta remember that next time." He looked at her, the geek with purple-streaked white-blond hair and a tiny, pointed beard, and made her realize not just parents could make you feel eight and stupid.

And flipped her last button.

"You know, I've had enough of this *crap*." She threw out her hands where the spurt of temper had light snapping from her fingertips. "I didn't bring on the Doom, I didn't ask to be the freaking Savior of the world or spend my life fighting, but that's the goddamn reality. That's the freaking, fucking world. So when I pull off a high-risk, high-reward operation, I don't appreciate being treated like a kid who missed curfew because I didn't clear it with every-damn-body first. I *am* the leader, and it's my head."

She kicked a chair because it was there. It levitated a foot off the ground, trembled there, fell with a *thump*.

"And that's just the way it fucking is."

Chuck said nothing until he'd sucked down some of the mango juice and ginger ale he'd grown fond of. "Feel better?"

"Not one damn bit."

"Too bad. Here's what I don't appreciate. Being put in the position of having to think and act like a tight-assed adult."

He shot out his index finger with its WTF tattoo.

"Then don't!"

"Uh-uh. I'm there now, and since I am, I'm going to say you can either do a little mea culpa-ing to smooth this out, or you can keep riding that high horse until your nose bleeds from the altitude. You got stuck with leading, well, sucks for you, but a leader who doesn't respect who they lead doesn't get much respect back."

"Damn it." She wanted to kick the chair again, but she already felt like an idiot. "I do respect them—you— all of them, and especially the Originals. Beyond words. I wasn't sure I could do it until I was sure, then I needed to act, not take a meeting. And—" She thought of her father's words. "Two-way street."

Maybe she would kick the chair again.

"You're not wrong."

"So when I— What?"

"You're not wrong," Chuck repeated and sucked up more fizzy juice. "We're not wrong. Give a little, get a little. Plus, I've about used up my adult quota for the week. I want to get to this."

He swiveled to his workstation, rubbed his hands together. And Eddie came in.

"Here's more," Fallon grumbled.

"We just wrapped up the spanking." Chuck winced. "I didn't mean that in a creepy uncle way."

"Then I'll just say ditto. Plus. Dude." He gave Fallon a light head slap before he turned to Chuck. "Have you picked anything up?"

"I'm about to commence getting started on working on trying to do just that."

"Before you do, Fred's been working on something." He held up a sealed jar filled with dark liquid. "She wanted you to try it out."

"Okeydoke. What've we got?"

"You tell me." When Eddie unsealed the jar, it let out a hiss, bubbles rose up. When he poured some into a cup, the air above it sparkled.

Chuck took it, sniffed. "It couldn't be." Looked at Eddie with what Fallon read as desperate hope. "Couldn't be. Could it?"

He took a small, testing sip. Closed his eyes—and whimpered a little before he took another, deeper sip. "It's a miracle. A genuine miracle."

Popping up, he danced, shoulders bouncing, hips rocking.

"What the hell is it?"

"Taste the miracle!"

Curious, Fallon took the cup, sipped. "Oh, oh, it's good." Strong, sweet, unlike anything she'd tasted. It gave her a little head rush. "What is it?"

"Fred's version of Coca-Cola," Eddie told her with a grin. "She's been working on it since we got the Tropics up and going. Your mom helped some, and I've been taste testing. I think we got it."

"It's better, even better than Coke Classic. Oh, it's been so long. Come back to Papa." He took the cup, drank again. Danced again. "Even better. It's LFC. Little Fred's Cola."

"I like it."

Chuck eyed the jar. "Can I keep it?"

"All yours, dude."

"I feel tears coming on. Lemme tell ya, armed with LFC, I'm going to rock this job here." He drained the cup. "Whoa, better take it slow." He sat again, rubbed his hands again.

Began to work controls.

"These codes you wrote? How accurate?" he asked Fallon.

"As close as I could manage. It's not my strongest suit, but I know they're close."

"Let's start with the Oval Office. I mean, go for gold if you're going."

She waited while he keyed in codes, fiddled, did things she'd never understand. Through the speakers came nothing but a steady electronic buzz.

"Think I see the problem. Another sec."

He adjusted the code, twice, and the buzz turned into a kind of rumbling.

"Magick-type bugs. This one's a what again?"

"Leaf."

"Huh. Organic eavesdroppers. Kick my ass and call me Sally. Give it a little boost there, champ. Just a little. Gonna interface the magicks, get me?"

"Maybe."

She nudged. The rumbling became a blast.

"Back off—a lot. Just, like, a touch."

"Okay."

From blast to a squawk then to a murmur.

"Got it. I got it. You can ease it off. Here we go."

I've had it with this bullshit, Carter.

Mr. President—Commander—if I could—

I said I've had it. We're expending too many resources for too little. I want results and get excuses and demands for more resources.

Sir, if you cut our resources, pull more personnel off the MUNA project, it's the same as shutting us down. We're already cut to the bone.

That's the idea, Carter.

Sir, what we've learned and can learn, the progress we've made and will make, it's essential to controlling the Uncanny threat. Our research—

Hasn't produced tangible results in twenty damn years. The so-called leaders who sat at this desk wasted years on their debates, negotiating, compromising with scientists like you. Weaklings, all of them. Soft-bellied weaklings. I gave you a chance, Carter, against my better judgment.

If you could see your way—

I'm sitting in this chair because I act! Hargrove's voice boomed out. *I'm done wasting time, done coddling those freaks of nature. Our resources and personnel are better utilized to eradicate the threat once and for all. Containment, research, experimentation? For what? So the freaks can continue to breed, to attack our cities, our people?*

Without our work, without science, we'll never understand the phenomenon.

Fuck your bullshit science, and fuck the phenomenon. It's time to end them.

Commander Hargrove, sir, we have over two hundred specimens in our facilities here alone, and we believe we're close to creating a serum that will essentially sterilize the Uncanny, prevent them from breeding.

You said that six fucking months ago.

We're closer. A few more months.

You've got two. If you don't come through, Carter, I'm not just cutting back your resources, I'm shutting you down, and neutralizing your specimens along with every one of them in other facilities. Every goddamn one.

Yes, sir. Thank you, sir.

Science, my ass. Debra!

A squeak of a voice responded. *Yes, Commander Hargrove.*

Contact that idiot Pruitt, and tell him I'd better have a progress report on negotiations with White and the PWs by the end of the day. And if he keeps pussyfooting around, he should remember what happened to the idiot he replaced. I'm going out to look at the training grounds, give the troops a little pep talk. Send my security in. Now!

Now Fallon heard movement, doors opening. Yes, locks releasing. The sound of gunfire, shouted orders before the doors shut, locked again. And silence.

"Jesus Christ." Chuck blew out a long breath. "How the hell did they put him in charge?"

"Fear," Fallon said. "Fear of us, fear of another plague, fear of power."

"Maybe so, maybe, but most people aren't like that, like him." Eddie rubbed his hands over his face because it felt numb. "Not like him and White, not most. He's talking about sterilizing people. He's talking genocide."

"We're not people to him. We're freaks."

"My kids," Eddie said. "And a lot of other people's kids. They won't stand for it."

"They have to know about it first, and they will." Lectures be damned, Fallon thought. She'd gotten what they needed. "He gave that Carter, that torturer two months. What he doesn't know is that's all he has."

She turned to Eddie. "He's never going to touch your kids."

"You're damn right he's not."

"Keep monitoring, Chuck, all the devices. He's looking to pull the PWs in. We'll want to know how that goes for him. We know they've got over two hundred magickals contained in or around the White House. They'll have more at other locations."

She stared straight ahead. "Two months, and I swear by all I am, we will tear them down."

December brought the first snows and preparation for Yule, Christmas, the New Year. And the battle to come. New Hope hung their wreaths, burned their logs, decorated their trees, created and bartered for gifts. And trained relentlessly.

On the bright afternoon of Christmas Eve, Fallon met with Arlys after her weekly broadcast.

"It was good," Fallon told her. "Hopeful and strong."

"If you can't be hopeful at Christmas, when? Chuck, can I have the room?"

"Yeah, sure. I've got some Christmas shopping to finish up. Hargrove's taking a holiday," he added. "He's hosting fancy parties for key players in his freaking dictatorship. There's not much going on anyway, but we're monitoring."

"Let him eat, drink, and be merry," Fallon said. "His time's nearly up."

When Chuck went out, Arlys rose to wander the basement. "Chuck's played recordings of any important bits I missed. You already know Hargrove feels he's close to a deal with White."

"He won't finalize it before we strike, and it won't help him."

"He also plans for White, after the deal's struck, to be

assassinated. He'll claim it was one of us, and provide the appropriate patsy for execution."

"It won't happen."

Arlys continued to wander, picked up one of the action figures, set it down again. "The government lied during the Doom, and right after. But I believe, I have to believe, it lied in a misguided, even arrogant attempt to control panic. This is nothing like that. Hargrove's a psychopath, and as obsessed as Jeremiah White."

She gestured to the monitor, and now Fallon read both misery and conflict on her face.

"I understand why I can't broadcast anything we've learned through the bugs, but it brings me back, Fallon. It takes me back to sitting at the anchor desk in New York and knowing I lied to anyone listening."

"You're not lying now, and when we take D.C., you can broadcast all of it."

"I understand the reasons. I even agree with them. My Theo, my boy, is going to war."

Arlys pressed a hand to her lips, waved Fallon off when Fallon stepped toward her.

"I'm terrified. I know Will, I know he'll look after Theo as best he can, but my son, my heart, is going into battle, and I'm terrified. Rachel's oldest, too."

"I know. I just spoke with her. I was coming to talk to you even before you asked me to come. I don't have a son or daughter, but I do know what it's like for you. I see it in my mother, and I know it's the hardest thing there is."

"I believe in you. I believed in you before you were born, when I saw you through Lana. I believe in you." She let out a breath. "I know why Theo's going. I know why I can't broadcast the horrors Hargrove perpetuates, the horrors he plans. But I can broadcast what we do about it. I want you to embed me when we attack D.C."

"You can broadcast from here," Fallon began.

"By relay, when someone's able to tell me something, anything. Not good enough," Arlys said, with steel in her voice. "I go, and I tell people, show when I can, as it happens. I show them when you go down to the containment center, what Hargrove and his bastardized government have done. I show them you, Fallon. I show them The One. For most people, seeing's believing. You need this, and I've earned it."

"Have you talked to Will about this?" At Arlys's cool stare, Fallon rolled her eyes. "Not because he's a man. Because he's your mate, and a commander."

"Okay. Yes, we talked. He didn't have an argument that overcame mine. You don't, either."

"No, I don't. You're my mother's friend. I believe in you. I believed in you before I met you because I saw you through her. You can't take Chuck."

"I understand. He won't like it, but he knows he's essential here. I want one more thing."

"What?"

"I want to interview Hargrove after you've taken him. I know you want him alive, and if he's alive at the end of this, I want an interview."

"That's an easy one."

When she went out, Fallon stood in the winter sunlight looking at the snowpeople kids had built in front and side yards, at the cheerful wreaths on windows or doors. Handmade menorahs graced a few windows. She could hear shouts—no school—from nearby as people sledded or threw snowballs.

She spun around when one of those snowballs hit dead center of her back.

And nearly jolted when she watched Duncan brushing the snow off his hands as he walked down the sidewalk to her.

"A coward shoots in the back."

"Or an opportunist," he said. "It was too good to miss."

"I didn't know you were here."

"Just for a couple hours. You look good. It's been awhile."

"Awhile."

"I was going to head over to your place, but Hannah said you were in town. Let's walk."

She fell into step with him. He looked . . . tougher, she decided. Honed. "You've gotten all the intel?"

"Yeah, right up to this morning. I'm looking forward to smashing their plans. Ballsy move to bug the White House. Sorry I missed it."

"It had to be done."

"Sure it did." Even as she let a little satisfaction in, he continued. "Too bad you didn't think of it sooner. We've been able to recruit off the rumors—we're caging them as rumors—Hargrove and White are working toward a deal."

"If that gets out—"

"We're not morons, Fallon. We're saying we got it from a captured PW."

"Your numbers increased with your alliance with the First Tribe, with Meda."

"More than numbers. I've never seen anyone who can ride or fight on horseback like the First Tribe." His words might have been briskly delivered, but admiration shone through. "They're helping train in that skill. We had some troops who could barely sit a horse a month ago. Now it's, you know, ride 'em, cowboy."

"You have four hundred and forty-two troops now."

"Five hundred and three. We added in the last few days. I figured to tell you in person."

"It's a good number, and from a remote location." She stopped to study him. "How?"

"Meda's got ways of getting word to more First Tribe. I've had scouts, myself included, traveling or flashing to where we've heard may be some settlements. I can tell you, since we've been able to pass along the rumors, recruits have come in steady. We may have more, some ready and able to fight, before the second."

They walked toward the gardens.

He'd shaved, she thought, for his family visit. And smelled clean, like the snow. The desert sun had given his skin a warm gold color that made his eyes greener.

"Are you ready to come back? To New Hope?"

He looked over the snow, the greenhouses, the playground. The memorial tree. And realized he'd stood nearly in this same spot when Petra had killed his closest friend.

"After D.C. Yeah. I've been away long enough."

"You helped build the army that'll take D.C."

"That's right. I'll help build more from here, and give my family some time. If I need to be somewhere else, I'll go somewhere else. But it's time to come back, for now."

"Your family misses you."

"I miss them. I miss New Hope. The desert—it's an amazing place. But I miss home. But that's not all I'll come back for. I told you when I left, I'd come back for you."

She shook her head. She didn't step away; that was cowardly. "I can't think about anything but January the second. Ten thousand depend on me to lead them to battle. And you, Duncan, to lead them."

"And we will. After, you and me?" He flicked bits of snow off her shoulder. "We have to deal with this."

"You make it sound like a chore."

"I don't know what it is." He took her arm before she turned away. "I don't know, but it's been inside me since the first time I dreamed of you. I'm beginning to think that started with my first breath. I want you, and everyone else I've ever wanted? They're like smoke, just easily brushed away. It doesn't seem right, but that's how it is. It's you."

She understood that want, because she felt it. "Do you know how much of my life has been laid out not just at my first breath, but hundreds, thousands of years before that breath? Can you understand I might resist having who I want laid out, too?"

"Sure, because I feel exactly the same. That's why we deal with it."

She didn't object when he took her shoulders, pulled her in, took her mouth. She wanted it, wanted to feel again what she'd felt the night he'd left. That heat, that rise.

But when he drew her in, just held her until the heat slid softly down to warmth, it left her shaken long after he stepped away again.

"So." He tucked his hands in his pockets. "I've got the coordinates for the second. We've been drilling with the maps you sent. Since we're too far away for otherwise, we'll flash the entire five hundred, and two hundred horses. We've already started prepping the NMs and horses."

Easier, she thought, less complicated to talk of battles. "You're confident you can flash that many?"

"It's the only way to get there, so yeah, I'm confident. I need a heads-up from you, to me directly, not through an elf. You're planning to strike at dawn, so we'll be ready to go two hours before dawn. But I need the go." His eyes, greener, steady, held her. "Direct from you, Fallon."

"You'll have it. We're going to win this, Duncan, because we have to."

"It's a good plan. Freaking bold, and that's what we need. You picked your base commanders well. I include myself in that," he added with a grin that flashed on, then off. "Every one of them knows how to lead, knows what's at stake. When we win, because yeah, we have to, who knows how many DUs we take down with that police state they call a government. Who knows how many magickals we'll free from containment."

"They have two hundred in the White House facility."

"They— What?"

"That's intel from the listening posts. The scientists who work for Hargrove are trying to create a serum that will sterilize them."

"For fuck's sake."

"Hargrove gave them a deadline. If they don't come through, he wants them exterminated."

Everything in him hardened and burned. "What's the deadline? How long ago did this come through?"

"The day after we planted the bugs. He gave them two months."

"You've known this for weeks?" His eyes fired as he raged at her. "You knew this goddamn deadline slaps right up against the strike? And you don't tell me, or any of the commanders? Because I'd have heard if you had. Who the hell do you think you are?"

"The One."

"Bullshit on that. Bullshit." He stormed away, then back again. "You had no right."

That rage, that storm, blew over her, blew through her, but she held her ground. "Maybe not. Maybe not the right, but the need. If I'd told you, and the others, what they're trying to do, if I'd told you we learned just days ago they're forcibly impregnating magickals to study them through gestation, to study the infants born, that they've experimented on newborns, how many would break ranks and push an attack before we're ready, before we can win?"

It sickened him—she could read it on his face—felt her own stomach quiver.

And he looked at her with contempt. "You're a fucking cold one, aren't you?"

"I'm not." Her voice broke, and so did the wall of will she'd so effortfully built. "I'm not. Babies. How many? I don't know. I didn't know they had them right in the White House, right there where they once had a bowling alley, a movie theater. They have labs and cages now, and I didn't know. I stood above them that night, and didn't know."

She covered her face with her hands. "If I had, I would have had to leave them. I would have had to because even if I could have saved a few, somehow, the rest would be lost."

"Okay. All right."

"It's *not* okay." Now she raged. "It's not all right. But it's necessary. Now I do know, and I hear babies crying. I hear them in my sleep. So how can I sleep?"

"Stop." He took her shoulders again, a firm grip that gentled as he ran his hands down her arms and back again. "Stop, now."

"I want to drive my sword through their hearts." She gripped him in turn, her fingers digging into his arms. "From D.C. to New York, from ocean to ocean, and over the oceans to every corner of the world. And I swear I will, I swear on my life I'll cut out their hearts and the heart of the beast that uses them like toys."

"Not alone, Fallon."

"No, no, God, I don't want alone. But if I know myself, and what my own rage, without control, can unleash? I know yours just as well. I swear to you, I swear, we have to strike on the second. Not a day sooner. It's one circle in many, Duncan. Not the first, not the last, but one in many."

"I believe you." Because she trembled, he laid his hands on her cheeks, kept his eyes on hers. "I believe you. But here's where you're wrong. I said before you chose your commanders well, and you did. Every one of us would have argued for an earlier strike. But," he said before she could speak, "we'd have listened to your reasons against. Jesus, Fallon, do you think I didn't learn control after all those months with Mallick? He's the king of control."

"It used to piss me off."

"Yeah, I joined that club. But it works." He dropped his hands, stepped back once more. "I want the coordinates for the containment facility. Once they realize D.C.'s falling, somebody down there could panic. They'd start killing prisoners. Which," he added, "you've already thought of."

"I planned to tell the other commanders what I told you. We'll have a rescue force take the containment center, free and transport prisoners to Arlington. You were already on it."

He nodded. "I'm going to share this with my key people when I get back today."

"Pick two for the rescue team."

"Can do. I'll also tell the troops when we're ready to flash to D.C. The rage will pump them up. I have to get back, spend a little more time with the family before I leave."

He looked around. "You know, I didn't figure I'd miss the snow. But I do." His eyes locked with hers. "Merry Christmas."

"Merry Christmas."

When he turned, she scooped up snow, balled it, winged it. The impulse, and his over-the-shoulder grin made her laugh. "Now we're even."

"Until next time. I'll see you on the battlefield."

When he walked away, she thought: Not just the battlefield of D.C. They would see each other on so many more.

CHAPTER TWELVE

Just before dawn on January second, Fallon stood in front of the barracks. More than two thousand spread out with her. Some mounted horses, others straddled motorcycles. Foot soldiers moved into formation.

Breath expelled in clouds swirling the air in mists.

The dying night hung cold and clear, the waning half-moon sailing low as the stars shimmered out. A fresh snowfall lay like ermine over branches while men and women trampled it underfoot to move into position.

She saw Marichu take hers, quiver on her back, eyes already fierce.

Those who would stay behind had already said their good-byes, embraced their loved ones, and waited now in the shivering dark.

When she felt the sun waking, she mounted Laoch, called Taibhse to her arm, and Faol Ban to her side.

She turned her horse to face the troops.

"What you do today, you do for all. Every blow you strike is a blow against persecution, bigotry, suffering. You are the brave and the true. Today you fight for all who are hunted and caged, tormented and slaughtered, and what you do this day will ring the bells of hope and freedom through the smoking cities, through the forests and over the hills, the seas.

"We are warriors of the light." She drew her sword, lifted it high as the air rang with cheers. "And today, as surely as day breaks the night, our light strikes back the dark. *Solas don Saol!*"

Thousands of voices echoed the call. *Solas don Saol!*

As the sun shimmered, blooming rose over the eastern hills, she enflamed her sword.

And struck the first blow in the heart of D.C.

Within seconds, the air filled with shouts, screams, gunfire, the flame of arrows, the thunder of horses, a roar of engines. Much of the city, already in rubble, smoked from fights waged through the night.

Overhead, the crows circled and cried out in a kind of jubilation. Taibhse shot off her arm, a white missile, tore through the smoke and ripped at the crows with beak and talon.

Fallon rode toward power. She felt it pump, black and vicious, pushed through the oily stream of it toward a woman striking out with bolts of red and black at oncoming troops.

With her shield, Fallon slapped a bolt to the ground, where it burrowed in the rubble. And with one swipe of her sword she ended it as Laoch soared over the fallen body and the charred stones.

A man with a bat studded with nails rushed forward, struck down one of the government militia. "Resist!" he shouted, and behind him poured a dozen more as Fallon rode into the chaos.

Arrows flamed and flew through the dull morning light. Fire burst from the thunder of explosives, quaking the ground as brick and stones avalanched from ruined buildings. Their dust spumed up, another smearing haze so thick soldiers became ghosts.

She pounded through wherever she felt that pulse of dark power, striking down, battling back. As war cries echoed, she thought of nothing but the next foe, the next inch of ground. Sweat and blood rolled through the frigid wind as powers clashed, as steel rang and bullets sliced.

Her forces drove through the barricades, north, south, east, west. Dozens of ugly battles flooding a city that no longer stood for its people, no longer honored the blood spilled, the lives sacrificed for centuries to preserve the rights of its people.

Monuments defaced, parks scorched to ash, the dome of the Capitol broken and blackened.

In that dawn, through the bitter morning, they fought savagely against the government forces, the Dark Uncannys, the cold hands of cruelty that had choked all life, all hope from a once shining city.

She took Laoch up, dived over the base, heaved down fireballs.

From her height she could see holes in the enemy lines, holes in her own defenses. Relayed orders to exploit the first, close up the second.

In her mind Duncan shouted, *We need to move on the containment center. They could start executing prisoners. We need to move there now.*

Now, she agreed. She shot down on Laoch, leaped from him. "Fight," she told him, and flashed.

Men and women scrambled to secure vials, samples, equipment. In what she took to be a holding cell, a boy—no more than sixteen—struggled against his chains. She heard the echoes of shouts beyond the main lab.

A woman running for a steel door, pushing a wheeled crate, saw her, shrieked.

"You should fear me. You should be afraid." Like a backhanded slap, Fallon knocked her to the ground with a wave of power.

Alarms screamed. One of the men, his black uniform pristine against the flapping white lab coats, drew a sidearm. She melted it in his hand so he dropped to the floor.

The rest dropped to their knees, threw their hands in the air. She heard the rescue force battling, knew with all she was they wouldn't fail.

"Carter," she said, and read the fear in one pair of eyes.

As she stepped toward him, tears leaked from his eyes.

"Please. I was only following orders. President Commander Hargrove himself—"

"Torture, rape, mutilation, genocide. Experimentation on infants. These are your orders?"

"Please. I'm a scientist."

"You're a war criminal." And because he deserved the insult—and so much more—she rammed her fist into his face.

Face coated with soot, eyes as fierce as they'd been at that break of dawn, Marichu pushed through. Those eyes and the arrow already nocked made her purpose clear.

Fallon simply shifted in front of Carter, said, "No."

She turned to the holding cage, opened the locks, dropped the chains away. The boy staggered out.

"Give me a weapon. Let me kill them."

"We don't kill prisoners. We're not like them." She turned her gaze to Marichu. "We won't be like them. Into the cage," she told the rest, and gestured to Carter.

"Drag him with you. Quickly, or I may change my mind and give this boy one of you after all."

She turned to the boy. "Can you fight?"

"Yes."

"Then fight." She gave him her knife. "I'll need that back. Let's move." She led him toward the sounds of combat, stopped short when she saw Arlys.

"You're supposed to be—"

"Right here." In flak jacket and helmet, Arlys recorded. "Right here. Finish this. For God's sake, finish this and get these people out of here."

"It's done." Duncan swung his sword left, right, and did what Arlys asked. He finished it.

"Secure the doors," Fallon ordered. "You," she snapped at Marichu, "help secure the doors, and don't make me regret I gave you your wish."

Cells, glass walled, ran at least fifty feet on either side of the space. People crowded into each section, some unconscious, some glassy eyed, others shouting for release. Children, separated from the adults, huddled together. In another, six infants squalled in clear containers with locked lids.

Like animals, Fallon thought. Even the babies caged like animals.

"We're going to get you out. Those of you who can fight, move out and to the left when we get the doors opened. We'll get the others to safety."

She gripped Duncan's hand. "Help me."

They joined, power to power, purpose to purpose.

"Magickally sealed," he murmured.

"Yes, I feel it. But we have more."

At her call, Tonia, blood splattered on her thick jacket, joined hands with them.

The glass began to hum, to ripple, to vibrate.

"Open, not break. There the locks, here the key. Turn the key to set them free."

The glass moved, a fraction, an inch, a foot, section by section, row by row.

People poured out, supporting, even carrying others. Some ran to the children, gathering them up, weeping. Over the clash of voices, languages, Fallon pitched her own.

"Stand together! We have to move quickly!" She noted more than a dozen walked to the left, prepared to fight. "Hold on to the children, the infants, the injured."

"Where will we go?" someone cried out.

"Arlington. They're waiting for you. Stay together, trust the light. Take them," she said to Tonia. "With Greta and Mace, as planned."

"We've got it." With the two other witches, Tonia focused power. "We'll be back," she said, and flashed the rescues.

Fallon walked to her father, laid a hand on his arm to heal a wound. "Give them weapons. Lead them. Take this house."

"Your standard's going to fly over it tonight."

"Secure the prisoners in the cells. We'll be bringing another." She looked at Duncan. "It's time to cut off the head. Are you with me?"

"You know I am."

She took his hand, spoke in his mind. His brows shot up.

"You know where he is?"

"Yes. They rehearsed only last week. The bunker's magickally sealed, so—"

"Together."

"Together." She pulled the location into her mind, flowed it into his.

Light sparked from their joined hands as they stood, eyes locked, mating power with power. Her blood hummed with it, all but sang as the link flowed through her. She felt his heart beat inside her own. And so, that merged light peeled away the layers of the dark.

Then it burst.

While prisoners herded into the cells they'd used to cage others, while troops rushed out to fight, she flashed with Duncan.

Hargrove stood in a small room behind four armed men and a thick steel door. Like the officer in the lab, he wore black, more uniform than suit. Medals glinted across the chest, gold braid wound at the cuffs.

His shoes shined like mirrors, those of a man who never walked through the dust and mud of the city he'd claimed as his own.

His eyes went wild when she slapped power at the guard who fired on her. The bullet pinged off her shield and shot back into his chest. Even as he fell Duncan slashed out, sword singing. In seconds, the guards lay, finished.

Hargrove cowered back, one hand held up. "You need me to—"

"We don't." Fallon flamed the gun he whipped from behind his back so he screamed, fell to his knees. "But I want you to taste what you've served."

She dragged him to his feet, flashed him back to containment and into a cell. "You're deposed," she said. "Arlys?"

"Right here. I'm getting all of it."

"When we have control of the communications here, can you broadcast without Chuck?"

"Oh yeah. I'm writing copy in my head right now."

Fallon continued to study Hargrove, who sat in his

fine suit, his false medals glinting while he cradled his burned hand. No power in him, she thought. Only what he'd stolen, what he'd killed for, what he'd grasped.

Now his hands were empty.

"Why don't you do your interview now. You might want to get some statements from the others. We'll send a medic to treat the wounded."

"It's more than they did for prisoners," Duncan noted.

"Yes. We're more than they are." She turned her back on Hargrove. "Communications?"

"I'm with you." Duncan took her hand.

The battle of D.C. waged from dawn to dusk. More than four thousand lost their lives and more than three thousand were wounded in the bloodiest day since the Doom.

LFL forces freed more than two hundred prisoners, and their strike forces found and freed another fifty from secondary containments, and sixty more, primarily children, held in an underground section of what had been the National Gallery of Art.

Resistance forces, numbering approximately fifteen hundred, joined with the LFL to defeat the government troops and the DUs.

General Dennis Urla formally surrendered the city. He, James Hargrove, Dr. Terrance Carter, Commander Lawrence Otts, and other key figures in the city's rule, along with two thousand enemy troops, were taken as prisoners of war.

With her father, Fallon stood in a vault, stared with some wonder at the stacks of gold bars, of silver, the wink and glint of jewels set in more gold for adornment. Cases of diamonds, cold and white.

"I wanted you to see," she told him. "We found another,

full of art, old masters. I recognized some from books. Duncan recognized more."

"Hoarding it all. Hargrove's personal treasure house. He—or somebody—looted the museums. Maybe at first—give them the benefit—to protect, but this? Hoarding, and for what?"

"He—and those like him—would still see this as wealth, and in wealth, power. The metal and stones can be useful, for engineering, building, mechanics, and in magicks. The art should be preserved. One day, it should be housed again, where people can see it, students can study it. It belongs to no one because it belongs to everyone."

Simon tapped a gold bar with a battle-stained finger. "There are some who'd kill for this. It doesn't matter you can't plant it, eat it, keep warm with it."

"Yeah. White kills for bigotry, for his wrathful god, but still draped Arlington in riches as he saw them. Hargrove kills for power and this. And this." She gestured around the vault. "Because for him and those like him, those bars of metal can make one man a king, and the lack of them makes others slaves. That time is over."

Arlys recorded all of it, with footage of the battle, of the condition of government prisoners and their rescue in her broadcast from the White House. She ended with a shot of the white standard flying through the battle smoke over the ruined city.

With Fallon, she sat with Hargrove in his cell. With her camera on a tripod, she took notes.

Though pale, he'd recovered some of his arrogance. "You've committed treason against the United States of

America. You will hang for it. Our military and our allies will, I promise you, cut through you and wipe you off the face of this earth."

"Allies like Jeremiah White and his cult? Allies that stand by while you sign orders to torture, maim, kill? Orders directing children be locked away in the dark and half starved? You kept infants locked away, infants born after you forcibly impregnated women. Six infants in this, once the people's house. And embryos, fetuses, found in jars in your laboratories here.

"How many more people, children, infants, unborn are locked away by your orders?"

"You're not people. You're not human."

"I bleed, I breathe, I think, I feel. I know right from wrong, light from dark. How many more, and where are their locations?"

"I am the president of the United States! I am the commander in chief."

"Self-appointed following a military coup on what was left of the government and this city," Arlys said briskly as she took her notes. "They weren't much better than you."

"No," Fallon agreed, "not much better. If we were like them, like you, like the Dark Uncanny you've both used and fought against, I would cut you down with a thought."

He paled at that, drew back. "White's right about you. You're from hell."

"No, but you? I see the dark in you, the human dark, the dark with no power but force and cruelty. Your time's done." She rose. "You don't have to tell me where you hold prisoners. There are other ways to find them."

"Torture. Black magicks."

He believed that, she realized. Believed every word

of his own lies. "You're alive. Your hand's been given medical attention. You'll be humanely treated. But you'll never know freedom again. I don't want your death. It's enough to know that you'll be here, under this dead city, for the rest of your life."

"I have a couple more questions. Mr. Hargrove," Arlys began.

"I am the president commander!"

"There is some dispute over that, but as president you'd swear to uphold the Constitution. Isn't it a violation of the Constitution, of basic human rights, of all decency, to forcibly impregnate females detained and contained for experimental purposes?"

"They're not human! Freaks! Abominations!"

"You consider the half-starved children I recorded being released from what's essentially a dungeon abominations?" Arlys crossed her legs, settled in. "Let's talk about abominations."

Fallon left him to Arlys—skilled hands, she knew. She left the others who'd followed him, taken his orders, ignored their humanity in the glass cages and walked back into the lab area.

Mallick waited for her.

Her heart lifted. "I'm so glad to see you. Glad to see you unharmed."

"You have the city. Even the crows have deserted it. It was once a seat of power. Will it be yours?"

"No. Those like Hargrove destroyed its light. It'll never shine again. Now, it's a prison. We'll secure it, hold it, but there's no center here."

"I agree."

"The issue will be feeding, housing, securing, treating medical needs for the prisoners. My last report numbered them at four thousand. We can't hold that many here, not humanely."

"I have a thought on that. I should say Duncan and I had a mutual thought."

"I'd like to hear it. Not here." She looked around at the remnants of torture. "I want air and movement. Let's go out to the base. I'm more comfortable with a military base, even if it was the enemy's."

As they walked upstairs, through the building, she watched her people securing areas, transferring supplies, taking more up to what would serve as a temporary infirmary for those not seriously wounded.

"I'm told you've ordered anything of real historical value to be preserved and secured."

"We have some with knowledge helping categorize," she confirmed. "This house, this city, the country, the world? It won't ever be what it was. Still, we need to value history, and art, and remember."

"You learned well."

"You taught well."

She walked outside with him into the cold, breezy night. Much of the base had joined the rubble—she'd destroyed some of it herself. But it could and would be rebuilt, as needed.

"You'll station some here."

"Yeah. Straight shot to New York. Soon, Mallick. We have the momentum. And we'll have more weapons, more troops. I only heard part of Arlys's broadcast earlier, but that will bring more to us."

"And more against you."

"It's time to dig them out."

"You hope for one in particular."

She looked out into the night. "Two. Not just Petra. Her mother along with her. In my heart, in my belly, I yearn for it."

He let out a sigh that had his breath expelling in a cloud. "Such yearnings dim the light."

"Do they?" Didn't her shield hang on her back to defend, her sword wait at her side to strike? "Inside me I feel they're the way through to the black, the very absence of light that crouches and watches. Is it because I want it to be, or because it is? I don't know."

"Nor do I."

"They bring death, madness, pain, grief. While they exist, that won't stop. Petra and Allegra won't stop until I stop them." She shook it off. "But it won't be today. What we stopped today is part of them, but only part. Your idea?"

"Duncan and I discussed the problem of prisoners. The numbers—and how those numbers will increase. How much of our troops, resources are involved in keeping them."

"We can hardly eliminate them."

"There are places, islands. Remote, all but inaccessible to non-magickals. Places with natural resources. Food, materials to build shelters. Land that could be farmed and grazed."

"Island prisons."

"Ones more easily supervised, again remotely. Provide them with basic tools, materials. Their life would be what they make of it."

"Saving us from using troops and medicals to guard and treat, resources to feed and clothe. Do you have locations in mind?"

"I do."

"I'd like to see them. If we do this, we should start with prisoners we feel are capable of living without locks and walls to hold them. Travis and other empaths could help select the first we placed. Some will have families, Mallick."

"Yes."

"Then they and their families can be given the choice." She shoved a hand through her hair. "God, if we can relocate even a few hundred for now, it would relieve some of the strain."

"Some will swear allegiance to you."

"And some will mean it. Those who do increase our number. How many were forced to fight? How many didn't know what they did in there? How many pretended not to know? And how many knew and deemed it good? We'll find out."

She studied him then, realized he looked tired, a little worn around the eyes. "I need to go to Arlington, see the rescues, the troops, then home. New Hope. Eighty-two I led from New Hope this morning won't go home again. Some of them had families."

"They'll be mourned and honored."

"They will. Does Duncan know the islands you have in mind?"

"I showed him."

"All right, he can show me. You go back to the cottage."

Surprise crossed his face, followed quickly by annoyance. "I don't believe my usefulness ends this day."

"No, and because it doesn't, because I need you, go home, Mallick. One week. It's what my father calls R and R. Take a week, tend the bees, drink wine by the fire. Then come back to me."

"And you, girl, do you take a week for bees and wine?"

"I'm damn well going to take a day or two. A week for you, old man." Before he could evade it, she wrapped her arms around him. "I'll need your guidance, your strength. Please, take a week."

He touched a hand to her hair. "Then take the two days."

"Deal. Starting tomorrow. Now I need to find Colin, take him back to Arlington. Should I have someone bring your horse?"

"I can get my own horse. Bright blessings on you, Fallon Swift."

"And on you, Mallick of Wales."

He flashed away, and she went inside.

She found not only Colin but Flynn and Starr in the Residence, divvying up cups and plates. And with Flynn, standing close to his side, a wolf.

Not yet full grown, she noted, a smoky gray with gold eyes that shifted to her, watched.

"Flynn."

He turned, teacups in his hands, bruises on his left cheek, dried blood on his right.

"He came to me only yesterday," he told her. "He walked out of the wood and waited for me." Flynn set the cups down, laid a hand on the wolf's head. "He's from Lupa. I can feel it. One of the sons of his sons, blood of his blood."

"Yes, and he's yours. His name?"

"He's Blaidd."

"Wolf in Welsh."

Beside Flynn, Starr, who rarely smiled at all, grinned. "Mallick sent him. Flynn felt it. Mallick sent him on the path to Flynn."

"I want to tell him I'm grateful. There wasn't time in the battle."

"I've sent him to his cottage for a week. I wanted him to rest a few days."

Satisfied, Flynn reached for more plates. "I'll detour there on my way back to base."

"I need you in New Hope now. Who can take your command?"

Flynn looked at Starr.

"Do you want it?" Fallon asked her, and at Starr's nod, said, "The command's yours. And with it I hope to send you a hundred resistance fighters."

"Then you really are going to need all these fancy dishes," Colin commented. "You'd better find something to use to carry them. Mick's called for some of the cooking stuff. He wants to set up a secondary camp."

"You've seen Mick?" Another breath of relief. "He's okay?"

"Yeah, he's good. We're going to need some of the sheets and shit for Arlington if we're going to handle the rescues for now."

"Let's get what you need and go. I want to see all the commanders in New Hope tomorrow—" She broke off, remembering she made a deal. "No, in two days. Flynn, can you pass the word? And let my parents know I'll be home either tomorrow or the day after?"

She gathered sheets—and towels—with Colin.

"You're okay?" she asked him.

"A to the okay. Hell of a fight, Fal. Some of them ran like rabbits at the end of it. I had a couple of DUs homing in on me. I've got a couple of witches to thank for that block."

He stopped, grinned. "We took fucking D.C. Who's president now?"

"Still not you." And, taking his hand, took them to Arlington.

Fallon toured the houses where they relocated rescues. Volunteers and soldiers had hauled in extra beds, cots, mattresses. In kitchens, more volunteers made soups, teas while medicals treated injuries.

In one large family room, Fallon counted twenty-five beds. Some slept, some ate, others simply sat huddled under blankets.

The air—she could breathe it—tasted of their fatigue,

confusion, fears, hopes. Volunteers moved through, offering tea, soup, and sometimes just a hand to hold.

She saw Travis sitting with a woman. Long gray hair, withered face. Murmuring to her as he draped a blanket over her shoulders. Nearby, Hannah tucked in two children together. They clung to each other.

Travis rose and, clipboard in hand, wound his way through the beds to come to her.

"I'm working on getting names, ages, abilities, whatever I can. Stories. It's . . . it's so fucked-up. It's beyond fucked-up."

Feeling his fury, she put a hand on his shoulder. "They're safe now. We'll take care of them."

"How do they get through it? The woman I just talked to? Susan Grant. Empath, like me. She was a teacher, lost everyone in the Doom. She got out of Dallas with a small group—a couple of her students with them—and ended up in east Tennessee, where they decided to settle. She started a little school. She said she never explored her other powers because they spooked her. She just wanted to teach, you know?"

"How long has she been in containment?"

"She's not sure. Five or six years, she thinks. Government forces swept in—night raid. She thinks some got away. They used electric shock therapy on her, Fallon. Put her in isolation—sensory depravation. And she thinks they did some kind of brain surgery. She can't remember. But after, if she tried to feel, to get a sense of someone, she'd get a blinding headache. They took what she was, and made it pain."

"They won't touch her again."

"How many more?" he demanded. "How many more like her, like the rest we got out today? Jesus, can't you hear them screaming?"

She did the only thing she could think of. She pulled him into her, pushed calm into him. "You need a break."

"They didn't get one. Sorry." Breathing deep, struggling to settle, he drew back. "It's getting to me. Some of them can't even remember their names until I push in deep enough to find them. The bastards did everything they could to erase them. To make them nothing."

He drew in another breath. "Yeah, you're right. I need a break or I'm not going to be able to help. I'll take a walk, get some air."

"Good."

"While I'm at it, I'll pass what I've got up the chain for the records. I'll be back."

"You could use some sleep."

With eyes full of feelings, he looked around the room. "None of us are going to get much sleep tonight. I'll be back."

When he went out, Hannah came over.

"I didn't want to interrupt. He's taking on a lot. These rescues, they're just so full." Fatigue leached her face of color, compassion glowed under it as she pressed a hand to her heart. "You know what I mean? And Travis can't help but take it in. Did you talk him into calling it a night?"

"No, but he's taking a break. What about you?"

"I'm going to bunk down here. We're stationing medics in every rescue area tonight."

"Where are the babies, the rest of the kids?"

Hannah took her arm, drew her a little farther away. "Rachel and your mother took them back to New Hope. Nobody knows who the babies belong to. Some of the women remember being pregnant, but they don't remember giving birth. They'd take them into the lab, from what we're piecing together, put them under. We need to go through the medical records."

"We have them."

"Not all of the women came back. And not all of them were at term when they were taken away. Fallon, I always knew, but . . . I guess some part of me wouldn't believe anyone, anyone could do what's being done. Now I know it's worse than what I thought I knew."

"They'll pay. Those who sanctioned it, those who ordered it, those who carried it out. There'll be a reckoning."

"I believe that. And I hope what we did today sends shock waves through every single one who's had a part in this. For now . . ." Absently, she rubbed at the back of her neck. "I'm going to take the next who wants a shower and a change of clothes. Do you see the woman Lydia's bringing back? The blonde?"

"Yes."

"You should talk to her before you go. She was taken in the first sweeps. She's been in containment for twenty years. She's Nadia."

As Lydia settled the woman on a cot, and Hannah helped another to the shower, Fallon made her way through.

Several reached out to touch her hand, her leg. It made her feel humble and strange even as she paused to say a word. Nothing she'd been through touched what every one of these women and children had endured.

The blonde with pale blue eyes stared at her as she approached.

"Nadia. I'm Fallon. Have you eaten?"

"They gave us soup and bread and tea. Thank you."

Hearing the accent, she sat, spoke in Russian. "I see the light in you. And the tiger."

"It's been twenty years since I've heard the language of my birth." Tears swam into her eyes. "I came to America, to D.C., to the embassy to work. I was twenty-six."

"Your family?"

"My brother also. Our parents and the rest in Moscow. My brother died in that horrible January. Most did. I did not. My friend—we shared an apartment—when she became ill, I took her to the hospital. You still had hope. The city was already in flames, but you still had hope. But she died, too. I tried to call my parents, but nothing went through."

Nadia's fingers rubbed at the blanket over her lap, restless, wondering.

"I felt what was in me, saw it in others. But I didn't understand. See?" She shifted, drew down the shoulder of her shirt to reveal a tattoo of a crouched tiger on her back. "I loved the tiger, always, but I didn't understand. Such madness, such joy. And all around the dying, the killing, the madness, the flames. Crows circling and smoke rising."

Because she understood, Fallon took her hand. "My mother lived through the Doom and became. She and my birth father escaped from New York."

"So you know. You've heard stories like mine."

"Tell me the rest of yours."

"There was a man I knew. I'd slept with. It was just beginning, not really serious. But I went to him. I was afraid, so I went to him. He worked for the government. He said he would help me. He called the soldiers. They said they would help me, and I believed them. I didn't resist. There were twelve of us they took from the city that day."

"They took you out of the city?"

"To safety, they said."

"All magickals?"

"No, some magickals, some immune. Out of the city, but I don't know where. Something in the water they gave us, I think. Somewhere, I think, underground. And it started. Just tests at first—taking blood, urine, asking questions. It seemed almost benign, even when they kept us separated and closed in. They gave us food, spoke softly. All for our own good, they said. To find a cure. I believed them, even as the months passed and the doctors changed."

"Changed?"

"New ones came. Military. And the tests weren't so benign. They brought the pain, and brought the tiger. I'd try to get away, to strike out, and they'd shock me, or tranquilize me—just enough. They made me sleep, took me to another place with others who could change into spirit animals. Then another place, then another."

"And here again," Fallon prompted.

"Yes. I didn't know I was back in Washington, but others they brought in knew. We couldn't get out. There were rapes and beatings, drugs and chains. Some they took out and didn't bring back. They made me pregnant. The child would be eight years if the child lived. I kept track then. Carter, they called him. He did his cruel tests on me and others like me. And one day, they took me. When I woke, there was no child in me."

She lifted her shirt to show the scar of a cesarean section. "They took the child out of me. Every day for months they strapped me down, pumped my breasts. I told myself the child lived, the child drank my milk. But they wouldn't tell me. I thought to find a way to end it, end myself, but then I thought, if the child lived . . .

"I wanted the hope of that. Some among us could speak in the mind. They spoke of you, of The One. The day would come when The One would strike with her sword and the light would burn away the dark."

CHAPTER THIRTEEN

By the time Fallon walked into the quarters arranged for her, dawn streaked over the east. Nadia's hadn't been the only story she'd heard through the night, and all of them circled in her head. Her heart.

Tales of torture and despair, of families torn apart. But through those tales she thought she might be able to pinpoint other containment centers.

She needed her maps. She needed a clear head. God, she needed a shower. A drink. One night's sleep.

Even as she reached for the wine some considerate soul had left on a desk under the window, someone knocked on her door.

Her first thought was: Go away. For five minutes just go away. But she walked to the door, opened it.

Duncan stood, as battle-grimed as she.

"Colin said you'd just gotten in."

She said nothing, just stepped back to let him in.

"I know you sent Mallick back to his cottage for a few days, and that's a good call. We're going to need him when he's had his time. And I know he talked to you about the islands. The fact is we can't spare the troops to handle the number of POWs we've taken, and we damn well can't keep people locked up for-fucking-ever anyway, or we're not much better than they are. That's number one. Then there's the resources we'd need to house, feed, treat, clothe. We can't spare them, not indefinitely."

"Duncan."

He kept prowling the room, stirring up the air, the energy. Stirring everything.

"We need a solution. One we can live with, and one where those resources are used for the rescues, the troops, the people who're just trying to live through this fuckfest."

"Duncan," she said again.

He spun back to her, fury and fatigue all over him. "What?"

"Shut up." She grabbed him, locked around him. "Shut up, shut up," she repeated as she crushed her mouth to his.

His hands gripped the back of her jacket, balled into fists. Then streaked up to take her hair in that same furious hold as he dragged her head back. His eyes, sharp and green, met hers.

"Don't ask me to stop."

"Shut up," she said again.

She grabbed his belt, tugged until his sword and sheath clattered to the floor. His hands got busy as she yanked at his shirt. He threw one out to lock the door before her sword fell with his.

She had a farmer's knowledge of mating, but already knew this would be more. She wanted more. She wanted all.

"Touch me. God, touch me."

"Trying." He fought off her jacket, shoved her onto the bed. Covering her, his mouth feasting on hers, he took her breasts in his hands.

Another rise, sharp and hot, streaming from her center, spreading, spreading everywhere. Oh yes, here was more. Should she have known—how could she have known—the feel of his hands, so hard and rough, would lift her up, so high, so fast?

She pulled at his shirt even as he yanked hers off. Now his hands—those hard palms, those strong fingers—took flesh. Took her breath. Arching up, she pressed her aching center to his.

Like the merging of powers, that joining, humming, humming, humming in the blood.

Her body, taut, lean, quivered under his. Those muscles, well honed, rippled strong. The feel of her—finally, finally, the feel of her—so long, so smooth, so hot, as if flames sparked under her skin.

Her heart galloped under his hands, then his mouth. God, the taste of her—dizzying. It rushed through his system, hot whiskey after a bitter chill. She bore bruises, cuts, burns left untreated from the battle. Half-mad, he healed as he touched, as he tasted, as he roamed the body he'd wanted longer than his own memory.

Her hands, as eager and questing as his, slid down, dug into his ribs. A stabbing shock of pain jolted through him. He hissed it out as he fought open the buttons of her pants.

"You're hurt."

"Now you shut up."

His mouth came back to hers while he worked her pants down. And he felt her warmth slide into his injured ribs, soothe, mend. They healed each other as they pulled clothes away. Frustrated by boots, he slapped power out, sent two pairs tumbling across the room.

He wanted to see her, absorb her, savor her, but need blinded him. And she was already reaching for him, taking him, opening for him.

"Now," she said, her eyes like smoke. "*Anois ag deireadh.*"

Now at last.

He plunged into her, deep and desperate, and swore his soul leaped. Light burst, brilliant and bold, through the window, through the air, from her, from him. There came a crack of thunder, a swirl of wind. Flying on it, she found his hands, gripped them in hers.

She gave herself to the light, to the storm, to him. Took him through the whirl of bodies, minds, powers mating. The thrill tore through her, keen as a blade, then rolled and rolled like a swamping wave. Rising on it, soaring, she tasted freedom so heady and sweet she cried out.

And the cry was joy.

Breathless, drunk, drugged, staggered, he lay over her. The light, softer now, spread over them, glowed and flowed between them like liquid. He felt her trembling, not from cold or pain, but from that same overwhelming rush that had stormed through him.

Half dreaming, she sighed. "I was so tired and sad. Now I'm not. You had a cracked rib."

"Now I don't." He wanted to stay as he was, but pushed up to study her face. He felt it, as he'd known he would, simply overwhelm him again. "We've seen each other like this before."

"Yes."

"Dreams and visions."

"Reality's more intense." Her gaze roamed over his face, and some of the light dimmed in her eyes. "If you're going to regret it, we'll just chalk it up to battle fatigue."

She lifted a hand to shove him aside, and he took it in his, squeezed hard.

"This is it. Goddamn it, this is it for me. You. So give

me a minute to deal with that. To deal with the fact it doesn't matter why. I've pushed back on that all my life. We'd end up here, sure. But then . . . I don't know what the hell. Now I know, this is it for me, and it doesn't matter why."

So frustrated, she thought as her heart melted. She lifted her free hand to his face, brushed it back through his hair. "No, it doesn't matter. Duncan of the MacLeods," she murmured. "*Tha gaol agam ort.*"

He dipped his head to brush his lips over hers. "I don't know what that means."

"Duncan of the MacLeods should learn a little Scots Gaelic. I love you."

He rested his brow on hers while emotion swirled through him. "I can probably butcher it in Irish from what I learned back in school. But I'll stick with English. I love you."

She drew him down to seal the words, the promise of them with a kiss.

He rolled over, tucked her against his side. "I just wanted to see you. Needed to talk to you about the island, but that was mostly an excuse. I just needed to see you. I didn't expect you to jump me."

"I wanted a drink, a shower, sleep. Then I saw you. Bloody, bruised, broody. And I only wanted you. I think if you hadn't come to me, I'd have taken the sad into sleep instead of remembering the good we did today."

"I get the drink, shower, sleep. Why were you sad?"

"What they did to those people, Duncan. Listening to what they went through—"

"I know." He rubbed his hand up and down her arm. "I talked with most of the rescues."

"One I talked to was taken in the first sweeps, in D.C. Some of the children were born in that place. They've never known anything else, only the dark."

"We'll show them the light. There must be a way to find out if any of the women have kids we rescued. I don't know if Rachel knows how to do that medically, but magickally."

"Some won't want them."

"Others will." He sat up, and because he saw the sad again, gray clouds in her eyes, he pulled her up with him. "Others will, Fallon. How many times have we seen it? Look at Rachel and Jonah with Gabriel—biology doesn't mean a damn. That kid's theirs. Look at Anne and Marla with Elijah. There are hundreds more like that. We all know them."

"You're right." Those clouds whisked away. "You're absolutely right. I'm so glad you're here."

A shoulder, she realized, good sense. And thank all the gods, sensibility.

"Oh, we've got so much to do. I think I can work with what I learned from some of the rescues who were moved around to locate other containment centers. And you and Mallick are right, we need to relocate the POWs. We need to talk about how to do all of that. How and when to—"

He pulled her to him, kissed her quiet. "We'll do all of that, but we're going to take a couple hours. We'll take that shower and find out what it's like to have sex when we're not bloody and banged up."

"That's one plan."

"It's a good one. We can grab something to eat."

"Eat." She pressed a hand to her belly. "I'm starving."

"See, good plan." He pulled her to her feet. "Then I can take you to the islands Mallick and I have in mind. We'll work out the rest."

He paused, let himself take her in. Long, lean, naked. "Jesus, I was in kind of a rush. You've filled out really well since the last time I saw you naked."

"You weren't impressed at the time."

"I lied."

She smiled, and with his hand in hers, walked toward the bath. "I know."

Late morning, energized—again—fed, she met with Colin in his HQ to explain the basics of the plan for POWs.

"Islands." He pushed away from his computer. For reasons that annoyed her, he had an easy skill with technology she lacked. "Tropical islands with resources, shelters or the means to build them."

"They'd still be supervised. We wouldn't put guards on the islands, but there are ways for us to watch them, to maintain control."

"I get that." He stood up, shoved his hands in his pockets. "Some of them don't deserve any kind of freedom."

"We'll determine that. We can't keep them all locked up indefinitely. Not only because it's just not who we are, but we can't spare the men or the supplies. I have to see the locations first, so Duncan's going to take me. But it seems like a good solution."

"Not Hargrove or Carter." He sent her one fierce look. "Not those two. I'm laying down a line there."

"You don't need to. They'll live out their lives in prison. I'm going to look, then when we all meet in New Hope, Duncan and I will present the plan to all the commanders. We need to look ahead, Colin. Not just to the next battle, but to the world we want at the end of it."

"You worry about the world. I'll worry about the next battle." He shrugged, paced.

Moved like a solider, she thought, looked like one with the tough build, the straight back, the warrior's braid. The soldier had always been in there, in the annoying and beloved brother who collected odd treasures and loved basketball.

She started to say just that when he glanced back at her over his shoulder.

"So, you and Duncan."

"He's already been to the islands, and Mallick's on R and R so he'll give me the tour, and we'll see."

"Yeah, yeah, I mean you and Duncan finally did the deed. Got, you know, down to it."

"What?" Shock came first, then the bone-deep embarrassment only a sister can feel when faced with a grinning brother. "How do you know?"

"Shit, Fallon, everybody knows. It was like the freaking sun exploded. And did you look out here?" He jerked a thumb to the window. "That tree behind the memorial stone."

"What do you mean everybody knows? What does a tree have to do with—" She looked now. "A tree of life," she murmured.

It bloomed, like the one at Mallick's cottage, full of flower and fruit.

"I'd've been cool with it anyway. He's a good guy. But it's hard to argue with shit like that. Dad now."

"Let's not go there. I need to see the islands and get back to New Hope. Don't let Travis take on too much. It's harder on him. He feels . . . everything."

"I've got him." He added a smug smile. "He'd have felt it when I short-sheeted his bed last night, and that'll have him working out how to pay me back."

Brothers, she thought. They were what they were.

"Safe trip and all that," Colin added. "Oh, wait."

He went back to his desk, opened a drawer. He took out her knife and the sheath Travis had made for her thirteenth birthday. "Kid said you lent him this, and asked if I'd get it back to you. Marichu brought him in. She handled herself," he said in a way that told Fallon he did, indeed, have a little thing there.

"Thanks. The boy's okay?"

"In the barracks. One of our new recruits."

Nodding, she clipped the knife to her belt. "Train him strong. I'll see you in New Hope."

"Hey, Fallon," he said as she walked to the door. "We've got them on the run."

"Let's keep it that way."

She got home at dusk to find her mother stirring something that smelled like heaven on the stove. So normal, she thought, after the blood and the battle, after a day of wonders.

Grateful, she rushed over to wrap her arms around Lana, press hard against her back.

"There's my girl."

"Here's my mom."

Lana turned, hugged just as hard before drawing back with a smile. The smile changed as she studied Fallon's face, a face she cupped in her hands as she said, "Your first time."

"What—"

"Duncan. Of course Duncan."

"I—you— How do you know?"

"I had a first time, too. You've got knowledge in your eyes, along with the stars. He made you happy."

"Yes." The initial awkwardness dropped away. "I love him. He loves me."

"I know."

"It was wonderful." As it rushed into her again,

Fallon spun in a circle. "I didn't know I could feel so much. You can read stories, or listen to soldiers' sex talk, I could even see the way you and Dad look at each other, but I couldn't know. I couldn't know until he touched me."

With a sigh, she laid a hand on her heart. "And then he did. When we're together like that, I'm not the Savior or The One, or anything but . . . I'm just me."

"I know," Lana said again.

"It's like that with Dad, for you?"

On a sigh of her own, Lana put a kettle on, chose teas. "All the months we were together, the time before you were born, and after, he never touched me, never asked. He wanted me, and I knew. Just as he knew I needed my grieving time for Max. And through that time, I fell in love, slowly and completely."

She got out cups, and the honey Fallon loved. "It was the day Mallick came. The new year. The end of Year One. When we were alone again, the three of us, I told him I loved him and wanted our lives together to really begin. That was our first time together. And when he touched me, finally, I was just me."

"You never told me."

"It would have been just a pretty story before. Now you understand. We're lucky, you and I, to love and be loved by good men. Through all this, the war, the loss, the victories, we can still be women in love with good men."

She set out the tea, added cookies, and sat to talk, to listen.

"I wasn't sure I'd know what to do—I mean other than the mechanics. There's so much more."

On a laugh, Lana bit into a cookie. "Thank the goddess for that."

"Or that it would *feel* so good. Everything. We were still banged up and bloody, and it didn't matter."

"Might have added to it," Lana replied.

"Then in the shower, we . . ." She trailed off, stirred honey into her tea. "Is it weird hearing this?"

"I'm patting myself on the back right now for being the kind of mother whose daughter feels comfortable talking to her about this. But . . . let's not share the details with your father."

Talk about awkward, Fallon thought. "Will he know, like you?"

"Unlikely. Let me ease him into it."

Better, Fallon thought, much better to leave that part to her mother. "Good idea. Oh, I forgot. When we, the first time, when we— Well, the light just exploded. It burst everywhere, and through me, through him. Outside, the tree behind the memorial stone changed. It's a tree of life, like Mallick's."

"Ah." Lana sat back. "That explains it. Our memorial tree, it did the same. I thought it was a sign of victory, but now I see. Then again, love's a victory." She put her hand over Fallon's. "Without it, all the battles mean nothing."

"There'll be more battles."

"But you'll go into them with one more thing to fight for."

"I was worried it would make me weak, but I was wrong. I feel stronger. I'll need to be. There are things coming—I can't see clearly, but coming. A flame from the north, a madness brewing, a blackened soul behind a mask of innocence. Can you see? A bolt through a faithful heart. The black dragon bringing its long shadow to smother hope. What bargains must be made, what loss suffered, what sacrifice given for the light to burn through the dark?"

Fallon lowered her head. "I can't see, but I know it's coming."

"When it does, we'll meet it." Lana took both of Fallon's hands. "Every one of us."

"There's so much more I need to talk to you about. You, Dad, Travis. Ethan, too. Even before we meet with the rest of the commanders, and the New Hope Originals."

Lana looked over as the door opened. Simon came in. "You're in luck. We'll just—" Something in his face stopped her. "Ethan."

Simon walked to Lana, laid a hand on her shoulder. "He's fine. He headed over to Eddie's. Babe, it's Joe."

"Oh. I'll—"

"Lana, Ethan says it's time."

"Oh no. But—"

"He said Joe's ready. He just needs Eddie to let him go."

Tears swam into Lana's eyes. "I need to be there."

"Go." Fallon stood. "You go. We'll finish making dinner. Go be with Joe."

Lana didn't hesitate, she didn't rush for her coat. She flashed.

She found Eddie, Fred, all the kids sitting on the floor of the living room in the farmhouse. Joe's head rested in Eddie's lap. Ethan, her strong, sweet boy, knelt, stroking a hand over Joe as the dog's breath labored in and out.

She knelt beside him, laid a hand on the old, faithful dog. And knew her son was right. It was time. She met Eddie's eyes, and her heart broke at the hope in them.

"He won't eat. Maybe you could . . ."

"He's so tired, and everything aches." Ethan spoke gently, stroking, stroking. "He won't leave you until you say it's okay. He'll fight not to rest because the love's so strong. He still dreams. He dreams of chasing balls and sticks, and going for long walks, playing with you, with kids."

With hands gentle, tireless, Ethan comforted the dog, read Joe's heart. "Jem and Scout and Hobo run and play, but he can only watch. He wants to run again, play again, but he won't unless you tell him it's okay. He misses Lupa, and knows Lupa's waiting for him, waiting to wrestle with him and run with him. But you need to tell him he can go."

"Do you believe that?" Eddie swiped at the tears on his cheeks. "That he'll go somewhere he can run and chase balls, play with Lupa. Do you really believe that?"

"I know that. Our Harper and Lee are there now. They want to meet him."

"Can he have a red ball?" Willow buried her curly red head against her mother's shoulder. "Can he please have a red ball?"

"Of course he can." Weeping, Fred pressed a kiss to Willow's hair. She took Eddie's hand, kissed it.

"Okay. Okay. Y'all say good-bye now." Eddie took a breath as Joe looked up at him with eyes full of love and trust. "You saved my life. I guess we saved each other. We've sure had some adventures, haven't we, boy? You go ahead now. You take a rest, and let it all go. Then you find Lupa, and meet Harper and Lee, and all the rest. You chase yourself some squirrels."

Joe licked Eddie's hand and on a sigh, he went to sleep.

Later, as she walked back home in a borrowed coat, she put an arm around Ethan's shoulders. "He couldn't have done it, couldn't have let Joe go, without you, Ethan. I'm not sure I could have, either."

"I didn't want to let him go, but he needed to." He glanced back. "They're lighting candles in the windows to help him find his way."

"We'll light them, too. Look." She gestured ahead. "We already have."

"He'll come back, you know. Find his way back after a while. Back to Eddie. People do, some animals do, when they love enough."

He looked at her. It gave Lana a jolt to realize her baby boy now stood eye to eye with her. "It's why they can't beat us. I don't know why they want to kill us, destroy everything that's good. I can feel what they feel, but I can't understand it. I know they can hurt us, take from us, but they can't beat us because we can love a good dog enough to let him go even when it hurts. They can burn the land, but we'll plant it. They can burn it again, but we'll plant it again. They can't stop us. They can't win."

"Oh, Ethan." She drew him closer as they walked toward the lights in the windows. "That's exactly what I needed to hear tonight."

"I need you to let me go with Fallon."

"Not what I needed to hear."

"They need support staff to deal with the horses, the hunting and fighting dogs. I can fight, but I'd be more useful freeing up a better soldier. You— It's time, Mom, for you to let me go."

"You've already talked to your father."

"Now I'm talking to you. All of you go, and I stay."

"What you do here is—"

"Important, sure. But I'm not a kid anymore, and I have abilities that can and will help during a fight. I need to use them. You need to let me."

"The gods ask for so damn much." She looked up at

the stars. "Talk to Fallon. I won't stand in your way. Give me this. We have dinner without any talk of war. We'll tell Joe stories. After, we'll talk about this, and whatever your sister needs to tell us."

"Is she going to tell us she and Duncan got naked?"

"I— Ethan!" His grin brought back her baby boy. "How do you know about that?"

"A little bird told me."

She had to laugh. "You're one of the few who can say that and literally mean it. Just keep that to yourself." She paused at the door. "I'm serious."

"Dad doesn't know."

"Just Joe stories," she repeated, and opened the door.

After the meal, with the dishes cleared and all the stories dulling the sharpest edge of grief, Lana poured wine for herself and Fallon. Travis, back from Arlington, got a beer for himself and Simon.

Ethan looked at the tea in his cup.

"Why can't I have a beer? Fallon had a beer when she was my age."

"A bit older," Lana corrected.

"And she'd just decked a two-hundred-and-fifty-pound man," Simon recalled. "No magickal assistance. You do that, I'll personally serve you your first beer. Meanwhile . . ."

"Meanwhile," Fallon repeated. "There are some things I want to go over here before the formal meeting. I want to hear about the status of the wounded, and the rescues, but before that, I need to talk to you about the POWs."

"We've debriefed about sixty so far," Simon told her. "Some hard-asses in there. And some who were conscripted, if that's what we're calling being rounded up and forced into service. You've got some barely older than Ethan, taken from their families, put into training camps where they're hammered every day about the Uncanny threat. And most of them, nearly all, have family, magickal family members."

"They turn them, or try to, against us." Eyes hard, Travis tipped back his beer. "To them we're the same as the DUs. Shit, plenty of them are waiting for us to torture them the way they do us, or just call down a lightning strike and kill them on the spot."

"They're indoctrinated, brainwashed. We know this." Fallon lifted a hand. "We can, and have, successfully turned some back. It's vital we continue trying. But for those committed to wiping us out, we need another solution. For some, like Hargrove, that's life in prison. We can't sentence potentially thousands more to the same. There can be a choice, for us, for them."

"Such as?" Simon asked.

She told them about the islands, about the basic outline, one she and Duncan had refined.

"It may be we use one for the harder of the hardasses, and the other for those we think, or hope, might build another kind of life."

"It's pretty radical," Travis began, but Simon shook his head.

"Not without precedent. The English sent people here—what was the Colonies—and to Australia."

"Without a choice, and as indentured servants. We'll give them a choice," Fallon added. "And they'll have a kind of freedom. Maybe it's not a perfect choice. Prison or relocation. We'd need a council of some sort to determine who would be eligible for the choice. And to determine who would be given the choice to come back, and when. We'd need to calculate how much in the way of supplies, equipment, and resources to send with them.

It's going to be complicated, and there will be more than one who argues against giving any enemy combatant a choice."

"But it's the right thing." Though she'd said nothing throughout, Lana had listened, weighed, searched her own mind and heart. "On the way here, the first time, I saw those, with powers and without, who could never be redeemed. Even before the Doom, it was the same. But I saw people who were afraid or desperate and did things out of fear and desperation they'd never have done otherwise. I've used my power to harm, to kill, and will again. That's a choice we all live with because what we fight against demands it. But we're not what we fight against, and when there is a choice, we choose what's right. This is right."

"Couldn't have said it better." Simon toasted her with his beer. "Let's work it out so when we run up against those arguments, we've got the answers. Do you want Duncan in on this?"

At Ethan's snicker, Fallon sent him a threatening glare. Simon simply looked puzzled. "What?"

"It's nothing." With a smile, Lana gave Travis a magickal, motherly buzz. "I'm sure Katie's happy to have Duncan around. Let's leave that for tomorrow. So where are these islands, exactly?"

"I've got maps." Rising, Fallon went for her bag, then spread the maps on the table.

By the time she went downstairs, she felt they had more of those answers, and with unified family support a strong force against any dissenters.

When she opened the door to her room, Duncan rose from the chair, set his sketch pad aside. "Took you long enough."

"I didn't know you were here. We were working out

more details on the islands. You should've come up—in. Oh well."

"It's a little weird with your family upstairs, and then there's the idea that if your dad catches me in here, he'll kick my ass. But."

"But." She sealed the door, and went to him.

CHAPTER FOURTEEN

As the commanders arrived, Fallon wondered how long the celebratory air would hold after she laid out the proposed agenda.

She greeted Mick and, amused, tugged on the side braid he'd dyed a bright blue.

"It's an elf thing," he told her.

"If you say so."

"A lot of the shifters are going for tats of their spirit animals. It's a way of—"

"Embracing heritage," Fallon finished. She looked around at the mix of people. "And a statement. Magickals won't hide who and what they are. I like it."

Duncan moved to her, laid a hand on her shoulder in a way that had Mick's grin fading. "Mick. Like the blue. Mallick's here."

"Oh." Fallon shifted to look for him. "I wasn't expecting . . ." She looked back, saw the hurt in Mick's eyes, felt it. Before she could speak, he stepped back, stiffly.

"I've got stuff."

"Hard for him," Duncan commented, and had Fallon turning.

"What do you know about it?"

"Jesus, Fallon, I've got eyes. I see the way he looks at you, probably because I look at you the same way."

"Did you come over here to tell me about Mallick, or what, stake your claim?"

"Both."

"Ass."

Unoffended, Duncan shrugged as she cut through the room to Mallick.

"You left your bees."

"They'll be there when I get back. I thought you might need me here today."

"I do. I'm glad you came. I expect some strong objections to what I'm going to propose today."

"Is it a proposal?"

"What I saw in D.C., beyond the battle. In the chambers of power, such as they were? We won't go back to that."

She thought of Mick's blue braid, of tattoos of spirit animals. "Tribes are forming, Mallick, and pride in them. They need their voices heard. And still . . ."

"They must be led, and united in purpose. There must be laws established for peace to hold when peace is won. That is for you."

"Then I'd better get started. Will you sit by my side?"

"Always."

She caught her father's eye as she walked to the big table, nodded. He gestured to Colin, brushed Lana's arm.

As they took their seats, others followed.

"I know you all have stories of the battle of D.C.," Fallon began. "We've buried our dead, treated our wounded. I'm grateful to all of you for your leadership. It's that leadership that will take us from this victory to New York."

She listened to the cheers and battle cries, the thumping

of fists on the table. Tribes forming, she thought again, and war drums still beating.

"We led ten thousand into D.C." She lifted her voice over the din. "We'll lead ten thousand and more into New York. The Dark Uncanny rule there, and Raiders burn and pillage its boundaries. While Hargrove's rule is over, there are still military that hunt us as mercilessly as they do the DUs, who forcibly conscript non-magickals to increase their numbers, and PW enclaves that hold slaves and executions."

"There won't be so many of them when we take New York." John Little gave the table another fist pound. "We'll cut them down. We'll lock them up. My troops are ready."

Fallon nodded, and took the opening. "We'll all be ready. But we need the ten thousand and more. And more," she repeated. "Some we've locked up were conscripted. Forced to fight. They would fight with us, or serve as support."

"How many of us did they kill?" Little demanded.

"How many of them did we?"

Duncan took his cue. "Jamie Patterson," he began, "seventeen, NM. Taken from his family in a military sweep, conscripted. They took his family, too. His sister, an elf, age fourteen. And his parents. They told him his sister would be held in a containment camp. His father would go to another training center, his mother to another. After five years, they'd be released from service. If he attempted to desert, refused to fight, he and the rest of his family would be tried as traitors and executed."

"Maybe that's his story," Little began, "but—"

"His truth," Duncan corrected. "His sister, Sarah Patterson, was in the D.C. prison. Do we keep him locked up? Do we tell her he fought against us—sure, he was forced to, but that's the breaks?"

"There are dozens more with similar stories." Simon spoke up now. "Isn't that what we're fighting against?"

"Look, man, I've got a heart." Little rubbed one of his big hands over his face. "But how do we trust them?"

"How do we trust any who come to us?" Lana asked. "Not everyone who weaves into our communities has good intentions."

"Kurt fucking Rove," Eddie muttered. "You're going to have the shitbirds, but you can't toss them all in the same bucket, dude."

"They can and should be given a choice." Fallon waited a beat. "Those able and willing to fight should fight. Train under trusted commanders. Those unable or unwilling would serve in other ways. If they have a skill, they offer the skill. And those who have families will know, will have our word, that we'll do whatever can be done to find those families and reunite them."

"We have a couple of shifters, twins." Mick drummed his fingers on the table, didn't meet Fallon's eyes. "They came in a few days after we took The Beach. They'd been in containment about six or seven years—lost track. They got out in the confusion when a bunch of whacked-out Raiders hit the containment center. They were about eight when the military grabbed them up. The parents tried to stop them, fought back. Soldiers killed their mom right in front of them, burned the house, dragged their dad off. They'd shot him, so they don't know if he's alive."

He looked at Little, around the table. "We've all heard stories like it. I don't see how we can make prisoners out of prisoners, because that's what they were."

Little huffed out a breath. "Some of them are going to be assholes."

And Mick grinned. "If we lock up the assholes, where does that leave you and me?"

Little laughed, waved a hand. "Okay, okay."

Thomas leaned toward the table. "How do we verify they were conscripted, or have families they claim?"

"We've got records." Chuck spoke up. "We're still going through them. We got a shit pile of docs from D.C., so it's going to take some time."

"We're making progress." Arlys, as always, took notes. "Most are conscripted between the ages of fifteen and thirty-five. It's a practice that's gone on for nearly twenty years. Some who were taken were also indoctrinated. They acclimated whether by nature or time, who knows. But we found no one who was released. Once they pulled somebody in, they didn't let them go."

She put down her notes. "There are also numerous records of trials and executions. Some who tried to escape, some who just didn't satisfy the command. They used them as examples to 'motivate' the troops."

"Fuckers." Little sat back. "You got ones that acclimated or whatever the hell you call it, we can't cut them loose and hand them a weapon."

"I agree," Thomas said, and the murmurs started around the table.

"How long do we keep them locked up?" Eddie demanded. "How many troops do we cut out of the fighting force to secure them? Then you gotta feed their asses, give them medical, clothes?"

"And after we win this thing?" Will put in. "What then?"

"There are so many already." Troy looked around the table in turn as people spoke over each other. "Where will we put more?"

"We can't cut them loose and we sure as hell aren't going to start executions. It's a lock and a cage," Little insisted. "That's it."

"It doesn't have to be. There's another way." Fallon turned to Mallick. "Would you show them?"

He lifted his eyebrows, clearly surprised she deferred to him. "Very well."

He rose, and after a moment's consideration, spread his hands, lifted them, and conjured a two-sided map. "This is the world. A large place, land masses, great oceans and seas. Much of this world is now empty of people."

"How many, Kim?" Fallon asked.

"Huh." Kim pursed her lips. "Most reports calculated an eighty percent wipeout from the Doom. Even in the years since, given births, deaths, war, you wouldn't have much population growth. A couple billion. Sounds like a lot. It's not when you consider the Earth's about two hundred million square miles."

"Once a nerd," Poe grumbled, and got an elbow jab.

"How much of that's water?"

"About seventy percent."

"Vast." Fallon looked back at Mallick. "And our ability to travel over the vast seas isn't what it once was. Lack of fuel, skill, equipment."

"In the vast are islands," Mallick continued. "Some are, and were, inhabited. Many are not, or no longer. And here, and here, are two." With a gesture, he had two small islands glowing on the map. "They are habitable. There is game, fresh water, natural resources, land that can be planted."

Interested, Thomas studied the islands, the positions. "Transportation?"

"Wait, wait, wait!" Little waved his hands. "You want to give POWs a vacation on a tropical island? Shit, sign me up."

"Hardly a vacation," Fallon corrected.

"Palm trees, beaches?"

The argument rolled around the table, hot words, cold ones, temper.

"Enough," Mallick snapped when Fallon remained silent. "I've lived a very long time. I've seen the rise and fall of powers, wars upon wars. Even in my sleep, I witnessed. The light must always seek the light. In that light are shadows that must be carefully chosen. What does it matter to you if those we defeated feel warm breezes or can pick fruit from a tree? The shadow we choose is isolation. Some will never see the home they knew again. And if some build a life, even find contentment, does it harm you or yours? It softens the shadows we chose."

"Hargrove—"

"Will live out his life with that lock and cage," Fallon said to Little. "As will those like him. But some are soldiers, John, just like all of us. Some have families, some may make families, and with the making come to see what wrong they did."

"Can I say something that's just the straight practical end of it?" Duncan shifted. "Supplies, security. This way, we give them enough to get them started instead of cutting into our own resources for the duration to keep them held humanely. Do the math," Duncan suggested. "How many pounds of meat, grain, gallons of fresh water, medical supplies, and staff? I've been to those islands. Yeah, they're pretty. You've also got sand fleas, snakes, a rainy season, and hurricanes. You're going to have to plant your own crops, build your own shelters, hunt your own meat, fish, figure out how to live surrounded by miles of ocean."

"How about security?" Mick asked.

"Merpeople, primarily," Duncan told him, and Mick nodded.

"I can live with that. We've got to be better than they

are. If they get one of us, they'll kill us, or toss us in a hole until that killed us. We have to be better than that."

"I might like it better if we talked islands in the North Sea." Colin shrugged. "But Mallick's right. Warm or cold, it's no skin off ours."

"Are we agreed?" Fallon looked around the table.

"What do we supply them with?" Troy asked. "How much, for how long? What if there are children?"

"We have most of that worked out. But we need to agree on the concept before we move to that."

"You're The One," Troy pointed out.

"But I'm not alone in this fight. Everyone here has a voice."

"Then mine's in agreement."

Agreement rounded the table until John puffed out his cheeks. "Maybe we can toss that North Sea idea in there."

Fallon smiled. "Let's see how this works first."

They worked on logistics, with Kim and Chuck—the nerd and the geek—assigned to calculate how much in supplies would be needed per man. Her father, Travis, and other empaths would work together to determine which prisoners were most suited to the choice—with Arlys helping confirm through the records, and Rachel clearing candidates medically.

With an optimistic goal of moving the first five hundred within ten days, Fallon shifted to New York and battle plans.

With her new maps over the table, Fallon looked over in annoyance at the interruption when Ethan and Max burst in.

"Sorry," Ethan said quickly, "but you need to come outside. There's somebody here and . . . you need to see."

With a hand on the hilt of her sword, Fallon reached the door with Duncan, and with Mick.

A woman stood in the snow-covered garden. Flaming red hair curled and spilled nearly to her waist. She wore a long white coat edged with fur at the collar and the cuffs, and looked like something out of a fairy tale with the icy sparkle of diamonds on her fingers, her ears.

She carried no visible weapon, but the two men flanking her—both in unrelieved black—had swords in sheaths crusted in jewels.

Fallon felt the pump of power that matched the confidence in the bold red lips, the emerald eyes.

She spoke with a charming lilt of France. "I bring you no harm, Fallon Swift. I am Vivienne of Quebec. I have come to offer you an alliance."

Fallon watched her gaze shift to Duncan, to Mick, saw those jewel-toned eyes sparkle with flirtatious approval.

"May we speak? Perhaps we will leave our very handsome men, and have, you and I, a little tête-à-tête?"

"All right."

"Fallon, hold on."

Fallon patted Mick's hand away from her arm. "It's fine. Would you tell my mother I have a guest and ask if she wouldn't mind bringing coffee to the living room?"

"How kind." Vivienne walked—all but glided—over the snow. Fallon caught her scent—rich—assessed her beauty. Flawless.

Fascinated, Fallon led her around to the front of the house. "You've come a long way."

"Yes. My escort Regis is a witch, so we do the snap."

Flashed, Fallon thought. "You're not a witch. A shifter."

"You see quickly. I see also that you have two very handsome men in love with you. I have men in love with me. It's pleasant, yes? I thought The One would be hard and—what is it—battle-worn? But you are very lovely."

Fallon opened the door. "Please come in."

"Ah." As she walked inside, Vivienne looked around the entranceway, toward the living room and the crackling fire. "How . . . cozy."

"Should I take your coat?"

"Please, yes." She wandered as she unfastened it. "I thought you would have more—*fancy* is the word? Yes, The One would live more grandly."

"There are people still living in caves or whatever shelter they can manage. This is grand."

"*Bien sûr.*" Beneath the coat she handed to Fallon she wore more white, a dress that skimmed down a curvy body to the ankles of white boots. "But The One is not people, no?"

"You're wrong about that. Please, sit. *Préférez-vous que je parle français?*"

Vivienne's eyebrows lifted as she let out a light, musical laugh. "*Vous parlez très bien français.*"

"*Merci.*"

"But I would like to speak in English. I wish to become more, ah, proficient."

"All right." Fallon turned, took the tray from Lana as she came in. "Mom, this is Vivienne of Quebec. My mother, Lana."

"I am so pleased to meet with you, the mother of The One. I've heard many stories of you."

"I've heard a few of you," Lana returned.

"I am flattered. And you've troubled for me. *Merci.*"
She sat as Fallon set down the coffee tray.

"I'll leave you two alone to talk."

"No, stay." Fallon took Lana's hand. "Just us girls, right, Vivienne?"

"Delightful."

"Milk, sugar?"

"Both, and the little cakes! I have no willpower against the sweet. I like the sweets and the pretty and the handsome men. Do you take both your handsome men for lovers?"

Fallon poured out the coffee. Sat. "No. Just one's enough."

"Me, I'm very greedy." Vivienne took two of the frosted cakes as if to prove it. "I was a child when the Doom came, and there was hunger for some time after. My papa died in it, and *Maman* and I had to hide as I became. She feared for me, you see. And feared of me as well. I was only ten. She was killed before my thirteenth birthday."

"I'm very sorry."

Vivienne acknowledged Fallon's sympathy with a nod. "The ones you call Raiders. I was not quick enough to save her, but I killed them all. And it was then I vowed, an oath on my mother's blood, I would no longer hide, no longer live hungry or cold or afraid."

She sampled a cake. "I would make a place, I took this vow, where no one killed a girl's mother. I used what I have to make what I needed. Now I have Quebec. Or enough of it for now. A fine house and soldiers. Lovers."

She bit into a cake with a smile.

"Slaves?"

"No. One has no right to own another. Servants, yes, I have servants. But they are free, they are not forced to give service. They have food, shelter, clothing. I give them work if they want it, and they are free to stay or to go. We offer protection from the Dark Uncanny, the Raiders, and the rest. These are my people, understand me. I do not go hungry, nor do they.

"This is very good coffee, thank you. We don't have so good the coffee. We have traded for some, but not so good as this."

"We'll give you some beans to take back with you," Lana said.

"That is very kind and generous." Delicately, she bit

into a second cake, licked a bit of icing from her finger. "*Maintenant*, my rule may not be as yours, but still we fight the same enemies. You have won a great victory. I would offer you an alliance. I have two thousand soldiers. Almost," she added with another smile.

"You offer an alliance *after* a great victory."

"But yes. If you had been defeated, my soldiers, my people would have suffered with yours. My council and my generals advise that you are most likely to advance on New York within the year. Perhaps within six months. I would be your ally. I would give my allegiance to you. I do not give it lightly. And I've chosen the light," she added. "Not so bright, it may be, as you, but the light."

"And for your allegiance, your two thousand, what do you want in return?"

"Quebec." Vivienne folded her pretty hands with their sparkling rings in her lap. "Safety for my people, my realm. The promise you and your soldiers will not invade or take from me what I've made. What I may make still. You go north, those who fight there may go more north. May covet what I have. So, an alliance. Promises. Terms. My people will fight with yours, and you will respect and help protect what is my country."

"I fight with my people. Do you fight with yours?"

"I'm not a warrior, but a ruler. Still, I guard what's mine. I'll kill to protect it."

"Show me."

Daintily, Vivienne set down her coffee, dusted crumbs from her fingers. And shifted.

Fallon studied the flame-red dragon with the glittering green eyes.

The red flame from the north, she thought.

"Impressive. And only the second I've seen."

Vivienne shifted back. "We are few. I don't know why. You saw another?"

"Twice. Larger, black. Of the dark."

"It saddens me that when we are few, any would choose the dark." With a delicate shrug, she lifted her coffee again. "Ah, well. I will not keep you, but I trust you will think about my offer."

"I will."

"I'll get you some coffee beans."

"You're kind." Vivienne offered a hand to Fallon as she rose. "I'm not unkind. I'm not unselfish. But I don't see those as . . . Ah!" On a gesture of frustration she rattled off a phrase in French.

"In opposition," Fallon told her.

"Yes, thank you. They are not in opposition. I am known to lie. To a lover, when it is . . . simple? I do not lie about life and death, about dark and light. I may lie to you," she said with a gay smile. "But not about that."

When Lana came back, she took the cloth bag offered, slipped it into her pocket after sliding back into her coat. "Thank you, very much. I will have a gift for you when I see you next. And I would send to you General D'Arcy if we proceed with the alliance. You will find him very clever."

"Safe travels, Vivienne."

"And to you, Fallon Swift. Madame."

Fallon watched her walk out, move to her men. And, standing between them, flash.

"She's . . . interesting," Lana decided.

"And complicated. She has shadows, but she isn't of the dark. Not like them. Not quite like us. An alliance. Two thousand troops."

Fallon shut the door. "She has more than two thousand or she wouldn't have offered two thousand."

"Now that you say it, that wouldn't surprise me. She's canny. Canny is a good ally."

"It could be. Let's see what else anyone's heard about

her, what else we can find out. It's going to be worth, at least, meeting this general."

"You're likely to get an argument from some quarters."

"What else is new?" As they started back, she looked at her mother. "From you?"

"No. You're going to need alliances. New York isn't the end of it. You never told me about the black dragon again."

"It was in a vision dream, with Petra."

Lana stopped, gripped Fallon's arm. "Petra."

"She rode it, I think. It's not all the way clear, and I wasn't sure until now it was real. I need to talk to Mallick."

"Let's take some food down," Lana suggested. "An alliance with a dragon queen might go down easier with some stew."

"You've got a point."

CHAPTER FIFTEEN

While the others ate, Fallon took Mallick and her father aside, related the meeting with Vivienne.

"I've heard of her," Mallick confirmed. "Bits and pieces, rumors, gossip. From what I know, she has her realm, her palace and people, and they're loyal to her. She is, or has been, content with that. If she's come to you I suspect she's concerned about invasion."

"We push the DUs out of New York," Simon agreed. "They may head north. She'd be more vulnerable. You're serious about the dragon?"

"Yeah, and she's impressive."

"Adding a dragon and two thousand to our ranks against New York wouldn't hurt a thing. And," he added, "it's likely she has more than the two she offered."

It added to Fallon's confidence that she and her father thought alike. "Exactly."

"Just as likely, she has other alliances."

"I wondered about that, too. She's both forthcoming and cagey. Clearly, she wants to preserve her own, and why wouldn't she? If her advisers estimate we're moving on New York within a year, maybe six months? The enemy likely thinks the same. If we can add her in, and potentially others she's hooked with, I'm looking at six to eight weeks."

"You didn't tell her that?"

"I'm standing here with two men who helped teach *me* to be cagey, so no. And we'll just keep that to ourselves until we're sure of her. Can you go?" she asked Mallick. "She talked about sending one of her generals here to negotiate, but I want a better sense of her and her people, her place. You could get that. She'd respect you, and you wouldn't fall for any bullshit."

"Of course. When?"

"As soon as possible. She popped in here, we'll return the favor. I'd like you to take Travis with you." She looked at Simon. "As an empath he'll feel as much as see or hear. And he's diplomatic, political."

"He'll love it, and he's a good choice. I'm not going to say Mallick and Travis can't handle themselves if anything goes shaky, but you need another, at least one more."

"I was thinking Meda. Female, and one who led her own tribe. And Arlys. Our chronicler. Travis will see, hear, feel, but Arlys won't miss a detail. She also knows how to negotiate and lead."

"Well chosen. Do you agree, Simon?"

"Yeah, it's a good mix."

"Great. Let's make it happen."

Everyone had a voice, Fallon thought later. The fact that she would defend that right with sword and shield didn't make it less of a pain in her ass.

Still, after the grumblings, objections, second-guessings, she had her negotiating team set and preparing to head north.

As the commanders left, Fallon broke away to find Mick.

"Got a question." Duncan took her arm, drew her outside. "Why aren't you sending me to Quebec?"

"A couple reasons." She looked over toward the barracks, but saw no sign of Mick. "First, Vivienne would try to seduce you."

"Jealous?"

She looked back, nearly laughed at his smug expression. "If I thought you'd fall into her bed, I wouldn't invite you into mine. But it would be a distraction, and this needs to go smooth. Second, it's a good balance. Third, I'd like Travis to work with Mallick more. And last, you, Tonia, and I are going on a hunt."

"We are?"

"For a black dragon."

"Now we're talking. When?"

"Tonight. But right now I need to talk to Mick."

"He took off," Duncan told her. "When you were talking to Arlys and Chuck about digging up more intel on the redhead."

"But—" Not even a good-bye, she thought. "I can't leave it this way. I need to fix this."

"You can't fix everything, Fallon. The guy's in love with you. It ought to piss me off but, hell, you've got to like him. Plus, he fights like a son of a bitch."

Maybe she couldn't fix everything, but this? This was different. "I have to try. I can't explain how sad and lonely and angry I was in those first weeks with Mallick, how much I missed my family. And Mick was there. It mattered. He matters."

"I get it, but—"

"What should I say to him?"

Thrown off, Duncan stared at her. "You want me to tell you what to say to a guy who's in love with you?

Jesus." Shoving his hands in his pockets, he paced away. "Damn it, Fallon, you're mine." Eyes hot, he strode back to her, gripped her face in his hands. "Mine."

How could the words, the anger in them both thrill and infuriate her at the same time? "You don't—"

"Hell I don't. You're mine. And I'm yours."

With that, the thrill drowned out everything else. She took his wrists as his mouth came down on hers, felt his pulse beat in time with her own.

She eased back, brushed her fingers down his cheek. "That's the point. So help me, please, help me try. What would you need to hear when someone you loved couldn't love you back the same way? I've hurt him, Duncan. What should I tell him to ease the hurt?"

"Damn it." He shoved his hands in his pockets again. "Tell him the truth, and don't use any bullshit like 'it's not you, it's me.'"

Baffled, she threw up her hands. "But it is me."

"Don't go there, it's insulting. Don't pull the can't-we-just-be-friends line out, either."

"But—"

"Did you ask for my help here?" he shot back.

"Yes." Still, she raked her fingers through her hair, twice. "Yes. All right."

"Just don't do the let's-be-pals crap unless you want to stick a knife in his ribs. Tell him straight. He matters, he's always going to matter. And for Christ's sake, don't expect him to snap back like a bowstring."

"Okay. All right. I'll go to The Beach, talk to him now."

"He didn't go with his crew. He and Mallick flashed out."

"Oh. Oh, I know where he is. If you could get Tonia, we'll talk when I get back."

"And go dragon hunting."

"Yeah. I need to try to fix this first." She laid a hand on his cheek again. "Thanks."

He dragged her in for another kiss, and if it was staking a claim, so the hell what? "I'm not going to say anytime because this better be the last time."

"Okay."

"Don't leave room for hope—it'll just hurt more."

She nodded, stepped back, flashed.

"Because who the hell could ever get over you?" he murmured, then turned when Simon came out of the house, gave him a cool-eyed stare.

"Looks like we need to have a conversation."

Though he'd rather have faced a horde of DUs, Duncan braced himself. "I guess we do."

Fallon walked through the green light of the faerie glade toward the pool where Mick sat cross-legged, brooding into the mists rising over the water. He bounded to his feet, and when he saw her, the hand on the hilt of his short sword fell away.

"You didn't say good-bye."

"You were busy."

"Mick." When she started toward him, he stiffened, so she stopped. "I'm sorry."

"For what?" His shrug was a sharp jerk of movement. "For not being with me like you are with Duncan?"

"Don't ask me to be sorry for loving him, because I can't, but I'm sorry it hurts you."

"Why him?" Mick demanded while the pixie lights blinked nervously in the green shadows. "Why not me?"

The truth, Fallon reminded herself, and found it. "Because what I feel for you is different. It's real and it's deep and it's true, but it's not what I feel for him."

"So, I'm just your good old pal Mick," he said bitterly.

"You're the one who was with me when I found each of my spirit animals. You're the one who made me laugh when my heart ached for my family. You're the boy who gave me my first kiss, and the man who fights with me. You gave me my first tribe outside of my family. You're an essential in my life. You always will be."

"But you're never going to love me."

"I'm always going to love you. You know that."

"It's not the same."

"No, it's not. But it's real and deep and true."

"I thought maybe there was a chance." He looked away from her, out over the misted water. "Now I know there's not." He turned back, met her eyes, but kept a wall between them.

"I'll fight with my last breath for The One. But I can't be around Fallon right now. Mallick will get me back to The Beach, and we'll be ready to strike New York when you say. You could pass any orders through Jojo for now."

"All right. I— If you and what you feel didn't matter, I wouldn't have come. If you and what you feel didn't matter, I wouldn't go. Blessed be, Mick."

She didn't go directly home, but called to Laoch. She took an hour for herself to clear her head, and her heart.

She flew over fields, some fallow with winter, others overgrown with neglect. And over roads and highways with cars and trucks long since abandoned, bridges crumbling into rivers. Herds of deer and wild horses roamed freely.

A hawk soared nearby, then dived with an echoing cry to claim its prey. After that small death, silence. A world of silence.

Here and there she spotted signs of humans, small camps and communities, and the glint of solar panels on roofs as the winter sun beamed down.

And the ash and smoke left in another by a raid.

As a matter of course more than hope, she turned Laoch toward the smoke to check for any survivors. She heard screams, engines, and through the smoke saw a man sprawled on the ground while Raiders circled a woman on their bikes.

Three bikes, two with double riders, she noted. And all of them armed. An even better way, she thought, to clear the mind and heart.

Like the hawk, she dived on Laoch.

As she leaped from her mount, sword flashing, she sent the first bike and its two riders flying. Spun and used her shield to block a peppering of bullets before decapitating the lone rider.

The last whipped a tight circle, the male riding pillion jumping off to try to take her from behind while the female driver, dozens of braids streaming, shrieked, eyes mad with the kill, and barreled straight toward her.

Idiot, Fallon thought, leaped aside, flipped, and slammed her shield into the woman's face. Spun again, planted a kick in the belly of the one trying to take her flank.

He stumbled back, but regained his balance. The female, blood spilling down her face, got to her feet, drew a knife. One of the first riders limped forward while he shouldered the rifle he'd had slung over his back.

Just like fighting ghosts at Mallick's cottage, she thought.

"You still have a chance to live," she said as they circled her. "Put down your weapons and surrender."

In answer the female let out a war cry and leaped, the gunman fired, and the third slashed down with a blade.

She downed the woman with a sweep of her sword at the knees, flung the bullets back at the shooter with a punch of magic. Even as she blocked the slashing sword with her own, more shots rang out.

His body jerked in place as blood bloomed on his chest. And he fell.

The woman they'd circled knelt, the gun of the headless rider clutched in both hands. Her face, gray with shock, dark eyes wide with it, held frozen in a grimace of fury.

"You won't need that now," Fallon said gently. "It's over now."

The woman dropped it as if it burned. "Johnny!" She scrambled up, ran to the man who lay sprawled in the ash-covered dirt. "They killed my Johnny!"

"Let me see." She had to push the woman's hands away to search for a heartbeat, for light. "He's alive. Let me help."

He'd been shot, but the wound wasn't mortal. He'd been beaten unmercifully, and those injuries could be if she didn't heal enough to bring him back.

"Help him. Please help him."

"I am. I will. He's Johnny?"

"Yes, yes, Johnny." She cradled his head, kissed his battered face.

"What's your name?"

"I'm Lucia. Lucy."

"Talk to him, Lucy. Let him know you're all right."

While Lucy murmured, wept, stroked, Fallon opened to the most serious injuries, began, as she'd been taught, to heal slowly, layer by layer.

The skull, fractured. Her own head roared with pain, forced her to back off even more. Slow, so slow, so careful, mending, easing. Jaw broken, and the nose, cheekbones. Wrist, arm, ribs.

When he moaned, stirred, Fallon eased back.

"It's enough."

"No, no, please. Help him."

"I did. Trust me. He's stable enough now. I can get you to a doctor, to healers. He'll do better there. You're hurt, too."

"Just a little. It's Johnny—"

"I know a place where you'll both get help, both be safe. Laoch!"

He trotted over, and at her signal lowered himself. "Get on." Fallon read fear in Lucy's eyes, but she climbed onto Laoch's back. Carefully, Fallon lifted Johnny, stirring the air to bring him up so he lay over Laoch's back.

"You . . . You're of the Uncanny."

"That's right." Fallon glanced back at the bodies. No life left. Their choice, but still she wouldn't leave them for the crows and vultures. With a flick of her head, she set them to flame, then mounted. "I'm Fallon."

"Johnny told stories, but I didn't believe in them. I didn't think you were real."

"Now you know. Don't be afraid. I won't let you fall."

As they rose up, Lucy leaned over, wrapped her arms around Johnny—to protect him, Fallon thought, as much as herself. "He wanted to come to you, to fight with you, but I begged him to stay with me. And now—"

"He'll be all right. You were brave. You could have run when I fought them. You stayed, and fought back."

"When they came, Johnny told me to run, to hide, but I wouldn't leave him. He wouldn't leave me. He could have left me when they came. He can run so fast, but he stayed, he tried to fight. He's of the Uncanny, like you."

"An elf, yes."

"We ran away. My grandmother, she lived through the Doom. I was only a baby, and she protected me when everyone died. She's very strict, and doesn't believe magick can be good, like Johnny. She isn't bad, she wouldn't hurt anyone, but—"

"I understand."

"'You have to stick with your own kind, Lucia,' she'd say. Even though once she helped hide a family from the PWs, and the little boy had wings. She says they're evil, the PWs, but the Uncannys aren't like us, and we have to stick with our own kind."

"One day she might see differently."

"That's what Johnny says."

She landed outside the clinic in New Hope. "Wait here. I'll get a doctor."

Fallon ran inside, spotted Hannah.

"You're bleeding."

"Not me. Maybe a little," she realized. "I have a man outside. Gunshot wound, severe beating. I need help getting him in."

"I'll get a gurney. Jonah!" she shouted as she dashed for the gurney. "Fallon has wounded outside. GSW."

He came on the run, headed straight out with Fallon.

"He had a fractured skull, and I did what I could. I hesitated to do more. The GSW's not fatal, but he lost a lot of blood." She rattled off the other injuries she'd found.

Hannah maneuvered the gurney while Jonah and Fallon lifted him down and onto it.

"Please, don't let him die."

Jonah secured Johnny on the gurney, searched for life or death, then looked up at Lucy. "He's not going to die. Let's get him inside, Hannah."

"They're doctors?" With the awkwardness of someone unused to riding, Lucy struggled to dismount.

"They're medicals, and really good ones. Believe me, if Jonah looked you in the eye and said Johnny wasn't going to die, he's not going to die. Go on in."

"You're not coming?"

"You're okay now. I'll see you both tomorrow."

"Thank you. I need to— Thank you," she said again as she ran inside.

Because Laoch wanted a run, Fallon rode home at a steady gallop. Fields, she thought, as she had when she'd flown, but while some rested for winter, horses, cattle, goats, sheep roamed. And mists curled out from the Tropics, where summer never ended.

The maintenance committee plowed the roads, and would again, she knew, as she smelled snow in the air. And smoke from chimneys, growing things in greenhouses. She could feel the pulse of life here, not just in the trees and grasses that slept, in the spruce and pine, but inside the scatter of houses where people cooked or crafted, tended children, read books. Where they argued or laughed.

So different, she thought, from the emptiness she'd flown over, so different from the mindless violence that roamed that emptiness looking for prey—not like the hawk for food and survival, but for sport.

It lifted her mood, that pulse, and lifted it higher when Taibhse swooped overhead and Faol Ban streaked out of the trees to run alongside her.

She pulled up outside the stables, slid off the alicorn to give the wolf a rub. "We'll hunt tomorrow." She looked over at the owl when he perched on a branch. "In the morning, we'll go on a hunt together, for fun. But tonight, we'll go on a different sort of hunt."

And thinking of it, she took Laoch into the stable

so he could rest and feed. She found her father inside, grooming Grace.

"I took her out for a while." He continued to brush, his back to Fallon, as he spoke. "We both needed a ride."

"Me, too. Well, a flight. Head-clearing time. So much talk. Fighting's a hell of a lot easier than talking about it."

"Maybe, but there's still some talking to do. You and me," he said as he stepped over to the stall where she rubbed down Laoch with a cloth. "I need to— Whose blood is that? What happened?"

She looked down, saw the blood on her jacket, her pants. "Crap. Raiders. Five of them about two hundred miles west of here. I spotted them after they'd burned out a couple—young male elf and his NM mate. They're at the clinic. She's not seriously injured, but he'd been shot and beaten."

"Are you hurt?"

"No. Might've picked up a couple of bruises. They were stupid. Now they're dead." She rubbed her cheek against Laoch's. "I gave them a choice, they chose death."

"You saved two lives."

"Yes." Lives taken, lives saved. She went back to the rubdown. "I saved two lives. They're in love, those two lives. Her grandmother doesn't approve of mixed relationships, so they ran off together. I think they'll be fine now."

He set a hand on her shoulder. "We need to talk."

"Is something wrong?" She set the cloth aside. "I wasn't gone that long."

"I saw you leave. I was about to come out, happened to see you and Duncan."

"Oh." Then it hit her. "Oh," she repeated. "Dad—"

"Hold on. Just hold on."

Like Duncan—so like Duncan, she realized in a *huh* moment—he shoved his hands in his pockets, paced away, paced back.

"You're a grown-up," he began, a war clear in those changeable hazel eyes she loved. "More. You're a warrior, a leader. You're not an idiot. You've never been, I don't know, flighty or careless, and . . ."

He stopped, and with his face covered in frustration, stared at her. "You're still my baby, damn it. You're still my girl, so I've got things to say."

"You disapprove." And his disapproval, his more than anything or anyone, would cut her to the bone.

"No. Yes. Shit! Yes, on a general level, because my baby, damn it. Specifically Duncan? No. I'm not an idiot, either."

"You're not making sense."

"Why the hell should I have to make sense?" His hands flew out of his pockets, into the air. "Sense, my ass, when I look out and see—and realize—"

"I thought Mom had, you know, prepared you."

"Yeah, yeah." Hands back in pockets, more pacing. "She reminded me, but I didn't really . . . I just figured, okay, a little puppy love. It doesn't matter I knew better somewhere in my head, it was a nice buffer until I look out and see his hands on you, and the two of you. My baby.

"Buffer?" He took his hands out again, mimed an explosion. "And I get, on some level, why you talked to your mom about it and not me, but you didn't, so it smacks me in the face, and I've got about thirty seconds to adjust before I grill Duncan."

"You . . . you grilled Duncan?"

"It's my fucking job, Fallon. My goddamn job."

"Yes." Touched, amused, a little horrified, she got an

apple out of the bin, carefully cut it in half for Laoch and Grace. "It is. How'd he do?"

"He did all right," Simon replied. "He's not an asshole."

"Good to know."

"Maybe I knew this was coming. I've seen the way he looks at you, from the time we got here, when you're not looking. I know that look because I used to look at your mother when she wasn't looking the same damn way. But—"

"Really?"

"I'm not going there, adding to the damn stars in your eyes. It's too much for me. I know he's a good soldier. I know he's a good son, a good man. I know when he tells me he loves you, he believes it."

"So do I. I love him. I had feelings for him pulling at me since the first time I saw him in a dream. The reality's stronger. I know he's loyal to The One, to the light. There's no question of it. But he sees me, Dad. He sees Fallon Swift, and he loves her."

She stepped to him. "You were the first one to hold me. You were the first man to love me. To love Fallon, just Fallon. You showed me, all my life, what it was to be a man with strength and heart and courage. I couldn't love a man who didn't pass the bar you set. I could want, but I couldn't love. So I know, with all that's asked of me, all that's happened before, all that's to come, I've been blessed. You're the love of my life, Dad. And now I've been given another."

She put her arms around him, nestled her head on his shoulder. "Two loves of my life."

He wrapped around her hard. "You're still my baby."

"I was born in the lightning, in the storm, as it was foretold, and your hands were there to bring me into the world."

He eased back to look into her eyes, into the visions.

"You were there for the mother, there for the child, and you loved without demands or restrictions. That is love pure. It is light beyond power. And with the sun of that morning, after the storm, while the mother slept, you held me on your heart, and I knew you. You are the father given me, a gift from the gods."

She came back, let out a breath. Smiled at him. "Daddy."

And like Duncan, so like Duncan, he just lowered his forehead to hers.

With Simon, Lana stood in the cold with the first snow-flakes drifting while Fallon called Taibhse to her arm.

"Are you sure about this? We could come with you."

"It has to be the three of us. Well, six." She laid a hand on Laoch's neck while Faol Ban sat at her feet.

"Maybe you could have Mom and Hannah over for a while," Tonia suggested. "I think Mom's having some sad because of where we're going."

"Of course." Thinking of her friend, Lana pushed at the hair spilling loose over her shoulders. "I should've thought of it. Are you going to be warm enough? It's bound to be colder there, and probably damp."

"We're fine." Fallon already wore the knit cap and scarf at her mother's insistence. "It's really a scouting mission."

"With a black dragon in the mix," Simon added.

"If we're lucky. We'll be back as soon as we can. Don't worry more than you can help it. Ready?"

She caught the look her father sent Duncan, nearly laughed before they flashed.

And there the dark held deep, the wind sliced like

angry blades, cutting through the trees that bowed and creaked, throwing up the snow lying thick on the fields so it flew in ragged curtains.

There, things breathed in the night, in the dark, that watched. That waited.

There the circle stood, its center black and slick as oil.

"My gods," Tonia uttered. "Feel that? It's like a black heart beating."

"I want to say we can close it, we could try, but . . ." With the wind blowing, streaming through his hair, Duncan stared into that heart and shook his head.

"We'd fail. I don't know why it can't be done now, and over. I just know we'd fail if we tried now." Fallon glanced toward the woods. "And if we fail we wouldn't be able to try again."

"It lives here. There are some animal tracks." After tugging her own cap down on her head, Tonia gestured. "But not nearly as many as you'd expect. And not one sign of a human."

The crows came to circle and scream. On Fallon's arm, Taibhse, his great eyes golden flames, stirred restlessly. "Not yet," she told him. "Their day will come, but not yet."

"It's in there."

Tonia looked toward the woods where Duncan stared. "Then let's go say hello."

"Yeah." Fallon circled a hand, conjured a bright ball that illuminated the snow, tossed the dark woods into relief. "Let's see how it likes a little light. Stay together," she said as they trudged through knee-deep snow. "Separating us would be a win."

"It's not going to win." Duncan drew his sword when they reached the edge between light and dark.

With the next step, the air dropped from blustery

cold to biting and bitter. Ice coated the trees in lizard scales that cracked and re-formed with a sound like gunshots through the deadening silence.

"No tracks." The thickness, the fog unrolling over the snow, turned Tonia's voice into a muffled murmur.

"No life," Fallon responded. She pressed her hand to the trunk of a tree, found no beat. She gestured to Duncan. When he pierced the trunk with his sword, a black liquid bubbled out of the wound.

The air stank with sulfur.

"It's taken these woods." Calmly, he cleaned his sword with snow. "Whatever's unlucky enough to wander in here doesn't wander out again."

Fallon guided the light left, right. "We'll pick a direction and—"

The wolf picked for them, moved left. She urged the owl to Laoch's saddle so she could have her sword in hand. So they followed the white wolf through a world of dead trees that shivered in their scaled coats of ice, through brambles crawling with thorns hidden under mounds of snow and creeping fog, through silence that echoed with the hollow breath of the dark.

"There's something." Neck prickling, Fallon gestured to the dark stain on the snow, a scatter of entrails. "Frozen solid, but they can't have been here very long. There's no snow over them, no snow over the blood."

"And where's the rest of it?" Duncan wondered. "It's not enough, more like another animal dragged a few bits here. And the bits are too big for a rabbit or fox. More like—"

"Human. A girl." Fallon fumbled out a hand for Duncan's as Tonia's came to her shoulder. And with their power joined with hers, she saw clearly. "Sixteen, only sixteen. Lured away in the night. Pretty music, pretty lights."

The hair on Faol Ban's nape rose up as he let out a growl.

Fallon snapped back from the vision, scanned the woods.

"We're being stalked," Tonia whispered, and nocked an arrow.

The wolf, black as the night, slunk out of the dark. Then another, and another. Thirteen, Fallon counted, that surrounded them with bared fangs and mad eyes ringed with red.

"They're not real."

"Those aren't illusions," Duncan said.

"No, they'll rip us to shreds, but they're born of blood magicks."

"If magick created them, magick can destroy them. I've got a quiver full of bespelled arrows ready to prove that theory."

"Get ready," Fallon advised, and Duncan enflamed his sword.

When the first wolf sprang, Tonia's arrow struck its heart. Faol Ban, gold collar burning bright, leaped at another's throat. Guarding Duncan's back, Fallon impaled another, heard the scream of one more trampled under Laoch's hooves.

The air seemed to howl, fetid with smoke as, like the tree, black ooze bubbled from the wounds until only that black pool remained.

Duncan set two burning. While they writhed and howled, he spun to protect his sister from another. And was spared the effort as Taibhse tore it open with talons.

Fallon struck down the last, then stroked a hand

down Faol Ban's fur. "They took a beautiful animal and twisted it into something evil."

"They?" Duncan repeated.

"Whoever lured the girl. There. That's what they were guarding."

"Someone broke a trail." Tonia moved closer. "Magickally, right? It might as well have been plowed. Why?"

"To make it easier for the victim to get where they wanted her to go. One set of prints, human." Fallon looked to Tonia, the best woodsman among them, for confirmation.

"Yeah, and, Jesus, she was barefoot."

"Maybe she's still alive."

He would always think first of rescue, Fallon thought, though he had to know no one lived in this place now but the six of them.

"We'll follow the trail. They lured her from her bed," Fallon continued as they walked. "Out of the window. In a trance, and she dreamed she flew like a faerie."

"Why have her walk once she was in here?" Tonia wondered.

"For sport." Grim, because he did know, Duncan watched for a new attack.

"For sport," Fallon agreed. "And so as they let her wake from the trance she'd be afraid and confused. Fear adds power to the ritual."

As they moved deeper, they saw symbols hanging from branches or carved into trees. Now she felt a beat, heavy and deep. The pulse of black magicks.

"What holds this place doesn't perform rituals." With a lash of temper, Duncan sliced down symbols, sent them burning. "It has rituals performed for it. They brought the girl here, offered her."

Fallon touched his arm, felt the ripple of tensed muscle nothing would soothe. "You brought me to the stones the first time so I'd make my choice. I chose to fight to stop this. We will stop it."

"I know it." Though far from soothed, he took her hand in his. "I know it."

"We need more light." Tonia added hers to Fallon's.

In the glow they saw the circle ahead, one burned deep into the floor of the forest. And the rough altar of stone in its center. What remained of the girl lay splayed over it.

"We couldn't save her, but we can destroy this."

Duncan drew his hand from Fallon's. "We're not leaving her in this fucking place. I'll get her."

"Duncan—"

He whirled on Fallon. "I said I'll get her."

Because she understood his fury, she didn't flinch from it. "I have a blanket in the saddlebags. You could wrap her in it. Give her to Laoch. We'll take her out with us."

"Okay. Sorry. I'm sorry."

Fallon just shook her head, turned to Tonia. "We'll destroy the symbols with fire, then the circle. There's salt in my bag, too. An athame, some fresh water, some crystals. Blood magick did this, and blood magicks— ours, blood of the light—will destroy it. We can do what we need to do."

Her own heart sick with helpless rage, Tonia watched Duncan begin to wrap the remains in the blanket. "He's always hated seeing innocents hurt. It's harder yet since Denzel."

"I ask myself why wasn't I pulled here before this happened, and there's no answer." She shot out a hand, released her own rage to send symbols flaming. "There's no damn answer."

When they joined hands, mixed the blood of the Tuatha de Danann, said the words, brought the light, something roared through the woods. Not in pain, but fury.

They didn't hurt it, not yet, Fallon thought as their joined powers poured through her. Only angered it. But they would hurt it. They would.

"And here the light burns through the dark. And no more will the earth carry its mark. By our blood, by our power we cleanse this space."

The altar broke, crumbled, and the earth they opened swallowed its curling dust.

"So from this day, from this hour, no innocent life can be taken in this place. Hear the voices of we three. As we will, so mote it be."

And they salted the earth.

"Its power's less. Not gone," Tonia said, sniffing the air like a wolf. "Not gone, but less."

"We need to find out who or what did this. We shouldn't take her back to New Hope." His eyes drenched in sorrow now that his wrath had dissolved, Duncan looked at the body. "She's probably got family around here. We can't just take her. And I . . . I want to go to the house, the farmhouse. I want to see it before we go back."

"So do I. Maybe—maybe it's stupid, but there might be something in there we could take back to Mom. Just something she could have."

"I don't think it's stupid. It's loving," Fallon said. "We need loving after this."

Something loving, she thought, to take away the sorrow. "We'll go to the house. And after, we'll try to find some people. Someone who knows about the girl."

"And about any DUs in the area," Duncan added. "It won't be the last time we come here, so we should get the lay of the land before we come again."

"Yeah, we should know our battleground." Fallon

looked around, the dead wood, the ice-slicked trees, the salted ground. "It'll gather again, and someone will find a way to feed it again. But for now, we're done here."

Again, she put a hand on Duncan's arm. "If we can't find anyone who knows her, we'll bury her at your family's farm."

CHAPTER SIXTEEN

Dark, deserted houses were commonplace in the world Duncan knew. But this one, this rambling house with its time-weathered outbuildings, blank, blind windows, and overgrown land, stood apart from all the rest.

Family had built this with stone, wood, sweat, lived here, slept and woke here, worked the land acre by acre, generation by generation. Until.

"I half expected it to be burned down." As she felt much the same as her twin, Tonia took his hand. "Or torn down for materials. It just looks like it's . . ."

"Waiting," he finished. "Well, wait's over."

As they approached the back door, Fallon gave them a moment, then followed. The spirit animals would guard the body.

He'd expected to find it locked, but the door opened with a long creak. He swore he felt the house itself release a long-held breath. He brought the light, a quiet one, and stepped inside.

In that quiet light, beneath the dust of time, he saw a large, tidy kitchen. Counters cleared, a table with a pottery bowl—bright blue under the dust—centered on it and chairs neatly tucked in. Curious, he opened a cupboard, found stacks of dishes filmed with spiderwebs. In another, glasses.

Tonia opened the refrigerator. Empty, scrubbed clean so the faintest whiff of lemon wafted out with the sour smell of disuse.

"There's a pantry here—cleaned out," Fallon said. "No food left to spoil or go to waste."

"But dishes, glasses, pots, pans, all of that." Tonia continued to explore. "Someone survived, at least long enough to do all this. To clean, to take the food out."

"It's been alone a long time. Waiting a long time." He could feel it, both the grief and the joy. "They had pride in their home, in the land, in the legacy."

"You're the legacy," Fallon said. "You and Tonia. Hannah, too. This is yours. They left it for you."

"It's full of them. The voices." As they murmured inside him, he moved on, into a dining room. "They'd have had that last dinner here, New Year's Eve. Mom said they always had a big dinner before the party."

The room held an old buffet. Candlestands and what he thought must be pieces passed down still stood on it among the dust and cobwebs. A cabinet with dulled glass doors displayed what had been the company dishes, or those for special occasions.

"The six of them that night?" The image of those company dishes carefully set ran clear through Tonia's inner vision. "Can you see them?"

He could, ghosts around the table, with a sparkle of champagne in glasses, fat pheasants on a platter, bowls and dishes holding food as they toasted each other. A fire crackling, and the scents of the roasted birds, the home-cooked dishes, perfume, candle wax.

"The farmer at the head," he continued. "His wife

at the foot. The twin brothers, the wives who are like sisters. They're friends here as well as family. Their children and children's children aren't here tonight, but scattered after the holiday visit. Not Katie, who had to stay home with the twins she's brewing inside her. So it's the six here, old friends, good family, toasting the end of the year, not knowing it would be the end of all."

"They loved each other." Tonia, tears in her eyes, tipped her head to Duncan's shoulder. "You can see it, feel it."

"It's already in him. Ross MacLeod." Duncan gestured to a seat. "He doesn't know, but it's in him, dark and deadly."

"In all before the plates are cleared. I'm sorry." Fallon kept a step away, letting the twins have their time. Because it made her unbearably sad, she whisked away the dust, the cobwebs.

Duncan met her eyes, a world of sorrow in his, then moved on.

The living room—or would they call it a parlor?—proved as tidy as the rest. Wood stacked neat in the hearth with kindling beneath as if waiting for the match to send it crackling.

Tonia walked to the mantel, took down a framed photo, wiped away the dust. "Duncan. This must have been taken the year before, or maybe the year before that. It's all of them, with the Christmas tree. Mom. This must be . . . Duncan."

He studied it with her. Hugh and Millie—the farmers. His grandparents, his great-uncle and great-aunt. Cousins they'd never known. His mother—so young! And beside her, his arm over her shoulders . . . "Our father."

"We've never seen a picture of him," Tonia said.

"When Mom went into labor, she didn't have time to take anything. New York was in chaos, and she was alone. She didn't take anything when she drove to the hospital. Her Tony was already gone. He's so handsome."

"You should take it to her." Again, Fallon kept a few steps back, gave them room. "Nothing would mean more than a picture of her family together."

They went through the rest of the house, finding each room carefully left. Beds made, towels folded, clothes hung or tucked into drawers.

"We'll come back," Duncan decided. "After it's done we'll bring Mom back, and Hannah. They'll want that."

"So do I." Tonia squeezed his hand. "I want to see it in the light. It's a good place, Duncan. It needs to live again."

When they stepped back outside, Fallon drew her sword. The hooded figure standing beside Laoch held up her hands. "I'm no harm to you. My granny sent me to fetch you." Her voice, thick with the country burr of Scotland, shook a little as she eyed the sword. "I only waited, not wanting to intrude."

When she drew back her hood, Fallon saw a young girl, around the same age as the one they'd found on the altar. A young faerie, she realized, with bright hair, eyes wide with apprehension, and no dark in her.

"Your granny?"

"Aye. She said you'd come, and for me to wait and ask you to visit. We're just down the road a bit. Dorcas Frazier, she is, and I'm Nessa. She knew your family, and would dearly love to have a visit with you. Would you come, please? She's a hundred and two, you see, and I wouldn't have her coming out in the cold."

"Of course we'll come." Fallon sheathed her sword.

"She'll be so pleased. It's not far, and it's safe enough now."

"Now?" Duncan repeated as they walked with her, the animals following.

"Aye, now." She glanced back at the blanketed burden Laoch carried. "I think that must be Aileen. She was a friend, and I feared for her when she couldn't be found."

"Do you know who did this to her?" Duncan demanded.

"It's best to talk to Granny, but those who did it are gone for now. You're the twins. Katie and Tony's. Granny knew them, and your grandparents, and the rest of the MacLeods."

They walked the dark road, past a cottage or two. Fallon saw candlelight gleaming, smelled smoke from chimneys, and animals bedded down in stalls and pens.

"How many are you?"

"We're near to a hundred, but it's a quiet place. Some move on, and some move in, you could say. There's good land to farm, and good hunting, fishing."

"Any trouble with DUs?" Tonia asked.

"I don't ken."

"Magickals," Fallon explained, "who bring harm."

"The Dark Ones. Granny will tell you. She has such stories." She looked shyly at Fallon. "She's told me many of you. This is our cottage. The rest of our family is there, and just a bit farther up the road. But I stay with Granny and help her tend the cottage and the animals."

She led the way to a pretty little house with magickal charms painted on the door, and others hanging from the eaves to click and clack and chime in the wind.

"You are very welcome here," Nessa said, and opened the door.

Though the hearth—the heart of the room—was

small, the fire roared in it. Candles lit the room with both charm and cheer.

The old woman sat near the fire, a plaid blanket over her lap, a red shawl around her shoulders despite the heat pumping. She had a thin, fluffy bowl of white hair around a face mapped with lines, and eyes as clear and blue as a summer lake.

Those eyes clouded with tears as she held out a hand. "You brought them, my good lassie. We'll have whiskey, won't we? And some cake. Please be welcome and sit. Oh, Katie's babies. How excited your granny was for you to come into the world. A good woman was Angie MacLeod, I hope you know. You have your grandfather's eyes, girl. Sit, sit."

"I'm Tonia." She took the hand offered, then a stool by the chair. "Antonia."

"For your father. I met Tony more than once. Oh, a handsome one, and a good heart inside him with a sense of fun along with it. So in love was he with your mother, and how he made her smile. Did they live, child? I haven't been able to see."

"He died before we were born."

"I'm sorry for it. Rest his soul. Your mother?"

"She's well."

"And that's a blessing. And you, boy, with your father's fine looks and your mother's eyes."

"Duncan. It's nice to meet you, Mrs. Frazier."

"Duncan, for the MacLeod end of things. You'll give your mother my best, won't you? The best from old Dorcas Frazier, who lived just down the road and used to give her ginger biscuits."

"Yes, ma'am."

"Your family were friends to me. I knew the Duncan you're named for. Flirted with him when we were younger than young. Sit here now, there's a lad."

She drew a breath and, clear again, her eyes met Fallon's. "I wondered so many times why I would live and live, wake every morning to a new day. So many new days. Some reasons, I thought, were for my Nessa. How could I leave my sweet lassie? Now I know I lived and lived and lived some more so to welcome the MacLeods back home. And to welcome The One into mine. Bright blessings on you, Fallon Swift."

"And on you, Dorcas Frazier."

She took Mrs. Frazier's hand and marveled at how bold and bright the light burned in a body so stiff and bent with age. She took the chair offered as Nessa passed out whiskey and cake.

"The whiskey's good," Mrs. Frazier told them. "We still know how to make it around here. And the cake my own Nessa baked just this morning."

"You said we'd have guests tonight, and to put a little extra love into it."

Her grandmother cackled. "So I did. My Nessa is full of love. To the love, we'll drink then, and to the light."

They lifted glasses, and Fallon learned the whiskey was indeed good.

"You'll have questions. You sit now, Nessa, for you should hear the questions and what answers I can give."

"How is it the house hasn't been touched? There are things inside," Duncan continued, "that would be of use to you and others."

"The house is of the MacLeods. Those of us who come from here respect that, and those who've come since are told. I think the house itself holds others out. It let you in, you ken. You're blood, after all. Hugh died within two days after your family left for home and for London on business. Millie, ah, a strong woman was she, lived two more. I nursed her, as when the sickness came,

I only became stronger. So I nursed her, and then Jamie, your cousin."

"You cleaned the house," Tonia said. "Cleaned it, made their beds."

"As a friend would do for a friend. My son and my granddaughter, who lived, helped with it. We took the food, but nothing else."

"Thank you." Duncan took her hand again and, following his heart, kissed her thin fingers. "For tending to our family, and our home."

"We buried them, and so many others, in the church-yard. There was hope in some that it would pass and things would be as they were. Fear as well, and no word from outside for some time. Some fled, never to be seen again. Others came and stayed. Those like we here, and those who accepted that magick was back in the world.

"I know the day you were born," she said to Fallon. "I saw it that night, that last night with the party lights and the celebrating. I took Ross MacLeod's hand, and saw. A good man, and none of his doing, not of his knowing. But it would start with him. And on the night he died, in that moment the dark struck, your light burst free, sparked by the blood of the Tuatha de Danann, the blood the MacLeods would pass down to theirs. You would be born in the storm, and delivered not into the hands of the one who sired you, but into the hands of one meant to rear you."

She sipped more whiskey. "You've known loss, all of you, and still so young. You'll know more. Loss can shake faith if you let it, and the dark gloats when faith seeps out with loss."

"The dark comes here, too."

The old woman nodded at Fallon. "It does. They come to the *sgiath de solas*."

"Shield of light."

"Aye, the circle, the shield, the evil they unleashed. And every year, near to the time it opened, they come and make a sacrifice to the dark."

"Granny, they found Aileen."

"Ah." A long, long sigh as she reached for Nessa's hand to comfort. "I feared it. Since the first year after Year One, they come. They lure a young one, usually a girl, but not always, into the woods. The woods were once green and full of game, a good place. Now cursed by what lives there."

"What lives there?" Tonia asked.

"It has no name I know. No face, no form but what it steals. It's a dead place now, that wood, and no one dare enter. I don't know what they do to the poor girls there. I can't see, or it may be I won't see."

"They tried for me only last year," Nessa said. "But Granny has charms on my window, on the door. And I wear this." She gripped the charm around her neck. "Still I felt the pulling, I heard the music, so bright and fun. I went to Granny and stayed all night in her bed. It was Maggie went missing that night, and never found again. She was but twelve."

"Who are they?" Fallon asked. "Has anyone seen them?"

"The first year there were two, a man and a woman. Both handsome, but a false front, that beauty. Scarred they were under it, and beneath the false front and scars, souls dead and black as pitch."

Shivering, she drew the shawl closer around her shoulders. "I saw them fly over the MacLeod farm, him on black wings, her on white, and she threw flames at the house, but they bounced away like balls as they flew on. To the circle, to the wood. It was that night the first of the children went missing."

"Eric and Allegra," Fallon stated.

"You know them?"

"They killed my sire. They've come every year in January?"

"Each year. But the next after that first they had a baby, and they became three who fed the dark. The child grew—pretty as a plum—but with hair dark on one side, pale on the other. As were her wings."

"Petra." Duncan's hand balled into a fist.

"There's more in her than in them." Because they trembled a little, Mrs. Frazier used both hands to lift the whiskey to her lips.

Nessa added wood to the fire, whiskey to the glasses.

"More dark in her," Mrs. Frazier continued, "and a madness you can feel wild on the air as she passes over. Only days ago, they came, but like these last few years, only the mother and daughter."

"I killed Eric. Or I wounded him," Fallon corrected. "My father—my life father—finished him."

"As is just."

"Only those?" Tonia asked. "No other DUs—Dark Ones?"

"We hear tales of Dark Ones, others, but none have come here but those three. Now two. I see them, though in the week they're known to come, I close the cottage tight. But I see them." She tapped her temple. "And on the night they feed the dark, storms rage."

"Granny says . . ." Nessa hesitated, then continued at her great-grandmother's nod. "She says they leave us be so we'll stay, and we'll keep having children they can take to the wood. We're taught not to listen to the music, to wear the charms, but some don't really believe, or the lure is too strong. Can you stop them?"

"We'll stop them. Have you seen the black dragon?"

As the glass tipped in her granny's hand, Nessa reached out to steady it. "Is it real then? I thought it a fancy. I've seen it soar over the wood, and into it, but no one else has. And in a dream I saw it sleeping inside the stone dance, but there's been no sign of such a creature."

"It guards the source." Fallon's eyes deepened as the vision rose. "It spies, in dragon shape and man shape, and plants dissension like weeds to grow and choke off the light. It serves its master as does its rider, as does the pale witch. It mates with the mad one, and in her seeks to plant the seed that will become the child. In the child, the source reborn so the dark rules all."

Fallon got to her feet. "We will strike them down, with sword, with arrow, with blinding light, with the blood of the gods, because we must. Look for the light, *Granaidh*," she told the old woman. "When you see it burst like the sun, when the tree of life blooms on MacLeod land, you'll know it's done."

"I will look. I will pray, and we will send our light to you."

She took the woman's hand. "Thank you for your hospitality. Can you tell us where to find Aileen's family?"

"Nessa will take you." She kissed Fallon's hand. "Safe journeys to you, to the children of the MacLeods. May all the gods go with you."

Lana had done as Tonia asked, so when they returned, they found Katie and Hannah with Lana and Simon, with wine and a fire. And waves of relief when they came in.

"The dragon slayers," Hannah said with a smile.

"Not tonight. There's a lot to tell anyway, but first . . ." Tonia went to her mother, offered the photograph.

"Oh, oh God. Oh, this is from the Christmas before. The last time I was there." She pressed it to her heart, rocked. "I never thought I'd see them again."

She tipped it down. "Your father. It's Tony. Do you see?"

"Let's get some more wine." Lana rose, signaled to Simon, to Fallon. "We'll give them some time. Where did you find a picture?"

"We went to the house. The MacLeod farm. I wouldn't mind the wine. It's been a night. Like Tonia said, there's a lot to tell. We should do that all together, after they have that time."

"And maybe a little something to eat."

"I wouldn't say no."

Simon got the wine, rubbed a hand on Fallon's shoulder. "There's blood on you again."

She only sighed. "Demon wolves. We'll get to them, and all the rest." But to make things easier, she swiped her hands down, vanished the bloodstains.

Duncan came in. "Appreciate the tact. And you were right, Fallon, there's nothing we could have brought back to Mom that meant more than that picture. If you could all come back, we could get through this. She and Hannah have a lot of questions."

Lana picked up a tray of snacks. "So do we. Duncan, Fallon, grab more glasses and small plates, would you?"

When they were alone, Duncan ran a hand down Fallon's back as she opened a cupboard. It surprised him how much he needed contact, but he didn't question it.

"It's going to take some time to walk them through it all," he began. "And after, I'm going to need to stay with Mom. She's handling it, but it's stirred things up."

"I can't even imagine it. You think you can because you've heard all the stories, but you just can't. She lost everything, everyone, so fast, so hard."

"I thought I understood, but I didn't. Not until I went into that house and felt it, felt them. So Tonia, Hannah, and I need to stay close tonight."

"It's going to be the same here, once my mother knows about Allegra and Petra." She handed him a stack of small plates. "More stirring things up. I promised my three a hunt tomorrow. Maybe you'd like in on that."

"I'm doing a couple classes at the academy in the afternoon, but I've got the morning."

"First light, east woods?"

"That works. Buy you breakfast at the community kitchen after."

"That really works."

As they carried in the dishes, Duncan realized he'd—inadvertently—obeyed Simon's *strong* suggestion during their conversation. He was taking Fallon on a date.

For two brisk, bright hours past dawn, Fallon rode the woods with Duncan. The night's snowfall left a fresh, fluffy six inches over the forest floor. The air smelled of it, of pine and purity, as they followed the tracks of a wild boar.

Taibhse glided, white wings spread, through trees with branches laden with snow and glinting spears of ice while Faol Ban slipped in and out of sun and shadows.

Here, the woods pulsed with life. The heartbeats of trees slow and steady in their winter rest, the quick beat of birds on the wing, of animals small and large, the bright pulse of pixies dancing through the ice and snow.

Light and life here, Fallon thought, unlike the dark and death in the wood on MacLeod land.

They didn't talk of the dead wood, of war or ghosts, of tactics or strategies, but argued books and DVDs, exchanged bits of gossip. It occurred to her they'd never just ridden through the woods, with a hunt more of an excuse to be together than a real purpose. They'd rarely talked of inconsequential things or explored each other's thoughts on them.

People had done just this once—maybe not with sword

and bow—but they'd spent time talking about so many things that didn't lead to life or death. Now, when war drums beat constant, taking an hour or two for only that became precious.

She'd remember it.

Because she would, she reached over, drew him closer, and kissed him with the owl soaring overhead, and the sun streaming onto untrampled snow. He got a better grip, added some punch to the kiss—oh yes, she'd remember it.

Then he eased back, put his fingers to his lips.

She caught the scent, too, and waited while he drew an arrow from the quiver on his back. The boar nosed through the trees. His bad luck, Fallon supposed, that the wind carried their scent away from him.

Duncan loosed the arrow, took it down, shot Fallon a quick grin. "That ought to pay for breakfast."

"And then some."

They took the boar to the community kitchen, where Duncan bartered for breakfast, some dry goods, and a portion of the meat. When they settled down to eat, she noticed a couple of those injured, treated, and not back to full duty sharing a meal along with a handful of recent rescues. It reminded her to go by the clinic and check on Lucy and Johnny before she left town.

Fred popped in, a rainbow-colored cap on her explosion of red hair, her youngest on her hip.

"Hi. Can I sit a minute?"

Duncan patted a chair. "You want some breakfast? I've got a little credit left."

"No, thanks." With the ease of experience, she stripped off the toddler's coat and cap as she talked. "I just dropped the kids off at school, and Dillon at the playground. The preschoolers are building snowpeople."

She set Willow down, unearthed some wooden blocks

from an enormous bag. "Build us a castle, cutie. Your dad made her those blocks for Christmas," she said to Fallon. "She's crazy for them. He and Eddie are working on the tractor—again. The alchemists are working on the corn fuel, and they think it'll work. Anyway."

She blew out a breath, side-eyed to make sure Willow remained engaged with her architecture. "I had coffee with your mom, Fallon. She caught me up. I haven't talked to Eddie yet, but anything that has to do with Allegra, he'll want to be part of it."

"From what we learned, she and Petra only go there once a year, so we've missed them. And that's the first substantiated sighting we've had in over a year."

"They're not done—and I don't mean just with the awful things they're doing in Scotland. I know Arlys is on her way to Montreal, but when she gets back, I think she and Chuck should, I don't know, put out an alert. Allegra and Eric worked with the PWs on the first attack on New Hope. They may be with them now, or still."

"We'll find them, Fred," Duncan assured her with a hard gleam in his eyes that spoke of vengeance.

"They'll come after you. You, Tonia, Fallon, Lana, especially. They want us all, but especially you."

"And that's to our advantage." Fallon finished her eggs. "Neither of them are what you'd call cool heads, and we will be. Neither of them are quite sane, and we are."

"I believe in you, and I believe the good always beats back the bad. But crazy and bad? It's unpredictable, so, you know, be a little wary."

Once Fred gathered up the baby, the blocks, Duncan studied Fallon.

"We didn't talk about it, about them."

"No. I want to say I know how much Denzel meant to you, and I understand the need to even the score."

"It can't be evened."

"No, it can't. I know how I felt when I struck out at Eric, and what blew through me was dark. It was revenge more than justice. I had to pull away from that, and so will you. You'll need to be a little wary, Duncan, because it's a powerful feeling. It's seductive."

"I need to end her, for Denzel, for that girl we found and all the ones she laid out on that altar. It'll be justice. Whatever else I feel when I do end her is mine to deal with."

FAITH

Yet I argue not
Against Heav'n's hand or will, nor bate a jot
Of heart or hope; but still bear up and steer
Right onward.

—John Milton

CHAPTER SEVENTEEN

It worried her, but Duncan was right. It was his to deal with. If she asked him to believe in her, she had to believe in him, believe his light, his heart, both strong enough to resist that dark surge.

She knew its pull, and had to admit she'd felt it tug inside her the night before when she'd seen what had been done to a young girl.

Murder, slavery, torture, mutilation, those were horrible crimes. But human sacrifice? An even deeper evil. So yes, she wanted to end them, this mate of her uncle, her own cousin. She wanted to spill the blood of her blood, and knew she'd have to beat back that dark surge to come out whole again.

Another choice, she thought as she rode to the clinic. One that might prove the hardest of all to make.

It surprised her when Taibhse dropped down to Laoch's saddle after she dismounted, and Faol Ban stood on guard. She'd expected them both to go on their way.

"You don't have to wait," she told them. "But if you do, I shouldn't be long."

No one sat in the waiting chairs, which she deemed a

good thing as she made her way to the offices. She found Rachel at a desk reading some paperwork with her half-glasses on her nose.

"Slow day?"

Rachel took off her cheaters, sat back. "At last. Hannah and Jonah are doing some routine exams. Not one emergency this morning," she said, rapping her knuckles on the desk three times. "We were able to release a few more this morning, so it's actually pretty quiet. Quiet enough I was just going over the supply list for the expansion. It's going to take some doing, but Bill Anderson and his team of miracle workers—which includes your father—say they'll make it happen so we can, potentially, break ground this spring."

Fallon walked over to the detailed sketches pinned to a bulletin board. In them she saw potential and vision, and most of all, faith.

"You're going to need more medicals."

At that Rachel let out a satisfied sigh. "I have a pediatrician—yay!—in the rescues from D.C. She's not ready, physically or emotionally, to work yet, but she will be. And I have another healer from the same group. Best of all?"

Fallon glanced back. "Best of all?"

"I've put together a series of exams, mostly from memory. I want Hannah to take them next month. If she passes, as I know she will, she'll be a doctor. As officially as we can make it. I've talked to Katie, and the town council. We're all agreed."

"I think that's definitely best of all."

"She's young. Awfully young, but she's been training, seriously training, since she was thirteen. She's got a natural talent, and the passion."

"Does she know?"

"I told her this morning. I want her to have time to

study. The exams aren't a cakewalk—shouldn't be and won't be. She'll have earned her M.D."

Rachel had let her hair grow a little longer since summer, had it pulled back in a short pouf of a tail. Now she rubbed the back of her neck under the pouf.

Quiet morning or not, the town doctor and founder of the clinic worked long, hard hours.

"Maybe you could give the paperwork a rest."

"Well. We're putting in a holistic area, and a physical therapy area. When we do, I swear to God, I'm getting a massage every week."

"Meantime." Fallon moved behind her, rubbed at her neck and shoulders.

Rachel shut her eyes, let out a sigh. "Come live with me and bring your magick hands."

"You can call on them anytime. I'll look for Hannah before I leave. I wanted to check on Lucy and Johnny—the two I brought in yesterday."

"She's cleared, but we got her a bed so she doesn't have to leave him until he is. He's awake, and lucid. Some blank spots in his memory, which isn't unusual given the head trauma. From what Jonah told me, what you did in the field made the difference. I examined him this morning, and he's stable. We'll keep him awhile, but barring something unforeseen, he'll make a full recovery. And they've both asked for you."

"I'll go by and see them. Is that better?"

"It was better in about two seconds, I just liked the rub." Laughing, Rachel reached back, gave Fallon a pat. "Let me walk you down. Oh, and more good news," she added as she rose.

"I'm always ready for it."

"Lissandra and Brennan—the preemie? They've officially moved into the apartment over Bill's. A lot of people ask for a different place when they find out there was a murder in it, but she's happy to have it. She said she'd been caged, and now she and her son are free. Plus, she hit it off with Bill—who doesn't? He loves having them upstairs."

"That's very good news."

"She's learning how to knit so she can contribute, and since Bill's a baby softie, she's taking Brennan down and helping him at Bygones a couple days a week."

"That's good. Good for all of them."

"It is. I advised her to wait until spring before she did any serious volunteering or work outside. It's better for the baby to stay out of the cold for now, but going right downstairs is fine. She's a good one, Fallon."

She paused outside a door. "I wanted to give these two a little privacy, and with all the releases in the last few days, I could give them their own room. It's small, but they have it to themselves."

Rachel knocked, eased open the door. "You've got a visitor. Don't stay too long," she murmured to Fallon, and stepped back.

"Oh, it's you!" Lucy, hair washed, pulled back in a tail, her face no longer carrying that gray tinge, popped up from a chair. "Johnny, it's Fallon Swift. We're so glad to see you. So glad."

Fallon barely stepped into the room before Lucy embraced her. "You saved us. Jonah said Johnny's going to be fine. Rachel said so, too."

"That's good."

The man in the bed didn't look fine, but he looked a hell of a lot better than he had. He sat up in the hospital bed, and though shadows dogged his eyes, they'd healed much of the bruising. He wore a white T-shirt, his arm in a sling, an IV drip in the back of his other hand.

"You're The One." His eyes swirled with tears as he reached out to her. Though his grip was weak, he clung

to her hand. "Thank you for the life of the woman I love.
Thank you for mine. I—I couldn't stop them."

"There were too many of them."

"You stopped them. When I'm able, I'll fight for you."

"We'll talk about it when you're better."

"No, please." Lucy moved closer, brushed a hand at
his hair. "We've talked. I was wrong to ask him not to
fight. We want to stay here, so we'll fight. I don't know
how—my grandmother wouldn't let me—but I'll learn.
We'll learn. I can sew, and cook, and garden. I can help
until Johnny's well."

"I'll have someone come in and talk to you about that.
And when the medicals say you're well enough, we'll
see about the rest. How far had you traveled?"

"Three days, west to east," Johnny told her. "We'd
been in the house we found for two days before the Raiders found us."

"And where you came from? How many people?"

"Maybe a hundred. I'm not sure." He looked at Lucy.

"People like my grandmother didn't want the Uncannys to mix. We had our place, and they had theirs, with
the river between."

"If I brought a map, could you show me?"

"I could." Johnny nodded. "If you went there, some
would fight for you."

"I'll bring a map then. For now, get better."

She considered as she left them. A small, segregated
community. She'd seen them before. It would be worth a
visit, worth trying to rally the willing and able.

She started out, as she'd kept her animals waiting
long enough. She saw Hannah in the waiting area with
a boy. A pretty little boy, cheeks pink from the cold,
blond hair curling out from under a red cap with snow-
men dancing over it. Hannah had one of his mittened
hands in hers.

"Of course I'll go see her. Just let me get my coat and a medical kit."

"She's really sick." He had a slight, endearing lisp, and big blue eyes. "She coughs and coughs. And her head's really hot."

"We'll get her some medicine. Hi, Fallon, this is Bobby. His mom's sick."

"I'm sorry to hear that."

"She doesn't feel good. She sent me for the doctor." He stared up at Hannah with those big, blue eyes, a boy no more than six or seven. "You can make her all better. You need to come now."

Fallon started to put her hand on his shoulder in comfort, but he jerked away, pushed closer to Hannah.

"Where is she?" Fallon asked easily. She stared into his eyes, fascinated she could see neither dark nor light. Just the face of innocence. "My horse is outside. He can get you there very fast."

"Just Hannah! You need to come now!"

"It's okay, Bobby. We'll go now. It's all right." She smiled at Fallon, but surely didn't see her. Not with those blank eyes.

"Sure. Wouldn't want to get in the way."

She moved fast, shoved Hannah back, threw power at the boy. He screamed at her, and those blue eyes went black as a crow's wing.

"The bitch is mine!" With his child's hand, he tossed a stream of fire at Hannah. Fallon simply caught it, crushed it. When he heaved the next at Fallon, it crashed against the shield she threw up.

"Do you think your power exceeds mine, imp?"

"I want her!" He pounded against the barrier, little fists full of hate. "I want her, I want her! Give her back!"

"Go to hell," Fallon suggested as she heard the sound of feet running behind her. "Stay back."

"It's not fair!" Tantrum tears spurted from those black eyes. "You're mean, and I'm gonna tell. We'll kill you all! You'll burn and burn and burn."

"I see you now. I see the dark in you."

"It'll eat you up. Chomp, chomp, chomp." On a scream of laughter, he tried to flash, then looked wildly around when he stayed in place.

To Fallon's astonishment, he dropped down to kick his feet, beat his fists in the air. "You're a mean girl, mean, mean, mean. I wanna go home! Let me out, you shitty-head."

"Christ, what a brat. You're not going anywhere, so calm the hell down. Who sent you?"

Temper stained his face an ugly red, tears turned it blotchy. But those black eyes gleamed into Fallon's as he rolled into a crouch.

A little spider, she thought, poisonous for all its size.

"The Princess of the Dark has a message for you. Eat this, Cousin!"

He gathered himself, pulling, pulling power, sucking it in as he might suck in air to blow. Even as Fallon warned, "Don't," he unleashed a flood of fire.

She saw his face, the shock and fear on his face, before the flames struck the barrier, flew back, and consumed him.

"Oh my God." Rachel, still kneeling beside a shaken Hannah, scrambled up.

"No." Fallon gripped her arm. "He's gone. There's nothing you can do."

"He—he was just a child."

"Age doesn't change it. He was a Dark Uncanny cloaked in innocence."

"There's nothing left, not even ash."

"Hellfire doesn't leave ash. You'll want white sage, salt, a cleansing ritual." Digging for calm, she turned away, helped Hannah to her feet. "I'm sorry I knocked you back so hard. I had to get you clear."

"What happened? What was that?"

"What do you remember?"

"I . . ." She pressed a hand to her temple. "I was just finished with an exam. I heard my name. Somebody calling me, and there was a little boy, crying, then . . . nothing."

Hannah pressed her fingers to her temples as if to push out the rest. "I don't remember anything. I was on the floor, and he—that thing—was screaming."

"He had you in a trance. He had power, and skill, despite his age. He wanted you to go with him. He told you his mother was sick in bed, needed a doctor."

"I— Yes, I think. It's foggy. He was going to kill me."

"I don't think so. I think he was sent to take you to her. To Petra. A bargaining chip."

"To get to Duncan and Tonia, to you, but absolutely to them." The shock and confusion on her face shifted, instantly, to cold rage. "That little bastard."

"How did he get through security?" Rachel demanded.

"I think that's why she sent a child. Small enough to slip through the security posts, and she'd shielded him. Even I couldn't see into him at first. And that's when I knew. She's not as clever as she thinks. In any case, we'll fix that. You're okay?" she asked Hannah.

"Yeah. I feel it." She winced as she rubbed her ass. "Small price to pay."

"Have Duncan and Tonia make you a charm. They'll know what to do. Wear it, twenty-four-seven."

"Right now, we're going to exam so I can look you over."

"I'm fine, Rach. I landed on my butt. But maybe a little something for the headache."

"It's from being pulled out of the trance abruptly, and not by the one who put you in," Fallon explained. "The herbal remedy's better for that than the chemical."

"Got it covered. Come on, Hannah."

"Okay, okay. Thanks, Fallon."

Rachel led her away, glanced back. "So much for the quiet morning."

Fallon went directly to Will to report the breach, left it to him to work out how to tighten security. Then she went to her mother to work together on a magickal over-layment.

That left her little time to check on the prisoner transfers and the progress of the delegation to Quebec. She spent the evening trying various locator spells, searching the crystal, but could find no trace of Petra or Allegra.

"I'll get through," she said aloud. "Sooner or later."

By the time she dropped into bed, the two hours in the woods, the simple kiss, the quiet, seemed incredibly far away. And very precious.

She'd just drifted off when she felt a snap in the air.

"Just me," Duncan hissed before she hurled something nasty at him.

He lay down beside her, wrapped around her. "Hannah. I'm stupid grateful you were there."

"She's okay, right?"

"Thanks to you." He kissed the nape of her neck. "I can't stay. I want to stick close another night."

"You made the charm for her."

"Yeah. Had to be pretty—she insisted." He nuzzled Fallon again. "Tonia handled the design so it would be. So it's pretty enough for Hannah, and effective."

She shifted around to nuzzle back. "Mom and I worked out an overlayment for security. I think it's effective, too. We thought we had enough already, but—"

"Kid demon from hell. Who expects that? Fucking Petra."

"I can't find her, Duncan. I looked, but I couldn't find her. I will."

"We will. Nobody messes with my sisters." He kissed her cheeks, her lips. "I can't stay. But I could take an hour."

Her lips curved against his. "This is a really good way to spend an hour."

Fallon spent time with her maps, huddled with her father, Will, Eddie, and others over battle plans. She worked with her mother on potions, with Kim on herbals.

To keep her hand in the game, she visited the barracks for some sparring, the academy to monitor a class on spell casting.

And while she continued to search for Petra through the crystal, she roamed through it to mark other areas, study, consider.

When her mother came in, Fallon sat with her maps at the dining room table. "Back at it?"

"Yeah."

"Want some tea? After a morning in the community kitchen I'm ready for some."

"Sure. Thanks."

"It's wicked cold out," Lana continued as she moved to the stove to put on a kettle. "I think it's a night for beef stew. Will you be here for dinner?"

"Should be." Fallon rose as Lana ran her hands over a teapot to warm it. "Mom, I have something to ask you."

"All right." Lana opened a cupboard, considered her teas. Chose a ginger spice.

"I've pinpointed the area where Lucy and Johnny

came from—the segregated community I told you about."

"Mmm. Some people never learn, do they? We're all in this together. Working, living, loving together makes us whole."

"It's that, how you're an example of that, know how to communicate that—it's why I want you to go."

"Go?" Lana glanced back.

"To what Lucy calls Riverbend. There are at least a hundred people, and they've managed to defend themselves against the occasional raid. Some, on both sides of the river, will fight if they're given a reason. I need you to give them one. You and Dad."

"You want me and your father to go, try to convince people who refuse to mix together to fight together."

"It won't be the first time, and I can't think of anyone better suited. You, Dad, and Ethan."

"Ethan."

"A family. A blended family."

"The One's family."

"That's a factor," Fallon agreed, and moved in to measure the tea. "A witch, an NM soldier, a young animal empath. Two people who survived the Doom and made a life. The son who's grown up in the world they've helped build and protect."

"Have you talked to your father about this?"

"You first. It's harder for you because I'm asking you to take Ethan. I've seen what you gave up to leave New Hope, and I know what you gave up to leave the farm and come back here. You did it for me, but not only for me. You did it because it had to be done. I need you to show these people what has to be done."

Lana stood back while Fallon poured the boiling water into the pot.

"That's not all."

"No. There are two more settlements. I've mapped them. Every person you can rally to fight increases our numbers. I'm asking you to go, talk to strangers, without being sure of your reception, and convince them to put their lives on the line, to send their sons and daughters to fight."

"When would we . . ."

"I'm hoping you'd be willing to leave tomorrow."

"Tomorrow? But . . ."

She had a rotation in the community kitchen, and needed to pick up some things from the Tropics. She'd promised to work with the herbalists on—

And the fact she had those things to do, could have them, had helped build the structure for them? The very reasons Fallon asked her to go.

"Don't you want to wait until the others are back from Quebec?"

"They're due back in a day or two. We'll know if we've got the support from the north. We've got the un-tapped in the Midwest. I'm asking you to begin to tap it. I'm asking you to leave home again. Only for a few days, maybe a week, but to leave home again."

"The farm's where we left it, and New Hope's right here. Of course we'll go. We'll need to talk about—" She broke off at the knock on the kitchen door.

Starr stood on the other side of the glass with Marichu, the fast, young recruit. "Two more cups," she told Fallon, and went to answer.

"Hi. Come in. It's freezing out there. I thought you'd gone back to Forestville, Starr."

"Tomorrow."

"We're just making tea."

"We don't want to bother you," Starr began, then looked at Fallon. "You should talk with Marichu."

"Sure. Have a seat."

The girl looked around the kitchen, carefully, warily. She'd changed the red in her hair to a forest green, stood in the sturdy boots elves and other cobblers made for the troops.

"Let me take your coats." Knowing Starr didn't like to be touched, Lana simply held out her hand. "Fallon, why don't the three of you go into the living room. I'll bring the tea."

"You don't need to bother."

"It's not a bother." If Starr said she needed to talk to Marichu, Fallon thought, and gestured for them to follow, she needed to talk to Marichu.

She'd neglected the fire, she realized, while she'd worked with her maps, so flicked out a hand to send it flaming again, and added a log.

The girl studied the room as she had the kitchen.

"Sit," Fallon invited.

Starr, her face carrying scars from burns so deep even magicks couldn't erase them, hesitated, then took a chair. Her body carried scars, too, Fallon knew, from Petra's attack. And her heart and soul carried more, from childhood wounds.

Outside of training and battle, she trusted and interacted with few. Marichu struck Fallon as much the same. But clearly they'd clicked.

Lana brought in a tray. As Fallon walked over to take it from her, she murmured, "Stay."

Fallon set the tray on the table. "Cookies, too. We're in luck. I've got it, Mom," she added, and began to pour out the tea. "So what do we need to talk about, Marichu?"

"I need to fight when you go to New York."

Fallon set the first mug down in front of Starr, poured another. "The age you listed is a little shy yet for combat."

"Not that much, and I'd have just lied if I'd known you had some stupid rule about it. I fought in D.C."

"And you broke ranks. You weren't on the squad for the lab and containment center."

"So what?"

"That's not the way," Starr replied.

"I fought in D.C.," Marichu insisted. "I'm faster than any-damn-body who isn't an elf. I'm better at hand-to-hand than most of the older recruits. I won the last archery tournament, and I'm better with a sword than most. You said so."

"I said you'd improved with a sword. She has," Starr said to Fallon. "I've stayed since D.C. to check on progress with the recruits, and I'm going back to the base tomorrow. Marichu's improved in every area."

Fallon poured tea for her mother, herself, then sat cross-legged on the floor, took a cookie. "You broke ranks," Fallon repeated, "and would have put an arrow in Carter after he'd surrendered and posed no threat."

"I—" One hard glance from Starr had Marichu cutting herself off. "You're right, and I've been disciplined for it. I deserved to be. And you were right, what you said in the lab. We're not like them. We can't be like them. I'm asking to fight, to prove myself."

"New York's going to make D.C. look like a scrimmage. The DU forces were strong in D.C., but they've dominated in New York for over a decade."

"I know," Marichu snapped back. "I was born there."

Gaze level, Fallon bit into the cookie. "Were you?"

"My parents were resistance. My mother was killed when I was twelve."

"I'm sorry," Fallon said.

"She was a soldier." Pride rang in the girl's voice. "She died fighting. They found the safe house where we kept the kids. She and the others beat them back, protected all of us. She died fighting. After that, my father wanted to get me out. We argued about it a lot, but he said he was going to get me out, get me to New Hope."

"Here?"

"Everybody knows about New Hope, but mostly doesn't believe it. Everybody knows about The One, but mostly doesn't believe it, either."

No longer able to resist, she leaned forward for a cookie. "But they fight anyway. My dad made me leave. Sometimes they smuggle out kids or the old or the ones who can't take it anymore. He made me go with a group, and said he'd find me when he could. But once we were out, everything went wrong. The crows came, and the black lightning. Everybody scattered. Then there were PWs, and they were taking everybody they could or just killing them. I got away. I'm fast, so I got away. But I couldn't get back into the city."

"She was hurt," Starr said.

"It wasn't that bad. I told you it wasn't that bad."

"She was hurt," Starr repeated, "and got lost in the smoke, couldn't find the way back in. Some resistance scouts found her, took her to their camp. Then to a small base farther south."

"They wouldn't take me back to New York, so I took off when I could. And . . ."

"And," Fallon prompted.

"I should've stayed with them. I understand that now. But then, I just wanted to get back to my dad. So I took off, and I couldn't get back to New York. I figured I'd try to come here—Dad drew out a route. It wasn't exactly right, but I followed it. I ran into more PWs, and . . ."

"They hurt you," Fallon finished. "Really hurt you that time. Damaged your wing."

"They were going to execute me, but I got away. I still got away. Then your scouts found me."

"Why didn't you tell anyone before, about New York?"

"I didn't know you."

"Fair enough."

"All of it," Starr encouraged.

"Okay, okay. I figured, at first, I'd learn stuff here, more skills, and I'd take off again, try for New York. But then . . . I know that's not the right way. I can't do it on my own. Nobody does it on their own."

"A good lesson," Fallon allowed.

"Do you know Chelsea?" Lana asked her.

"Yeah. Our group stayed mostly on the lower. We had other groups on the upper and the mid."

"I lived in Chelsea." Lana held out the plate of cookies.

"I know. There are lots of stories. It's not like it was—my dad said it's not, so it's not. But I know how it is. I know where you can find resistance who'll fight. I know where the PWs have a stronghold in what was Brooklyn, and where the military bases are in Queens."

"I've got maps in the other room." Fallon rose. "Show me."

"I'll show you if I can go and fight."

"Show me," Fallon repeated, "then we'll decide."

It took more than an hour, and when they left, Fallon pored over the maps, the notes, the new markings.

"I need more map paper. I have to redraw—"

"You're going to let her go." Lana sat, hands folded on the table. "She's so young, and still headstrong. You can see the headstrong even though she's trying not to show it. Maybe not to be it, quite as much."

"Her father's in New York, and I'm going to hope she

learned her lesson, won't make the same mistakes. Still, I told her she needed to sharpen her skills with a sword, and she'd need the go from every one of her instructors."

"You're going to let her go. I know you," Lana said.

"All right, yeah. What do you think she'd do if I said she had to sit this out? She'd take off. If I said she needed more discipline, same thing."

"I know that, too. Just as I know Duncan and Tonia, and most of the others, were already in the fight by her age. But with so many joining, we've been able to up the age for combat, give them more time."

"Her father's in New York," Fallon said again. "Everyone she really knows, the world she considers home. I can't stop her, so I use her, yes, but she goes back with an army. She doesn't go back alone."

"And still, it makes me sad. I can know you're right, that I'd very likely do the same, and still be sad. I'll get your paper."

Rising, Lana stepped over, pressed a kiss to the top of Fallon's head.

With the new information, Fallon huddled with her parents, Duncan and Tonia, Will. She added Katie, Jonah, Rachel, and Fred for their knowledge of old New York.

"Tony and I lived here." Katie laid a finger on the old map. "My parents here, his here. This is the hospital where you were born."

"DU Central now," Duncan said, then immediately looked at Katie. "Sorry, Mom."

"No, that's the reality. New Hope's home, where I raised you and your sister, where we made our life. They've twisted and burned what was my home, but that doesn't mean we can't and won't take it back."

"I lived here, started out here," Rachel said, "but I wanted my own place, and an easy commute to the hospital. I didn't grow up there like Katie, and wouldn't know the area nearly as well as Jonah would, as he drove those streets every day as a paramedic."

"We were based here, covered this section." It took him back, those street names. "I imagine some of the buildings are gone, some of the streets destroyed, but the layout's the layout. We took the boat from here to get out, decided to try for Hoboken."

"Hell of a night," Rachel said, and laid her hand over his.

"Yeah, it was."

"We could get troops into Brooklyn by water. Boats, merpeople."

Jonah nodded at Fallon. "There were bridges, tunnels."

"Marichu says the tunnels, for the most part, are for the dead and the lunatics. The bridge from Manhattan to Brooklyn, destroyed, leaving Brooklyn essentially cut off. If we come in as you left, by the water, we can retake what they've claimed. From the outside in, while we flash more troops into the center. We do the same in Manhattan."

"Arlys and I worked here, in Midtown. She lived close enough to walk to work. It all happened so fast," Fred remembered. "People dying, people killing, people running. The magickals—well, there was a lot of confusion at first. I mean, one day you're an intern, learning the ropes of broadcasting, running around New York with a cool job, a dumpy apartment you love, and the next you've got wings. It's not like being born knowing. It's a rush, and a little scary at first. Some couldn't handle it, just went crazy, others went dark."

"You didn't," Eddie reminded her. "Not my Fred."

"You could have left," Tonia pointed out. "Why didn't you?"

"Arlys, the people we worked with. They needed me.

After that last broadcast—God, that was awful—Jim, he was in charge then, said that Arlys had to get out, and I just knew I had to go with her.

"We walked down to Thirty-fourth—here." She showed them on the map. "And walked the PATH tunnel to Hoboken."

When she pressed her lips together, Eddie laid a hand on her thigh, rubbed.

"We got through it." She put her hand over his for a quick squeeze. "The thing was, Hoboken was pretty deserted, but it wasn't destroyed. Not even looted much."

"PW base now, according to Marichu. We take it out," Fallon said, "make it ours."

"We're fighting on a lot of fronts, Fallon." With the others, Will studied the maps, old and new. "PWs in New Jersey, DUs and PWs in Brooklyn, military in Queens, and all of that in Manhattan."

"That's why we'll win. Not in a day, not in a week, not in a month, but we'll win. We'll drive them out. I was conceived there, like Duncan, Tonia, Hannah. Ross MacLeod traveled back from Scotland to die there. The firsts of New Hope found each other there, and found their way out. Now it's time to go back."

She looked at Fred. "You could have escaped when the time came over the water on wing, but you went into the dark because a friend needed you. And you, Jonah, on the edge of despair, chose life because a stranger needed you. Arlys chose truth rather than the safety of lies. Chuck gave Arlys and Fred shelter and a way out. Katie gave a helpless infant a mother and family. Rachel stepped into the unknown because she was needed. My mother left everything she knew and loved, met a stranger and his dog on the road, and helped them. That's what we take to New York. And that's a powerful weapon."

"Can't argue with it," Will admitted. "But I'd feel better going into this with a shitload of swords, arrows, bullets, and soldiers."

"And we will. But we'll also go with the light, strong and powerful enough to shut down the dark."

CHAPTER EIGHTEEN

It felt a little strange, and altogether amazing, to sit in Fallon's kitchen while she fixed breakfast. Just the two of them, Duncan thought, in the big house. Her parents and Ethan had left the day before, his mom had steadied up—with the framed picture of her family on the mantel.

He'd be a fool not to take advantage of some Fallon time. And he was nobody's fool. For the first time, they'd spent the night together in that big house, and now the morning after.

He wondered if she wondered if this served as a kind of gateway into their future. And just where the gate would lead.

He let her cook because she made it clear he sucked at cooking. He didn't think he was that bad, but why argue? Besides, he liked watching her—the confidence, even a little flair.

She set the plates on the counter, sat beside him.

"Looks great, smells great." He sampled a forkful. "Tastes— Wow. What is it?"

"Pesto and roasted tomato omelette with some goat cheese."

"Take after your mom. She's the best cook in the world."

"She'd say there's not a lot of competition."

"Are you worried about her, about them?"

She tasted the omelette, found herself pleased she'd pulled it off as she'd been taught. "No. I worried I'd worry, if you get me, but I'm not. It's all steps somehow. I just wanted to fly, to take some time to think, and there was Lucy. Now through her maybe we get a couple hundred soldiers. And maybe one of them points us in a direction that gets us a couple hundred more."

"We'll need them. Is that what's worrying you? New York. I hear the worry."

"I'd be stupid not to worry. It's a big bite. And what Will said the other day isn't wrong. It's not enough to be right. We need soldiers and weapons."

He said nothing for a moment as they ate in the quiet hum of the kitchen, in the warmth of it while winter held cold and hard outside.

"They can't always understand," he began. "Will's a hell of a commander. Tough, smart, courageous, committed. I learned how to fight from him—learned how to fight smart—but he can't always understand. He accepts and respects magick. That can't always be a snap, either, right?"

"I guess I don't always think often enough from their side. Just listening to Fred, how she talked about those weeks in New York when everything changed. How she changed."

"Will, Eddie, the other NMs—with the big exception being your dad—are always going to think the conventional way first. Even after twenty years in this world, they lived that long and longer in the other. I figure that's a good thing."

Curious, she shifted to him. "Why?"

"Because that's how the world works now. The mix. We're a mix of conventional—or what was conventional— and magickal. It works best when everybody accepts. You and me, we've got that mix right inside our own families. So does Will, so does Eddie. I figure that's how it's going to be now."

"That's another reason we'll win."

"Check that. I've spent some time at the barracks and the academy since I came back. Some students, some recruits are going to need more seasoning. You've got some like Denzel."

It gave him a pang, always did, when he thought of his friend.

"He was never going to be a soldier," Duncan went on, "but he thought—hell, lived to be one. Because he figured combat was exciting, dangerous, just plain cool."

She thought of how desperately she'd wanted to use the sword hanging over the hearth in Mallick's cottage because . . . cool.

"Didn't you at first?"

"Maybe." He added a half laugh. "No, hell yeah. Got that knocked out of me, thanks to Will."

She got up to get more coffee. "We need the numbers, Duncan."

"I hear you. Are you going to eat the rest of that?"

"Yes." She poured the coffee, sat, picked up her fork. "The numbers determine how soon we can move on New York. Can you work directly with the ones you feel need that seasoning?"

"Sure." Since it didn't look like he'd get the rest of her omelette, he took his plate to the sink. Assumed, correctly, he'd take cleanup since she'd cooked. "I could use Mallick."

She sighed. "I really wanted to give him some time at his cottage, but you're right. He's needed."

When she finished, she cleared her plate, wandered to the glass doors. "I'll spend some time on it, too. I need to go to the elf camp near the cottage, check in there, and up north. I thought Meda and I should scout in the West. We could pick up more. And I need to go back to the farm, the village. God, I miss the farm."

Leaning on the door, she looked out at winter, the snow-covered garden, the woods beyond. "I don't know if it'll be home for me again. It's like your mother talked about Brooklyn. It's not home for her anymore. I don't know if the farm will be for me, even though I miss it like a limb."

"I'll make a home with you."

It took her breath so she had to steady herself as she turned to face him. He held a dishcloth, but, God, he'd never look domesticated. The winter sun streamed through the windows, pale as water, and flowed over the sword he wore, as she did, as routinely as another wore shoes.

"We can make a home. Here, there, somewhere else."

"You'd leave New Hope if—"

"It's you I won't leave, Fallon."

It trembled through her, the solid certainty of him, in him.

"Loving you makes me afraid," she told him. "Afraid of what's to come, where I'm leading others to go. Are you afraid?"

"Of dying in battle? Of losing someone else I love? Damn straight I'm afraid. And afraid doesn't mean dick. Doing what's next, that's what counts."

She let out a half laugh. "You're the only one."

"I'd better be."

"No—such an ass—you're the only one who measured up."

"To what?"

"My fathers."

He tossed the cloth aside as he crossed to her. "You're calling your fathers asses?"

"No, that's just for you." She gripped his hands. "At fourteen, I opened the Book of Spells, and all it held blew into me in a storm of power and knowledge. With that I leaped into the Well of Light to take the sword and shield from the fire."

"Now you're just bragging."

"No, no." She laughed, squeezed his hands. "All of that, all of it, is no more magickal than being able to stand here with you, knowing I can be afraid with you and we can do what's next. Knowing we will do what's next."

She brought his hands to her lips. "I'll make a home with you. Here, there, or somewhere else."

He started to draw her in to hold that moment. And they both felt it.

"They're back." She let her hand lay on his heart another second. "Mallick and the others."

They gathered in the war room after Duncan went to get Will. As her mother's daughter she made coffee, tea, lit the fire, and struggled to be patient until everyone settled in.

"I want to thank all of you for making this journey," Fallon began.

Travis gestured with his mug. "I want to say, straight off, the snow queen's got, you know, style. Her HQ's the next thing to a palace."

"Excessive." Meda chose tea, black, no honey. No frills.

"Yeah, maybe, but it didn't hurt my feelings to have a little taste of luxury. Which she definitely has."

Arlys, prepared to take notes, shot Travis an indulgent look. "She's converted what was a five-star hotel in the heart of Montreal to her headquarters, her home. She lives the high life, literally, in the penthouse suite—and takes the entire floor. However, she's also seen to it her people have housing, food, clothing, medical attention. Other buildings we toured have been converted into clinics, schools, greenhouses, tanneries."

"She indulges herself, a great deal," Meda put in with clear disapproval. "Fancy clothes, dripping jewelry. But."

She jerked a shoulder in what Fallon read as reluctant respect. "Her people aren't neglected or misused. They have food, shelter."

"And she listens to them," Travis added.

"Yes, in her way. They use, primarily, wind and solar energy. Their training facility could be improved, but their security's strong."

"She was very gracious," Arlys put in, "and seemed receptive to Meda's suggestions on their training facilities and methods. It's certainly a different feel from New Hope. Her center's very urban, and she's most definitely in charge. She has advisers, but it's not the sort of setup where they do any more than advise. She rules."

"And how do her people feel about that?"

"They love her," Travis said. "They trust her, and they feel safe. She loves them. It's not bullshit. Their safety and well-being are important to her."

"Did you? Trust her?"

"Yeah. She's an easy read."

"She tried her wiles on him," Meda added.

"Is that so?"

Travis grinned. "She's too . . . fancy," he decided. "Hot, yeah, but too fancy and not my type. And it was more of a test. She likes sex, a lot—another easy read. But it was more of a test. Same with Mallick."

"She—" Fallon's gaze flew to the sorcerer, who sat silent and placid. "Really?"

"Just a test," Travis continued. "Maybe with some thoughts in there on gaining a little advantage if she could bag Mallick the Sorcerer and the brother of The One. Anyway, not my type."

He shot a look—close to a leer—at Meda.

"Act your age, little man."

"This is acting my age. I like hot warrior chicks."

"I think we can move on from that. Mallick, other than attempting to seduce you and a teenager, were there negotiations that apply?"

"Yes. She wants your allegiance very much. She's very aware she needs you more than you need her. Her concern for her people is, as Travis said, very real, and very deep. She is particularly concerned that the children in her region are not only safe and educated and sheltered, but happy. Her ambition is not slight. She wants the region, and believes she can bring it safety and prosperity."

"She's not wrong," Arlys said. "She's ensured loyalty because she gives it. It may be a kind of benign dictatorship, but we're in a different world. I didn't see any cruelty in her or her rule."

"She offers two thousand fighting troops for that allegiance."

"Three now." Mallick poured more tea. Winter chilled his bones now in a way it hadn't for centuries.

"Three?"

"She has four," Travis told her. "An easy read. But we agreed she needed to hold back a portion to secure her city, her people."

Mallick nodded. "There are old and young and others unable to fight who need protection. As well as the city itself. The three thousand come with arms—and her forges will continue to produce weapons. As you suspected, she has other alliances. With these negotiations, she brought in those leaders. They are both smaller groups, but we have, between them, another fifteen hundred."

"Over four thousand." Feeling the surge, Fallon sat back. "What did we promise in return?"

"We recognize her rule and the sovereignty of the other alliances. If needed, we assist them against our common enemies. We open trade with them, while respecting their borders. A small side deal with Vivienne is her request we assist her people in creating a tropics area and the means to begin growing coffee beans, tea, cacao, pepper, citrus, and so on."

"Smart," Fallon decided. "Not only will she have that capability, but she'll be able to trade directly with her other alliances. I'd prefer if we sent a coven up to create it rather than giving them the means to do it themselves."

"Which is what we agreed to. She's satisfied with that."

"Good. Over four thousand and, with luck, nearer to five when Mom and Dad and Ethan get back."

"From where?" Travis demanded. "I thought they were just busy somewhere."

"They are. Just not in New Hope."

She explained the mission, listened to the back-and-forth. Then rose. "I want to thank all of you. By successfully negotiating these alliances, you've given us a strong advantage. We have allies in the north, and thousands of troops who'll fight with us. We'll need them to take New York. Meda, would you be willing to go west with me to find more? To hopefully find and forge other alliances?"

"I answer the call of The One."

"Travis, I need you on this one."

He sent a wide grin to Meda, who answered it with a stony stare. "No problem."

"Arlys, I'd love to read what you'll write on this in *New Hope News*."

"It's all but written. I promised Vivienne a copy. They have very, and that's very, rudimentary IT, but Chuck will figure it out."

"Okay then. Mallick, if you could stay for a minute."

The rest headed out, Duncan and Travis to the barracks, Will and Arlys back to New Hope, and Meda to prepare for the next journey.

Fallon poured Mallick more tea, moved to sit beside him. "Three words to describe Vivienne."

"Vain, ambitious, loyal."

"I can work with all of those."

"I'll add she envies you."

"Me?"

"Your power and position. With the envy is genuine admiration, and a little fear."

"I can work with those, too. Is there any reason to think, if we help her secure Quebec, establish herself as head of that state, she'll want more?"

Pleased she thought beyond the battle, he picked up the tea. "I think not. Quebec is personally important for and to her. More would require more work. I believe she'll be a staunch ally. She sent you a gift."

Rising, he walked to the bag he'd brought in, took out a small pouch. Intrigued, Fallon opened it.

The moonstone pendant glowed white. Carved on it, as if as one, three figures blended. The owl, the wolf, the alicorn.

"It's beautiful." The stone was set in silver, the words inscribed on its back read: WISDOM, COURAGE, LOYALTY. THE SPIRITS OF THE ONE. "And, like Arlys said, gracious. I've never seen work this fine outside of the vault we found in D.C."

"Her craftsmen do more than make the practical.

She has jewelers, silver- and goldsmiths, those skilled in working with silks, velvets, furs. Quebec will be a monarchy under her. I believe she'll rule well."

Because it touched her, Fallon hooked the pendant onto the chain with Max's wedding ring, Simon's St. Michael's medal. Rubbing her fingers over the faces, she spoke casually. "She didn't tempt you?"

"She's too fancy for me," he said, clearly amused. "And not my type. What do you need to ask of me?"

She looked at him then. "I wanted to give you time at your cottage, but instead I'm asking you to stay in New Hope, to help Duncan season some of the recruits. I'm sorry to—"

He waved her off before she finished. "Fifteen centuries I've waited to fulfill my duties. This is what I'm made for." In a rare show of affection, he closed a hand over hers. "I answer the call of The One."

"You could have Colin's room while you're here."

"Now, that does tempt me. But I'd do better with the seasoning if I stayed at the barracks. Perhaps I'll be invited to a meal when your mother returns."

"I'll make sure of it. In the meantime, I can tell you they eat well at the barracks. We've seen to that."

"Then I'll join Duncan and Travis, and get a meal. A safe journey west." He rose, retrieved his bag, then looked back at her. "You've done well, girl."

"High praise from the old man."

Alone, she sat a moment longer. Not just battle plans now, not only training, readying troops. Now alliances, politics, diplomats, borders. Now visions for the tomorrows must come through the smoke. She had no desire to be a queen, to rule over the re-forming world. But if she took up the sword to lead that world to war, she needed to know the ways to embrace the peace, and hold it.

Once, she'd drawn back the curtain to show Colin the

blood and battle, the worst the dark demanded. She held the hope that one day, she'd draw it back to peace, to unity, to all the light offered.

But for now she rose to prepare for the journey, for her quest to find more souls to lead to war.

While Fallon packed provisions, Lana sat in the pristine living room of Tereza Aldi, Lucy's grandmother. A handsome woman, her stone-gray hair coiled in a braided bun at her nape, she sat stiffly in a chair.

She offered no refreshment.

A wood-burning stove, obviously scavenged and added after the Doom, squatted in the corner and sent out some stingy heat.

Still, the chill in the room came as much from the woman as the winter.

"I appreciate you seeing me, Mrs. Aldi."

"I've told you we have nothing to say to each other, but you're persistent."

"Women raising children in this world have to be. I'd hoped you had some message you'd like me to take to Lucy."

"She made her choice."

"She told my daughter you once hid a magickal from Purity Warriors."

"We're not heathens." She lifted a hand to the cross she wore around her neck. "Or fanatics, like that godless cult."

"It was an act of kindness, of humanity, that involved considerable risk."

"They would have killed the boy—one no more than ten. We don't wish your deaths, Mrs. Swift. We only insist you keep your distance. We live quiet, peaceful lives here."

"You have a lovely community. As do the magickals who live across the river."

"They stay on their side, we on ours." She kept her hands folded, implacably, on her lap. "The boy wandered over, and should have known better."

"I have three sons," Lana said with a smile. "I can't count the times they should have known better. I have a daughter, too."

"I know who you are. Know who she is, and what she claims to be."

"She doesn't claim, she is. But more directly to you, she saved your granddaughter's life."

"I told you I have no desire to hear—"

"But you will hear." Lana's voice changed, snapped. She'd tolerate the chill, even what she considered the rude, but she wouldn't tolerate ignorance. "You'll hear, then I'll go. The child you raised—"

"*You* hear!" Tears as much from anger as grief sparked in dark eyes where lines fanned out in deep grooves. "I raised Lucia. I raised her because her father died in the Doom, and her mother, my own daughter, my only surviving child, changed."

In turn, Lana folded her hands in her lap. She considered the temper progress when measured against the cold stone wall she'd hit before. "How?"

"Became like you. Cursed, she was. Cursed, and mad with it. The world dying around us, friends and neighbors sick or already buried. My husband dead, my two sons dead. And my only daughter wild, wild and violent where she'd once been kind and loving."

When Mrs. Aldi looked away, her knuckles white as bone on her lap, Lana said nothing. Better to wait, Lana thought, let it all come out.

"She tried, my loving daughter, tried with fire from

her own hands, to burn down the house. Burn it down while the baby she'd wanted so much screamed in her crib. The baby's room, she started that fire in Lucia's room, and laughed like a mad thing, wept like a mad thing. Reason couldn't stop her, pleas couldn't as I rushed in to grab the baby, as others rushed to put out the fire. She only laughed and wept and threw more flames from her hands. Those flames struck one of the men who'd come to help, and she laughed and laughed as he burned. Laughed and wept as others dragged him out to try to save him.

"And when she turned to me, to the child I held in my arms, I saw what she meant to do. I shot her. I killed my child, one I loved with all my heart, to save her child.

"So don't speak to me of witchcraft and magicks."

"I'm sorry for your daughter, for all you lost, and for the terrible choice you had to make."

"You know *nothing* of it."

"You're wrong," Lana said quietly. "I've seen the madness. I faced it. I understand loss. I suffered it. I've known evil, with power and without. All of us who survived had to make terrible choices. The boy your granddaughter loves made a choice, like yours. To try to save the child you saved, he made a choice. It was Raiders, Mrs. Aldi, not magickals who attacked them. Just men, cruel men. Johnny could have gotten away, he could have left her and with his elfin abilities, run or hidden. Instead he fought to save her, and nearly died in the attempt. Would have died, as she would have if my daughter hadn't come to their aid."

Mrs. Aldi looked away, but those tightly pressed lips trembled. "He took her away."

"It seems nearly the other way around, according to Lucy. Johnny wanted to fight against the Dark Uncanny, against the dark that threatens us all. Lucy begged him not to leave her. They left the home they know because you forbade them to love."

"No good can come of mixing."

"Oh, I so disagree. My husband isn't magickal, our oldest son isn't. We're a family, Mrs. Aldi, one I love, one I'm proud of. We're in this world together, and if you push back, push away from that world, your own becomes smaller and smaller. Has the community across the river offered yours any violence?"

"We leave each other alone."

"Except when you hid a frightened boy, or when they offer healing balms or other aids to people here. You should ask your neighbors," Lana said when Mrs. Aldi blinked in shock. "Ask yourself if your pride and your bias—and it is bias—is more worth clinging to than the child you saved at such a terrible cost. A child who loves and misses you. She asked me to give you this."

Lana rose, laid a letter on the table by the chair.

"Thank you for seeing me," she said, and left the woman with a choice to make.

Fallon spent ten days in the West. Despite the purpose, she found time for amusement watching Meda flick Travis away like an overeager puppy. She enjoyed watching Taibhse glide through western skies, over land that offered mile after mile of open. They often slept in that open, under stars so brilliant it made her throat ache, drifted off to the music of coyote and wolf.

She found the potential for a base in Sedona, a place she hoped to revisit, with the staggering beauty of the red mountains, the magicks that whispered in the air.

In the canyons, by boiling rivers, Faol Ban raced and hunted. Near crystal lakes that reflected the spearing mountains, hawks cried and circled overhead, deer roamed thick through forests, leaped through high grass with white tails bobbing. Elk bugled at dawn and swarmed like an army over grasslands with no fences left to block their path.

Bear larger than she'd ever seen fished in streams while cougar and lynx hunted over rocky slopes.

She watched the majestic flight of an eagle, the stunning dive of a peregrine, and understood the wonder Duncan had felt during his time in the West.

In settlements and camps, she spoke to leaders, conversed when it suited in Arapaho, in Sioux, and once, to an old woman's delight, in Dutch.

They roamed through ruined cities, empty towns where ghosts roamed as thick as the deer and elk. It amazed her how many useful supplies had been abandoned, like the cars and trucks, the ranch houses, the cabins, even the weapons inside them.

Wild horses ran the plains in living rivers of speed and grace. Buffalo, hides thick with winter, cropped the swaying grasses.

"Generations ago, this land was taken from my people." Meda scanned the land, the mountains, from the saddle. "We'll have it back. It won't be taken from us again."

"Do you think that's what I want? To take?"

"If I did, I wouldn't fight beside you. But like the North Queen wants what she sees as hers, me and mine want what *is* ours. There won't be reservations. We won't be driven off again. This is home."

"And for those, not of your tribe, who see this and believe it is or could be home?"

"There's room." Meda shrugged. "There's room for those who respect our sacred places, who work the land with respect, or leave it as they find it. I've already given you my allegiance. This isn't bargaining. It's truth."

"I've already given you my allegiance," Fallon returned. "This isn't bargaining, but another truth. The land here, or in the east, over the oceans, the oceans themselves, isn't mine to give. But it will be held in the light by your people, and all people."

"I pray for the day we see that truth. But we have a war to win first."

As she rode on, Travis let out a long sigh. "She just gets hotter."

Fallon rolled her eyes, and nudged Laoch into a trot.

Later, as the sun dipped, sent its first roses to bloom over the peaks in the west, she spotted a settlement tucked into the basin near the foothills of what her map told her was the Sierra Nevada.

"Should be good farming land," Travis commented. "Good pasture."

"Whatever's left of Reno's to the northwest. And Lake Tahoe. It could be a good spot for a base." Fallon scanned the houses, the farmland—probably ranch land out here, she corrected. "Let's see if we can convince them to join up, maybe we can spend the night here before we head north."

"I don't see much security." Meda continued on in an easy walk.

"We're still, what, a mile away?" Scanning, Fallon looked for any sign they'd be met with hostility. "They've got cook fires going. I can smell them. Meat cooking. No electric power. I can see solar on a few roofs, and somebody built a couple windmills. We'll ride in slow, so they have time to look us over."

And the crows came.

With their first shriek, an alarm sounded with the manic clanging of bells. Even as Laoch leaped into a gallop, riders on horseback poured out of the trees, headed for the settlement. The air rang with gunfire, tore with screams. Fallon saw a flash of fire streak from one of the houses, take out a rider.

On the gallop, Meda nocked an arrow, took out another.

"Travis! Grab that kid, three o'clock."

He looked where his sister indicated, said, "Oh hell," and veered off toward the little girl who stood frozen with her hands over her ears.

Fallon drew her sword and rode into battle.

At least thirty, she thought, most armed with handguns or rifles, a few with axes or swords. They shot wildly, indiscriminately, and even without Travis's empathic ability, she sensed a kind of desperation.

She blocked bullets, slashed with sword. If she enflamed the guns, she'd disarm the defenders as well. Even as she considered it, Faol Ban leaped on a rider, tore him off his mount. She caught the symbol of a PW tattooed on his arm.

On another slap of magick, a fireball whizzed by. She felt the heat from it—entirely too close. She wheeled Laoch, shot her own fire at another PW. When he fell to the ground, a woman rushed outside, began to pummel him with her fists.

As she charged a swordsman, Fallon had to throw up her shield to block an arrow. She glanced up to the boy perched on a roof with a bow.

"Goddamn it, watch it! We're the good guys."

It took less than ten brutal minutes. At the end of it, bodies littered the ground, blood soaked into it. She looked up at the crows, circling under an endless sky painted with reds, golds, pinks, and a magnificent beauty.

"You're done here." She thrust her sword up, and added their bodies to the rest. "It's done," she called out. "They're down. Travis?"

"A-okay. They're not all dead," he added.

"Good. I want to know where they came from. Meda." She turned. "You're hit."

"A graze." With as much disgust as discomfort, Meda looked down at the sleeve of her jacket, torn by the bullet, stained with the blood from the wound. "I bartered my ass off for this jacket."

"I'll fix it, and you. It's done," Fallon called again. "We're here to help. I'm Fallon Swift, with my brother Travis, and Meda of the First Tribe."

A man stepped out on the porch of a house. Maybe thirty, she thought, with a scruffy beard, a mop of brown hair under a cowboy style hat.

"Yancy Logan. Thanks for the assist."

"Glad we were in the neighborhood. Are you in charge?"

He took off his hat, dragged his fingers through the mop before he set it back in place. "I might be, seeing as they killed Sam Tripper, who more or less was."

A woman stepped out behind him with a wailing baby on her hip. Fallon felt a quiet power from both of them. "You're welcome here. Yancy, she's The One."

"Okay, honey." He blew out a long breath. "I guess we should start cleaning up this mess out here."

CHAPTER NINETEEN

They burned twenty-two PW bodies and three from the settlement they called Bright Valley. Fallon worked with a healer on wounded, both friend and foe.

She tended last to the knuckles of the woman who'd run out to use her fists on a downed PW.

"I don't think we'd have held them off if you hadn't shown up, so thanks. I'm Ann."

"Ann. You're welcome." She glanced over as Yancy's wife—Faith, half-Apache on her mother's side, Fallon remembered—brought her a mug of tea. "Thanks. I gave some balm to Wanda, your healer. You should use some a couple times a day for a day or two."

"They feel fine now."

"The balm will keep it that way. I noticed you're mostly women and children."

"Out of a hundred and fifty-six—sorry, fifty-three now—we have fifty-five men over eighteen. We haven't had much trouble before." Faith handed Ann another mug. "Small groups of nomads or Raiders, but nothing like today. We thought we were ready, but we weren't."

"We got complacent," Ann decided. "I haven't seen a PW raid since I got here."

"How long ago?"

"Almost five years now." Ann, a small, diamond-shaped scar on her left cheekbone, flexed her healing knuckles. "We got hit by one outside of Reno and had to run for it. I had my sister and little brother—not blood, but heart."

"I understand."

"Well, we got out. Lost everything but what we could carry and ran for it."

Fallon heard the bitterness, understood the pummeling fists. "Sometimes you fight, sometimes you run."

"My brother got horses. He's got a way with horses and animals altogether."

"An animal empath. My youngest brother—blood and heart—is the same."

"Then you know. We rode south and ended up here. Bright Valley, it's a good place, with good people."

Ann paused, rubbed both hands over her face. Her voice wavered. "Sam, I want to say Sam was a real good man. One you could depend on, and everybody here . . ."

She dropped her hands again, straightened her shoulders. "He's going to be missed. People around here aren't bloodthirsty, but they're going to want to hang the ones who killed him that aren't already dead."

"Yancy will calm everybody down," Faith predicted with a steadiness that rang with truth. "He's got that way."

"If anybody can, Yancy can."

Faith smiled at that, then the smile died away. "But I don't know what in hell we're going to do with them. Where we'd put them, how we'd deal with them."

"We'll take them."

"Where?" Ann shifted her attention back to Fallon.

"I'll explain, but we need to talk to the prisoners."

"Yancy's got Sal watching them. They're tied up tight in the sheriff's office—Sam's office. Sam," Faith said and pressed her fingers to her eyes for a moment. "We don't have a jail, but they're tied up, and Sal won't let them pull any crap. Ann, can you take her? I'm helping ride herd on the young ones."

"Sure, I can."

They went out of the small building into the street, where blood still stained the ground. But people worked to board up broken windows or led horses back to a town paddock. She signaled to Travis and Meda.

"Will he lead?" she asked Ann. "Your Yancy?"

"I'd say he and Sal will help run things, as much as they're run. Yancy's quiet, but he's nobody's fool. And Sal doesn't take crap for certain."

They walked to a box of a building with two chairs on a narrow porch. Inside, the prisoners sat on the floor, bound hand and foot.

Sal had her booted feet on the desk while she sipped whiskey. She'd been a redhead once, Fallon noted, as streaks of ginger still wound through the gray of her long braid. Like Yancy, she wore a cowboy hat, hers tipped down over her forehead. And a gun belt with a pistol rode on her narrow hips.

"Hey there, Ann, how are those knuckles?"

"Just fine now. This here's Fallon Swift, and—sorry, I didn't get the other names."

"That'd be young Travis and Meda. Had my ear to the ground," Sal added. "I'm pleased to meet you. Maybe a little sorry you figured you should heal up these assholes, but pleased just the same."

"It's easier to talk to them if they're not bleeding."

"Got nothing to say to you, devil whore." One, black-bearded, potbellied, spat on the floor. "Or any of your like."

"Oh, I think you'll have plenty to say." Tapping her fingers on the hilt of her sword, Fallon circled the bound men, arranged back-to-back on the floor.

The potbellied one wore boots with toes as pointy as needles, a fancy flag—red, white, and blue—sweeping up the sides. And soles worn so thin they showed holes at the balls of the feet.

She decided to start with the youngest—bearded as well, but scraggly, patchy. He wore a faded denim jacket that carried a poorly embroidered PW AND PROUD! on the back.

He'd taken an arrow in the hip, and though she'd healed it, she hadn't taken the pain. She imagined it ached like fire.

He couldn't have been older than Ethan.

"What's your name?"

"Ain't got nothing to say to you, whore."

She gave Travis a glance, then crouched down to stare eye to eye. "I can smell your fear."

"Fuck you."

"You follow Jeremiah White."

His eyes, a faded blue, held hate as well as the fear and pain. "He's gonna wipe you and your like off the face of this earth."

"How many have you killed? How many women have you raped in your quest for purity as defined by Jeremiah White?"

He twisted his mouth into a sneer that helped dampen any pity for his pain. "Many as I could."

"You tell her, Ringo."

She glanced to her left, to the bald man with a grizzled gray beard.

"Really? Ringo?"

"He goes by that," Travis said easily, "because it makes him feel badass. His name's actually Wilber."

"Looks like a Wilber," she said as he shot a wide-eyed glance at Travis. "I'm going to call you Wilber. Where'd you come from, Wilber? Where's your base? How many in your base?"

"Fuck you, whore!"

"Excuse me." Travis nudged by Ann, walked over, slammed a fist into Wilber's face. "Call my sister a whore again, I'll pull your guts out through your broken nose."

The move surprised her, she couldn't deny it. Travis preferred diplomacy over fists. But at the moment, the glint in his eyes didn't have a hint of the diplomatic.

"That's all right, Travis. Being called a whore by a cowardly rapist named Wilber doesn't bother me. You know these people want to string you up like you've strung up the innocent magickals you've tortured."

She cocked her head, smiled in a way that drained the color bravado had put into Wilber's face. "Maybe I'll let them. After all, their community, their rules. Or I could try to reason with them if you tell me what I want to know. Where's your base?"

Though tears leaked from his eyes, blood streamed from his nose, he said nothing.

"California," Travis supplied. "The northern part, sort of central, he thinks. They called their base Second Eden."

"Shut your mind down, asshole," the black-bearded one snapped. "That demon's pulling thoughts out of your head."

"Try shutting your own down . . . Pete," Travis suggested. "Wilber here's afraid of the rope."

"He oughta be." Enjoying herself, Sal drank more whiskey. "It's something we've got plenty of around here."

"How many on your base?"

When Travis punched Wilber again, Fallon brushed him back. "Jesus, Travis, enough."

"You didn't hear what he was thinking about you and Meda, and these other ladies. Trying to keep his mind off the question. Give me a minute, they're all thinking at once. Earthquake. Ah, okay, okay."

Travis shut his eyes. "They had about two hundred. The bald guy—hi, Tom—he and some others made it up there from the L.A. area. Earthquakes there drove them out. Then *bang*, they get hit with another in their Eden. Leveled the base, killed most. The ones they rode in here with lived through it. They've been riding for weeks—lost a few on the way. Haven't had much luck hunting, mostly because they're dicks, got good and lost a couple times. Again, dicks. They've been out of supplies for days now, then spotted the settlement here."

Nodding, Fallon rose, circled them again. "I can take it from there, follow the logic. They'd kill everybody they could, rape and enslave the rest, take the food, the horses, cattle. Maybe settle down right here until they figured where to go next."

"Time to get that rope." Sal tossed back the rest of the whiskey, winked at Fallon.

Wilber began to blubber, literally blubber, with tears and snot leaking.

Fallon walked over to ease a hip on the corner of the desk. Ann leaned in to whisper in her ear, "She doesn't mean it."

"I got that. Would you mind if we talked outside, Sal? And maybe Ann could find Yancy. Travis and Meda can stand guard here."

"I could use some air. That's some trick you've got, young fella," she told Travis. "And you got a solid right jab along with it. Ann, I think Yancy went on down to the livery."

When they stepped outside, into star-struck night, Sal hissed out a breath. "Sam Tripper was a friend of mine, a good friend. I'm not going to tolerate any lynching, but we're not going to cut those bastards loose, either."

"I have a solution that should satisfy you and the rest."

"Is it a dark hole where they'll never see the light again or have one minute of joy? Because, goddamn it, Sam was a friend of mine."

"I think it's close. Tell me this before Yancy comes. How many of the women could be trained to fight, and be willing?"

"All of them." No hesitation. "Every blessed one."

"Good. I can send someone to help with that, and with your security. How many would you estimate are battle-ready now?"

"What kind of battle?"

"Major."

She took off her hat, slapped it over her thigh a few times. "Maybe a dozen here could handle that. Maybe."

Fallon watched Yancy walk, a lanky stride, from the paddock. People rushed toward him, obviously asking questions. He took the time, she noted, to answer before moving on.

"Would he be one of the twelve?"

"He would. He's not as placid as he looks. He can ride like a son of a bitch, and shoot the same. Got a level head on his shoulders."

"That was my impression. And you?"

"Yeah, I can handle myself. Yancy," she said when he joined them.

"Sal. Ma'am, I want to thank you and those with you for helping dig the graves. We'll have a memorial in the morning, say some words. I asked Old Eb to say them, Sal."

"That's a good choice."

"My Faith'd like to have you all to supper. You're welcome, Sal. We can get somebody to watch the prisoners."

"Will you let me take the prisoners?" Fallon asked.

"I'd be happy to give them over."

"Just hold on," Sal interrupted. "I'd like more particulars there."

Yancy puffed out a breath, looked up at the stars. "We can't keep them here, Sal, and that's a fact. Somebody's bound to get their blood up and do them in. Too much of me, I gotta say, wants to let them, and be done with it."

"We have prisons," Fallon explained. "Travis and Meda can take them back tonight. They'll be locked up. They're murderers. They'll be locked up for life. We have the means, the system. It's your place, your people, your decision, but I can promise you if you let us take them, they'll pay."

"You talking bars and locks?" Sal demanded.

"I am. We have other facilities for prisoners of war, those who qualify. But these aren't POWs. They're killers. Bars and locks."

"I can live with that. How many you got locked up?"

"Including POWs? Several thousand."

Sal's mouth dropped open. Yancy simply stared out of narrowed eyes.

"You don't have any outside communication," Fallon decided.

"We get someone comes through now and again," Yancy said. "Maybe brings some news in. Heard some rumors about fighting back east, about you. We got Carrie—she sees things. She says she's seen you fighting, an army with you, but she didn't know where."

"There's been more than one fight. You don't know we've taken D.C."

Sal gripped Fallon's arm. "Girl, you took those government bastards down?"

"We did."

"You're the answer to prayers I've been afraid to speak. I've got a pile of questions for you."

"They got Sal's son, the government did, and my sister."

"I'll answer your questions. Let me arrange to have Travis and Meda transport the prisoners. I'll stay the night. We have a lot to talk about."

When she got home, snow fell in fat, soft flakes. And she saw her mother coming from the greenhouse with a basket, moving along a shoveled path.

Her hair bundled up under a red cap that matched her knitted gloves, Lana kept her eyes on the ground to watch for slick spots. On a surge of love, Fallon rushed toward her.

"Mom."

Lana's head jerked up. She very nearly lost her balance, then beamed and opened her arms. "You're home! You're finally home."

"Just this minute. Let me get Laoch settled—and I promised Faol Ban one of your biscuits."

"I'll get it for him." She met the wolf's patient eyes while Taibhse glided—white through white—to one of his favorite perches. "I'm so glad to see you all. This calls for some serious hot chocolate."

"With whipped cream?"

"It's not serious without it. Don't be long. Come on, boy, I've got a biscuit with your name on it."

Home, Fallon thought as she scooped grain for the alicorn, gave a carrot treat to the faithful Grace. Not the farm, but still, home. Stepping out again, she looked through the snowfall toward the barracks. Duncan should be there, she thought.

She sent her mind toward his. *I'm home.*

Moments later, she heard his voice in hers. *I'll be there as soon as I can. I missed you.*

So smiling, she walked through that snowfall and into a kitchen that smelled of chicken soup, bread, and, gloriously, chocolate.

"Have you eaten?"

"Not since breakfast. I stayed a little longer than I'd planned."

"Then it's soup first."

"I'll get it, for both of us. Where's Dad?" she asked as she got bowls, ladled them with soup.

"Hunting party. Ethan's in town. He's had this idea to hold a kind of vet clinic. They'd both be here if they'd known you'd be home today for certain."

"I stayed longer to help with some basic training—combat and magickal. Bright Valley's an interesting place."

"So I hear. Travis filled us in. Earthquakes in California?"

"Apparently severe enough to destroy a PW base. I flew over to see for myself. It's rubble. The prisoners?"

"In the Hatteras facility. It seemed the best choice for now. Hard cases," Lana said as she turned the hot chocolate to low, sat to eat with her daughter. "Travis said their minds are, at least for now, hardened. Even the young one. He also had a lot to say about the land out west. The mountains, the plains. He enjoyed every minute of the trip—and said you'd managed to recruit over five hundred."

"A lot of the five hundred are green and greener than green. But they can be used as non-combatants. I want to hear about your trip."

"Well, it cemented I'm an East Coast girl. All that flat land, miles and miles? I like the hills. And my God,

Fallon, the wind. It just screams over that flat land. And so much of it empty," she said. "It brings it home just how desolate the world is now. You can forget, living here in a busy, thriving community, that there are miles and miles of nobody."

"And Riverbend?"

"Small and segregated, as you said. I tell you, when you see those miles and miles of nobody, it shows how ridiculous it is to live barely a stone's throw from other people and behave as if they're not there."

"Bigotry comes in all levels. It's never right or smart or productive. You talked to Lucy's grandmother?"

"The formidable Mrs. Aldi. A very tough nut to crack."

"Did you?"

"I'd say some cracks opened. She does love Lucy—or Lucia, as she calls her. DUs attacked when Lucy was just a baby, so Mrs. Aldi's prejudice has its roots there. And Lucy's mother came into power. A witch."

As if she just needed to touch, Lana reached out, ran her hand along Fallon's arm. "Like too many in the beginning, the change drove her mad. She tried to burn down the house, with the baby in it."

"Oh my God."

"Mrs. Aldi saved Lucy, and to save her, killed her own child."

"To have to make a choice like that . . . It's no wonder she's bitter."

"It's a terrible burden, Fallon, a terrible price to pay. I had more sympathy for her when she broke enough to tell me. In any case, after we talked, and after she read Lucy's letter, she gave me one for Lucy in return. She isn't giving her blessing, but she's giving her acceptance. That's the gateway."

She's so beautiful, Fallon thought. She'd seen it all

her life, knew it went beyond the physical, but in that moment, over soup in the kitchen, it simply struck her hard.

She leaned her head toward Lana's shoulder.

"She saw something in you. She had to see it."

"I don't know about that, but she heard me. Finally."

"And on the other side of the river?"

"Not as stubborn," Lana told her. "The sentiment there seemed to run from apathy to resentment for their neighbors. I'll say you were right to send your family. It gave us weight and status we wouldn't have had otherwise. And Ethan, along with an injured puppy, helped turn the tide on the NM side."

"How is that?"

"This poor little pup had been mauled by a larger animal. They were going to put him down, and the little girl who loved him begged and begged her father not to kill him. He was suffering, and they didn't have the means to help the poor little guy. But Ethan intervened, was able to keep the puppy calm, begin to heal him until I got there. The little girl hadn't named him yet—the little guy was barely weaned. He's Ethan now," she said with a laugh.

"A sweet little mutt named for our boy—who showed them in a very real and simple way that magick can be kind and compassionate.

"The upshot is, we have forty-eight willing to fight. And your dad thinks others will come along."

"That's really good news."

"Oh, I have better." Lana rose to finish off the chocolate. "We found the other communities you earmarked. Add seventy-three more. And best of all?" She tipped her finger in a bowl of cream to whip it. "We found—or they found us—a band of nomads who'd traveled east from Idaho, down through Colorado, into Kansas, picking up more along the way. This way, Fallon. They were coming east to find you, to fight with you. Nearly seven hundred."

"Seven hundred?" Fallon's spoon clattered against her bowl. "That's more than I ever hoped for."

"There's more. Mick sent word he's added three hundred, bands migrating up from the south—again on their way to find you. Every base is adding more. The light, my baby, it spread, even through those miles and miles of nobody. They're coming to fight for you."

She felt the lift, the thrill of light spreading. "We'll take New York. We'll take it back from the dark. We'll take it for the light, and for you, Mom. For you and Max."

She looked over as Duncan came to the door, pulled it open. "Welcome home. Hi, Lana."

"Hi yourself. Come in and shut the door. We're about to have some hot chocolate."

He stomped snow off his boots. "I could go for some, thanks."

As she got the mugs, Lana studied the way they looked at each other. Love, she thought with an inward sigh, that came with longing and a healthy dose of lust.

"And for the goddess's sake, kiss the girl."

"Good idea." He strode across the kitchen, lifted Fallon off the stool, circled her once. And kissed the girl.

He couldn't stay long, but had a little more time with Fallon when she walked back to the barracks with him. She watched the troops train. Battles didn't wait for fine weather, so they held their mock fights in the snow, taking on Mallick's ghosts and each other.

Others did the same, she thought. In the West, the

Midwest, the South, the North. And more, still more, would come.

At Lana's invitation, Duncan and Mallick joined the family for dinner. She put on a hell of a spread—a kind of welcome home, Duncan imagined—with a rack of lamb, potatoes that looked like accordions—which, it turned out, Ethan called them—roasted with butter and herbs. Kale, nowhere on his list of favorites, done in some creamy sauce that made him a convert, a fancy salad crunchy with sprinkles of grain. Bread, wine, and the promise of lemon-berry tarts for dessert.

With all of that, it wasn't hard to follow Lana's rule of no war talk during dinner. Instead, they talked of the plans for expanding the clinic, Ethan's addition of a veterinary clinic, Hannah's upcoming exams. And the practical joke some of the recruits had tried—and failed—to pull on Mallick.

"They figured they'd catch Mallick in his shower," Duncan relayed, "and one of the magickals would flip the water to ice-cold."

"Some objected to training outdoors in the recent ice storm," Mallick explained.

"Wouldn't bother you." Relaxed, Fallon wagged her fork. "Even when I got an actual bathroom—after a *year*—Mallick still used the stream, which equaled an ice bath from October to May."

"Refreshing." Mallick lifted his wine.

"They'd hoped for shouts and curses, got nothing," Travis said between bites. "But that's not the best part. When the recruits hit the showers after training, turned on the water, it wasn't just water that came out."

"Snakes," Duncan said with a grin. "You can bet there were shouts then. Screams, shrieks, pandemonium.

We ran in there—Travis and I—figuring we were under attack."

"And holy shit! Wet, naked recruits—from both sides—running around, skinny little snakes slithering all over the place. And this guy?" Travis jerked a thumb at Mallick. "He just sort of glides in, Mr. Dignity, poofs the snakes, then glides out again. Never says a word."

"I believe they understood without any."

"I like snakes," Ethan said cheerfully. "Dad doesn't."

"They should have feet like everybody else." Simon shot a smile at Mallick. "Remind me not to get on your bad side."

"I'd tolerate a great deal in exchange for an invitation to a meal such as this."

"And we haven't even gotten to dessert."

When they did, Lana lifted the ban on war talk.

"I'd like to see the cowboys," Ethan mused. "And the buffalo, the mustangs."

"They're pretty magnificent," Fallon confirmed. "I asked Meda to go back, to help get them battle-ready. She agreed."

"That's a good choice," Simon decided. "The nomads have people who can work with the communities in the Midwest, but you should think about making an appearance there. Let them see you."

"All right. In the next few days."

"I've got a tidbit I haven't had a chance to pass on." With enthusiasm Travis dug into his tart. "When Meda and I transferred the prisoners to Hatteras, I poked them a little more. Easy reads," he added. "White was at their base before the quake. Just a couple days before."

"White, in California?" With a frown, Fallon nudged her tart aside. "We don't have any intel putting him in California."

"Now you do. You remember the younger one?"

"Wilber. The one you punched in the face. Twice."

"Yeah, that one. He's hoping White will come save him—all of them—lead them to their righteous victory. He kept thinking how it was the biggest day of his life when he heard White, in person, preach at the base in California. The dude's a true believer. It's not even so much he sees White as what you'd call a conduit to this asshole god of vengeance and bigotry he worships. More like White *is* his asshole god. That's who he's praying to anyway, to come bust him out so he can kill you personally for White. It's what he imagines doing to you before he kills you that earned him a punch in the face. Twice."

"He has to be flashing." Since Travis had already told him what the man had thought about Fallon—and it wasn't the sort of thing you spoke about at dinner—Duncan moved on. "No way he could get all the way to California otherwise without our getting some word on it."

"He's been known to work with DUs before. How does he, how do his followers justify that?" Fallon wondered.

"Ends, means," Simon answered. "The man's been preaching his ugly racism and twisted god for more than twenty years. Plenty did the same before him, before the Doom. He's just taken it to a new level."

"We're cutting into his numbers, and after New York, we'll hunt him down. He can join Hargrove in prison. We cut off the head of the snake."

"There is always another snake," Mallick said.

"One at a time." Deliberately, she pulled the tart back, took a bite. "He's poisoned the world long enough."

CHAPTER TWENTY

Winter raged on, week by week with brutal cold, icy winds, long nights with bulging clouds, pregnant with snow, that smothered the sun, the moon, and stars. No hopeful February thaw broke the bitter, so the world seemed cased inside a snow globe constantly shaken.

Fallon considered waiting another week, two weeks, to launch the attack on New York. Indeed, some she respected advised just that.

She went out alone, cast the circle, stood inside it under the blank sky and called the gods.

"Fill me, gods of peace, gods of war, into me your wisdom pour. For this world you've placed in my hands, I accept all your commands. To help me guide this world to light, open the curtain to my sight. This I ask with humility, for as you wish, so mote it be."

She let the vision come.

The once great city burned and smoked, its flames and ash whirling through the wild wind of a blizzard. Red lightning streaked over the black sky, staining it like blood blooming on a dingy cloth. The battle, brutal and bitter as the night, raged below the murdered sky with a roaring as vicious as the gale. Men and women fought on the streets with filthy snow heaped like mountains. Rats, toothy and fat, scurried under those streets to feast on the dead and dying piled in tunnels. Dogs, feral as the rats, prowled and snapped. Inside buildings or the rubble of them that formed caves, the very young and very old huddled in terror. Balls of fire exploded, turning men into shrieking torches.

Overhead, she saw the sweep of a black dragon. For an instant his eyes, red against the black, met hers. He turned his sinuous body, graceful as a swan. And breathed his killing fire.

On his back, Petra rode with her hair streaming, her face exultant. Her laugh, savage bells, rang and rang and rang.

The curtain closed. She had her answer.

Fallon waited another moment, letting the vision fade, then closed the circle. Duncan stood, wind streaming through his hair, just outside it.

"I didn't know you were here."

"You were a little occupied. I couldn't sleep, then wake-dreamed of you standing here. I saw what you saw."

"We can't wait."

"No. But I was never on the side of waiting."

"No, you weren't. We attack as planned, when we planned. Midnight tomorrow." With her eyes gray as the smoke, fierce as the battle, she held out a hand. "Let's take tonight."

At midnight, in the raw whip of February, Fallon sat astride Laoch, Taibhse on her arm, Faol Ban beside her. Troops stood or mounted, as did those in Arlington, on The Beach, in forests, on plains, in fields, on rocky rises.

She looked at her mother and Ethan, who'd stay behind for now. Healers and support would be needed in waves, just as fresh troops would be needed.

She knew her mother's thoughts: Come home safe. Bring your father, your brothers home safe.

But Lana said, "Fight well, fight strong."

She saw Arlys gripping Bill Anderson's hand. She wouldn't risk the chronicler or the elder on this launch. Fred, not only with her brood but the children of others who stood ready to fight, sent a smile full of faith toward Eddie.

Katie moved to Lana so the women slid arms around each other's waists. Hannah and Jonah, she knew, waited at the clinic, beside a mobile with a team for the signal.

It was time to give it.

She drew her sword, cast her mind to every leader in every base. "Fight well," she said as her mother had. "Fight strong."

Lifting her sword to the sky, she flashed. Thousands flashed with her.

Lightning exploded in the sky. The spires that still stood bled red in its savage light. Smoke choked the frigid air, spewing up from fresh fires whose heat churned the snow into ash-black sludge. Buildings along the wide avenue that bisected the city into east and west huddled battered and broken where wild laughter echoed.

A rumble of engines, the blast of explosions, tortured screams ripped from the west. As planned, her troops fanned out along the grid of what had been Midtown.

A small army of Raiders on snowmobiles, in burly trucks roared in.

You first, Fallon thought, and charged.

Duncan veered his horse left as she took out the lead rider with one killing slash and sent the rumbling vehicle and its pillion rider tumbling through the air.

He fought his way to the first truck, smashing power

at the windshield, following it with flame. While the driver and his companions screamed, he surged through the trampled snow to the back of the truck, broke the locks to free the half a dozen people locked inside.

"Get clear!" he shouted as the crack of gunfire, the whiz of arrows in flight ripped through the city's canyons.

A girl of about sixteen, blood running down her face, leaped out. "Screw that." She grabbed for a charred piece of wood and, wielding it like a club, rushed into the fight.

He felt the first slap of power whip toward him, whirled to meet it with his own. As those magicks, dark and light, clashed, the air bloomed bloody red. He pushed into it, sword flaming, power pulsing.

Dealing with a group of Raiders, he knew, was only the beginning. As he took the next truck, burst the doors open so prisoners tumbled free, black lightning rained from the sky. With it came a new surge of power on dark wings.

He saw the face, contorted with glee, the eyes, black, piercing. Even as he braced, sword and power ready, an arrow winged out, struck the enemy in the heart. The wind tore through the great, edgy wings, tattering them as power died. Duncan looked toward Tonia when the body fell into the soot-stained snow.

"I could've handled it."

"I did." Guiding her horse with her knees—she'd been one of Meda's top students—Tonia nocked another arrow. "Ready?"

"For this? All my life."

Together, they led their brigade west.

As Duncan and Tonia moved west, Simon east, Fallon south, block by brutal block, Colin fought in Queens, Mallick in Brooklyn. By boat, on foot, on horseback, Mick's troops surged on lower Manhattan from the east, Flynn poured his in from the west.

War cries ringing, resistance fighters teemed into the streets, climbed over rubble, many armed with nothing more than clubs or fists. While crows screamed, while magicks clashed as violent as swords, they stormed the city held by the dark for a generation.

Faeries swooped through fire and smoke to fly wounded out of the fray, to lift children, the elderly out of the war zone. Some struck down had to be taken out through lightning strikes, through sudden, shocking explosions.

Hour by hour, foot by agonizing foot, they drove the enemy back. When they lost ground, lost men, they regrouped, pushed on.

At first light, weak, dull, smeared with smoke, Fallon drew her exhausted troops back, called in fresh.

The first strike in the battle of New York raged for fourteen hours with a toll of five hundred dead or wounded. For the price they regained the heart of the city, several sectors on its fringes.

Fallon ordered a triage set up for wounded, a shelter for the horses, guards posted to hold the lines they'd drawn. Troops from the first wave were billeted, fed, ordered to rest.

She stood outside a building in that heart and, curious, used the sleeve of her already filthy jacket to wipe at soot.

Magickal symbols, she noted. Protective symbols, still beating, still carrying light. She moved to glass doors, waved a hand, and when they opened, walked inside.

Large, echoing, marble and gilt dulled with time, but undamaged. Many doors—elevators, she corrected. Photos of people, smiling through layers of dust, lined the walls. Some had fallen—vibrated off from explosions, she imagined.

She opened herself, searched, searched, but could

find no scent, no taste, no remnants of dark. So here, she thought, she'd make her HQ.

She turned to Travis. Like her, he was soaked with blood, grime, wet from the snow. But, and she thanked the gods, unharmed.

"This'll work. It's protected, and whatever protected it was strong enough to hold that light all these years. We can billet more troops here, and wounded who haven't been transported or treated."

She rubbed at the dirt on her face, managed to make it worse. "We need to send elves to the other commanders, get updated sitreps."

"You need sleep. Hey, me, too."

"As soon as we're set up. We need to hold the ground we took today. And I need, as soon as possible, a list of the dead, a list of the wounded. I need to talk to the resistance fighters we picked up today. We need to coordinate."

She squeezed the back of her neck, tried to roll the worst of the ache out of her shoulders. Her eyes stung so each blink felt like a swipe of sandpaper. So much to do now, right now, she thought, with this breath between the fight between life and death.

"POWs need to be transported."

Travis pulled off a wool cap, dragged a hand through his filthy hair. "I don't know if we've got any yet."

"When and if. We need a team to handle the bodies. Ours, theirs. Any minors, any too old, sick, or unwilling to fight should be taken to safety."

"They're already on that. You chose those teams before we left New Hope, so they're already on it."

"Good. Travis, I need to get word to New Hope, I need to be sure, then send word back that Dad and Colin are alive, Duncan and Tonia, Eddie and Will, and—"

"I know. I'll send some elves out. What was this place?" His eyes, red-rimmed like hers, scanned the space.

"I'm not sure, I need to check the old maps and find out. Because it was important enough to earn strong protection. I'm going to go through it, find the best place for a kind of command center."

"You're sure it's clear. I don't feel anything, but—"

"It's clear."

He took her at her word. "Then I'll find you once I've got the reports."

She searched out a stairway, empty and echoing with her bootsteps as she walked up. She found offices, most with desks, some with other furniture. Desks separated with partitions in big open spaces.

Dead plants, framed photos coated with dust, computers Chuck might revive, strange little notes, their edges curled, the paper crisp as bacon.

Bagels for 8:00
Table read 1/3

Mike (maybe) 212-555-1021

Another echoing area had rows of seats, rows and rows, and a kind of stage, big lights overhead, a large . . . camera?

A . . . performance space? she wondered. A theater? A studio?

She'd need someone who'd lived through the Doom to study it.

On another level, she found more desks—no partitions—the remnants of computers—destroyed—more lights, another camera, screens like Chuck had in his basement. Monitors.

She wandered through, then into a large office space—big desk, she noted. It would serve well. The dirt and soot lay so thick on the big window she couldn't see through it. So she laid her hands on the glass until it cleared.

She could see fires still burning, a large blaze to the east, smaller spurts to the west and south. Below, troops carried the dead through another snowfall that swirled in high winds.

Others transported supplies to another building. Elves blurred by. Archers held positions on roofs, or through the broken windows on high floors.

"Yes, this'll work," she murmured.

She shrugged off the saddlebag on her shoulder to a sofa. Sent up plumes of dust. They'd clean, she thought. Clear away the dust, the grime, the spiderwebs. But for now she waved her hand to clean the desk, the desk chair. She pulled out her maps, sat.

She spread out the newest one to mark the progress of the first strike. Then, weary, laid her head on the desk.

She'd close her eyes for a minute, just a minute.

She fell asleep instantly, and dreamed of war.

Duncan found her there, set the New Hope version of MREs down on the desk, dragged a blanket out of her saddlebag to throw over her shoulders. Then, without bothering to clean it off, he stretched out on the dirty couch to grab some sleep for himself.

He woke to the smell of coffee and hot food, blinked his eyes open to see Fallon awake at the desk. She spooned in soup while she watched him.

"How could you sleep on that filthy couch?"

"It's no dirtier than I am."

As he sat up, she held her hand over the second MRE to heat it.

"How can you sleep sitting?" he wondered, and got up to grab the food. "Your dad and Colin are fine," he began.

"I know. Travis told me." She tapped her head. "Tonia,

Mick, Mallick, all of them, holding their own, holding the line. It'll be dark soon. The troops in the first wave should be rested and ready."

"We took them by surprise, the enemy, with the first strike." He thought the soup the most excellent ever made in the history of soup. "They'll be ready now, too. We got to Times Square. It doesn't look like the DVDs or books now, but we got there, and we're holding it. What I hear is Mallick's forces sent the PWs running to hell. But there's a pack of shifters, DUs, giving them some grief."

He ran through what he knew, and Fallon adjusted her map accordingly. "We'll send more shifters to Mallick, have the merpeople cut off the PWs' escape route by water. We're going to need to take the tunnels, but for now, we can close them off. I still need to go over the old maps. There are landmarks still standing, and we can use them. Taking the city's more important than preserving specific sites, but whatever we can preserve will matter later. Especially to those who lived through the Doom."

"It still beats," he said as he ate. "Not like D.C."

"Yes, it still beats. And this place mattered," she added. "Enough to cloak it in protection strong enough to hold back the DUs, the military, the crazies."

"This may sound a little crazy, but I think this is where Fred and Arlys worked."

Frowning, she shifted to face him. "Fred and Arlys? Why do you think that?"

"I grew up on the stories. I know you've heard them, but probably not as often or in the detail I did. I drew a sketch once, of Arlys at the newscaster's desk, with the dead guy beside her. You know that story, right?"

"Her last broadcast from New York."

"Yeah. I was about twelve, and thought it was really cool, so I drew it—the way I saw it in my head. When

I showed it to Arlys, I realized, not so cool, not for her. But she said I got it right, and asked if she could keep it to remind her to tell the truth even when it's scary."

He took Fallon's hand. "Come on."

He led her out of the office, into the place with the desks, the long counter under the lights, in front of the camera.

"Put Arlys and the dead body up there, and that's my sketch."

"That's why," Fallon acknowledged. "That's why it's here for us, why it's here to serve as the center of command. Fred protected it, Arlys told the world the truth. They held back the dark, and now so will we."

For two weeks in the bitter cold, war ripped claws through the already torn city. It rampaged through the boroughs like a wild thing. In the third week, the Light for Life forces lost fifty troops in an ambush when they worked to clear a crosstown tunnel. Fallon led in a hundred more to beat back the alliance of DUs and Raiders in the green glow of faerie light.

She emerged into winter sunlight that struck the huge mounds of snow her troops had cleared from the streets and entryways. The crows still circled, smoke still spewed skyward, but the tide was turning. She felt it in her bones, and with it a hope that drove away the fatigue.

She started to mount Laoch, paused at the call of her name. Starr streaked toward her.

"You need to come. It's Colin."

"No, he's not—"

"Alive, but he's hurt. He's hurt bad. You need to come." She who rarely touched, gripped Fallon's hand. "He's with Jonah and Hannah. They got him to the mobile, but—"

With her hand vised on Starr's, Fallon flashed them both.

Colin lay on a gurney, his face bleached white, his eyes glazed, his body trembling. With horror Fallon saw the tourniquet above the elbow of his left arm, and Hannah holding compresses to the stub beneath.

Jonah submerged that arm, wrapped in gauze, sealed in a bag, in a tub of ice.

"The bleeding's slowing down. You're going to be all right, Colin," Hannah assured him. "We're going to get you back to New Hope. He's in shock. Starr got him here fast—and the limb, but . . ."

Fallon turned, looked directly into Jonah's eyes. "Will he live?"

"I don't know." Jonah laid a hand on Colin, obviously willing the vision of life and death that had once nearly driven him to take his own. "It's just not clear, it's not yes or no the way it usually is."

"Then it's not no. Can you reattach his arm?"

"Not here, and . . ." He drew her toward the back of the mobile. He kept his voice low, kept it calm. "We haven't done anything like this at the clinic. I don't know if Rachel can or not. She'll try. Like Hannah said, Starr got him here fast. We've cleaned the arm, done the emergency treatment, but this is massive, complicated surgery, Fallon. And we can't flash him back. The blood loss, the shock. He wouldn't survive it."

"Then he stays here. Starr, I need you to get my mother. Get someone who can flash, and get her here. She needs to bring her cauldron, three white candles, carnation petals, bay leaves, fresh earth, blessed water, three bloodstones, a white cloth, and leather. Enough leather to cover his arm right down to over the fingers. Her healing balm, her strongest healing potion. Have you got all that?"

"Yes. It was a sword strike," she added. "It took his arm, and still he killed the enemy before he fell. I'll be fast."

"What are you going to do?" Hannah bathed the cold sweat from Colin's face. "I cleaned the wound, and Jonah's protected the viability of the severed limb, but we need an OR, and even then—"

"He's not going to lose his arm." After nudging Hannah aside, Fallon leaned over her brother. "Colin, look at me. Hear me, see me. I can give you back your arm, but it has to be your choice. It won't be the same as it was. Do you understand?"

"No. Son of a bitch!"

"You'll have to relearn how to use it again," Fallon persisted. "And it's going to hurt like hell. Pain's part of the price. It's your will, Colin. You have to want it, be willing to go through the pain. You need to be awake and aware. You're strong. You can do this."

His teeth chattered, and his eyes swirled with pain. "Can't they, like, sew it back on?"

"They're not sure, and we're not sure how long it would take you to get back to New Hope." As she spoke, she opened herself to his wound. Pain, searing, even with whatever Hannah had given him to dull it. But clean. She'd done her job well. "But I'm sure. Trust me."

He closed his eyes for a moment, and before he opened them again, she felt that will inside him, steely, snap strong.

"Maybe you could toss some magick in. Make it like a super arm."

"Let's just get you whole again. I need more room. We need to move him outside."

"Out—" At Fallon's swift, ferocious glare, Hannah bit back the objection.

She could hear the battle raging, only blocks away

from the safety zone in Midtown. North now, Fallon knew, moving slowly, steadily toward the great park. As they set the gurney in what had once been a promenade near the ice rink where during the winter months people had spun and circled, slipped and tripped, Starr flashed back not only with her mother, but Ethan.

Good, she thought, the more family the better.

Lana rushed to Colin. "There's my boy. Mom's here. Let me see."

"We need to cast the circle." Fallon took the satchel her mother carried. "And fast."

"I need to see. I might be able to—"

"You can't." Brisk to the point of cold, Fallon cut off her mother's words, the voice that struggled not to shake. "I've looked. But we can. The Book of Spells is in me, that knowledge. There's a chance, but we cast the circle first. Ethan, you'll help. Set the candles in a triangle at Colin's head. Light them. Starr, roust some of the troops off rotation. Magick can draw magick. I don't want any interference."

"How can we help?" Jonah asked.

"Get your weapons, stand guard. Mom, the circle."

"All right, all right. You hold on." As the scarf she'd tossed on snapped in the wind, Lana pressed a kiss to Colin's brow. And with Fallon and Ethan, cast the protective circle around her oldest son.

"Float the cauldron over the candles," Fallon told her mother. "And in the cauldron put seven carnation petals, seven bay leaves, one bloodstone."

Fallon took the white cloth and, pricking her finger with her knife tip, carefully wrote Colin's name.

"This is my brother, blood of my blood. Know his name." She wrapped another bloodstone in the cloth, added it to the cauldron. "This is water, blessed by the mother. Know her love. This is earth, given brother to brother." She nodded to Ethan. "One fistful," she ordered. "Know his faith."

She lifted her hands and the wind came in stronger, in circling whirls. "This is air, stirred by the sister. Know my devotion. And now this air lifts the flames on candles white and pure, to offer these elements. Rise, rise, rise, flame and power, rise, rise, rise, a healing tower. Merge water, earth, wind, and fire, rise straight, rise true, rise higher."

As the flames shot up, lances of light, what was in the cauldron began to bubble and smoke. In it she slid the leather, and the third stone.

She sheathed her knife, drew her sword, one taken from fire, one lifted in faith.

"We are three and family, this healing spell we seal."

She held out a hand for Ethan's, and without hesitation he offered it, kept his eyes on hers when she scored his palm so his blood dripped into the cauldron. "Here, in a brother's blood, is kindness." She scored Lana's. "Here, in a mother's blood, is selfless love." Then her own. "Here, in a sister's blood, is faith. We are three. We are family. This spell we seal, this wound to heal.

"Unwrap the wound," she told her mother. "Coat it with the balm. Then take his right hand, push all you have into him when I say. Ethan," she continued as she took the arm from the ice bath, "at his shoulders. Hold him down, give him all you have."

She unwrapped the arm, pushed away the doubt and fear that wanted to creep under the shield of power.

"He's going into shock again," Hannah called out. "Let me—"

Fallon merely flicked a hand, shoved Hannah back two steps, then drew the leather, now slick as skin and shimmering, from the cauldron.

Her eyes, dark, lit with power, met Colin's. "Your

will," she told him, "your courage. Let them see your power, your heart."

Holding out her hand, she caught three of Lana's tears in her palm, let them fall on the wounds as she pressed them together.

"Hold him down. Push!"

When she laid the leather over his arm, the sudden, searing pain ripped a cry out of him. His body arched against it, his eyes went wide and glazed.

"Will it," Fallon snapped at him. "Want it. Take it. I call upon the power of light," she shouted as she ruthlessly coated his arm, from fingertip to elbow, with the shimmering, smoking leather. "Restore your warrior for the fight. Knit and join to heal, skin to skin now merge to seal. By the power you granted me, as I will, so mote it be."

Light flashed from her hands, streaked over his arm.

She heard the crows, ignored them. The lightning that flashed at the circle others deflected. She kept her hands clamped on Colin even as his pain cut through her and the wind snapped with keen teeth.

Then it died, like a switch flipped, and the pain, the terrible burning of it, fell to a pulsing ache. His pulse, she thought, one she felt through his arm.

"Do you see me?" She leaned in close. When he nodded, pale, breathless, she laid a hand on his sweat-slicked face. "I see you, brother. The light in you is mortal and human and stronger than any dark. Give him the healing potion, Mom."

Weeping, Lana lifted his head, brought the vial to his lips. "Drink now, my baby. My boy."

"Am I moving my fingers? I can't tell."

"You have to will it," Fallon told him. "Retrain your mind to work with your arm. It'll take time, and it may not function as easily or as completely as it used to."

"I'll make it work." He stared down, obviously puzzled by the leather that covered him from fingertip to elbow like skin. "Is it like a cast?"

"No."

He looked at Fallon with eyes going a little goofy from the potion. "I got a leather arm now? Cool."

"Yeah, cool. Sleep now." Fallon put him under. "We close the circle, then—"

Lana, eyes still streaming, reached out across her sleeping son to grip her daughter's hand. "I've never seen such power. In all I've seen, all I've known, I've never seen anything like what you were able to do. You were hurting him, hurting yourself, and I tried to stop you."

"It doesn't matter."

"It does. The lack of faith, even just for that second, could have cost him. It won't ever happen again. I need to stay with him."

"We'll move him into the HQ. You can help him work on getting movement back. He'll get pissy about it, so better you than me."

"I'm staying, too," Ethan said. "I can help with the animals, with Colin."

They closed the circle, gathered the tools. When Hannah as medical, Starr as guard, helped take him to the HQ, Fallon sat on the ramp of the mobile.

"It's clear as day now," Jonah said. "It got clearer and clearer during the spell. Life. I think it depended on you, and Colin, on all of you being able to do what you did, so it got clearer and clearer. Then there's that."

At his gesture, she looked at the statue of the god overlooking the ice rink. Where the war and black magicks had turned it into a fanged demon, coated the gold with oily ash, Prometheus shined again.

The gods, Fallon thought, had heard, and answered.

He laid a hand on her shoulder. "You look like you could use a little magick elixir, too." He went into the mobile, came out with a flask. "Not your mother's elixir, but it can't hurt."

She took it, sipped whiskey, let out a breath.

A golden god, a rink of ice, a pulse in an arm.

Her head hammered with the aftershocks of the spell.

"I need to get word to my father, to Travis that he was hurt, but he's okay."

"We'll do that." But he sat beside her, put an arm around her shoulders.

Though it didn't surprise Jonah, it did her when she pressed her face against him and wept.

CHAPTER TWENTY-ONE

Colin, being Colin, did get pissy, especially when Fallon refused to let him back into the field of battle. He managed, after two days, to wiggle his fingers, and after a week to make a loose fist.

Colin figured that was good enough. Fallon disagreed.

"It's not my sword arm anyway," he argued, stomping around the room so the beads dangling from his warrior's braid clicked and clacked together. "What's the BFD?"

Fallon, marking the latest map, nearly regretted that her brother had recovered enough to be on his feet—and hound her.

"You can't even lift a cup of coffee with your left hand yet."

"I won't be drinking coffee. I'm going to die of boredom, and the goddamn war's going to be over before I'm back in it at this rate."

"I wish the second part were true."

He moved, restlessly, wiggling, wiggling, wiggling the leather fingers of his hand. "We've taken Queens, Brooklyn, most of lower Manhattan, all of Midtown."

"We've lost fifteen hundred men, and have another three hundred, including you, medically unfit for duty. We've yet to be able to advance above what was Fifty-eighth Street on the west side."

He paced, now working, working, working the fingers of his restored arm into a fist. "We need to take Central Park. It's their last real stronghold. Once we do, they're broken here."

"I'm aware. I'm working on it. Get battle-ready, Colin, because when we're secure here, I want you to take a thousand troops and root the enemy out of Pennsylvania."

He stopped pacing, flexing, scowling, turned to stare at her. "The whole state?"

"That's right. They're scattered there, but still a presence. Run them to ground. Vivienne's troops are going into upstate New York, I'm going to have Mick move into Georgia."

She gestured him over, showing him her plans on the maps—and intrigued him enough he stopped bitching.

She turned when Arlys and Fred came in.

"I didn't think you were coming until later," she said to Arlys. "I didn't know you were coming at all, Fred."

"I wanted to see. I've got friends riding herd on my herd until tomorrow." Fred slipped a hand into Arlys's.

"I can't believe it's still here. So much of it's still here. Even after they got word back to us, I didn't believe it." Arlys walked to the window, pressed a hand to the glass. "So much gone, but so much here, too."

"I didn't want you to come until I felt we'd secured enough, but Mom kept pleading your case. She knows how much it means to you. She knows what both of you did here."

"Not alone," Arlys added. "Jim, Carol, Steve. They could have left, but they stayed. God, I wish we knew what happened to them."

"They got out." Fred moved up to slip her arm around Arlys's waist so they stood at the windows, heads tipped toward each other.

"God, I hope so."

"I just know they did. I just know they found a way."

Comforted, Arlys drew Fred with her into the newsroom. "When I first started working here, it was a high point of my life. And I was, by God, going to work my way to the anchor desk."

"You did," Fred reminded her.

"Not the way I imagined." She walked to it now, to where she'd sat for that final broadcast.

They'd cleaned it, she thought as she skimmed her fingers over it. But she could still see the blood and gore, still feel the way that blood had rained warm on her face when Bob, poor Bob, had chosen despair and madness and death.

Had that been what had woken her up? she wondered. Had that warm slap of blood reminded her to dig for the courage to do her job?

To tell the truth.

She looked out now, into the eye of the camera. It was still her job.

"I want to broadcast your victory from here, Fallon, from this same desk, in this same newsroom. I want to tell whoever in the world we can reach we've reclaimed New York."

"Maybe Jim and Carol and Steve will hear it."

With a firm nod, Arlys took Fred's hand again. "Or T.J. or Noah, or someone who worked in that shop in Hoboken where you left the thank-you note. We can bring Chuck up—he should be part of it, and he can figure out how to make it work."

"I can help write the copy." Fred's wings peeked out to flutter.

"Damn straight. When you're ready to declare victory, Fallon, I want to report it. You and me and Chuck, Fred. The three of us are going to close that circle. Then we'll turn this place, and the reporting done from here, over to someone else. Because we're New Hope now."

It was, Fallon thought, exactly what she'd hoped to hear. "Mom said you would. You're earlier than I thought—and like I said, I didn't know Fred was coming. Will and Theo are going to be here in about an hour. I can have Eddie come in, too."

Now Fred's wings fanned out, sparkled. "I can't wait!"

"Let's get some news for New Hope while we do," Arlys suggested. "How about we take a little stroll around Midtown, Fred?"

"Colin can take you—secured areas only."

"Great, you can be our first interview," Arlys told Colin. "Go on, Fred, I'll catch up."

"I really like your arm." Fred took his leathered hand, beamed up at him. "It's super cool. I bet the girls think it's sexy."

That got a grin. "Now that you mention it," he said as they walked out.

"Fallon, I just wanted a minute. I wanted to say that even after all this time, all that's happened, there's so much about magick that baffles me." Watching Fallon, Arlys ran her fingers over the anchor desk. "But something I know, absolutely, right down to the bone? What happened here mattered. It matters that of all of New York, you chose this place. And it means everything, Fallon, just everything to know it mattered."

She had to pause, gather herself as tears spilled. "When I sit at this desk again, tell whoever can hear or see that the light is back in New York, it'll close that circle for me. I know that doesn't end it, but it'll close that circle, and I know, absolutely, right down to the bone, that matters, too."

Arlys let out a breath, swiped the tears away. "Now I'm going to do something I never thought I'd do again. I'm going to walk in New York."

"You could stop off in the triage on the first floor. My mother should be there. I think she'd like to take that walk with you and Fred."

"I'll do that." She walked over, embraced Fallon. "It all matters."

Alone, Fallon went back to her maps. She had a plan, needed to refine it. And help close that circle.

Surreal, Lana thought, as she walked down Fifth Avenue with Fred and Arlys. One building rubble, the next soot-streaked, graffiti-scrawled, but standing. Who chose, she wondered, what would stand, what would fall?

The rising temperatures and stiff winds of March shifted and slowly melted the high hills of snow, and lethally long icicles dripped and shrunk as they jabbed down from eaves. Sentries patrolled, the occasional support troop rode by on horseback or on electric scooters. Some carted wagons of supplies that rumbled and bounced, but in this sector, won back and held by LFL forces, along the avenue once thick with traffic and tourists, the voices of three women rang clear as church bells.

She could smell the smoke from distant fires, hear the echoing *rat-a-tat* of gunfire from the north, the sudden blast of light from a bolt streaking across the sky.

And thought of the scent of roasted chestnuts, the blare of horns, the colorful displays in shop windows.

The sea of people, moving, moving, moving along the sidewalks, so many busy places to go.

"I bought my winter coat there." Fred pointed to a

hulled-out building across Fifth. "They always had good sales," she remembered. "And there was this guy who sold fake cashmere scarves on the sidewalk right down there. I got one to go with the coat. Ten bucks."

"I shopped there, too," Arlys remembered. "I'd usually head downstairs and get a latte from the Starbucks after. And I treated myself to an outrageously expensive pair of over-the-knee suede boots at Saks that last Christmas."

She turned, studied what had been a Fifth Avenue landmark. War had sheared off the top floors, shattered the windows. Oddly, a couple of naked mannequins sprawled like the dead behind the broken glass.

"I hope some resistance fighter looted my apartment and got them, and everything else."

"Where did you shop, Lana?"

Lana smiled at Fred. "I was a downtown girl. The Barney's on Seventh practically applauded when I went in. God, I loved to shop—to buy. Shoes, big, big weakness."

She looked down at the sturdy, laced leather of the elf-made boots that had served her, and well, for three years.

"Oh well."

"Do you miss it?" Fred asked. "I sort of miss shopping—the looking and touching and discovery. You don't think about it really but, seeing all this, it brings it back so I kind of miss it."

She hooked her arms through theirs. "We'd have had fun with it, the three of us. Shopping, trying on clothes, stopping for lunch."

They watched a scavenging team haul out bags and crates from what had been—if Arlys's memory served—a Banana Republic.

"But scavenging's fun, too," Fred decided.

"I'm amazed there's anything left to scavenge."

Because there was, because it seemed there was always something else to find, Lana's mood lifted. "Well, it is New York." She gave them each a hip bump. "Let's go shopping."

With her father, Fallon refined her battle plan, then called in her available commanders. After more than an hour's debate, she sent them back to prepare their troops.

Will stopped, laid a hand on her shoulder as he studied her floating map. "Basically the same tactics as Arlington."

"It worked."

"Damn straight. Well, I'm going to find my wife before I head back."

"She's with mine," Simon told them. "Give me a minute and I'll go with you." He turned first, pressed a kiss to Fallon's forehead.

"What's that for?"

"We'll say luck."

Reaching out, she gripped his hand. "Are the numbers right?"

"As they'll ever be. We'll get the word out. Buy you a drink later? It's tradition. A drink before the war." He glanced at Duncan. "You, too."

"Sure." Duncan waited until Simon walked out. "He's warming up to me."

"He's always been warm toward you."

"Warmer before I got naked with his daughter. But he's warming up again. After the drink, let's have another tradition and get naked before the war."

"I'm for that. It's all in, Duncan."

"And it'll be all in and done. It's the right move, the

right time. We're ready." He gave her a quick yank, took her mouth, took them both away for just a moment. "More of that later."

Alone, she walked back to the map. She expected she'd have another heated argument with Colin, but she would keep him solidly on support on this one. She had additional fighters with the resistance—undisciplined for the most part, but fierce.

"Hey."

She glanced over. "Mick."

"Sorry I couldn't get here sooner. We had a little distraction."

Since mud and blood streaked his face, his clothes, she doubted it had been little or merely a distraction. "Are you hurt?"

"Nah." He swiped the back of his hand over his face. "Some DU thought they could push us out of Chelsea— your mom's old neighborhood, right? We thought different. Got an assist from a small band of resistance, and tamped it down. But I couldn't get here for the briefing."

He wandered in, his forehead creasing as he looked at the map. "Is that my battalion?"

"Yeah."

"When do we strike?"

"Daybreak. Let me run it through."

While she did, he pulled a pouch of sunflower seeds from his pocket—offered her some, munched.

"You've got Poe leading Colin's troops."

"Colin's not cleared for combat."

"He's gonna be pissed. You know he's working on getting a tat on the arm—after we hoist the banner here. That's not going to screw up the magicks, is it?"

"It's the same as his own skin now. It is his skin now, so no."

"Cool enough. Shit, almost forgot. I brought one of the resistance guys back with me. He wanted to check, see if he can find his daughter. He got her out awhile back with directions to New Hope."

"Did he give you a name?"

"Funny name. I'm not sure—"

"Marichu."

"Yeah, that's it. I told him somebody around here probably had records, or could find out."

"I know her. She's here." Gesturing for him to follow, she started out. "What's his name?"

"Jon—nice and easy to remember. I never figured she'd be here. He said she's sixteen."

"She says seventeen now, but either way young. And persuasive." She found an elf runner, gave him instructions. "Let's find Jon."

They took the stairway. They had the elevators working on magickal power, but Fallon found them too confining and slow.

"We keep records in an office on the main floor. Support staff are trying to keep it updated. Rotating troops in and out, wounded, casualties. How's your father? And Minh?"

"Dad's good. Minh took a hit—nothing serious," Mick said quickly. "Just some shrapnel in the leg. He'll be up and running for tomorrow."

"Good to hear." She flicked him a glance. "We're okay, right? You and me?"

"Yeah." After only the briefest hesitation, he gave her an elbow poke. "It's hard to think of anything but the next fight when you're in the thick of it like this for weeks. Makes you realize . . . stuff. I'll be glad to get back to The Beach. Man, New York's just too closed in and covered with concrete or whatever. How the hell did anyone live here?"

"Millions did."

"Count me out. But that doesn't mean the assholes can have it. We're going all the way down?"

"That's right."

He grinned. "Race ya."

For a precious few minutes, she was back in the woods, in their faerie glade, in the youth, racing Mick to a finish line. When he edged her out, she shook her head and laughed. "You had a head start."

"Blew you away." He pulled open the door.

In one section of the gilded lobby, medicals treated wounded. In another, support staff issued new supplies when needed. On a higher floor, a commissary had been converted to a mess hall to cook for the medicals, the wounded, to prepare the MREs.

She started to direct Mick toward the back when he called out. "Hey, Jon! That's him."

Fallon saw the man—black beard with a sprinkle of gray, tired eyes, worn and muddied boots—move toward them. He had a limp, a slight one, and a rifle slung over his shoulder.

"They're checking." His voice, gruff, grave, held the fatigue she saw in his eyes. "Said it would take awhile and I could get some of the meal packs for my people."

"We're fighting the same fight," Mick said cheerfully. "This is Fallon."

"Fallon Swift." Jon scrubbed his hands on the thighs of his pants before offering it. "It's great to meet you. We never lost hope, but there were days, and nights, when it was hard to hold on to it. My girl—"

"Marichu," she said. "She reached us."

He closed his eyes, then pressed his fingers to them. "Thank God. Thank God. I had to get her out, make her go. I didn't see any other way to— She's okay?"

"She's . . . fast," Fallon decided as Marichu streaked through the main doors. "See for yourself."

"Dad." Colorful hair flying, she all but leaped over the marble floor.

On a choked sound, Jon grabbed her up. All the strain in his face just melted away.

"Let's give them some room," Fallon murmured.

Mick stepped back, but watched the reunion, draped an arm over Fallon's shoulders. "That's what it's about. That's the reason."

"Yes." Love, she thought, bright as the sun. And friendship. She circled Mick's waist with her arm. True as the heart.

That night she felt both lying in Duncan's arms, and when they rose, vowed to take that—the reason—into battle.

Power pulsed through her, around her, in those hushed moments before light broke the dark. She saw it in her mind's eye, the troops poised, positioned strategically around Central Park. The warriors crouched in other parts of the city, ready to block, to cut down any who tried to break through the lines.

They held, the men, women, witches, warriors, elves, faeries, shifters, all who'd fought for weeks for a city smothered in black magicks. All who'd fought to bring the light back.

Like the statue of Prometheus, she thought, this city could, and would, shine again.

As the light blinked through the haze in the east, through the towers that stood even after two decades of war, she drew her sword, set it to flame.

Saw the answering flame of Duncan's, the tipped fire of Tonia's arrow, the surge of light from every direction. At that signal, she pointed her sword east, pulled light from the burgeoning sun.

Day burst like a bomb.

And they charged.

They rooted the enemy from burrows, flushed them from trees, drove them in so her northern troops broke through to take more ground.

Swords slashed, magicks clashed over ground, melting snow turned into a bog that sucked greedily at boot and hoof.

PWs who hadn't escaped the city, who she knew were now used as DU fodder, ran in panic to be attacked by both sides. Taibhse swooped, tore strips from a panther shifter as Faol Ban joined to fight off a pack of wolf shifters. Through the scream of crows ripped the screams of men, so the melting snow ran red.

She took Laoch into a steep climb, rising into wind that whirled with those clashing magicks. She sliced through the wings of a dark faerie, sent her spiraling to the ground. Below she saw the ground shake under a platoon of her men, and hurled fireballs at the clutch of Dark Uncanny who worked to open the earth beneath them.

She wheeled Laoch in midair, saw that Vivienne's commander kept his word. His troops surged in from the north, trapping the enemy between walls of warriors.

Diving east she fought with her father, pumping power and flame against the hail of black lightning. It sizzled to the ground, scorched.

"Drive them in," she shouted, ignoring the enemy who fled. They would meet yet another wall in Troy's battalion.

"Keep the heat on," Simon shouted back. "We've got this."

Trusting he did, she galloped south.

She joined with Will, then Starr, pushed through to Poe in time to help fight off an attack led by the blur of rushing elves, a rain of arrows. She swept them back, sent them tumbling in a whirlwind.

"Fast fuckers." Poe swiped at the mud on his face.

"You're bleeding."

His breath came fast, but he shook his head, flexed his impressive biceps. "Just the meat."

In answer Fallon leaned over, pressed a hand to his arm to close the wound. "Drive them in."

"You got it, boss."

She raced toward Mick's troops, and charged a Dark Uncanny as he flashed lightning from his hands. Laoch impaled him on his horn, shook him off.

"We've got some wounded," he called to her.

"Medics and reinforcements are on the way." She pivoted to strike out at the next attacker, then streaked to Tonia. "Mick needs some help."

Gripping Fallon's hand, Tonia swung up with her. "Let's take a ride."

They flew up, circled. Tonia's arrows flashed down, finding mark after mark. "Like old times," she said.

"There, Travis is moving in to back Mick up. Drive them in," Fallon ordered. "Drive them in."

"Meda and her horsemen—women—are sure as hell doing just that. Jesus, Mallick and Duncan have merged, and they're kicking ass. Drop me off that way. I want in."

Tonia leaped down onto an outcropping of rock, arrow already nocked, then flying into the belly of a tiger.

Through the mud and the blood, the scorching flames, the cutting wind, they fought, pushing, pushing the enemy inward, closing in around them like the walls of a well.

She saw the spread, the rise of black wings, felt the streak of power slap the air. For a stunned moment she thought: Eric. But she'd buried the ashes of her uncle herself, had salted the earth over them.

Still, she sent Laoch in pursuit.

Up, up, high above the city, beyond the crows that screamed, he turned.

No, not Eric, but every bit as twisted and dark.

He smiled, lips curving in a face as handsome and smooth as a carved angel's. She realized almost too late he'd drawn her away, isolated her.

When he threw the first strike of lightning at her, she blocked it with her shield and pivoted to stream flame from her sword at the attacker who'd swooped in on her flank.

He swept away the fire as a third charged in.

She thought of Mallick's ghosts, wondered why neither of them had thought to practice in midair.

They combined power, heaved it toward her. She dived, felt the heat of it blow past her—and felt Laoch's quick start of pain. But he never faltered, streaking up, wheeling as she slashed out, caught a wing, followed through with a gale that tumbled the wounded one into the second.

As they flailed, she blocked a blow from the first, pushed back.

They regrouped, the handsome one, the wounded one, a female with dozens of flying black braids. She steadied Laoch for the next attack.

Duncan's voice sounded in her head. *Make room.*

"No, don't—"

But he flashed behind her, sliced his sword so the flame from it lashed out like a whip. It struck the one she'd wounded, seemed to curl around him as he shrieked. The fire simply enfolded him, left a trail of bitter smoke as he fell.

"Which one do you want?" Duncan asked her.

"The male. Son of a bitch."

She lashed out, again and again. A strike, a block, a sweep of power. He had more than he should—who knew what bargain he'd made with some devil to increase his power.

"We're wasting time. Give me your hand," she ordered.

"Busy here."

"Your hand!"

She reached back, gripped it. Light sparked from the joining, power meeting, merging. With it, she threw what she had at the dark angel, felt Duncan loose his own.

That power cut through them like glass. They didn't shriek. They made no sound at all as they fell.

"Are you hurt?"

"No. You are."

She didn't feel the pain until he pressed a hand to her hip to heal the slice and burn.

"Easy," she snapped. "Go slow. Laoch is burned—left hind leg. I need to get him down, tend to him."

Duncan shifted, looked down and back. "It doesn't look too bad."

"He's hurting."

She took him down slowly, started to search for the safest spot so she could see to him. "Duncan."

"Yeah, I see. Down's a good place to be. We've got what's left of them trapped, just the way we lined it up."

She landed softly, slid off.

"I've got him," Duncan told her. "I'll fix him up. You finish this."

"All right." She stroked a hand over Laoch, then moved through the thick circle of her troops.

There couldn't have been more than a hundred left inside that circle. So many more lay dead, dying, or wounded on the ground. A coven of witches ringed the circle, forming a shield against any dark magicks the vanquished might attempt.

Fallon stepped through them as well. She lifted her sword with one hand, her shield with the other.

She pulled power, more power, from the streaks of sun that burned through the haze.

"Feel the light entwine you. Know the light will bind you. Your powers I here block and on them close the lock."

She waited a beat, and the coven added their voices to hers.

"The net around you, one and all, holds tight. Restrained, rebuked dark powers by the light. For you have chosen this destiny. As we will, so mote it be."

She turned to Troy. "You're unharmed."

"Yes. And you?"

"Close enough. You know where to take them."

"We do. The evil in them remains even if their powers are locked." Almost casually, Troy flipped back her long spill of hair. "They'll likely kill each other before they're done."

"Their choice. The island we chose can sustain them, or be their graveyard. It's all a choice."

She turned away to check on Laoch. Mick fell into step beside her.

"We could both use a dip in the faerie pool about now."

She looked at him, herself, both coated with mud, streaked with blood, smeared with soot. "The faeries will have our asses if we washed this much away in their pond."

"That's a point. You had me worried up there."

She rubbed a hand on his cheek, smearing more mud. "I'm down here now."

He smeared mud back, grinned at her. "I didn't know you could do that. You know, lock up the dark magicks."

"We couldn't have if you hadn't cut down their numbers, gotten them cornered. And if we didn't have a full coven ready with the incantation."

She closed her eyes, breathed. "We took back New York, Mick."

"Sure as hell did. I'm going to go find my dad. Gonna clean up, drink a bunch of faerie wine."

"I'm right there with you."

He did a backflip, a series of tumbles that made her laugh.

And on the final spring, the bolt struck him. In the back, and through to the heart. He fell like a stone on the boggy ground of battle.

"No, no, no!" Whipping out both sword and shield, she leaped to him, raised the shield over him to protect him from the next bolt.

The black dragon glided overhead. On his back rode Petra.

She heaved fire, scattering troops, but her eyes, those mad eyes, never left Fallon's. Her hair, her wings flowed, black on one side, white on the other.

"You think this is over, *cousin*!" She shouted it, let her laugh ring out. "You think this matters? But he mattered, didn't he, you weak, stupid bitch. He mattered to you. Oops, gone now."

Fallon gathered her grief, let it wind with her power. Flung it into the sky.

"And me, too. Poof."

Both Petra and the dragon vanished an instant before Fallon's power blasted the sky, boomed across it like a comet.

"Mick. Mick." She lifted his head into her lap. "I'll fix it. Please. Let me fix it." Pressing her cheek to his, she rocked.

"Fallon." Duncan knelt beside her. "He's gone. I'm sorry. He's gone."

"No. No." She shoved Duncan back, ran her hands

over Mick's face, his hair, his chest, searching for life, for his light. "No. Stay away from me."

But he wrapped around her, held her, as she'd once held him when he'd grieved. So she wept in Duncan's arms on the bloody field, cradling her friend.

LIGHT FOR LIFE

Life is a pure flame, and we live by
an invisible Sun within us.

—Sir Thomas Browne

CHAPTER TWENTY-TWO

She thought she might drown in grief. She sank under the swamping waves of that grief so every breath poured in more until it saturated her heart. She barely felt it beat.

She sent for Mick's father, but she wouldn't have Thomas see his son lying in the mud. Instead, she took Mick to a triage tent, dismissed everyone, and washed his body herself, let her tears mix with the water as she bent to touch her lips to his.

She cleaned his clothes of mud, of blood, dressed him again, tenderly. Though her hands shook, she braided his hair.

"I like the blue," she managed, then touched her fingers to the bracelet she'd made him so long ago. "It wasn't enough. I wasn't enough."

Thomas stepped in.

She stepped back.

To honor his grief, she pushed down her own.

"I have no words," she began as he took his son's hand in his. "I have nothing to give you but my own sorrow, and you have enough sorrow. But I will pledge to you, take this oath that the one who took his life, his bright, joyful life, will pay for it with her own. I swear it to you."

She started to leave him, to give him his privacy, but Thomas reached out, took her hand in turn to stop her.

"He was bright, and joyful, and brave. And so clever. From the moment of his birth, he was my star, shining. He gave his life to fight against all that's dark and cruel and cowardly. A father should never outlive his child, but war often demands it. I would have given my life if he could have lived his in peace and freedom."

He let out a broken sigh as he brought Mick's hand to his cheek. "He died a warrior, a commander, a defender of the light. He deserves our pride as much as our grief."

"He has it."

"He loved you."

She couldn't push it down any longer, so the grief swelled up again. "I know. Thomas—"

He shook his head. "That love helped make him the man he became. That's our pride. I need . . ." His voice wavered. "I need to take my boy home, to the forest, to the green."

"Yes. I'll take you."

"You're needed here, for the living and the dead. Those who fought to free this city need to see you as much as they need the banners to fly. I'll make my way home with my boy. My son. I need time with him first, then we'll make our way home."

She moved to the opening of the tent. "I loved him, too."

"I know it. So did he."

Outside, the air was crisp and clear. Cleansed, Fallon thought, with the dark and cold magicks driven out. Some, like Mick, had paid for that cleansing with their lives. Those lives would be honored, and the city would be held.

And Petra, by all the gods, Petra would pay in pain and in blood.

She saw Mallick, muddied, bloodied, and straight as an arrow. They moved toward each other.

"Even in triumph, sorrow that deep cuts to the heart. He will be missed."

"The gods demand their pounds of flesh," she said bitterly, "their vats of blood."

His gaze, full of patience, stayed on hers. "Victory of light over dark requires sacrifice."

"Like my birth father, like Mick, like scores of others. I'm aware. What demands sacrifice will have it, again and again, until this is done. And I, who was chosen to order others to fight and die, will have mine."

"To kill with a sword coated in vengeance leads to the shadows."

"If I wasn't meant to feel rage, grief, fury, I shouldn't have been given a will, a heart, a mind. I'll do what's asked of me, Mallick. I'll cleanse the world as I have this city. But I will have my payment."

She looked out to see the banner flying white over the field. "The troops need to see me, and there's work to be done yet. Thomas . . . he wants to take Mick home. Would you take them?"

"Yes, of course." He laid a hand on her arm. "It's no comfort now, but in time it will be to know Mick is part of the light."

"No, it's no comfort now. He's dead. A statue of a god shines gold in the heart of the city, and another good man who loved me is dead."

She did her duty, walked the battlefield, visited the triage tents, the mobiles, the clinics to speak to the wounded, the medicals. With her grief frozen inside her, she did her best to give comfort to those who'd lost a friend or loved one.

She checked on Laoch, found Faol Ban and Taibhse with him. And going over the alicorn from ears to tail, found Duncan had indeed healed any wounds.

With the cheers of victory ringing hollow in her head, she made her way back to her headquarters, and to her quarters. She found her father waiting for her.

Simon opened a bottle of whiskey, poured two glasses.

"Thanks, but I need a shower more than a drink."

"Have the drink first." He handed her the glass. "I want to say first I'm sorry about Mick. He was a good man, a good friend to you, a good soldier. He deserves us lifting a glass to him."

Her eyes stayed as cold as fog over a frozen lake. "He deserves more."

"Start here. I've spent more time than I like to think about in combat, and plenty of that time commanding others. I know what it is to lose men, as a soldier, as an officer, and what it is to lose a friend."

Not the same, Fallon thought. Not the same. Not the same. "I didn't feel her, didn't see her coming, didn't anticipate. If I had—"

"That's bullshit. It's understandable bullshit, but still bullshit."

"She killed him because he mattered to me, because he loved me. I know what she is, but I didn't see this. I wrapped my power into the spell to lock down the DUs who would slaughter us, every one of us, so I didn't feel her coming."

"She didn't fight," Simon pointed out. "Didn't risk herself. Ask yourself why. Instead of asking yourself why Mick, ask why she didn't strike at you, or me, your mom, your brothers, Duncan."

"I don't know."

"Because you're not thinking straight yet. It was of

the moment, Fallon. It was convenient and low risk. He was with you. It was the easiest way to hurt you without putting herself on the line. She wants your pain, wants you to question yourself, blame yourself. Don't give her what she wants."

"I don't know what to do. I can't think past finding her, ending her."

"If that takes front and center, you give her an advantage. That's how she thinks, Fallon, and you're smarter. Where was Allegra?"

She looked up, stunned she hadn't asked herself the question. "I didn't think past Petra, the dragon. I've seen the dragon fly over New York, over the shield in Scotland—but not Allegra. I didn't think about Allegra."

"Is she dead? Is she alive but too weak or damaged to join an attack? Is she alive and well and on other business somewhere else? Can't know," Simon added. "But you can know she wasn't part of this. Petra did this on her own."

"Yes, it matters. The answers matter. Petra said she didn't care about losing New York, but of course she did. Of course she did," Fallon repeated as she paced.

Now she's thinking, Simon decided, and waited for the rest.

"She waited. She's no soldier. She's a killer, but not a warrior, so she waited. She must have been furious when we drove them out. She's waiting to take a victory lap, and instead watches defeat. Of the moment, you said, and yeah, yeah, that was blind fury. Mick's dead because she's a killer, because, like Denzel was to Duncan, Mick was important to me. She probably stayed close all these weeks. Not close enough for me to feel her, to risk her own skin, but close enough."

"She fears you, even though she thinks you're weak."

Fallon stopped. "Does she?"

"What would she have done in your place today? With the enemy trapped, defeated, helpless?"

"She'd have destroyed them all."

"You didn't, and she sees that as a weakness. You love, and that's a weakness to her. She struck down someone you love to exploit that weakness."

"She miscalculated."

"I know it."

"I can't think, Dad." Broken, she thought as she covered her face with her hands. Something broken in her. "I can't feel past the grief and the fury under it, bubbling under it. I know what has to be done, but—"

"You need a little time."

"I don't have time for time. But—"

"Not all wounds are physical, Fallon. If you don't take time, you'll go into the next weakened. Take a couple of weeks, because love and grief aren't weaknesses, baby. Every good commander knows when a soldier needs a couple of weeks to recoup. That includes you."

"We need to rotate in fresh troops, leave a security force here, bring in people to help the resistance repair some of the infrastructure, others to plant in the green spaces. The Beach needs a commander, and one who can start leading some of its troops south. We need—"

"It'll be a long list," Simon interrupted. "Get your shower, we'll get some other brains in on that list, get some food, and work it out. But first."

He held up his glass, waited.

"Okay." She let out a long breath, steadied herself. Then lifted her glass. "To Mick."

Duncan headed the burial detail. Some would be transported back to their homes, but so many had no home other than the bases they'd migrated to. For those, he claimed a section of the park, one where the ground rose, where the trees grew thick.

It was heartbreaking, soul-searing work, and so he'd asked for volunteers rather than issuing orders for the detail. It revived him, his flagging spirit, that he had more than were needed. He split them up into groups assigned to separate the enemy dead, others to dig graves, others to make markers.

He spotted Tonia, worked his way to her. "Give yourself a break."

"I will when you will," she said, and kept shoveling.

"There are easier ways to dig a grave."

"Sometimes you need to do something this way. We lost Clarence."

"Shit." Duncan felt his heart drop again as he thought of the boy they'd rescued from a cult, and the women who'd taken him as a son.

"And Keisha, Morris, Liah. Mick." Tonia swiped at her face, leaned on the shovel. "Have you seen Fallon?"

"Not since . . . No. Colin said she's holding, and they're meeting now to work on reconstruction, cleanup, expansion."

"Why aren't you in on that?"

"I need to do this."

"Me, too."

With a nod, he picked up a shovel, helped her dig.

After friends, loved ones, comrades had been laid to rest, Duncan supervised the purification and burning of the enemy dead. Dusk crept in by the time he went back to the graves.

This he'd wanted to do alone.

Pulling up power, he brought the green springing through the mud, a hopeful sea of it over what he thought of as sacred ground. There would be a ceremony in the morning—even now Tonia worked on those arrangements. Words would be said, tears shed. But tonight, he'd pay his own respects.

He'd chosen this spot for the rise of land, the trees, and the rough rocks pushing tall out of the ground. Some formed wide steps, others peaks.

He'd already sketched what he wanted in his mind, and now used his magick to bring it to be.

He smoothed some of the rough. He sketched a great deal better than he sculpted, so worried a little he'd muck it up.

But he smoothed, formed, carved, etched, polished, let the image flow from him into the rock.

He chose the form of a faerie for the grace, with wings spread, hands held out to those who lay beneath her.

He drew up more, still more, until water broke through the rock, to spill gently down the steps of stone, and formed a stone pool below for it to feed. Above the pool, he carved the fivefold symbol.

Finally, he stepped back, studied his work. "Best I can do."

He turned to leave, saw Fallon, the alicorn and wolf beside her, the owl on her arm.

"It's beautiful."

"I couldn't think of any words."

"It doesn't need any. Look, the faeries are lighting it."

He looked back, saw the dance of lights.

"You used Fred's face."

"I guess I did." He saw it now. "I didn't realize."

"It's beautiful," she repeated, and again felt tears pushing up into her throat. "It's right. Tonia told me you might still be here, and that she and some others have the details for a ceremony in the morning. I need to walk."

He fell into step with her but didn't touch her. The barrier he felt was as real as the stone he'd carved.

"You didn't come to the meeting."

"I needed to do this."

"Understood. Flynn's going to take command of The Beach and start moving troops south."

"You couldn't ask for better."

"No. He'll be gone for weeks, maybe months. I nearly asked you to take that post, but . . . I wasn't sure I could get through those weeks or months if you went away again."

"Then why don't you want me to touch you now?"

"I'm not sure I can get through the next minute if you do. I should have helped with the burial, the purification of the enemy dead. I knew you would take care of it, so I spared myself."

"Stop. Damn it. You want to feel sorry for yourself right now, you're entitled, but I took care of it because I needed to, wanted to. Some of those people died under my command, so just knock off all The One crap. We all did what we had to do, and we all lost friends today."

It weighed on him, more stone. "Those friends knew what they risked, and took this place back with courage. You demean that by sucking up all the responsibility. You demean them."

It sliced at her, the truth of it sliced. "That's harsh, that's cold."

"Maybe, but it's how I see it. Those men and women didn't die for you, they died for what you represent. They died for their families, their neighbors, their futures."

"Mick died because Petra wanted to hurt me."

"Then let's go get the bitch and her fucking hag of a mother." He wanted it, could almost taste the bitter tang of their blood. "We go back to Scotland, close the shield, and we take down that dark bastard in the woods. We draw Petra and Allegra out, and finish it."

She pressed her face to Laoch's neck. "It's not time."

"Screw that, Fallon. If not now, when?"

"I don't know!" And that sliced, too. "I just know it's not time. There's more to come. I can't—" She whirled on him, stopped. Drew a breath. "There," she said, and pointed.

And there where Mick had fallen stood a tree of life, blooming full, branches curving upward.

"Is that my solace?" she asked.

Now he whirled on her. "It's acknowledgment. It's gratitude and honor."

Tears burned the backs of her eyes, and she wanted to scream and shed them. "Yes, yes, you're right. The fact I can't feel that, just can't, is another reason I need to leave."

"Leave? Go where?"

"I need solitude, I need to restore my faith. I need a couple of weeks, Duncan, just some time alone."

"Alone?"

"Everything you said is right, but I can't feel it. I need to feel again, believe it again. And I can't lean on you until I'm sure I can stand on my own. She broke something in me, Duncan, and I need some time to heal. When she killed Denzel, you needed to leave."

"Part of that was distance from you, but okay, yeah."

"A couple of weeks," she said again, and though she felt his need, stayed behind the wall she'd built. "Will you stand for me tomorrow, at the memorial?"

"You're leaving now?"

"If I don't, I won't, because I want to lean on you, I want my family, my friends. But I know it won't be time to end this until I take back what she took from me today."

"We need to—I need to just sit the hell down with you. Take a minute."

"I can't. I just can't. I have to go."

"Where?" he demanded. "Where the hell are you going?"

"To the quiet." She felt his hurt, his need for more from her. But couldn't give it. She mounted Laoch. "After the quiet comes the fury, and with the fury the end. The end of dark, the end of light—this hangs in the balance. Know the fire, the famine, the rivers of blood should dark tip the scales. Know the song of peace a thousand years if the light shines true. Shine true, Duncan of the MacLeods, and you will know when the time has come."

She dropped out of the vision, looked at him under the streaming moonlight, the sparkle of stars that spread over the freed city.

"I love you," she said, and vanished.

"You said no," he murmured. "For the first time you said no."

Battles sparked as the Light for Life forces advanced in every direction. Duncan gave himself over to the fighting, joining Flynn's troops in the green mountains of Georgia, flashing to Meda, the shuttered city of Santa Fe in New Mexico, and on the windswept fields of Nebraska.

He nursed his own wounds when he got them, cleaned his sword, and looked for the next fight.

Fallon might have taken the quiet, but he wanted the fury.

"You need some downtime, brother."

He drank a beer with Tonia in the community gardens. Shrugged with it. "I'm sitting down right now."

"You know what I mean. You only came back today

to placate Mom. I know you've already grilled Chuck on where to find some action next. Maine, right? Vivienne's troops and ours about to face off on the coast."

"I'm needed there. I'm not here."

He heard Eddie's harmonica join in with someone's guitar riff. And Rainbow, now a leggy teenager, danced in the air with some faerie friends.

Spring, he thought. Plenty of those signs of spring around him with the greening trees, the young crops, the burst of flowers, the balm of the air as it neared May Day.

Spring bloomed everywhere in New Hope. He wondered if it bloomed wherever Fallon was.

He shoved that thought away, turned his head to look at Tonia. "Anyway, seems to me you were into it with me when we took on those combined forces in Georgia."

"I was needed. There's also plenty of need here. We're barely keeping up with training. And we're losing Colin again. He's taken Pennsylvania and going back to Arlington tomorrow. It's spring, and that takes Eddie and some of the other serious farmers off rotation for scouting. They broke ground on the clinic expansion."

"After Maine, I'll be back."

"That's what you said after New Mexico."

"And I came back." Annoyance bit through the words. "We're driving them down, Tonia. But the way they're combining forces, that's got to be a concern. We're seeing more and more DUs fighting alongside PWs. More Raiders grouping together."

"I can't argue with that. There's not even a pretext with the PWs now. It's not magicks they want to destroy. It's us. Did Chuck tell you about their latest dispatches, what they're sending out?"

"Yeah. How the Uncannys who fight with them have been purified and redeemed or whatever. Using their powers for the holy war, blah blah. White's a lunatic, and he's an idiot if he actually believes the DUs won't wipe him and the rest of the PWs out the minute they're not useful."

"A lunatic, an idiot, but he's still managed to keep his cult going for more than two decades."

"Fear and hate can work." He drank more beer, brooded over the colored lights strung around the garden.

"I know you miss her. We all miss her."

"It's not about—" The hell it wasn't, he admitted. "She said a couple weeks. It's been nearly five. I shouldn't have let her go alone."

"Let, my ass. You don't let her any more than I let you go to fricking Maine. You're worried, I get it. Jesus, Duncan, so am I. So's everyone. She's been the prime target since before she was born."

"Then stop making excuses."

"Not excuses. Reasons. I think living with being the prime target, with being The freaking One takes a toll. Like losing your oldest friend five feet away from where you're standing takes a toll. Like training recruits knowing when they're ready to fight not all of them will come back takes a toll."

"Sounds like somebody else needs some downtime."

Tonia heaved out a breath. "Maybe."

A fiddle joined the guitar, the harmonica. A few people started to sing a song he'd heard a few times about life on the farm.

Maybe Fallon had gone back to the farm. He could go, look. The hell with that, he decided, and chugged beer. He wasn't a dog who'd belly crawl back to the boot that kicked him.

She hadn't just left, she'd blocked him so he couldn't even touch her mind, not even in dreams.

The hell with it.

"How about you come with me to Maine," he suggested, "then when we drive those bastards into the sea, I'll come back with you. I'll take some of the recruits off your hands."

"I could use the help, Duncan, no lie."

Hannah came over, plopped down on the grass beside them. "Here you are. I've been going over clinic plans with Rachel and Mom, and I am seriously done. Where's my beer?"

Duncan handed her what was left of his. She sighed at the couple of swallows. "It'll do. Mom says she's making French toast for breakfast—with pig bacon."

While Hannah couldn't read minds, she knew her siblings. "Oh, come on. You just got back." She swallowed the last of the beer, poked the bottle at Tonia. "You, too?"

"We made a pact. I go shoot a few arrows with Duncan, and he comes back to take some of the training hours off my plate."

Hannah let out a sigh. "A deal's a deal. It's fairly quiet at the clinic. Need a doctor in Maine?"

"You're volunteering to take some of the heat off us," Tonia decided.

"The three of us go, the three of us come back—and stay," Hannah added, "for at least a full week. Mom'll take it better if it's all of us."

"Best sister ever." Duncan wrapped an arm around Hannah's shoulders.

"Hey!"

He grinned at Tonia, laid his arm over hers. "Plural."

The vocalists shouted out: "Thank God I'm a Country Boy." Eddie added a "Yee-haw."

And Garrett, a shifter once nearly hanged by the PWs, came on the run.

Shifted from cougar to teen. "Trouble's coming. I found Will." His breath came fast as all three surged to their feet. "He's mobilizing. He said Eddie was here, and I should—"

"What's the trouble?" Duncan interrupted.

"PWs, Raiders, and DUs with them. Maybe thirty miles beyond the checkpoint, moving this way."

"I'll get Jonah, Rachel, Mom." Hannah ran from the gardens.

"How many?" Duncan demanded.

"It looked like hundreds. We were just out for a run. We went past the checkpoint. I know that's against the rules, but—"

"We'll worry about that later. Thirty miles?" Tonia pressed.

"About. They're not moving fast, and we did once we spotted them. I told the others to peel off, alert the outlying farms. But the thing is, I think White's with them. I saw him once when they had me. I think I saw him with them."

As his blood heated—he'd wanted to take on White all of his life—Duncan shot a look at Tonia. Understanding, she gave him a nod.

"Tell Eddie, Garrett. He'll get things started on this end of town. We need to scout past the other checkpoints, see if they're coming in from other directions."

"I'll alert the barracks, and pull in who we need on the way." Duncan swung onto his bike, something else that came out in spring. "Get the Swifts, let Fred know." He revved the engine. "You take Flynn. I'll take Mallick in Arlington."

"Fast," Tonia said. "Even if they're moving slow, we don't have much time."

She flashed as Duncan roared away.

They'd trained for this, he thought as he all but flew out of New Hope. Every man, woman, and child had their emergency posts and duties. He alerted them along the way, eating up what he knew would be precious time skidding to a halt to call out the alert to the man tossing a ball to his dog, to the old woman rocking on her porch.

He caught some luck at the barracks when he saw Colin and Travis entertaining themselves by putting some troops through night maneuvers.

"Enemy forces spotted heading in from the south—less than thirty miles beyond the checkpoint. Indeterminate numbers, possibly hundreds. White may be with them."

"Well, hot damn." Colin managed to bring his two hands together in a clap. "All right, boys and girls, suit the fuck up."

"We've got this," Travis said. "Get Dad."

"Next stop."

He spun the bike in a circle, streaked toward the Swift house. Leaping off, he didn't bother to knock, but shoved open the door.

Simon and Lana broke off what looked like a pretty serious kiss.

"Sorry. Enemy forces moving in from the south." Even as he continued with the details he had, Simon rushed to the pantry, came out with a rifle, ammo. Lana darted into the mudroom for jackets.

"Ethan's with the horses. Simon will need one, so he'll tell him." Lana shoved her arms through the sleeves of her jacket, voice steady, eyes showing not a hint of the fear. "Ethan can alert Fred and the kids, I'll get Mallick. Duncan, you get Poe. Simon."

She gripped his hand, then let it go and flashed.

Simon clipped a holster onto his belt, met Duncan's eyes. "Go."

Ten miles beyond the checkpoint, the enemy halted. Silver hair streaming, eyes ablaze with fervor, Jeremiah

White climbed onto the roof of a truck. As planned, one of the DUs at his side illuminated him so all could see. His voice carried, full-throated, through the soft spring night.

"Fellow warriors, friends, patriots, tonight, at long last, we will eradicate the sanctuary of the demons that defile our world. Tonight, at long last, our blessed crusade to purify the land, the seas, the very air we breathe ends. We mark this night as God's wrath, delivered through his true children. We will strike them down, rip out this beating heart of their evil. Tonight, in our righteous fury, we avenge our fallen brothers. Arlington. Washington. New York. Philadelphia."

Others in the crowd shouted out names of other battles, other places as White spread his arms, lifted his face to the starstruck heavens.

"And our brothers will cry out from their graves, will rip the air with their gratitude as we wipe these demons and all who truck with them from the face of this earth."

"Burn the witches!"

As that cry rang out, over and over, the Dark Uncanny who stood with them remained stone-faced. No sense of irony leaked through.

"Burn the witches," White echoed. "Hang the demons. Strike them down as they flee. Root out the false prophet they worship as The One, for she will face our judgment. And with her death, as promised, as decreed, by her own fiery sword, we take back the world, we ride the glory.

"Tonight, New Hope burns!"

He drew his own sword, lifted it high, then sliced it down to point toward the glimmer of lights in the distance.

They spread out, squads to attack outlying farms, homes, families, others to circle or flash to the west and east to strike from those directions. Another handful to surge to the checkpoint, take down security as the main forces followed.

Still agile and fit, White boosted down from the roof of the truck, nodded to the pair of burly DUs who served as his personal guard.

"Let them burn, let them bleed, let them litter the ground of this cursed place with bodies. Through the flames and the blood we'll take her at last. When I strike the bitch down, we'll have all."

Troops swept by in a flood, eager for that blood. Others, according to plan, pushed in from the north, with advance teams striking at the checkpoints.

Seasoned, experienced warriors, White thought, some of whom had been with him since the earliest days. Raiders who killed and maimed for the thrill of it. Dark Uncannys who sought the end of Fallon Swift as much as the most fanatical Purity Warrior.

And all under his command.

He waited, his own eagerness growing, the thirst for vengeance searing his throat.

CHAPTER TWENTY-THREE

White heard the first snaps of gunfire, watched the first spear of lightning rip across the dark. The crows swarmed in.

Like music, he thought. Like triumph.

Like power.

Finally, what had risen from the dark would know all he was.

"Now. To the heart, straight to the heart to tear it out."

But rather than the gardens, as planned, the protective shield held. When power struck power at the checkpoint, the light spread. In the pale green the faeries brought, the troops, the people of New Hope, magickals, NMs, farmers, teachers, soldiers, weavers, potters engaged the enemy.

On the road to town, in the woods, over fields, on outlying farms, they struck back.

Colin and his recruits met the enemy rushing from the south. Flynn sprinted with troops from The Beach through the woods, turning the ambush back on the attackers. At the farm, Travis fought with Eddie while Fred turned the torches and flaming arrows meant to burn down her home to flowers. To the east, Will fought with his son, with Poe and his.

At the checkpoint, Simon fired from his sniper's nest, blocked out worry for Lana. She'd refused to join the second line of defense, and whipped her power against the dark on the front line.

White had haunted her and hunted her, he understood. And Mallick was with her. He had to trust.

Duncan wove his bike through the oncoming forces, sword slashing in one hand, power in the other. He swung back, the bike another weapon as Tonia loosed arrows from her own sniper's nest.

A pair of Raiders—and he could admire the chopper under them—barreled toward him. The one riding tandem heaved an axe. Veering to avoid the crash, Duncan flipped power, sent the axe flying back and into the skull of the lead rider. The speed, the sudden loss of control sent the chopper careening off the road, into the tree where Tonia had her nest.

"Watch it!" she snapped out.

"Sorry."

He spun around, saw a couple more Raiders, some PWs on foot, a couple on horseback pull back to retreat.

"No, not today."

He started to pursue, then saw White.

"Son of a bitch. Assholes in retreat!" he called out, satisfied when riders on horseback set off after them. He spun around again to confront White.

He looked dazed, Duncan realized. Likely from the crash into the shield. But the two DU's flanking him didn't have the same issues.

He threw up a block, and still the force of the power strike spun at him nearly unseated him. He gunned his engine, started to blast out his own.

Fallon dived out of the sky, Laoch's wings arrowed

up. Both the wolf and the owl leaped off to join the battle. And she, as Duncan fought to keep the flood of emotions inside him dammed, dropped the left guard with one strike of her sword, took down the one on the right with a bolt of light.

A swipe of her hand through the air blew White to the ground. "Sleep." With him sprawled, she wheeled Laoch around, looked at Duncan. "I'm back," she said, and charged into the enemy who remained.

"Yeah, I see that."

The attack meant to level New Hope was routed in under twenty minutes. New Hope suffered no casualties. Not a single building burned. They gained thirty horses, ten trucks, six bikes, a number of weapons, and more than six hundred prisoners.

Including Jeremiah White.

Fallon looked down on him where he sprawled on the road to New Hope.

"I know we need to talk," she said to Duncan. "But we have to deal with this first."

"Yeah. To both." He took a step back when Lana rushed to her.

"Fallon."

"Warrior Mom," she murmured, holding tight. "Dad." Still in Lana's embrace, she reached for him as he dropped down from the sniper's nest. "We'll talk, I promise. Mallick. I'm glad you were here."

"You timed your return well."

"I saw—in the fire. We need to check on the other lines, on the houses and farms."

"Word's coming in, elf to elf." Like Simon, Tonia dropped down. "We have some injuries. No casualties reported so far. We're still chasing down a few. Hi, pal."

She gave Fallon a light punch on the arm. "Nice entrance." She looked down at White. "And top prize."

"Let's get him into town. The gardens I think." Fallon looked at her mother. "It seems appropriate. Arlys is going to want to report on the attack, the capture. We're going to broadcast it far and wide."

"I'll take him." Duncan set a boot on the back of White's neck, flashed them through.

"He's feeling a little rough," Tonia said.

"I know. I'm sorry." Fallon sighed. "I'm sorry. Let's get this done."

Lana laid a hand on her arm. "What are you going to do with him?"

"Part of me wants him dead, but that's not the way. I'm going to question him, here, in front of as many as possible, so any who want to hear can hear. I'm hoping Chuck can find a way to record it so we can send it out. So more can hear and see and know."

"We'll get the word out," Simon told her. "I have a feeling everyone in New Hope wants to hear."

She kept him sleeping; it seemed best. Under the colorful lights of the gardens, people gathered. She saw Lissandra, with her son at her side, Garrett, who bore the brand White ordered burned into the flesh of captured magickals. Anne and Marla, still grieving for the son lost in New York, stood with their remaining two children. Her mother, who'd fled what had become home to save the child she carried in her.

Before she moved forward to pull White out of sleep, she heard a murmuring through the crowd, one that grew louder.

"God, Jonah." On a gasp of breath, Rachel gripped his arm. "With Eddie. Is that . . ."

"Kurt Rove." Jonah put a hand on his youngest son's shoulder. "It's that son of a bitch Rove."

Eddie, his face hard as granite, dragged the bound man through the crowd. Then shoved him to the ground in front of Fallon.

"This here's Kurt Rove. Maybe he didn't kill Max Fallon directly, but he was part of it. He betrayed this town and everybody in it. He killed the good, sweet woman my oldest girl's named for. Shot her in the back while she used her own body to shield a child. He'd have killed your mama if he could, and you with her. You need to know that, Fallon. You need to see him, and know that."

"I do know it, Eddie." She looked down at Rove, at the bitter face scarred by hate, at the eyes radiating it. "I do see him."

"I wanted to kill him when I saw he was one of the prisoners. Wanted to just put a bullet in him and be done. But I couldn't kill in cold blood. I couldn't do that and face my wife and my kids."

"It's what makes you the man you are, and not a man like him."

"I'm gonna ask you for one thing. He doesn't go to some island to make a life. He doesn't get that after what he's done. I'm asking you to lock him up, so he lives locked up, like we've done for men like Hargrove, like you'll do for White. He earned it, so I'm asking."

"It's done."

"Okay then." Tears swam into his eyes, and his jaw trembled, but he nodded, sharp and firm. "Okay." He walked back to Fred, to the arms she put around him.

"You ain't gonna lock me up, lying bitch." Rove spat at her. "Everybody knows you burn the righteous alive with your hellfire."

"You'll be disappointed when you find yourself in prison for the rest of your life. We don't execute prisoners. We don't enslave them, torment them."

"Lying spawn of hell. I should've cut the throat of your whore of a mother when I had the chance."

Fallon clutched the hilt of her sword. "I wish you and your twisted soul a long life in the dark you've chosen. No, leave him," she said when Will moved forward to take him away. "Let him hear what the one he follows has to say."

She walked forward to White. "Wake."

Still dull from the spell, White's eyes blinked open. As they cleared, as he struggled to get to his feet, found himself bound, a violence came into them.

Hate, deep and crazed, with fear riding with it.

"Things didn't go as you planned," she told him. "New Hope stands. You don't."

"More will rise in my place. Legions to strike you down."

"I don't think so, but they can try. There are people here tonight we freed from you and your followers. Children you branded and took as slaves, people you raped, magickals you mutilated and tortured."

She glanced around, saw Garrett, remembered the dream, years before, when she'd watched Duncan, Tonia, others from New Hope rescue him. She gestured him forward.

"What was done to you?"

"His Purity Warriors captured me, they locked me up with other magickals. They branded me. They tortured me, beat me, burned me, raped me. They were taking me to be hanged—they held ritual hangings at midnight on every Sunday, like . . . worship. The people of New Hope rescued me and the others. I was twelve."

"Spawn of Satan," White spat at him. "The Almighty will strike you down, you and all like you." He managed to push up to his knees.

"You don't deny imprisoning, torturing, branding, raping, executing children?" Fallon asked.

"They aren't children! They aren't human. Demons! Demons spreading their infestation over the earth."

"Yet he lives here, as do others, causing no harm, while the Dark Uncanny you're in league with burn and kill. The Raiders who ride with you burn and kill. With Dark Uncannys in your number you attacked the peace of New Hope, trying to end me before I was born. You killed my birth father on this very ground."

The fanatical light burned like torches in his eyes. "It should have been you."

"It wasn't."

"It will be." He threw his head back. "Strike me down with your sword, demon whore. I give my life for the god of Abraham. Shed my blood on your demonic altar, rend my flesh for your hell beasts to feast on. I will walk in the kingdom while you burn in the fire."

"That's a lot of drama," Fallon said with a hint of amusement that had White's eyes glinting. "We don't execute prisoners, have any demonic altars. We sure don't feast on human flesh. You're going to have to settle for prison."

She felt it, in a snap of an instant, the quick pulse of dark power. And in that instant, threw out her hands to meet it.

Black met white with a force that set the ground to quaking. The bonds fell away, White's face and form fell away.

Allegra sneered as she rose.

"You fool. Eric killed White years ago. We took turns wearing his face, leading his idiots against you. And you never saw."

"I see now." All the beauty gone with no power to

spare to disguise the scars that ruined the face, the thin wisps of gray that exposed most of the raw, ridged scalp.

"Too late." And on tattered wings, Allegra flew up, slicing bolts of fire. "I'll be back with an army, finish you."

"It's not," Fallon murmured, as she and others extinguished the weak flames before they hit the ground. "And you won't."

Wings spread, as silver as her sword. Fallon rose up on them, drew Allegra's fire.

"Only dark magicks, blood sacrifice bring the wings to the witch."

"You're wrong," Fallon said. "Again." She blocked the bolts, held her own fire. Allegra was weak, she thought, obviously unable to draw the strength to flash. And not a little mad. "Pull back your power. Surrender and live."

"The dark protects me, with the blood of the legions shed in its name. Your light dims against it." She swiped at Fallon again. "You destroyed the father of my child, you gave her pain. Now watch the bitch who whelped you burn."

She used all she had to draw up a torrent of flame. She sneered down at Lana, drove that torrent toward the ground.

"No!" With power pumped by fear, Fallon pulled the storm of flame back. And threw up her shield to deflect it, felt the storm of heat lash out as it engulfed Allegra.

One shriek, sliced off short, then there was nothing. Just nothing.

On the ground, Arlys gripped a trembling hand on Chuck's arm. "Tell me you got that."

"Yeah." Though it shook a little, he kept his scavenged and rebuilt video camera on Fallon as she landed softly, folded in those silver wings. "I got it. I need a really big drink."

"We'll both have one when we check the footage." She stepped forward to stand with Lana. "Did you know she could do that? You know, fly?"

"No. I knew she had all magicks in her, but . . . We'll have to talk. Eric, now Allegra." Lana reached for Simon's hand. He'd stood beside her even as the fire spewed down. "Both here, where they killed Max."

"It's justice."

"Yeah." Steady and sure, Lana brought his hand to her lips. "It's justice."

People wanted to stay and talk, to Fallon, to each other. Apparently, she noted, Duncan wasn't one of them.

She embraced her family.

"So, wings," Colin commented. "They're the bop."

"The what?"

"It's an expression I'm trying out. It's going to catch on."

"No," Travis corrected.

"Wait and see. Let's round up the troops, get them back to the barracks. I'm due in Arlington tomorrow." With set teeth, focused effort, he lifted his arm, closed his leathered hand into a fist, and tapped Fallon's shoulder. "Nice work."

"I need to help with the horses." But Ethan came in for another hug first. "She was lost, and couldn't be saved."

"I know."

"She tried to call for Petra, but she couldn't pull enough power. If she'd stopped trying to kill you, kill Mom, she could have. But she couldn't stop. Glad you're back," he added, and moved off.

"Think about Petra another time," Simon advised. "If and when she comes, we'll be ready. I'm going to help Will with the prisoners."

"And I'll help with the injured." Lana brushed a hand on Fallon's cheek. "There's chicken left from dinner at home if you're hungry."

"I'll get to it."

Then Lana laid her cheek to Fallon's, whispered, "Go find him."

"I will." But she turned to Mallick first.

"You put the last weeks to good use."

"I traveled, and studied, and grieved. I needed to. I went to Wales because I wanted to see where you were born. That's where I found my wings."

"I didn't mean the wings. They were never lost, only waiting. You would have spared her life. Even when she left you without a choice, you didn't take her life in vengeance. You put your time away to good use."

He frowned at some dried blood on his sleeve, brushed it away like lint. "The boy, however, spent most of his brooding. I'm for a glass of wine and my bed."

"We'll talk tomorrow. There's still work to be done."

Since she couldn't find Duncan, she searched out Tonia.

"Excellent wings. Want a beer?"

"Not yet, thanks. I—"

"He went to help with the prisoners. Too many of them for the usual, so he suggested using Howstein's barn, putting a lockdown spell on it, doing a sleep trance on the DUs until we can start transporting them tomorrow."

"That's a good idea."

"He has a few." Tonia's MacLeod blue eyes softened. "He missed the hell out of you, Fallon. Go a little easy on him."

"I'm more hoping he goes a little easy on me."

She decided it was only fair to talk to him, if he was willing to talk, on his turf. So after the town bedded down for the night, she sat on the curb outside of his house to wait. He'd come back eventually.

It occurred to her she'd never done this, just sat in the quiet of New Hope. The fact that it could and did settle in again after a night of attacks, bloodshed, violence, illustrated its resilience.

It served, to her mind, as an illustration of the resilience of the spirit, of the unity forged by community.

Illuminated now by only moon and starlight, it slept. Parents had checked on their children, soothed them into dreams. Lovers shared beds. In the clinic, medicals watched over the sick or wounded.

The schools held dark, waiting for morning when instructors and students would file in. With the sun, shops and services would begin the day. The farms would stir awake, the community kitchen would smell of coffee and cooking.

There could be peace after war, she thought. There could be normality after nightmares.

And, she knew, there could be solace after the grieving. Renewal after doubt.

Hope after despair.

She heard the sound of the engine, the muscular roar through the quiet. Driving fast, she thought, driving home. And stood to meet him on her feet.

Like the first time she'd seen him, in dreams, with his hair blowing in the wind. But he'd been a boy then. The one who swerved the bike to the curb, cut the engine, swung off to face her was a man.

She'd considered a dozen ways to start this conversation, and at the sticking point tossed them all aside and said what came first. "I'm sorry."

He didn't approach her, but stood as he was. "For what?"

"For leaving when you wanted me to stay, when you

needed more from me than I could find in me to give. For staying away longer than I'd said I would. And for blocking you out while I was gone, even though I knew it would hurt you."

"I know why you left, or thought you had to."

His voice carried calm—he didn't put a bite or snap in it.

"I figure there's a reason you didn't come back when you said you would. I don't get why you blocked me. I don't get that, and yeah, you hurt me."

"I blocked you because I was afraid if I let you in, even for a minute, I'd come back."

More than a bite snapped out now. "Fuck that. I wouldn't have pushed you."

"No. I'm not supposed to say it's me, not you," she reminded him, "but it was. I'd have come back before I was ready because I wanted to be with you, and wanted the comfort you'd have given me. I needed you more than I needed to find my resolve again."

She lifted her hands, helplessly. "My faith and real purpose, lost in grief and a need for revenge. I lost it with Mick, and I had to find it again. I had to, Duncan, or I'd never be able to do what needs to be done. Everything I wanted was here. You, my family, my friends. If I hadn't left all of that, I'm not sure I'd have found what I needed inside myself to fight again. Or to lead again."

"Did you find it?"

"I did. But I'm sorry I hurt you. I'm sorry I worried my family and friends. I'm sorry I wasn't here to help."

"That's a lot of sorry."

"I have more if you need it."

Studying her face, he shrugged. "That might be enough."

And in two strides, grabbed her, dragged her in, took what he really needed.

"Oh, thank the goddess," she murmured and locked herself around him. "Come with me. Will you come with me?"

Without waiting for an answer, she flashed.

The light shimmered, pale green with the sparkling blink of pixies dancing. A pond spread, pure, clear as glass, with moonlight filtering through trees to spill across it. Mists, thin fingers of silver, rose from the water. The air, warm and sweet, held still.

"It's your faerie glade."

"It's where I was before I came back. Right before I—I'll explain later." Her fingers dived into his hair. "Can we just talk after?"

Since he wanted her naked, he swept his hands over her, left her clothes, her sword, in a jumbled pile with his before dragging her down to the carpet of grass.

This first, he thought, body to body, skin to skin. This first.

"Touch me." Her hands ran over him as she murmured against his mouth. "Bring me back to you. Come back to me."

Light sparked as they came together, over flesh, under it. She felt it pour inside her, fill all the spaces she'd emptied out. She'd turned from him to find resolve, and now, turning back to him, found love.

And pleasure. The beat of his heart, the strength of his hands, the shape of him, the taste.

Here, with him, she could yield, or demand. Abdicate control or take. Here, with him, she could feel all the joy she'd lost.

He gripped her hands to slow them, to slow his own. Looked down at her, at the moonlight mirrored back in her eyes. When he took her mouth again, he stripped off all barriers and let his heart pour into the kiss.

You're my light.

She melted under him, let her heart pour into his.

And you're my light.

They rose up, joined, cushioned on the sweet air, bathed in the soft, green light, with their own, united, shimmering like the stars.

When, once more, they lay together on the carpet of grass, their light quieted to a glow, she pressed a kiss to his heart. "I'm forgiven?"

"Probably." He trailed a finger down her spine, up again. "I wasn't mad. Well, off and on. I was worried, everybody was. Where did you go?"

"Everywhere." Now she rested her head on his heart. "At first I just needed to be alone, to be gone. The grief, it was so huge, and still only part of it. There's so much empty in the world, Duncan. It's not hard to find places to be alone. I've known what would be asked of me all my life, and I carried that. I've carried more since I turned thirteen. So I told myself everybody else would just have to handle it all for a while because I couldn't. And I knew you would. You, my parents, my brothers, Tonia, Arlys, Jonah, everyone. I knew you would. If it was selfish, well, the gods would just have to deal with that. Because I couldn't lead troops into battle when my heart was bleeding or ask anyone to follow me when I couldn't see where to go."

She pushed herself to sitting, looked through the mists rising over the pond. "When I saw what you'd done, the memorial you'd created, everything in me shook. I couldn't say all I wanted to say to you, or I'd have fallen completely apart. Then, the tree over where Mick fell. I wanted to feel comfort from it, but I didn't. It was anger, and the anger, the hunger for revenge blocked everything. I wanted to bring the lightning and burn that tree to the ground."

She paused, trailed her fingers over the cuff she wore, fashioned from another tree she'd destroyed with temper.

"I wanted to leave everything and hunt Petra, only Petra, until I could cut her to pieces with my sword. A sword of light and justice. How could I stay? How could I lead?"

"You could have told me."

"I couldn't. I couldn't even tell myself. I could only feel grief, anger, despair. Why, when I've done what they asked, when I've done all I know how to do, do they demand such payments? Max to Mick, with so many between. Why, why, why? How could I be the light when I couldn't feel or find it?"

She looked over at him when he sat up with her. "It wasn't just who Mick was to me, or what he was to me, how much I loved him. Though, God, as much as I did, it's not what I feel for you. What if it had been you?"

"It wasn't."

She shook her head. "But that question kept circling in my head. You, or my parents. Colin lost his arm— what if he lost his life? Travis, Ethan, Tonia, Hannah, Mallick, so many I love. What if one of you is the next payment?"

"I'd say you can't think that way, but you already knew that." He didn't have to like it, he decided, to begin to understand it. "And that's why you left."

"It's a big part of it. What grew in the grief, the doubts was worse. That hunger, that thirst to destroy what destroyed. Eric and Allegra killed Max because they wanted to kill me, inside my mother. They came back because they wanted to kill me, and destroy everything, everyone in New Hope. Petra killed to hurt you, and for the joy of it. And Mick."

She shut her eyes a moment. "She killed him to strike

at me. I think, I feel, if we'd lost him in battle, I could have taken it. Grieved, yes, but it wouldn't have shaken me to the core. But she chose the moment of victory. She chose to strike him down in his moment of joy. In a moment the two of us shared. It took me some time to understand that, to get through that hunger and understand."

"She won't win, Fallon."

"I know it, but I didn't know it then. I stopped believing in what we are. I went to mountaintops and deserts, to forests and to cities even the ghosts have abandoned, and wondered why we bother. Didn't people just find another reason to kill, or scar the land? Hadn't they driven magicks away out of fear?"

He tugged the ends of her hair. "That was some excellent wallowing you did there."

"It really was." She tipped her head to his shoulder. "But I started to see beauty again. The way the sun strikes the water in a stream or a bridge spans a river. I went to the mountains where Allegra and Eric attacked Max and my mother, Poe and Kim. The house is gone, but the land is beautiful, and there were signs of people working it, finding shelter, making lives.

"Why that mattered so much, why it started to open me again, I don't know. But it did. So I started to look for more of that. Resilience, faith, effort, caring. And I found it. There are a lot of empty places, Duncan, but there's land being tended, homes tended, families becoming. There's still strength and courage, and there's still joy. I just had to look to see it again. I nearly came back then, but I knew I wasn't finished. I wasn't finished because I couldn't make myself come here, where Mick's everywhere. I went to Wales instead."

"Mallick."

"It didn't begin with him, but so much of what I

am came from him. He never wavers. His faith had to have been tested countless times, but he never wavers. I wanted to see where he was born, where he walked as a boy, what he saw."

"You found it."

"I found it. They didn't take that. I found the stone cottage, centuries old, and the goddess who sits by the door. It's there, and I felt him there. He chose to devote his life to the light, to me, to us, to leave his home and put himself in the hands of the gods."

With her head resting on Duncan's shoulder, she watched the mists rise like spirits from the pool, wind through the air.

"I felt his faith, his courage, and feeling it restored the rest of mine. And that terrible hunger died, it just died. Anger, that can be useful, but that hunger is dangerous and destructive. Finally, I could let it go. When I did, and I poured wine in tribute to Ernmas, to the mother goddess, I felt the light pour back. And wings open.

"I could come here, say good-bye to Mick. I could come home to you. I wanted to bring you here, because I first met Mick here, because I sat here with Max. Because I love you, and I wanted to take an oath to you here. I won't turn away from you again, or block you, or leave you. I'll fight beside you, and when that's done, I'll build a life with you."

"Fallon." He lifted her hand, kissed it. "We're already building a life." He closed his own hand, opened it to reveal a ring in his palm. "Wear it."

The gold, white as the moon, gleamed in a circle. Etched on it was the fivefold symbol.

"Just like that?"

"You want me to ask? Do the one-knee thing like in the books?"

She considered, wondered if a heart could get any

fuller than hers in that moment. "No. I kind of like the way you handled it. Put it on," she said, and held out her hand. "I'll wear it."

"I'll take an oath, too," he told her. "I'll fight beside you. And when that's done, we'll keep building the life we've already started."

When he slid the ring on her finger, the light bloomed to seal the promise.

CHAPTER TWENTY-FOUR

She didn't waste time. In addition to solidifying her resolve and cementing her faith, her weeks of alone had produced more maps, more information. And a clear-eyed purpose.

She sat with her parents at breakfast, asked Mallick to join them. These three first—these most vital three first.

"I'm going to apologize for worrying you, and everyone, and promise to do a better job of that later. But right now I need to tell you some of what I found when I was gone. And, man," she added as she bit into her omelette, "did I miss your cooking, Mom."

"You could start by telling us where you've been," Simon began.

"Everywhere. I stood on the summit of Everest where the world's white and frozen, and saw elephants on the savanna in Kenya. I saw the pyramids and miles and miles of golden sand. The Dead Sea, the Australian bush, the moors of Cornwall."

"Well." Simon sat back. "You've been busy."

"Yeah." She paused, scooped up more eggs. "Everywhere," she said again. "At first, I just needed the lonely places, the silent ones, but . . . Wherever I went? There's so much beauty, so much light in the world. So much, whether it's a gift from the gods like Denali or through the sweat and ingenuity of man like a round tower in Ireland, it's there. Palm trees and clear water shining in the desert, a village carved out of a jungle so thick the air shimmers green."

Remembering it, just remembering it brought a glow inside her.

"Even in those first days when I didn't want to see it or feel it, I couldn't stop seeing, feeling that beauty, that light."

"You saw the world." And more, Lana realized. "A world that's not just war and loss, battles and blood."

"I want to show you. One day I have to show you. You showed me," she said to her parents. "With books, even the DVDs, with stories and maps. But . . ."

"Being there's different," Simon commented. "It's more."

"So much more. I saw a world that offers everything for the body, the mind, the spirit, if we just . . ."

She turned to Mallick, flicking fingers at the bangs she'd carelessly trimmed with her combat knife in a cave in the Anhui province of China.

"You can't see if you don't look. How many times did you say that to me? You told me how you'd traveled the world, but I didn't look so didn't see you'd traveled it to know it, understand it, honor it."

"So now you've looked."

"Now I've looked," she agreed. "And I see. The treasures, the dreams, the dangers, the glorious diversity of the world and those who live in it. She's a generous mother who offers all we need, and she's a child who needs our tending and care."

She reached out to Simon. "You always knew that.

Always respected, always tended. And you knew the world was worth fighting for."

"So have you, baby. You just needed a break."

"You were right about that, too. I wanted the three of you, my teachers, to know what I learned from you got me through. Because it did, once I looked, once I saw, once I started thinking clearly again, I spent more time studying where I was, thinking about where I'd been."

She got up to get the coffeepot, add more to the mugs. Because it was time, again, to speak of war.

"Here's a vital bit of that observation. There are skirmishes in Europe, in Asia, Africa, and so on. Small bands, well scattered, not particularly organized. Like here, there are people working to rebuild, to communicate, to connect, or those who prefer more isolation. But the dark magicks are barely a presence. Some Raiderlike tribes, but that's more the ugly side of human nature, and there's strong resistance there."

She scooped up more breakfast. "Unlike here, there's no sense of constant battle, no serious concentration of the dark. It's here, concentrated, because I am. We are."

"But in Scotland, you found what you believe is the source," Lana said. "And the broken shield."

"It's waiting there; it feeds there. It needs to be near the damaged shield because that feeds it, too. That's a theory, but it rings for me. It's where we need to destroy it. The dark's focused its forces here to try to kill me and mine, to eradicate any threat. Once eradicated, it can move on to the next shield, do the same until there's nothing left. It also keeps us focused here, fighting those forces."

"And keeps you from taking the fight to it."

Fallon nodded at her father. "Just exactly right. We've still got work to do before we move on that, but once you know the enemy's tactics—".

"You know how to adjust your own," Simon finished.

"You got it. We're going to keep them really busy, de-plete their numbers. The PWs may not be destroyed, but they're severely damaged after last night. They might lift up another leader, but they'll be weak and scattered and shaken by Arlys's broadcast."

"You could see that on Rove's face," Lana said. "You could see the shock, not shame but shock, when Allegra shed the mask, when he realized he'd been duped."

"He can spend the rest of his life in prison thinking about being duped." Fallon shrugged that off.

"A lot of them will crawl back into their holes, de-moralized." Simon gestured with his mug. "Some will try to hide or remove the PW tats, pretend they had no part in it. And some will try to rally. But they'll never be the threat they were." Fallon lifted her mug in turn— soldier to soldier. "We'll run them to ground when we need to. We've been finding and taking out the confine-ment camps, the labs, and we won't stop until we get them all. There's no one in charge there with Hargrove locked up. We're not, as we were, fighting on multiple fronts. But . . ."

She kept her eyes on her father. "I think we should form specialty teams to work on mopping them up. Forces geared toward hunting them down, the PWs, the militias, taking them out. And we do that before they can recover or regroup."

"That's good adjusted tactics."

"Will you head that up? Refine the training wherever you think it needs to be refined, and take command of that team?"

"You know I will."

"When he goes, I go." Knowing her man, Lana held up a hand to ward off Simon's argument. "They'll need a healer, and a witch, and I'm both. If the kids needed me here, I'd stay here. They don't. I go where you go. That's it, Simon."

"Don't pull the that's it—"

"Did. What's next, Fallon?"

"We're going to talk later," Simon muttered.

"Fine. Next?"

"Okay. Next is a small, special group that can be ready to mobilize and flash out anytime we get word of a Raider camp or attack. I'm going to ask Poe to head that. A third team should be ready to bug out if we learn of any confinement centers or labs we've missed. Starr and Troy, I thought. And on all of these, I'd expect our allies to give support if needed. I'll speak with Vivienne, firm that up."

She looked over at Mallick, calmly eating his omelette, a slice of toast with damson jam, the pretty fruit compote.

"You'll need other specialty armies, feeding out of your established bases," he said as he ate. "Not exclusively magickals, but primarily."

"Yes. I intend to spend time at every base helping with training."

"And would like me to do the same—and with less time here to enjoy your mother's excellent cooking."

Gray threaded through his hair, and creases had deepened around his eyes, his mouth. She wished she could give him his cottage, his bees—just as she wished she could give her parents the farm.

But the world needed them.

"I'll make it up to you. I'll be asking Duncan to rotate, too. I'd like to keep Tonia and Travis here—they're so solid at the barracks. And as New Hope's already dealt with three attacks by Petra or her parents, I think we need to keep the others right here, to defend. When Petra finds out—and she may know already—I killed

Allegra, she may launch another attack on New Hope. We should stay on high alert."

"As should you," Mallick added. "We had Allegra in our midst, and yet none of us saw beneath her false face. Not one of us saw through the disguise of White."

"She used all she had," Fallon told him. "For the disguise, to hide under it."

"Max hurt her. Hurt her and Eric," Lana said, "in the mountains before we came to New Hope. And after the attack here, I hurt them. Then you, Fallon. You added to that. She never recovered, not fully."

"That's right." It was just, Fallon thought, that the damage to Allegra's power had started with Max. As it had been just for her father to have ended Eric.

"It's why she couldn't attack, why she was weak when she did. It's why she's dead."

"She should have held it until she was away from you," Lana said. "She should've held that mask in place until she was in prison. The damage she might have done once inside to guards and security. But she couldn't wait. She didn't have the control to wait with you so close. Petra has more power and more control."

"It won't be enough." Fallon reached over to rub the back of her mother's hand. "I'll take care of the dishes. And rather than ask the commanders here, I'm going to talk to them all individually, at their bases, which also gives me the chance to apologize to each individually."

"Then if Fallon's got KP, I'm going to walk over to the barracks. I've got a few in mind for the specialty force you're after. That was great, babe. Thanks." Simon kissed the top of Lana's head after he pushed back from the table. "We're still going to talk later."

"Uh-huh."

"If you'll excuse me, I'll go with Simon. I have a few to consider as well. Thank you, Lana, for the meal."

"You're always welcome at our table."

When they were alone, Fallon shifted to her mother. "Before I start the KP, I'll start with the apology."

"There's no need. Your dad talked to me about it so I understood. I truly did. And everything you said here?" She sighed. "What mother doesn't want her child to see the world, and all its wonders?"

"I want to take you. I want everyone I love to pick a spot so I can take you where you most want to go."

"Won't that be an adventure?" Brows arched, she ran a hand over Fallon's hair. "Combat knife trim?"

Fallon brushed a hand through it in turn. "Is it that bad?"

"Hmm" was Lana's answer before she laughed. "So . . . instead of an apology, I'm hoping you'll tell me about the ring you're wearing. I'd always imagined you'd be full of excitement when you told me you were engaged."

"I didn't want to say anything until it was just you and me."

"Now it is."

"It's really more of a promise. I think, in some ways, we've been engaged since before either of us was born. But this is the promise, and the choice for both of us. And I am excited." She thrust out her hand, and for a moment, a precious one to Lana, was just a young woman in love. "Isn't it beautiful?"

"It is beautiful, and it's perfect."

"Don't cry, Mom."

"Just a little. He's exactly what I'd wish for you. Just exactly," she said and opened her arms.

Within three weeks, Lana joined Simon and the newly formed special forces team on a strike at a PW base in

Arkansas. They moved on to Louisiana, across Mississippi, through Alabama.

Near the ruined, flooded city of Mobile, troops from The Beach pushed in from the east to help drive the enemy to the barrier of the Gulf of Mexico.

In what would become known as the Summer of Light, Poe and his team mobilized to cut off Raider attacks in the Midwest, the Southwest. Troy and Starr with their band of magickals uprooted confinement centers.

Fallon, in steady rotation, joined each group in turn as they worked their way east and west, north and south.

Over three scorching days in August, where lightning strikes turned forests to blazing tinder, where the ground quaked and split like eggshells, she fought side by side with Duncan.

In the Dark Uncanny stronghold of Los Angeles, mansions had become palaces and prisons. Canyons jagged through the broken streets of Beverly Hills, and served as killing pits for those unfortunate enough to be captured. The stench from a decade of blood sacrifices on the black marble altar erected on Rodeo Drive stung the air.

In the flaming hills, faeries and elves fought to suppress the fires, worked to rescue any who'd managed to escape the city to hide in caves and canyons. And there, above the city where magicks clashed and slashed, the sky turned red.

Even as she fought, Fallon searched for the black dragon and its rider. But as they cut through the enemy's numbers, drove them to the beaches, to the wild waves of the Pacific, she saw no sign of Petra.

When she rode Laoch through that red sky, over the hills where fires still sparked, where blackened trees rose like skeletons through the smoke, she scanned the city.

Not dead like D.C., but deeply wounded, with its bleeding not yet completely stanched. Its broken bones might heal over time, its raw scars might begin to blend into the landscape in another generation. This land, this city would become what those who settled on it worked to make it.

But never again, never again would innocent blood be spilled there in the name of the dark.

Duncan, Tonia, and their handpicked team would transport the surviving enemy to D.C. Dead City, she thought. There, with their magicks bound, they would remain.

She flew down for Faol Ban, called to Taibhse, and with them, flashed home.

It surprised her to find Fred and her three youngest working in her mother's garden.

Fred pushed back her floppy yellow hat with its trailing ribbons and flowers the crown, waved a hand. She wore pink-lensed sunglasses in the shape of hearts.

"Hi! Welcome home. We thought we'd give your mom a hand with the garden, since she's so busy this summer."

"She'll appreciate it. We all do."

The instant Fallon dismounted, Angel, her hair as sunny as her mother's hat, ran over. "Can I brush Laoch, water him?"

"Sure. He's earned a carrot, too." And knowing the girl's love affair with all things equine, Fallon stepped back.

"That made her day. You could use some brushing and watering yourself."

"I guess so." It struck Fallon that the kids hadn't so much as blinked at the blood and soot all over her. Such was the world they lived in. She watched Willow fly out

of the garden and all but fall over the wolf with hugs—
attention Faol Ban seemed fine with.

"Max and Rainbow are training, aren't they?"

"Yes." Fred gripped her hands together, looked toward the barracks. "After the attack, they just . . ."

"This part is nearly over."

"Is it?" Fred shifted her gaze to her youngest two
while her boy tried to convince the wolf to fetch a stick.
Such things were well beneath Faol Ban's dignity.

"An end, a beginning. A chance, a choice. All of
those bathed in blood and tears. But its sinews are sacrifice, courage, faith. Its heart is now, then, always love."

As the vision ran through her, Fallon lifted her face to
a sky not of murderous red but aching blue.

"Here is the earth, the air, the water, the fire, and the
magicks that join them together. All of that, all, feed the
light. Watch the light burn like a thousand suns, Queen
Fred, and you'll know when the sword strikes, the arrow
flies, and the blood seals the end of the dark."

Fallon's eyes cleared, looked into Fred's. "You have a
new light inside you."

"Well, wow." Blowing out a breath, Fred took off her
hat, fanned it at her face. "Nobody expects a prophecy,
right? And that one was a *pow* with the wow."

Fallon pointed to a chair on the patio. "Sit."

"Maybe for a minute."

When she did, Fallon poured a glass of the sun tea
steeping on a table, chilled it with her hands, offered it.

"I'm sorry if I intruded. It just sort of beamed out
at me."

"That's okay." Fred sipped the tea, patted a hand on
her belly. "Yeah, one more time. Crazy, right?"

"No. You and Eddie make beautiful children."

"We really do. He's such a good dad. The kids are

missing him right now. He's with Poe. They're proud of him, but they miss him."

"You, too."

"I haven't told him yet. I only felt the spark—felt it often enough to know—after he'd gone."

"What a great welcome home he'll have." She crouched down. "You, from the beginning, Fred, you've been a light. You and Eddie. Your children will carry that light. You helped save the world. They'll help heal it."

"Is that another prophecy?"

"Not this time. It's faith."

She carried that faith with her into September when it seemed the fire and blood of battle would never end. She carried it with her each time Chuck intercepted another call for help, or the scouts learned of another stronghold.

She carried it to the clinic to keep the spark strong when she visited the wounded. She carried it to grave sites and memorials.

"We've got them on the run," Duncan said.

They'd finished a meeting with commanders, team leaders, and now she sat with Duncan and her father.

She knew what Duncan wanted—he wanted her to signal the time had come to finish it.

"The constant, focused attacks have paid off," Simon agreed. "We're still going to see some skirmishes, but we've broken the backs. The DUs are the primary problem at this point, like we discussed. We can't give them the time or opportunity to regroup."

"We won't. I don't know why it's not time to finish it, I just know it's not. We've had multiple and conflicting reports on Petra, but nothing concrete. She's part of the circle, and we'll need to confront her, defeat her, to fuse that circle and end it."

"Then we draw her to Scotland," Duncan argued. "It ends there."

His determination to finish it, his absolute certainty they could, spilled through the gears of her mind like sand.

Irritating. Irritating.

She found it difficult to keep the edge out of her voice. "On our timetable, not hers, on our terms, not hers. And we need to know more about how to finish it, and her. The black dragon. And what they feed in the forest. We can't afford to fail."

"We can't win if we don't fight."

And gave up the fight, led with the edge. "A year ago the DU ruled New York, D.C., Los Angeles, and more. The PWs and military hunted us like animals. Now they don't. We have fought, are fighting. Every day people fight, bleed, die. Do you think I don't want to end it?"

"Hold on—"

"You hold on," she snapped back at Duncan. "I'll know when I know."

On a flick of temper, she flashed away.

"She's tired," Simon said after a humming moment. "And frustrated—that was her tired and frustrated voice."

"I know it," Duncan replied.

"I guess you do. She's also worried. Not about winning this, but about sending more troops out, and burying more. It's a constant weight on her."

"I know that, too." Duncan pushed up to pace. "She's not alone in that."

"No, she's not."

"I feel something pushing in me, and I don't know if

it's because she's wrong and it's time, or because she's right and I want it to be time. Either way, she's pissed now and a lot less likely to listen."

Brooding, Simon noted. Well, he couldn't fault that, as he enjoyed a good brood himself from time to time. He held his peace, let the boy brood while he studied him.

Unlike a lot of the other soldiers, Duncan hadn't gone for the braid—or braids. His hair spilled and curled loose, midnight dark. No tats, either, no beads, no charms.

Like Fallon's, his sword was always at his side. And like her, he had a tall, rangy body, well muscled. Well, the male version, Simon thought.

His boots showed miles of wear and battle scars— literal battle scars. He was a damn good soldier, a canny commander.

Broody green eyes, scruff on his face. Simon scrubbed a hand over his own, knew he couldn't fault that, either.

And he couldn't find fault in the boy—man, Simon corrected—for loving his daughter.

"Take her flowers."

"What?" Duncan stopped pacing, stared. "Flowers?"

"Yeah, flowers. Something you pick yourself adds to it, so something wild. If it smells good, you rack up another point."

"Wildflowers that smell good?"

"That's right. It'll catch her off guard. She might still be pissed, but she'll be off-balance, too. Then state your case."

"Flowers are everywhere anyway."

"Trust me."

"Okay." Hesitating, he slid his hands in his pockets. "So. When this is finished, I want . . ."

"I knew this was coming." Simon sighed.

"When it's finished, I want us—Fallon and me—to get a place, make a place, find a place. Together. I'd like to get your blessing on that."

Simon sat back. "You're never going to be a farmer."

"No, sir."

"Well, I've got Travis and Ethan for that. Born farmers, both of them. She'll need some land though. She likes to grow things. She'd start feeling closed in if she lived right inside a town. Nearby, that would do for her, but she needs room to breathe."

"I love her, Simon. I'm going to do whatever I need to do to give her what she wants, what makes her happy."

"I wish I didn't know that was true, then I could say get the hell away from my baby, and I'd keep her with me. But I do know it's true. You can take that as a blessing." He rose, extended a hand. "One thing," he said when he gripped Duncan's. "No, two things. Finish it first, all the way. And don't be too much of an asshole with my girl."

"Deal. Both counts."

He brought her flowers. He felt like an idiot, especially since he'd tracked her to a meadow loaded with them, but he brought her a fistful of wild lilies.

She stared at them like she'd never seen a stupid flower before, and made him feel like more of an idiot. "What are those for?"

"They're for you." He shoved them into her hands, then followed up with a simple truth. "They're like you. Bright and beautiful and full of light. So."

Then he saw Simon had been right, by the way she smiled, the way she bent her head to draw in their scent. Just a little off-balance.

"I can be sorry for pressuring you. It's just . . . I feel something pushing in me. I feel it pushing harder and harder. I keep seeing the stone circle, the crows, the lightning. I feel it, Fallon, pushing in that dead wood, gloating in there, and my hand itches for my sword. Tonia, too. It's the same for her."

"I know it. I know it, Duncan, and it only makes it more frustrating to know not yet. Still not yet. I've asked. I've cast circles and asked, but it's the one question they don't answer. I've looked in the crystal. I see the dragon, the black dragon, Petra on its back. And nothing I do, nothing we do, stops her.

"I've looked in the fire, searched the flames. I see Tonia bleeding on the ground, the dragon breathing death, a rain of black lightning. And the circle, the center opens wider, wider, and more dark pours out. It pulls you in. I can't stop it. And I'm alone."

It was his turn to lead with the edge. "For fuck's sake. Why am I just hearing this?"

"I had to think. What does it mean? And I know it means that can happen if we don't wait. It can happen if we don't find the way to kill the dragon, destroy Petra."

"We're stronger than she is."

"I believe that, but what's there, in that place? It feeds her just as she feeds it. And the dragon—"

She broke off, eyes narrowing. "The dragon," she repeated. "We need to slay the dragon. It knows its own weaknesses, right? If you want to know how to kill a dragon, ask a dragon. I need to talk to Vivienne."

He grabbed her hand in case she intended to flash away, then and there. "No spell in you for dragon slaying? You're going to Canada?"

"I don't know what kind of protection it may have been given. I'm not going to Canada. I need to talk to Vivienne on my ground, not hers. I need Chuck."

She used Arlys as well to help her craft an invitation both diplomatic and flattering. She asked her mother to bake a Rainbow Cake. She took a ruby from the vaults in D.C., and with it crafted and conjured a gift for the Red Queen.

Vivienne, resplendent in emerald green, arrived with her entourage. Fallon met her alone, and chose the patio, as the gardens held their summer glory.

"How lovely it is here. Such a blooming. And, of course, your vegetables thrive."

"We're farmers," Fallon said simply. "Please sit. I give you my mother's regrets. She and my father were called away only this morning."

"Oh? *Qu'est-ce qui s'est passé?*"

"A small band of PWs to handle. *Ne t'en fais pas.* Before she left, my mother made a cake in your honor. We call it a Rainbow Cake." Fallon served a slice. "I thought you might enjoy it with some faerie wine."

"Perfect." Emeralds glittered at her ears as she nibbled. "And delicious."

"I hope you'll accept this token of our gratitude for your loyalty and comradeship. New York could not have been brought back into the light without your help."

"My people rejoiced with yours." She opened the box Fallon had tied with a fancy gold bow. Then wonder spread over her face as she lifted out the curled ruby dragon, laid it in the palm of her hand. "Oh! *C'est magnifique. C'est merveilleux! Merci, mon amie, merci beaucoup. Je suis*— Ah, English, I want to express myself in English. I'm touched, very deeply. I feel your light in this treasure."

"Duncan sketched the dragon—you—to help me with the creation. It's a gift, Vivienne, given in sincere gratitude."

"Yes. And it will be precious to me." She set it carefully

back in the box, nibbled more cake. "But I, as I'm a cunning woman myself, sense more than a thank-you."

"Yes, but whatever your answer, the gift is yours, and the light in it, yours."

"What is the question?"

"While we bring light to the world, there's still dark. And there's one who seeks, above all, to serve the source of the dark, which she does with human sacrifice. Children."

"*Mes dieux*. Any and all who prey on children are the evil, the deepest and darkest of the evil, whatever form they take."

"We're of one mind on that. This woman is my cousin, blood of my blood."

"*Je suis désolée*. You have my true sympathy. We have no choice in our blood relations, *n'est-ce pas?*"

"No, we don't. Above New York, at the moment of our victory, this cousin, this evil, struck down a friend, a brother of my heart."

Vivienne reached over, laid a hand over Fallon's. "I know of this. The young elf, so handsome, who was with you the first time I came to visit you. *Je suis profondément désolée, mon amie*. I know you sought solitude in your grief. I hope you have found comfort."

"I found it, and renewed purpose, and even stronger faith. I've seen her, in visions and dreams, in Scotland, at the shield. She rides a black dragon."

"This I've heard, of course." She trailed a finger over the carved ruby. "Some can turn even beauty into evil."

"To end the dark, to seal the shield once again, I have to destroy the source. To destroy the source, I must destroy my cousin. To destroy my cousin, I must destroy the dragon."

Fallon waited a beat. "How do I kill it?"

Vivienne lifted an eyebrow, sipped wine. "You would ask me?"

"I've seen, in these dreams, in the fire, in the glass, arrows, even bespelled, fail to penetrate the dragon. Aimed true at the heart, they break and fall. Magicks fall away as well. It feeds from the source. Yes, I would ask you. How do I kill it?"

"You would ask me?" Vivienne repeated, in a voice gone cold. "You would ask me to give you the means to destroy myself? You offer cake and wine, offer a symbol of what I am, then ask me to reveal how you might kill me should you want what I have?"

"I've given you my oath. What's yours is yours. Why would I wish to harm so valued a friend and ally?"

"There are others who might covet."

"You are and always will be under my shield, as will and always will be your people. Help me end this, so your people and mine, so all people can have peace. The gods brought you to me, I believe that, so we could prove ourselves to each other. And having proven, I could ask you this question. You would search your heart and give me the answer."

On a huff, Vivienne stood, stalked around the patio with her emerald gown swirling. "You ask me to put my life into your hands."

"She lures children, young girls most usually, out of their beds, takes them into a wood where only death and dark remain. She rends them there, on an altar, to feed the beast. The dragon protects her, kills for her, burns for her. Should I show you?"

Vivienne threw out a hand. "No. I've seen enough of what this evil can do."

"The last she disemboweled on that altar was just sixteen. Her name was Aileen."

"*Mes dieux, merde, ça pute!*" When she ran out of

curses—that took awhile—Vivienne turned to stare hard into Fallon's eyes. "Who will you tell?"

"Duncan and Tonia, also my blood."

"Like your whore of a cousin?"

"Nothing like her. You know that without me telling you. I'll tell the man I'm pledged to, and his twin, who's a sister to me. These two who, with me, wrapped Aileen's body in a blanket and took her to her family. The two who will go with me to finish it so together we can destroy the one who turned the glory of his spirit animal to the dark."

Vivienne sat again, poured more wine into her glass. She drank it all. "We are so few," she murmured. "I had hoped there would be a way to turn this one back to the light. At least to the shadows, yes? But children, young girls, sacrificed? There is no forgiveness for this."

She added more wine while Fallon waited, this time took only a sip. "In the stories, it's often a sword through the heart of a dragon. Or perhaps used to cut off its great head. *Mais non*. It may be the dragons of old could be killed in such ways, but not those of us who shift. I hope there are more of us. I must hope. Perhaps they hide, perhaps they still sleep."

On a long sigh, she took another sip of wine. "There is only one way to kill the dragon. It must be struck in the eye, pierced through. The left eye only," she added, tapping beneath her own. "Only then will it fall, will its flame gutter out. Only then will a sword cleave through its armor to take the head. You must burn the head to destroy it. These three things you must do, or it will not die."

"Thank you."

"Kill him, end this. I will have another glass of wine. And will take the whole of the cake home."

Fallon had to smile. "And welcome." Then she gripped

Vivienne's hand, let the truth inside her flow. "When I kill it—him—I'll do it in part for you, the flame from the north, to strike that blow for the beauty of what you are, and what he refused to be."

CHAPTER TWENTY-FIVE

She felt it moving on the air, stirring in her blood, whispering in her mind. In the weeks since she'd met with Vivienne, she and Duncan and Tonia had trained with the specific purpose of destroying a shifter dragon and its rider.

And still, she'd found no answers to when.

Yet she knew a storm gathered, dreamed of the lightning and the circle of stones. Of the spill of blood, and the throbbing heart of what waited in the murdered wood.

That throbbing heart whispered, too. She heard its alluring promises, its silky lies, saw the mask it wore that was handsome, seductive when it crept into her dreams.

It broke her sleep as she shoved her way out of fitful dreams to restlessness. Every night, she lit the candle Mallick had given her as a baby, to keep that spark of light constant, to keep the dark at bay.

When the fractured sleep and strain began to show, Lana made up charms and potions for rest, but Fallon didn't use them. Though it lied and lied, there might be something said or thought she could use to end it.

But when?

Come now, it murmured. *Come to me through the crystal. I wait to embrace you. We're meant to be as one, meant to know all pleasure, all power. Your blood released me. Come drink of the freedom you unlocked. Take it, taste it, know it.*

She woke, found herself standing, staring into the crystal that swirled with shadows. Had she been reaching for it? She couldn't be sure, but it had through nights and nights of stalking, found some weakness.

Shaken, she held her hand over the candle flame so that small light brightened, brightened and cleared the shadows.

She needed to take action, to try again.

She dressed, gathered all she needed, and went out into the night. Though summer held gamely on past the equinox, she scented the first hints of fall. Before long the harvest, the gathering, the sweep of color over the trees.

Thinking of it brought a deep yearning for the farm, the rambling house, the fields, the garden, the woods that had once held every adventure she could have wanted.

Would she see it again? Would she ever again sit under a tree with her nose in a book and her fishing line in the water? She wanted to know her mother would work the garden again, her father the fields. Wanted to know there would be bread dough rising in the kitchen, candles lit in windows.

She'd done all that had been asked of her, she thought. How much longer did she have to wait?

She went into the stables thinking to fly Laoch, but found the faithful Grace, already awake, her head—so much gray on the muzzle now—over the stall door.

"You couldn't sleep, either?" Fallon stroked her cheek, saw a world of love and patience in Grace's eyes. "All right then, you and me, just like we used to."

She saddled the horse, stowed her tools in the saddle-bag. "No hurry," she said as she led Grace out, mounted. "We can take a nice easy walk."

But when they reached the road, Grace broke into a trot, brisk as a filly. "I guess you're not feeling your age tonight."

As if to prove it, Grace lengthened into a smooth, rolling gallop. And nothing, Fallon realized, could have cleared the strain and fatigue more completely.

For just a little while, she was a girl again, and Grace a young filly. It wasn't the woods, the fields of home they rode, but there was freedom in the night, in the beating heart of the land, in the joyful speed of a faithful horse.

And in the absolute quiet broken only by the brisk beat of hooves, the soft, stirring sigh of the breeze over rows of corn, wheat, through trees and grasses.

Starlight sprinkled down on pumpkins growing fat on vines, on plump grapes in vineyards, glowed in the eyes of deer grazing late, on the slink of a fox on the hunt.

She heard the cry, looked up to see the wide, white spread of Taibhse's wings, the silver glint of Laoch's. Faol Ban leaped out of the shadows to pace the horse. Even the dregs of the dream faded as they made the last turn to New Hope.

She slowed Grace to a trot again, then to a walk as they approached the gardens.

"I don't know why I wanted to try this here," she said aloud. "Maybe just because nowhere else has worked."

After dismounting, she slung the saddlebag over her shoulder. "And I have to try."

She cast the circle, brought white candles to flame with her breath. In the center, she placed a small statue of the mother goddess, and her offering of wine and flowers.

With her athame she gestured north.

"Powers of the north, hear me. Powers of the east, I beseech thee. Powers of the south, I call to thee. Powers of the west, see me. I am your daughter. I am your servant. I am your warrior. I cast this circle in faith, in trust, in respect, and in honor."

In the center of the circle, she floated a small cauldron, filled it with blessed water, spread the flames under it. From a pouch she sprinkled crystal dust over the water's surface.

"Here for insight, for wisdom, for a clear eye. Now mix and meld and bubble and brew, stir away the mists for visions true. For strength," she said as she added herbs, "for knowledge, for understanding the reply. Now heat and boil and release your scent, now rise the wind to carry the question sent."

She stirred the air, brought it lifting.

"And now to seal this my quest, three drops of blood upon the rest."

She pricked her finger, let the three drops spill into the brew.

"At this hour, on this night, I renew my vow to carry the light."

Power whipped through her. She shot her arms up as shimmers of lightning woke above the western hills.

"In this place, in this hour, I call upon my source of power. Mother goddess, accept my offering from earth and vine. Hear your daughter, Ernmas divine. Grant me an answer, show me a sign."

Inside the circle, the wind wailed, pulled the smoke from the cauldron up, spread it like fog. For a moment, it seemed a thousand voices spoke, a thousand hands reached out to touch her with a power that nearly buckled her knees.

Lightning cracked across the bowl of the sky, and in

the answering roar of thunder, the fog cleared. Silence fell.

But she was no longer alone.

"Max." She breathed out his name. "Dad." And reached for him.

Her hand passed through him.

"I'm not corporeal." His voice held the faintest echo. "The veil's not thin enough."

"But you're here." Disappointment at not being able to touch him warred with gratitude. "You're here. I've tried so many times, but I could never find you."

"You didn't need to before this. Look at you. You've grown up. Beautiful, you're just beautiful. You're a woman now, and a warrior. You carry the sword."

She saw, clearly, both pride and sorrow in his eyes. More than anything she wanted to deserve the first, somehow ease the second.

"There's so much to tell you. The sword, the shield, the book. We took back New York. We— I don't know where to begin. It means so much to see you again. We came to New Hope. We're in New Hope."

"Yes." He looked toward the cornfield. "I know."

"If I'd known you— I shouldn't have done this here."

"I'm here because you did. I told you before, I have no regrets. How can I when I look at you?"

"He's dead, Eric's dead. Allegra, too. I'm sorry if it hurts you."

"No. I lost my brother in the Doom. What he became wasn't my brother." If there'd been regret in his words, on his face, it cleared away like the fog. "What he became would have tried again and again to kill you if you hadn't killed him."

"I didn't. Simon did."

"Simon." Max nodded. "Here? I can't see, but I can

feel. They came back here." Once again, he looked toward the cornfield, rustling, rustling in the autumn breeze. "Eric died here, as I did."

"Yes, here. And only a few months ago, I killed Allegra here. Maybe that's why this, I think, you coming again was meant to be here. They have a daughter."

"Eric had a child? Eric and Allegra," Max said, slowly now, "have a daughter." He looked up, seemed to search the stars. "She'll be like them."

"Yes. She's darker and more powerful than they were. We've come so far, Dad, done so much. The cost, it's a terrible cost, but we're winning this war. But I can't end it, I can't finish it until Petra, Eric's daughter, and what she serves is destroyed. All this power."

She pushed her hands through her hair, tossed them up. "All they've given me, but I can't have the answer to the one question I need. When to strike. I don't ask how, I don't ask the cost. I don't ask if I'll survive. I don't ask if the sister of my heart survives, or the man I love. Just when."

"You're wearing a ring."

"What? Oh, yes. Duncan."

"Katie's boy." With a nod, he looked out again, not to the cornfield, but to the gardens. "He makes you happy."

"Yes. You'd like him. I know he was only a baby when you died. I wish you could meet him now. He's on rotation, tamping down a flare-up of DUs—Dark Uncannys—out west."

"He's a soldier," Max murmured.

"A soldier, a commander, an artist. He's . . . everything."

"I see that."

"It has to be me, Duncan, and Tonia who go to the circle, destroy Petra and the source of the dark. It has to be the three of us who set the shield again. Our shared blood, the blood of the Tuatha de Danann. If we strike too early, too late, we'll fail. And I can't see."

"Trust your birthright," he told her, "and your blood. You were conceived in love and magicks at the very instant the dark brought death. Not a moment before, not a moment after."

"January second." She searched herself. "I knew that was when we had to strike New York, so I can see the logic in that, the closure. But it doesn't feel like the answer now, not for this."

"The gardens there, renewal and rebirth, year after year. My blood there, given to keep you safe. Your mother left all she knew to keep you safe. You came from us, but you were born on a night of storms and came into the hands of another. A father. And the light took her first breath of the world in those hands, on that night. There were three to love and protect you until you came to be. As there are three there." He gestured to the alicorn, the wolf, the owl. "You'll be three who fight the final battle of a night of storms. A night of power."

"My birthday." She felt it then, the answer, the knowledge. "It's nearly here," she acknowledged. "My birthday, because this is what I was born for. They sent you to tell me. You're the sign, and the answer."

"The messenger," he corrected with a smile. "I can't stay."

"But we've barely had any time." She grabbed for something happy. "Fred and Eddie have five kids, and she's going to have another."

"Eddie?" Max laughed, the sound rolling out into the night. "Eddie and Fred. I didn't see that coming, but now that I do, well, it's perfect." His grin flashed, quick, delighted. "Did you say *five* kids?"

So good to see him smile, so good to see that sorrow lifted. "Six come spring. They named their oldest boy Max."

His eyes, gray like hers, softened. "Tell them I'm honored. I can't stay," he said again. "But all I have will be with you when you lift that sword. Blessed be, my brave and beautiful daughter."

"But, don't—" He faded away, and she stood alone with magicks still thrumming. "Blessed be, Max Fallon, my brave and beautiful sire."

Fallon closed the circle, and with plans and possibilities circling in her mind, rode Grace home. It shouldn't have surprised her to find Mallick waiting in the predawn stillness. He stood at the edge of the garden as the first stars began to sigh away.

"You knew?"

"No." He slipped a hand in Grace's halter as Fallon dismounted. "But I felt the rise of magicks, the stir of powers, and with them, with you, I knew. They sent you Max Fallon to give you the answer."

"His image, his spirit, and only for a few minutes." She lowered her forehead to Grace's cheek. "No time, and so much I wanted to say to him. I couldn't even think of all I wanted to say, then he was gone again. I don't know if I'll ever see him again."

"It's common to say, so means little to hear, but he's always with you."

"I asked for a sign, and he was there."

"And what sign could be clearer? Who could have been sent who has more love for you and for the light than Max Fallon? Brood over the brevity later, girl. You have work to do."

Typical of him, she thought. Just get on with it. "I'm

not brooding. I'm . . ." Sulking, she realized, but wasn't she entitled? "Thinking. Considering."

"You know what to do next, go do it. I'll tend to Grace."

She handed over the reins. "You're figuring you can wheedle breakfast out of it."

"I don't wheedle," he said with considerable dignity. "I do expect the household will be stirring soon, and your mother, being gracious, will issue an invitation."

"Same thing."

"Not in the least," he objected when she flashed away. "You'll break your fast with extra oats," he told Grace. "And if I were to put pancakes in Lana's mind, that can't be considered wheedling."

She flashed straight to Duncan. She found him already up, dressed and strapping on his sword.

"Trouble?" she asked quickly.

"Not here. I dreamed . . . I saw you, felt you. I was just about to go, to check." She moved right into him, wrapped around him. "I shouldn't have gotten dressed."

With a half laugh she shook her head, burrowed in. "I tried again, asked again. They sent Max. Sent his spirit."

He eased her back, cupped her face in his hands. "Hard for you."

"Yes. And wonderful. Wonderful and hard. But he gave me the answer. The time's almost here, Duncan."

"When?"

"In nine days."

"Nine days. That's . . ." He did the quick calculation, and she saw the realization on his face. "Your birthday. Of course, it's your freaking birthday. We're idiots for not seeing it all along. The start and the finish."

"I came from three. Max, my mother, Simon. I was

given three. The owl, the wolf, the alicorn. Another three—the book, the sword, the shield. And given the answer with nine days. Three and three and three."

"And three go to the dance of stones, to the broken shield and murdered woods. The blood of the three, against the three that remain. The source, the dragon, the witch. On a night of storms the light breathed life. On a night of storms, the light strikes the dark."

He paused, shrugged. "You're not the only one who can prophesize."

"I know we've been preparing for this all our lives, but now it's down to nine days, and there's a lot to do. I need to get back, get started."

"I'll be right behind you."

"The DUs here?"

"Suppressed. We've got some scouts out hunting stragglers, and there are some civilians who need some help. I can organize that and be back in New Hope in a couple hours."

"That works. I'll get Tonia."

He grabbed her hand, yanked her in for a kiss. "In twelve days—keeping it in multiples of three—you and me are going on a date."

"A date?"

"Like people used to. Dinner, music or something, and sex."

"I like dinner, music or something, and sex."

She held on another minute, to that hope, to that promise, then left him.

They turned the war room into what Simon dubbed Magick Central. While troops continued to suppress flare-ups, instructors continued to train, people harvested crops, stored wood and supplies for the winter to come, Fallon, Duncan, and Tonia worked on spells and weapons.

Life went on in New Hope. Work on the clinic expansion neared completion, Arlys broadcasted to anyone who could hear. Chuck continued to search for any rumors of those flare-ups.

The three, united in purpose, focused all they had to be sure life did go on.

Hours every day centered on combat training where they fought dozens of Mallick's ghosts. If they defeated one, he sent three more, sent darker ones, more vicious ones.

Every night they nursed bruises, rattled bones, sprains, wrenched joints.

"They can't go into this weakened and exhausted," Lana argued.

Mallick watched as Fallon fought five at once, as Duncan pushed back the sweeping flame of a ghost dragon, as Tonia leaped off the back of an enemy to shoot for the eye. And when her arrow went wide as the slashing tail struck her, the force sent her tumbling to the ground.

"They can't win unless they're prepared for whatever comes. We can't know what form it might take, how many forms. They have to be ready."

"It's too much." Lana pushed out power, destroyed two ghosts. "It's enough. Enough!" Slicing her hands down, she shattered all of Mallick's ghosts.

"All you see are warriors," she snapped. "I see my daughter bleeding, the children of my friend bleeding. Again. When does it end? When will we stop watching our children bleed?"

Fallon pushed up from her knees, but Duncan was already walking to Lana. He put his arms around her.

"It's all right. We're all right. Nothing the old man can come up with is going to take us down. Nothing in

Scotland's going to take us down. We need you to believe that."

Tears in her eyes, she eased back, stroked her hand over his cheek. "Look at your face," she said, and healed raw bruises.

"Scary handsome, right?"

She stroked his other cheek. "You always were."

"My mom could use some company. She's pretty upset about all this, too."

"You just want to get rid of me."

"She's scared. She and Hannah are both scared. They could use you. Especially if you could get Arlys and Fred and Rachel. You're her circle, Lana. She needs her circle."

"All right." She sighed, stepped back. "I'll get Fred, we'll go into town." She looked at Fallon. "Stop holding back your power. Use it." She flashed away.

"I am using it," Fallon muttered, wincing as she rubbed her throbbing shoulder. "Judiciously. It's called tactics. Anyway, thanks," she said to Duncan.

"No problem, and straight truth."

"He's right." Tonia walked off the stiffness in her knee, in her hip. "Mom's wrecked over this. Trying not to show it—so's Hannah—but they're wrecked."

"In a couple of days, they won't have to worry." She looked back at Mallick. "Again." And swung her sword to meet the first strike.

The night before her birthday, Fallon prepared herself. She bathed in candlelight in water infused with sage, rosemary, hyssop, to purify her body for the battle to come.

She drank a cup of faerie wine from grapes harvested during a blue moon, offered another to the mother goddess. She lit the candle Mallick had given her, set it in the window, in the moonlight, and dressed by the twin glows.

"For this I was born. This is the path I chose to take, of my own will. For this I opened the book." She carried the Book of Spells to the candle, set it in that light. "For this I took up the sword and shield."

She hooked on the shield, strapped on the sword.

"By the heart of the sire, the heart of the mother, the heart of the father, I will not return here until I have done what I was born to do. Should I fail, I ask your care for my family. I ask that someone else open this book, take up the sword and shield, and fight on."

She hooked on her knife in the sheath Travis had made her so long before. Thinking of it, she got a pouch, added the painted tulip, the wind chimes Ethan and Colin had made her for that seminal birthday. A copy of *The Wizard King* with Max's words inside, his photo on the back, the stone she'd taken from Laoch's hoof that Mick had carved with her face. And the pink teddy bear.

Around her neck she wore the ring and medal—both worn by her fathers.

Talismans, she thought as she packed another bag with the tools of magick. Gifts given from the heart.

Duncan and Tonia packed their tools and weapons. Each performed their own private rituals and met outside their rooms.

"Ready?"

Tonia nodded. "Revved up and ready to go." She glanced toward the stairs. "This part might be harder than Scotland."

"Yeah. Let's get it done."

Katie and Hannah waited downstairs.

"I was thinking French toast for breakfast," Duncan began.

"And bacon," Tonia added. "Lots of bacon."

Hannah gripped Katie's hand tight. "I'll even do the dishes."

"Now we're talking. We've got this, Mom."

Katie held up her free hand to stop Duncan. "First, I have something for the three of you. Lana and Fred helped make them, so they've got magick from that, but what went into the making, I think that's magick too."

She squeezed Hannah's hand before releasing it, then drew three small pendants on chains from her pocket. "I used the wedding ring your father gave me."

"Oh, but, Mom—"

Katie shook her head at Tonia's objection. "He would have loved his three children so much. And I used the earrings Austin gave me his last Christmas. He loved you so much, too. So these are from the three of us— magickal number—to the three of you.

"My babies. I'm so proud of all of you. Hannah. Dr. Parsoni," she corrected.

Hannah took the offered pendant. "A caduceus. It's beautiful. It means so much."

"Duncan."

He took the sword pendant, held her eyes as he slipped the chain over his head. "You're the real warrior, Kathleen MacLeod Parsoni. Always have been, always will be."

"Tonia."

Tonia blinked at tears as she took the pendant of a bow with arrow already nocked. "You're the glue, Mom. You're the reason all of us are here."

They surrounded her, her three children.

Fallon hoped to say good-bye at home, but her family— including Colin—insisted on going with her to the community gardens to meet Duncan and Tonia. So they rode to New Hope together, as they had years before.

She nudged Laoch over to Colin. "I'm not sure how long I'll be gone. Could be a couple hours, could be days. It'd be good if you could hang around until I get back."

She didn't say *if* she got back, didn't allow herself to think it.

"Arlington's secure. I don't have to be magickal to know where I'm needed."

"Okay. How's the arm?"

He bent it at the elbow, managed to bring it to about a forty-degree angle. "Give it a few more months, we'll go some rounds."

"You'd still lose."

"Not unless you cheat."

"Not a chance. Just like you're still not president."

"Given that up," he said easily. "I'm thinking Supreme Global Commander. SGC Swift."

"You would." Oddly comforted, she rode into New Hope where the gardens were lit with lanterns, faerie lights, streams and beams of moonlight.

And where hundreds upon hundreds waited.

"I didn't expect . . ."

"Katie organized it," Lana told her. "And with your father, your brothers, Mallick, and some good friends, we refined it."

"Please tell me I don't have to make a speech."

"Not necessary."

No cheers rang out, but people moved back so she could ride through to where Duncan and Tonia waited.

When she dismounted, Lana embraced her one last time. "Your light changed me. All I have goes with you tonight."

When she stepped back to stand with Mallick, Simon hugged her. "Come back to me, baby. Fight strong, kick ass, and come home."

Before she could speak, Mallick and her mother

stepped forward. They lifted their hands, and she felt their power pulse and merge. From it, a flame rose, straight as a spear.

"This fire burns until the children of the Tuatha de Danann return. When their battle is won, this flame will be cast in stone, a flame eternal to symbolize the light."

People formed circles, the New Hope Originals innermost, those familiar faces illuminated by the fire's light, others spiraling out behind them, ring after ring.

"This is New Hope," Fallon decreed. "This is the center. This is why we can do this. Why we will."

Circle after circle, she thought. Unity and faith.

With Taibhse settling on Laoch's saddle, Faol Ban by her side, she joined hands with Duncan and Tonia.

Another circle, forged in blood, in trust, in purpose.

She felt the clock ticking toward midnight, closed her eyes. And when that moment struck, opened them.

As one they flashed from New Hope, and straight into the storm.

CHAPTER TWENTY-SIX

Lightning cracked, red and black, pounding the ground with hammer strikes, splitting the already blazing fields with fissures that belched smoke. The smoke rode whirling cyclones skyward to smother the moon and stars so the night drowned in black.

Crows streamed and screamed through it.

Duncan shoved a ball of light against the dark, then another, illuminating the stones and its undulating center.

"Looks like they're expecting us."

"Cast the circle!" Fallon shouted and, pointing her sword north, called the gods.

They set candle and cauldron, lit the flame, rang the bell, said the words. Defiant, releasing her anger, Fallon deflected bolts of lightning, power against power.

"On this hour of my birth, we challenge the evil that walks the earth. I am The One, born of power and light, destined by blood and choice to lead this fight."

"We," Duncan continued, "sister and brother who shared a womb, join with The One to build your tomb.

With blood and power the gods foretell, we send dark's creatures back to hell."

"We, children of the Tuatha de Danann, are the three," Tonia shouted. "And here and now accept our destiny. This place, this time, this night, we pledge all we are to the light."

"Blood joins blood," they said together as Fallon scored their palms. "Light joins light. Power joins power."

As they joined hands, the shock of merging snapped light from their palms. As the surge rocked them, swept through them, they gripped tighter.

"Hold on!" Duncan pitched his voice above the gale. "It's working."

The force of the wind nearly buckled Fallon's knees. She watched it snatch the band from Tonia's hair like angry fingers so the wild curls flew free.

And the undulating earth in the circle of stones began to open, to reveal the maw beneath.

"Finish it!" With the storm raging around them, Fallon drew in her breath.

"Now rise magicks, rise, rise, and strike the creature of death, of lies. Show us the path to find him, and into the pit we drive him and forever our blood will bind him. Here is the vow of the three. As we will, so mote it be."

The leading edge of the wind died, but what remained blew raw as winter. Inside the stones, the ground held still, and open.

"Is it enough?" Tonia wondered.

"It'll have to be." Fallon gestured to a thin stream of light leading into the woods. "We have the path."

"And we've got company," Tonia added, breaking the connection to nock an arrow.

Duncan enflamed his sword as dozens of Dark Uncanny surged from the woods. "We're going to need a bigger circle."

Energized, even eager, Tonia laughed. "Points for you," she said and let the first arrow fly.

"Keep clear of the pit." Fallon punched out power, took out three with one swipe. "They waited until we opened it. They want to push us back, into it."

She leaped on Laoch, shot up to attack from the air.

"I'll take the left flank," Duncan told Tonia. "You get the right."

"Deal." She dropped and rolled under a fireball, shot a light-soaked arrow.

With a sweep of his sword, Duncan swatted bolts back into the enemy, pivoted to meet the pulsing black blade of another. Sensing movement behind him, he swung to kick out. Faol Ban leaped for the throat of a shifted panther and saved him the trouble.

Fallon's fire and fury rocked the earth, cut swaths through oncoming power as Taibhse tore through the crows, sent them smoking, screaming into the pit below.

She dived, leaped off. "Take him up," she shouted to Tonia, then striking, cleaving, burning, moved in to fight back-to-back with Duncan.

"They're a distraction." Despite the cold, sweat ran down his face. "A damn good one, but a distraction. They want to drive us into the pit? We drive them."

She nodded, reached back to grip his hand. "Push!"

It poured out in a kind of rage, hot, savage, strong.

In the screams that followed, the howl of shifters, the flaming blur of elves, they battered them back, back. But worse, the sounds that came, no longer human, as they fell, tumbled, spilled into the pit, tore through the shrieking wind.

A handful broke off, ran.

"If they reach the village," Fallon began.

"I've got this." Astride Laoch, Tonia circled. "Go, go. I'll take care of this and be right behind you."

"She can handle it." Duncan looked at Fallon. "Ready?"

Together, they charged into the dead woods.

Shadows loomed, shifted. Some breathed, and that breath held death. They felt it, that beat, beat, beat of the dark heart. The pulse of the source.

The light, called by the spell, lay thin and winding.

"It knew it would come to this night." With sword and shield, Fallon followed the light. "It's always known. Maybe all of it, all the blood, the battles, the death and misery, was another distraction. Because this is what it's waited for."

You're what it's waited for, Duncan thought, and stayed close.

The ice-slicked, skeletal trees seemed to slink over the ground as if to block the path. Jagged fingers of branches jabbed out. Duncan sliced one aside with his sword, heard a quick, high-pitched shriek as the severed limb bled black.

"That's fucking creepy."

"Enough. Enough." Sheathing her sword, Fallon used her hands to slice the air. "Clear."

Those ice-coated trees went still, leaving the path open.

"Distractions," she repeated.

"Yeah. It's leading to where we found the girl, the altar."

"It wants us there. It thinks it wins. It wants us there. Can you feel it? Can you hear it?"

She gripped his hand. "Now I can," he answered as that pull, that tug nipped inside him like sharp fingers, as the voice echoed softly inside his head.

A woman's voice, a lover's. Promising, promising.

They moved on. The pulse beat, faster, louder, a voice of its own that shook inside the belly, that rumbled underfoot. The path widened, then spread to another circle of stones, and the smooth slab of rock resting on them.

On it, the inverted pentagram pulsed red.

"A new dance, a new slab. Petra's work," Duncan noted. *But not only hers*, he said in Fallon's mind.

Not only hers, she answered. *But she's here. She's close.*

Now, Fallon thought, and once again reached for her sword. At the roar, she looked up, saw the wave of fire, heard the wild laugh.

"And here she is now." The elation that spurted through Duncan died on sudden, sickening alarm. "Oh, Christ, Tonia."

She fell from the sky already bleeding, the arm of her jacket smoldering. She struck the side of the altar, tumbled bonelessly off to land at his feet.

"No, goddamn it. No." Dropping down, Duncan swiped a hand over the jacket to stop the burning, then ran them over his sister to find the wounds.

Fallon leaped forward, threw her shield over them to block a stream of fire.

"There's too much. I can't find it all. We need to get her back to New Hope."

"No." Tonia found his hand, struggled to close hers over it. "It has to be the three of us. Help me up."

"You've got internal injuries. There's so much broken. Fallon, help me."

"Let me see. Let me try." Her arm trembled holding the shield against the steady barrage of fire, but she closed her hand over Duncan's, over Tonia's, searched.

Blinding pain, unspeakable pain, and a light dimming.

"Help me." Her voice weak, her face pale as the smothered moon, Tonia closed her eyes. "We have to finish this."

In New Hope, the tower of light shivered, seemed to shrink. In the circle with her mother, Hannah fell to her knees. Around her neck the pendant symbolizing her power glowed.

"Baby." Katie dropped down beside her. "What—"

"Tonia. She needs me. They need me." She pushed up, grabbed the medical bag she'd set on the ground for the return. "Tonia. She's hurt. I can feel . . ." She closed her hand around the pendant. "I have to go. Lana, take me."

"You're not prepared. I'll go, bring her back."

"I have to go." Hannah held out the glowing pendant, then took Lana's hand. "She's my sister. I was chosen, too." She looked at her mother. "I was chosen, too," she repeated. "Hurry. She's hurt."

When Lana took her hand, Simon stepped forward.

"I can't. I can't take both of you, two unprepared non-magickals."

He nodded, forced himself to step back again. "Bring our girl home. Bring them all home."

"I love you." She looked at Katie, her heart in her eyes. "All I have to protect yours. I swear it. All I have."

Gathering Hannah close, she flashed.

"My babies." Katie pressed her hands to her mouth, all but fell into Arlys's arms. "My babies."

"You have light," Mallick called out. "You have a mother's light and love. Send it!" He drove his own light into the fire. "All here, you have light, you have faith, you have love. Send it."

Tears still falling, Katie straightened, reached for Jonah's hand, for Rachel's. "You helped me bring them, all three of them, into the world. Help me bring them home."

Jonah held Katie's hand but didn't meet her eyes. He hadn't been able to see life, or death. He hadn't seen anything but dark.

Then Fred took his other hand, murmured close to his ear, "They brought you back into the world, too. Believe in them."

Hannah nearly slid out of Lana's arms when they flashed to the altar. Though her vision grayed, she shook it clear.

Duncan might have cursed at seeing his other sister on the battlefield, but he was too busy working with Fallon to heal Tonia's most dangerous injuries.

"Stay back! I'll draw her off," he said to Fallon. "Help them with Tonia. Get her back to New Hope."

"You can't take it all on alone."

"I'm not losing you or my sisters." His gaze locked with hers, one last time. "Take care of them."

When he ran, shouting Petra's name, drawing the flame, she did curse.

"Men," Tonia managed weakly. "What can you do? Hannah, you shouldn't be here."

"You needed me. There's magickal tools in here, too," she told Lana briskly as she took out a bottle and syringe. "Fully equipped."

"No sedative." Tonia waved it away. "I've still got work to do. Tail caught me, freaking dragon. I missed my shot. Laoch tried to catch me, but it was too fast. He's burned. I don't know how bad."

Fallon rose. Fire streaked the sky. Lightning red as Tonia's blood rained from it. And in the woods that heart beat with deep, dark joy.

"Get her out of here."

"I'm not—"

"Clear of the woods," Fallon continued. "Follow the path of light, and get her clear. We're not losing you, Tonia. Hannah and my mother will make sure of it, but the three of you can't be in here for this."

"You need to hang on for another flash. It's not going to be a picnic for either of you, but it'll be fast." Lana looked up at Fallon, her child, her love. She'd promised that child she would never lose faith in her again. She would keep that promise.

"I believe in you."

Alone, with her mother's words still on the air, Fallon turned to the altar. "So now you have what you've wanted. Me alone. No more distractions."

She closed her eyes, let the dark crawl in.

She felt its spider legs walk along her skin, its sinuous fingers snake around her ankles. It brushed its lips over hers, breathed its cold breath over her eyes. And surrounding her, covering her, squeezing, gently, gently squeezing, it murmured in her ear.

They are not worthy of us. They are beneath us, these mortals, these weaklings, these pale magicks. Lie on my altar, child of the bright gods, and know the dark. Know the pleasure I offer only to you.

"There have been others before me."

Only to prepare for you. Lie with me, chosen one, and drink my dark, so rich, so sweet. I will drink your light, so bold, so bright. With our merging, we will be The One.

"I am The One."

The dark compressed, choking off her breath. *Do you wish pain when I offer so much? I will only feed on it. Take the pleasure, feel the pain, give me your light or I will take it. Give me your light, and I will spare the mother.*

She took an agonizing step toward the altar, laid a trembling hand on it, felt its iced surface, its alluring promise as the dark smothered her.

Through the curtain she heard Petra's mad laugh, saw the red glow of the fire scorching the sky. In her mind she saw sickness, death, war, murder, the plague of black magicks. So much loss, so much brutality.

It has always been so, and so it will always be. Brother killing brother over a patch of grass or a whoring woman. Children starving while others grow fat on fists of candy. The world burning for greed and ambition. These are who would hunt you, burn you, destroy you for what you are to save themselves. For your power. Come to me, lie with me. They are but toys to be played with, broken, and cast aside. We are forever.

"Can you hear them?" She took another step, another as the excitement of what wrapped her so close hummed over her skin, beat like moth wings. "Can you?"

Their screams? Their lamentations?

She felt the blood on her hands. Tonia's, Duncan's, her own. "Their song of faith." She pulled her sword, cleaved through the dark. "You won't drink my light. You'll burn in it." And, clasping the hilt in her bloodied hand, drove the sword into the pentagram and through the stone slab.

It writhed. It snapped and clawed. Screaming, she forced power through the blade, into the stone, into the heart.

"I am Fallon Swift. Child of the Tuatha de Danann. Daughter of Max Fallon, of Lana Bingham, of Simon Swift. I am The One. I am your end."

The slab cracked, spewed out blood and stink. The force of it threw her back, stole her breath as she slammed into the ground. The beat slowed; the pulse grew weak. Lungs laboring, she pushed to her feet. And her moment of triumph was stillborn as dark seeped from the shattered stone, rose thin, but rose, into the murky sky.

"No." She heaved light at the remains of the altar, turned it to dust, spread fire over the dust. Then praying, flashed.

Wounded or not, Laoch flew, with Duncan on his back. Near the circle, Hannah and Lana continued to treat Tonia. She raced to them, shield lifted to guard.

"It's wounded, it's weak, but I didn't finish it. How's Tonia?"

"Wounded and weak." Hannah's breath came fast, but she held tight to Tonia's hand. "I've done all I can here. Your mother's trying more. We need to get her to surgery."

"Not until we finish." Tonia spoke through gritted teeth. "Help Duncan."

"I will. I—" And she saw that dark crawl over the sky, saw it wrap around Petra, slide and slither into her. "Take this." She shoved her shield at Hannah. "Use it."

She spread her wings, shot up.

"It's in her! What's left of the source is in her now."

"Hey, cuz!" Eyes black pools with what lived in her now, Petra swung toward Fallon. "We've been waiting for you."

Fallon dived under the whip of the dragon's spiked tail, swooped beneath the armored belly. Before she could try to strike the eye, it spumed out fire.

"I am filled!" Petra flung out her hands, spewed out lightning from her fingertips. "Like fireworks! Like my favorite holiday. The Fourth of July, when my daddy killed yours."

With a flick of her hand, she batted away a stream of fire from Duncan's sword, followed it with a wind that nearly unseated him.

Petra's hair flew—black-and-white—then coiled like snakes to lash at the air. "You can't touch us with your puny powers now. I have the heart in me. All promised is mine." Lifting her arms, she called the crows to circle and swipe with smoking wings. "How about some of this!"

She threw out fire that speared into arrows and rained on the shield Hannah fought to hold.

"You have to help them." Tonia nudged Lana's hands away. "You have to help them. She—it—they're getting stronger."

"Keep that shield up, Hannah."

Lana ran out from under its protection, pushed power up. Flamed it out.

Me, she thought, frantic. Come for me. You won't have my child, you won't have Katie's. Come for me!

Petra flung bolts, fire, wind in all directions, her face bright with glee as the dragon's tail slashed. Whipped around as Lana's power rocked the air.

"Look who's here." With great good cheer, she shot bolts of lightning at Lana's feet. "Dance, dance, dance. You killed my mummy, bitch. Now you can watch me kill yours. Fire in the hole!" she shouted, and laughed as the dragon breathed it.

Fallon flashed down, called the whirlwind to send the flame over the already burning field.

"You can't spoil my fun. And you can't save both of them. Which one will it be? Eenie, meenie."

She shot a flurry of bolts at Duncan.

"Miney, moe." Another flurry at Lana.

"God, she's an asshole." Breathing through her teeth, Tonia fought to sit up. "You've got to help me, Hannah."

"You need to lie still."

"Hannah, that bitch has the heart of freaking darkness inside her and a dragon under her. You have to help me. Get an arrow out of my quiver."

The sky's on fire, Hannah thought as the ferocious heat washed over her. "Tonia. You don't have the strength, physically or magickally, to draw the bow."

"No, but I can aim." By the gods, she could still aim. "You're going to have to do the rest. Come on, Team Sister time. Nock it."

Even breathing hurt but Tonia sucked air into her lungs, pushed it out. "She's distracted, we're nothing right now. You have to keep me steady, brace me up."

"I can't do that and hold the shield."

"Put it down. It's all or nothing now. Nock the arrow, hold me steady." The world wanted to spin—she wouldn't let it. "You draw the bow, but don't release until I say. We've got one shot."

Because if we miss, Tonia thought, a pissed-off dragon's going to burn us to ash.

"One shot," she echoed, and blinked her eyes clear.

Seeing the fallacy of trying to draw fire away from the women, Duncan sent Laoch into a dive. He leaped off to stand with them.

"Together," he said. "Just let it rip."

"Wait." Fallon gripped his arm. She saw Tonia lift the bow, Hannah draw it. "Wait." She stepped to the side.

She could angle it for Tonia. Just a little. "Hey, cousin. How about a little one-on-one, just you and me?"

Fallon spread her wings again, floated up. And yes, Petra turned the dragon while she smiled, stroked its neck.

"We'll get there. We're saving you for last. You'll watch the others burn before I send you into the dark. I'll rule then. Me! As it was always meant. The dark will feast and feast and—"

Tonia homed in. "Keep talking, bitch. Now, Hannah!"

The bowstring sang, and the arrow winged through the air. The keen head struck true, pierced the left eye. And the shaft dug deep.

The toothed tail slashed madly, and the sinuous body bucked, bucked. It shook its powerful head, fighting to dislodge the arrow. As it fell, the dragon's dying roar shuddered through the air, swept over the burning grasses in the field, flattening them. On an answering cry, Fallon cleaved its head.

"Burn it!" she shouted at Duncan, but he'd already fired the flame.

Lana whooshed out wind to send the burning head of the dragon, the smoldering body of the man, into the pit.

"He was mine!" Petra barely got her wings out before she hit the ground. She landed badly on ground sparking with embers, screamed at the pain. "He was mine! We'll kill you. Kill you all."

"You're done." Duncan sheathed his sword, led with power only, pushed out with light when Petra flung out dark.

"Let him do this," Fallon murmured. "He needs it. Open," she said when Duncan drove Petra and what was in her back toward the stones. "Lock the dark." And she, too, sheathed her sword.

Petra's next flame dissolved when it hit the barrier.

"The circle holds. The light holds."

Face contorted, Petra charged at Duncan, beat fists bloody on the barrier. "You will not send me back!" The voice that roared out of her, no longer her own, thundered.

Petra, trapped by what she'd taken in, flung herself against the circle, raced around it in a blur until the blood of the woman soaked the ground.

"Enough," Fallon ordered. "It's enough."

"Get me up," Tonia insisted as Duncan moved into the circle. "I'm not missing this."

"You shouldn't— Never mind." Hannah got an arm around her. "Lean on me."

"I always have."

Her hair in tangled mats, Petra huddled on the ground, battered, bleeding. With eyes that had gone a sweet and innocent blue, she lifted her face to Duncan.

"It made me do terrible things. Look how it hurt me. Help me, Duncan. Rescue me."

"Not this time." He pushed, but more gently than he'd thought himself capable of, driving her back.

"Come with me." Smiling through bloody teeth, Petra reached out, and the dark heart clawed with her.

Fallon stepped in. "Go to hell."

Petra's hands, her feet left grooves in the ground as she fought against the push. Her scrabbling fingers caught the edge of the pit. With one last smile she looked at Fallon, spoke with the voice of the beast.

"We'll come back for you."

As they fell—a scream from what had once been a woman, a roar from what she'd embraced—Duncan drew his sword, sent flames to destroy both. "No, you won't."

"Hold the line," Fallon said to him, and walked over

to Laoch, took what they needed out of the saddlebag. "Are you up for this?" she asked Tonia.

"You're damn right. A little help? Legs are still wonky. Seems I broke both of them."

"I've got you. We only left the circle open for the three of us," she explained to her mother and Hannah. "We couldn't take chances. We have to close it, seal it, purify it."

"We'll wait." Lana slipped an arm around Hannah's waist.

They waited and watched while the children of the Tuatha de Danann closed the ground inside the stone. With merged blood, they sealed the shield, purified it with light.

With the sword she'd taken from the fire, Fallon etched the fivefold symbol into the shield.

As she did, light exploded in the sky. It burst like noon, bathed the world, fell warm and soothing over her face.

"Here, the grass will grow again and wildflowers bloom," she said as the light quieted, and night flowed back.

"The deer will come to graze, men may come to see. But the sign will remain, and the shield forged in blood and light will forever hold back the dark."

"This land is clean," Duncan said.

Tonia leaned against him. "This shield is true."

"Open." Fallon stepped out of the circle. "This place is open to all who walk or fly or crawl in the light. And forever barred, in and out, from any who seek the dark."

"As night follows day," they said together, hands again joined, "as day follows night, this world is guarded by the light."

She turned to her mother. "It's done. It's finished."

"I know." Tears glimmering, Lana cupped Fallon's face. "I know it."

"I never saw you here. Mom, I never saw Hannah. We couldn't have done it without you, both of you."

"And what came out of New Hope with you," Duncan added.

"Thought I heard singing." Tonia swayed. "You hear singing?"

"Something like that. How about you and Hannah take Tonia back?"

"Yeah." She sent Duncan a weak smile. "I can go with that now. Because . . . uh-oh."

Duncan caught his twin when she passed out.

"She just fainted," Hannah assured him as she checked Tonia's pulse. "We'll get her to the clinic. We'll take care of her. Here." With Hannah on one side, Lana on the other, they supported Tonia.

"It's going to take another flash," Lana warned her.

Supporting her sister, Hannah braced herself. "I can handle it."

"I know you can." She looked into Fallon's eyes, laid a hand on her heart, and flashed.

Safe. They'd be safe now. Fallon ran her hands over her filthy face. "It was in the altar. I could feel it in the stone. It wanted me to lie on the slab so it could suck the life and light from me. So I destroyed the altar, but I didn't kill it. Only weakened it. I—"

"It's done now. It's done."

It didn't seem quite real, not quite solid now that the tidal wave of power ebbed.

"I don't know how to feel. Relieved? All my life's been aimed at this moment, so what do I feel now that it's finished?"

She looked at him. Real. Solid. And everything steadied

again. "You're a mess. Bruised, bleeding, burned. I guess I am, too."

"We'll fix each other up." He took her hand. Light still shimmered between them, and he focused on that as he spoke. "I wanted her dead, and wanted to do it. For Denzel, for Mick, too. For so much and so many. But when it came down to it, she was just crazy. Pathetic. Evil, but pathetic. Ending her . . ."

It wasn't satisfaction, it wasn't pleasure.

"Relief's good," he decided. "Relief works."

"I'll take it, and now we need to— Laoch! Oh Jesus, Laoch. I need to—" She ran to him, ran a hand over the flank the dragon had burned.

Instead of a wound, even a healing scar, he bore, like the shield, the fivefold symbol.

"Sometimes the gods are kind," she murmured. She breathed out a sigh as Taibhse dropped down to perch on the golden saddle, and Faol Ban sat beside the alicorn to wait.

"We need to make sure I destroyed all of it in the woods, that there's nothing left that can—"

"Fallon." With a tenderness that surprised them both, Duncan pressed a kiss to her forehead, turned her around. "Look."

The woods lived again. They stood thick, the pines green, the oaks ripe with color under the light of the swimming moon. A moon, she realized, and stars that shined through a sky as clear as glass.

Through the trees, and over the fields no longer scorched and burning, lights danced.

"The faeries came. They're bringing it back. All of it back."

"We'll come back, too, bring Mom so she can see the house again. Open it up to the light again."

"Someone will farm the land again."

"Someone."

She smiled at him. "Relief's okay. Happy's better. I think I just got to happy. And finished? That's best of all. Let's go home, Duncan."

"Let's go home." He yanked her in, and they flashed to New Hope on a kiss.

EPILOGUE

On New Year's Eve, in a year that ended and would begin in light, snow lay in white blankets over the sleeping gardens, draped over the branches of trees like lacy handkerchiefs. The wind blew cold and clear over families of snowpeople.

Inside the house where Fallon's family had made a home in New Hope, friends gathered. Food for all and more covered tables, wine and whiskey poured generously into glasses. Music played jubilantly.

Fred, round with child, wings fluttering, danced with her oldest son while Eddie worked his harmonica, a dog at his feet, his youngest in his lap, clapping the time. For old times' sake, Poe and Kim argued over a game of Scrabble while their sons rolled their eyes.

Jonah watched his middle son finally work up the nerve to ask a pretty girl to dance, and nudged Rachel. On a sigh, she tipped her head to Jonah's shoulder, then reached out and grabbed Gabriel before he could dash by.

"Mom needs a hug."

"Dad, too."

On the lower level several gathered to play poker for pebbles and feathers and the high stakes of candied nuts. Colin narrowed his eyes at Flynn as Flynn raised him, yet again, ten nuts.

"No elf mind reading allowed, pal."

"Don't need them with you. You've got tells."

"Do not."

"Do," Travis corrected, frowning at his own hand. "You're jiggling your foot, so you're bluffing."

"I am—too," Colin said on a laugh, and folded.

Across the room, content to watch the party, the game, Starr stroked Blaidd. When Ethan settled on the floor beside her, she drew back a little.

"He likes when you pet him," Ethan said easily. "Not everybody or every animal likes to be touched. But he likes when you pet him."

She sat for a moment, cleared her throat. "You have such kindness in your mind. Not everybody does. I know the farm is your home, but I'm sorry you'll be going back soon."

"We'll come visit. New Hope's home, too."

Arlys, her hair styled in a smooth sweep for the party, and the end-of-year broadcast that had preceded it, weaved through the crowd. She carried a steaming mug to her father-in-law as he sat warm by the fire.

"Echinacea tea, for that scratchy throat."

"Tea?" Bill scoffed with insult. "It's New Year's Eve."

"Tea for the throat." She leaned down, kissed Bill's cheek. "The whiskey in it for the rest of you."

"All right then." He gripped her hand. "It's going to be a good year."

"Best ever."

"Will Anderson!" he called out. "Your father didn't raise a fool for a son. Dance with your pretty wife."

"There's an idea." Will swung her toward the music, then just wrapped around her and swayed. "A really good idea. Theo's flirting with Alice Simm's daughter. Can't blame him. Cute as they come."

"I noticed. Cybil's flirting with Kim's oldest."

He yanked back. "What?"

"Typical." Arlys pulled him right back. "It's your son, it's 'Woo-hoo.' Your daughter, it's 'Whoa.' I might have to write an article about that."

"Oh no, you don't."

She laughed, snuggled in. "Chuck's dancing. Not with anyone, and it's not actually dancing. But it's movement approximating the basic concept of dancing. Katie's in the kitchen gossiping with Lana. God, I'm going to miss Lana. Hannah went down to the poker game with Simon. And—"

She looked up at him. "The gang's all here, Will. We're all here, and I love you."

In the kitchen, Katie poured more wine, studied it. "I think I'm going to get sloshed."

"Stick with faerie wine. No hangover."

"Lana. Lana, what am I going to do without you?"

"We'll visit. A lot." Because it made her teary, Lana poured more wine for both of them. "And you have to visit us. I want you to see the farm. In fact, I hereby decree everybody comes to the farm this summer for a huge party. I demand it."

"I'm in." Katie blinked at tears. "We're going to miss you and Simon, the boys."

"Colin's going to stay in Arlington." Her smile bittersweet, Katie understood. "He's a soldier, not a farmer. So more visits there, too. And Fallon."

Lana breathed in, breathed out. Like giving birth, she thought. Letting a child find her way in the world wasn't all that different, really, from bringing them into the world.

"This will be her home now. This house, her home with Duncan."

"Are you—did they—"

"Just something I know. So visits, lots of visits. One day they might want a wedding or handfasting. Won't that be a party for us to plan, Katie? Our babies."

"I'll watch out for her for you. I love her, Lana. I love Fallon and your boys."

"I know. I love Duncan and your girls. We raised strong kids, didn't we, Katie?"

"Amazing kids. To your four and my three." She lifted her glass.

"Lucky seven," Lana said and lifted her own.

"Ladies."

Lana glanced over, laughed. "Mallick! You came."

When she circled the counter to embrace him, he patted her back awkwardly, but smiled. "I wanted to wish you, all of you, a happy New Year."

"How about some wine?"

"I'd be grateful. This home is full of light," he added as she poured him a glass. "They'll be happy here. I would offer a toast to two fine mothers and their excellent children."

"Thank you."

"And I would thank you for the suet cakes, and the recipe for them Fallon brought me on Christmas Eve."

It had touched him, deeply, to find her on the doorstep of his cabin that night, with the suet, and the feeder she'd made him from a branch of a fallen tree near his childhood home in Wales.

Because it made him sentimental, he cleared his throat, drank the wine. "I'm told there is a game of cards in the room below?"

"Poker?" Katie angled her head to study him. "You play poker?"

"I've lived a very long time." He smiled, gave them a slight bow, and went downstairs.

Duncan and Fallon sat on the steps where they could look down at the movement, hear the voices and music. They drank wine, shared a plate.

Simon paused at the base, then climbed up. "Why aren't you dancing with my daughter?"

"Well, we were—"

"I thought you were playing poker," Fallon interrupted.

"I was until Mallick came along and cleaned me out. Cleaned most of us out." He looked down to where Hannah mimed emptying out her pockets before plopping down beside Fred.

"Dad, he's a centuries-old sorcerer."

"And a cardsharp. Come dance with your old man."

"I don't see an old man, but I'll dance with you." She passed her wine to Duncan, took Simon's hand.

"I just wanted a minute." He pressed his cheek to her hair. "It's getting close to midnight. New year, new changes."

"I'll visit so often you'll get sick of me." She smiled.

"Couldn't happen. I want this for you, this life. Even that boy up there. He probably loves you almost as much as I do."

"There's still work to do. I'll depend on you for so much."

"Don't think about work tonight. Be happy." He gestured to Duncan, waited, then gave Fallon's hand a squeeze before he put it in Duncan's. "Dance with the girl," he ordered, and stepped back.

"I'm crap at dancing."

"Just hold me and sway."

"I can do that."

"This is good. It's good for everyone. Tonia's back all the way, and she's having fun."

"Yeah, she's— Who is that?"

"That's Filo. He was one of Mick's friends, and helped take The Beach."

"Well, now he's hitting on my sister."

"She's hitting right back." Deliberately, Fallon turned his head so they were face-to-face. "I'm hitting on you, so pay attention."

"I just want to—"

Tonia danced by, pinched Duncan's arm. "Mind your own business. He's gorgeous!" she told Fallon. "And he thinks I'm amazing. And he's transferring to the barracks."

"What—" Duncan began when she danced away again.

"Do you have a problem with elves?"

"Only when they're hitting on my sister. And who's that guy who just muscled in on Hannah?"

"I love you, Duncan."

"I just don't think—" He looked back at Fallon and fell, just fell. "And I love you."

"It's nearly midnight. I'll end the year with you, begin the new with you. And I promise myself to you all the years after."

"With you." He kissed her hand. "The end, the beginning, and all the years after."

"It's ticking by. Do you feel it?"

"Yeah. With you."

People began to count down, a unity of voices lifted in hope for the year to come.

He pulled her into a kiss that held as the old year died and the new was born.

And with the kiss, like the kiss, the light shimmered, settled, held.

BRUCE WILDER

NORA ROBERTS is the #1 *New York Times* bestselling author of more than 200 novels, including *The Becoming, Legacy, The Awakening, Hideaway,* The Chronicles of The One trilogy, and many more. She is also the author of the bestselling In Death series written under the pen name J. D. Robb. There are more than five hundred million copies of her books in print.

The stunning conclusion of
The Chronicles of The One trilogy from
New York Times bestselling author
Nora Roberts

After the sickness known as the Doom tore across the globe and civilization crumbled in its wake, magick has become common-place. And if this desolate, radically altered world has a chance of survival, it will need all the powers of the fierce warrior leader, Fallon Swift.

Strengthened by the wisdom of her mentor Mallick, and the troubling yet stubborn bond she shares with her fellow warrior, Duncan, Fallon has already succeeded in rescuing count-less shifters and elves and ordinary humans. Now she must help them heal—and rediscover the light and faith within themselves. For although Fallon, from the time of her birth, has been The One, she is still only one. And as she faces down an old nemesis, sets her sights on the enemy's stronghold, and pursues her des-tiny—to finally restore the mystical shield that once protected them all—she will need an army behind her.

US $8.99 / CAN $11.99

ISBN 978-1-250-12305-3

9 781250 123053

50899

Cover design by Ervin Serrano

Cover photographs:
background © Dmitriy
Ruslavenko/Shutterstock.com;
texture © iStockLoudRedCreative;
symbol © artdock/Shutterstock.com;
flames © iStock/Eduard Muzhevskyi;
shield texture © iStock/Nastasic;
shield © Peyker/Shutterstock.com

S